P9-ELS-037

# ACCLAIM FOR
## *Kathryn Lynn Davis'*
## BESTSELLING
## *TOO DEEP FOR TEARS*

"ENGROSSING . . . MOVING . . . Ms. Davis has filled the pages of this novel with pathos, interesting characters, and colorful settings. . . . EVERY WOMAN WILL FIND A PART OF HERSELF IN *TOO DEEP FOR TEARS*."

—*Rave Reviews*

"ELEGANT . . . LOVELY . . . Davis has done an enormous amount of research and easily captures the flavor of each disparate setting. . . . Her characters are richly drawn, and the relationships between lovers, friends, parents, and children are beautifully portrayed."

—*Inside Books*

"Davis' story is as richly textured as a fine old tapestry. The time is the latter half of the 19th century; the emotions and conflicts are ageless. . . ."

—*Chicago Tribune*

"Populated with unforgettable characters, *TOO DEEP FOR TEARS* sweeps the reader around the world and back in telling this compelling story of loss, betrayal, love, and discovery."

—*Affaire de Coeur*

"GET OUT YOUR HANDKERCHIEFS. . . ."

—*Dallas News*

"CAPTIVATING . . . A MAJOR NOVEL."

—*San Bernardino Sun*

"A compelling story. . . . You won't want to miss this richly detailed saga."

—*Midwest Review of Books*

**Books by Kathryn Lynn Davis**

Too Deep for Tears
Child of Awe

Published by POCKET BOOKS

POCKET BOOKS
New York London Toronto Sydney Tokyo Singapore

This book is a work of fiction. Names, characters, places and incidents are either the product of the author's imagination or are used fictitiously. Any resemblance to actual events or locales or persons, living or dead, is entirely coincidental.

POCKET BOOKS, a division of Simon & Schuster Inc.
1230 Avenue of the Americas, New York, NY 10020



ISBN: 0-671-72550-5

First Pocket Books printing October 1990

10 9 8 7 6 5 4 3 2 1



Printed in the U.S.A.

*To my husband, Michael,*
*Because in the eight long years*
*That this book was my obsession,*
*He listened endlessly, counseled wisely,*
*And never for a moment*
*Stopped believing in the magic.*

# Acknowledgments

*Child of Awe* is truly the book of my heart, begun long ago and lingering always in some part of my mind, no matter what else I might be working on. There are many people who, through their advice, unflagging faith and friendship, became part of the slow unfolding of the magic that has touched this project from the beginning; it made me believe, in the end, that this novel is worth every last moment of agony and joy. I want especially to thank these people:

Dorris Halsey, who had the patience and the faith to wait for this "child" to grow up. My dear friend Brenda Trent, who read and critiqued the novel so often she began to know it by heart. Laura Kalpakian, who, with great humor and sensitivity, sent me fourteen single-spaced legal-sized pages of comments after reading only the first two chapters. I still remember and make use of those comments every time I sit down to write. My mother Ann Davis, Camille Guerin-Gonzales, and Jana Thomas, each of whom read the manuscript more than once, gave me their thoughts and feelings and, by doing so, helped me understand the book's problems and strengths more clearly. The members of the History Department at the University of California, Riverside, especially Professor John Phillips and Connie Young, for their support and encouragement over the years. Jane Curtis, who, with great patience, listened while I read aloud all 526 pages of the original manuscript, and who often saw what I could not. Her husband Chick, an artist, who, as he read the book, sketched the characters one by one. The wonder is, they looked exactly as I had imagined them.

Finally, I want to express my gratitude to John Scognamiglio, who did a great deal of extra work—cheerfully—in order to make my rewriting easier. To my editor, Linda Marrow, for whom no detail was too insignificant to merit her attention and care. To Linda Susan Baker, who, with Muriella's kind of wisdom, always told me this day would come, and to Gretchen Van Nuys, who read and wept and brought back vividly the passion for *Child of Awe* which I first felt fourteen years ago.

# PROLOGUE

# Northern Scottish Highlands 1497

The mist swirled and eddied, obscuring the stars and shrouding the wan light of the moon on the night when the second Earl of Argyll heard that Alex Urquart had been murdered. The Earl did not care that the man was dead, but the fools who had killed him—that was a different matter.

Argyll had been on his way home from court after many months, craving the warmth of his hearth and his wife's soft body, but when the news was brought, he smiled grimly and turned at once toward Kilravok. He realized, as his horse's powerful muscles moved beneath him, carrying him surely through the treacherous Highland night, that he had been awaiting just such a moment, though he had not known it until now. Ever since the King had made his startling announcement, the Earl had been waiting for a chance, a turn of fate that would put the advantage squarely in his hands. Now the moment had come, and he intended to make the most of it.

His heart raced with exhilaration, and his pulse quickened at the thought of the battle awaiting him. No sword would be raised, no arrow would fly; his weapon would be words and he had no doubt about the outcome.

He burst into the tiny, ill-kempt keep of Kilravok with the Campbell men-at-arms behind him, clattering into the courtyard despite the feeble protestations of the guards. He did not wait for the word to spread that he had come, but swung his rich fur cape, heavy with mist, away from his shoulders and pounded with both fists on the barred double doors.

They swung open too quickly, and he exchanged a disgusted look with his men, but did not pause as he stormed over the worn and battered stone threshold.

"What is't ye want? Who are ye?" a woman demanded. When her gaze fell on the Earl's brooch, symbol of the Clan Campbell, the most powerful family in Scotland, she closed her mouth and clutched the child in her arms more closely. Behind her, four other women clustered, shivering and pale.

"Do the Roses of Kilravok leave the women to guard their doors, then?" Argyll demanded impatiently.

The woman straightened and met his gaze without flinching. "There's been some disturbance. My father is occupied. Our doors are not usually open to any savages who choose to come crashing through them at midnight."

The Earl contemplated the group of defenseless women. The one who had greeted him spoke steadily, angrily. Neither she nor her sisters had a weapon among them and the Campbells were heavily armed for travel. Yet he knew she would defy him, block his path if necessary, with nothing but her two hands, and those obviously cradling a baby. In spite of himself, he smiled. "Ye would dare to stand against me? Do ye know I am the Earl of Argyll?"

"I'm no' blind, nor am I daft," she replied. "But aye, I would stand against ye 'til I know if ye come as friend or foe."

"I'm Archibald Campbell," he murmured unexpectedly, using his given name for the first time. "And ye?"

"I am Isabel Rose—" she hesitated, "Calder."

The Earl regarded her intently. "Ah," he said. "The widow of the Thane of Cawdor." He paused. "Why are ye back in your father's house and no' with your husband's family?"

"Surely you've heard, as all Scotland has, that the Calders didn't want me after my husband died," Isabel replied tonelessly. "What ye may not have heard is that *I* did not want *them*. So I came home."

Argyll was surprised by her honesty—surprised and

pleased. He could not disguise his interest as he approached. She did not step back, but held her ground. "And this," he said, nodding toward the fur-wrapped bundle in her arms, "must be the Thane's child and heiress."

"'Tis *my* daughter," Isabel Calder said fiercely.

The Earl did not miss the slight emphasis on the word *my*. He tipped the fur away from the baby's face, admiring her downy white skin, thick, tousled red curls and unblinking green eyes. His face softened when he thought of his own wife and daughter, who shared the name Elizabeth—the companions of his solitude, the comfort of his days and nights away from court. "What is her name?" he asked gently, without bothering to hide the tenderness in his eyes.

Startled by the sudden change, Isabel replied without thinking. "Her name is Muriel, but we call her Muriella."

"A lovely name," he said, "sweeter and bonnier."

Isabel was touched by this unexpected gentleness in a man like the Earl of Argyll, whose reputation for ruthlessness was known all over the Highlands.

"What the devil is going on? How dare ye enter my keep unasked at such an hour?"

Hugh Rose's harsh voice broke the spell and Isabel stepped back while Argyll's expression hardened. He turned toward the Laird of the Clan Rose, noticing with disgust his sweat-stained saffron shirt and baggy trews. He wore no boots and his hand hovered above the hilt of his sword.

The Earl regarded his reluctant host with an icy stare. "Because I have business with ye, and because I am the Earl of Argyll. Where can we talk?"

Hugh Rose drew himself up taller and fingered the sword at his side. "I've no wish to speak to ye, even if ye were the King himself." He noticed Isabel and her sisters nearby and waved them away. "Leave us!"

Argyll raised his hand in protest, partly to annoy Rose and partly because he knew the wisdom of having the women present. "Let them stay. This concerns your daughter Isabel."

Hugh's face burned red with anger as he turned on his heel and headed for the library. "'Tis my house you're in now, Argyll. Ye can no' be telling me how to run it. Go!" he called to the women.

"Stay," the Earl repeated, sweeping through the barren hall and into the austere library. He noticed a motion out of the corner of his eye, but dismissed it. His attention was half on Rose and half on the sound of swishing skirts. The women had chosen to ignore the Laird's command and follow Argyll's. He suppressed a smile.

Isabel Calder's heart pounded dully as she followed the men. She began to fear that she knew why Archibald Campbell had come. No force on earth could have kept her from that room. Her sisters and sisters-in-law were close behind.

Quietly, Isabel closed the door and watched the two men face each other across the room.

Rose glared at his daughter, growled an unintelligible curse and peered warily at the Earl. "By what right do ye invade a man's home in the middle of the night and order his family about like servants?" Hugh demanded querulously.

Argyll remained unruffled. "By right of the King's writ. I've come on behalf of your grandchild—the Thane of Cawdor's daughter. King Jamie has named me her guardian."

Hugh Rose stared, eyes bulging. "'Tis a lie! We're her family."

The women gasped in chorus and the Earl glanced at Isabel. She stood in front, the baby in her arms. Her sisters looked stricken, pale and flushed by turns at his disturbing revelation. Isabel alone stood rigid, unchanged. The only sign of her distress was the slight tightening of her arms around the child. He nodded his approval and turned back to her father.

"You're protecting her well, I see, with guards half-asleep at the gate and your daughters waiting at the door to let me in." When Rose started to interrupt, the Earl silenced him with a wave of his hand. "But 'tis no' the only reason the King made her my ward." He lowered his voice. "The Calders are her family as well, ye see, and 'tis known they wish her ill. The King feels there's too much conflict about this little bairn. She's no' yet a year old, and already she has many enemies."

Hugh Rose let out his breath in a rush. "And ye one more."

Again, the Earl let the insult go by. "Ye would be wise to learn to recognize your friends, Rose. Ye'd be a far happier man."

Hugh snorted. "Ye don't give a damn about my happiness."

Argyll shrugged. "As far as that goes, ye can believe what ye like. But I *do* give a damn about the child. And I've no intention of letting ye endanger her. The Calders are becoming a bunch of outlaws determined to have their way. Ye can't hold them off if they set their full fury upon ye. But the Campbells can. For our strength, the King has given me her care."

"For your arrogance, I'll give ye naught. I could kill ye where ye stand or hold ye for ransom, saying ye attacked Kilravok without provocation. The King would pay a great deal to get ye back."

"Ye could, though 'twould be foolish beyond reason," the Earl said casually. "But ye won't."

"And why not?" Hugh was sweating and did not like the feeling. He did not like Argyll's certainty, nor the power he knew the other man wielded. Most of all, he did not like being backed into a corner like a helpless rat.

"Because," Argyll said softly, leaning negligently on a plain wooden chair, "the rest of my men await me on the road to Edinburgh. They have in their custody your oldest son Hugh and his brother David. Their tunics and daggers are stained with earth and the blood of Alex Urquart. They spoiled the lands of Cromarty tonight and killed the man in front of all the servants. They acted heedlessly, did no' even try to hide who they were, but rode out of the keep as they had ridden in, plaids flying proudly. The King does not like such lawlessness and he has no patience for fools."

Hugh Rose went pale with rage and fear—at his sons, who had grown up wild and greedy and careless. Now they had endangered the entire clan. A moment before he had felt like a cornered rat, but he was less than that to Argyll—a gnat, defenseless and easily squashed beneath the Earl's thumb.

Suddenly, a whirlwind of flailing arms and legs erupted from behind a screen in the corner. A small flame-haired boy ran for the Earl, striking his knees, biting, trying to knock him down. "I want my papa. Where've ye put my papa?" he shouted.

With difficulty, Argyll disentangled himself. Hugh Rose smiled; he couldn't help it. His four-year-old grandson had nearly toppled the mighty Earl to the floor. Argyll held him at arm's length, but the boy still struggled, biting the air, snarling and swinging his fists uselessly.

"Now you've met Hugh Rose the youngest, my first son's child," the Laird announced. When he saw the dangerous glint in Argyll's eye, he snapped, "Bridget! Take the brat and go."

"Hugh, lad, come away," Bridget said, moving from among her sisters. Her fear for her husband was momentarily diverted into concern for her son. The Earl's color was high and he did not look the slightest bit amused.

"But he took my papa! He'll hurt him. I know it. I want my papa!" the child shrieked.

Bridget backed from the room, the child snarling all the way. Argyll felt eyes full of hatred burning into his back long after the door had closed. It was something to mark for the future, he thought. Something to mark well.

Hugh dismissed his grandson without thought. "What are ye going to do?" he demanded.

"About your sons, ye mean?" Argyll spoke calmly, hiding his unease. "I am, as ye know, Justice General of Scotland. I didn't like Alex Urquart. I doubt that many will mourn his loss. Especially if the servants are made to forget what they saw. Ye know if anyone has the power to make them do it, I do."

Hugh waited. "And? What of my sons?"

"I'll keep the daggers and tunics, of course, to insure they don't forget how much they owe us. But if ye deal with me fairly, 'twill cost them no more than a small fine."

"What do ye mean by deal fairly?" Hugh asked suspiciously.

"Accept my guardianship of Muriella."

Even then Isabel made no sound. Her face had no color, and the lines between her nose and mouth were deeper, more pronounced. She was rigid, waiting, but her eyes showed no fear or weakness.

Hugh hesitated, though he knew he was trapped. "Ye already have land and wealth aplenty. To give ye Muriella would only give ye more. It makes my stomach turn to think of it."

Argyll was becoming irritated. "Your sons brought ye to this moment, not I. Ye'd best blame them. I'm offering ye a fair exchange. Their freedom for the girl. Ye have to choose—Muriella Calder, and the Thanedom of Cawdor someday in the future, or your sons now—your clan, your own survival. Choose."

Argyll could feel Isabel's breath withheld, feel its absence in the chilly air. But he did not turn. "Choose."

"Take the bairn," Rose snarled. "Take her!" He swung away, beating his clenched fist into his hand.

"No," the Earl murmured. He went to look once more into the child's innocent face. "For now, she'll stay at Kilravok. A girl-child should be with her mother, with the women of her own family." He wondered, fleetingly, if he were making a mistake, to put so much wealth into such unsteady hands. But Isabel's gaze was unwavering and he thought again of his own wife and daughter. He believed in this woman's strength. His gaze locked with hers, and there passed between them a promise—unspoken, but binding and real just the same. He reached out to touch the girl's soft cheek, smiled at her gurgle of pleasure.

Isabel sighed with relief and her grip on Muriella lessened.

"I don't want to take her from her mother 'til 'tis necessary. As long as ye can protect her, I'll leave her here, where she can grow and learn as she should. I need ye as an ally, Hugh Rose, not an enemy. I will give ye a bond of friendship. When ye have trouble, send word and the Campbells will come to protect ye."

"To protect *her,* ye mean," Rose snarled.

The Earl was looking at Isabel, though he spoke to Hugh. "All of ye. 'Tis what such a bond means, man." He smiled slightly, then whirled toward Rose, his face devoid of expression. "I'll have your vow that ye'll send word at the first hint of trouble, that ye'll use our strength to see that she is safe, that ye'll keep in your head always the Campbell motto—'Be Mindful.'"

He took his sword and held it, hilt out, toward Hugh Rose. The crusted ruby in silver winked in the pale firelight. "Swear and your sons will be free, your family safe. Swear!"

Hugh's lip curled and he felt ill as he reached toward the offered sword. Friendship indeed. When the Earl offered friendship it was best to turn and flee. But he had no choice. Damn his sons to hell. Briefly, he clasped the jeweled hilt of Argyll's sword. "I swear." He thought he would choke on the words, but they rang loud and clear through the room.

"Remember," Argyll said, "you're sworn to be ally to the Campbells, but more than that, you're sworn to keep Muriella Calder safe." He turned to Isabel one last time. "And now so are ye."

She nodded, stunned by the feeling of relief that swept over her—the first moment of peace she'd known since her husband's death. The turmoil had begun long before that, if the truth were told, since the moment she'd learned she would be John Calder's wife. She kissed her daughter's smooth white brow. "Aye," she murmured. "I swear."

"Then 'tis done." The Earl felt suddenly unutterably weary. To Hugh, he said, "She'll stay only as long as ye can keep her safe. No' a moment more! That's the pledge," he added with a face of thunder, a face many men had quailed at the sight of. "And don't even be thinking of crossing me."

Hugh averted his eyes. "No man would be such a fool."

Argyll smiled bitterly. "I have learned that most men would rather be fools. I suspect 'tis because they choose to believe themselves stronger than they are."

Rose looked up, lip curled. "Oh, aye, but 'tis only ye who's invincible, I suppose."

Argyll glanced from Isabel, with the girl-child in her arms, to Hugh with his smirking grin. "No," the Earl said sharply. "I'm neither blind nor full of false pride. I know I'm only a man, ye see."

He took a step forward and raised his hand. "Because of that I'll survive and prosper while others fall around me. Because of that, I can make certain that the bairn," he pointed toward the bundle in Isabel's arms, "reaches womanhood, marries and has bairns of her own." He started for the door. "Ye'd be wise to remember what I've said," he called over his shoulder as he disappeared into the long, dark hall.

Hugh, Laird of the Clan Rose, did not choose to remember, but his daughter Isabel never forgot.

# PART I

## 1509–1510

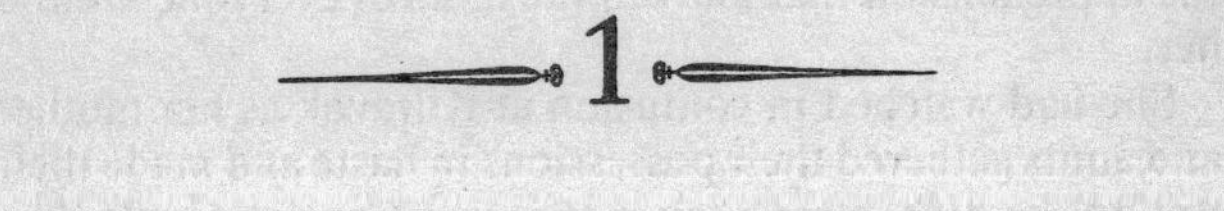

Muriella!"

The harsh voice echoed upward through the tower, bouncing off the walls until it reached the girl crouched in the recessed window of the circular room. As the sound dissipated in the late-afternoon air, Muriella Calder pressed herself harder against the chilly stone of the window. She shrank back on the ledge, hoping she would disappear somewhere beyond the reach of that voice and the other strident voices that joined it. The day was oddly warm for October, and she wanted to be by the river, away from the walls of the tower and the oppressive presence of her aunts. Her heavy skirts hung limp and her undergown clung to her thighs and ankles. In desperation, she had finally undone the intricate laces so that her gown hung open, revealing her damp kirtle.

She moved over carefully, an inch at a time, until she sat at the very edge of the embrasure. Turning her head, she peered down through the trees at the river. She could just see the water glistening through the layered leaves of hawthorns and oaks. As the sun struck the swells of water sharply, Muriella closed her eyes, giving herself up to the murmur of water on stones.

It was the only sound that could begin to soothe away the anxiety that had haunted her since her arrival at Cawdor Castle two days before. Her mother had told her they had come here to prepare for the girl's wedding to her cousin Hugh, which would take place on her fourteenth birthday, a little more than three months from now. But Muriella did not believe it was that simple. She had seen too many of the furtive looks cast her way in the past weeks, felt too much of the apprehension that marked the faces of everyone around her.

She had watched in confusion at Kilravok as her mother and aunts gathered their possessions in haste and made their way to the high, strong tower that was Cawdor Castle. She had listened in dismay to the unnatural silence that fell upon her relatives as they settled amidst the dust and long-unused furniture on the upper floors. She had held her breath, shaking her head in alarm, when she saw how many armed men had taken their meager furs and established themselves on the ground floor.

Muriella had not been allowed to leave the tower since. She had begun to feel restless under the weight of the somber atmosphere that still lurked in the corners of a place that had been so long uninhabited. She missed the tapestry-hung walls of Kilravok where she had grown up. The bare stone here was cold despite the warmth outside; Muriella felt that the tower was somehow unfriendly. There were not even rushes on the floors, and her thin slippers were little protection against the rough stone.

She shivered, remembering the room where she had slept. There was nothing but a bed there, from which the curtains had long been removed. The room was huge and cold and empty, and if her companion Lorna had not been with her, she might have been afraid. She could not help but be aware that she was watched always, and that Lorna was never allowed to leave her side.

For two days Muriella had wandered the tower, unable to stay still and unable to go out. She had pestered her mother constantly. "Why have we really come here?"

Her mother had frowned, answering abruptly, "Because we were told to do so."

"But who told us?"

Sighing, Isabel Calder had replied, "My father. 'Tis

dangerous just now at Kilravok, and he's afraid we aren't strong enough to protect"—she paused and looked away—"everyone." She added the last word stiffly, and Muriella sensed that it was not the one she had meant to use. But her mother would not explain further.

Then the girl had appealed to one of her aunts. "Why don't we go back to Kilravok? 'Tis too quiet here."

The aunt had shaken her head and snapped, "Leave me be. Tend to your embroidery."

Muriella had even sat down beside one of the men who sprawled on the dirt floor below, waiting. "'Tis dusty here and uncomfortable. Wouldn't ye rather be at Kilravok?"

The soldier had put a hand on her shoulder and said, "'Tis best we stay here where the men-at-arms have half a chance." He would say no more.

Finally she had sought relief in climbing to the room high in the tower where the hawthorn tree grew through a hole in the floor. Of course Lorna, who had once been Muriella's nurse, was with her as always, but the older woman sensed the girl's disquiet and left her to herself, sitting nearby on the floor. From her isolated spot, Muriella gazed through the aperture at the river far beneath her. With her knees pulled up to her chin, she tilted her head so she could just hear her aunts and her mother chattering near the window of the sewing room on the floor below.

"I tell ye, 'tis no' a good sign in her. She craves the water, like a Kelpie. And to be born on the stroke of midnight—I believe she is marked."

"She's only restless here." Muriella recognized her mother's voice. "'Tis no' healthy to keep her so confined. If only we could let her go out, she would be more at ease."

An aunt sniffed. "'Tis no' safe, Isabel, and well ye know it. The girl must be watched."

"Then perhaps"—her mother paused—"if we aren't strong enough to keep her safe, 'twould have been better to let her go."

The aunts gasped in chorus. "Ye must be daft! Father was a fool to make such a promise. She must stay here where she belongs."

"The old man is a fool, right enough," Isabel replied with a chill in her voice, "but I am more concerned for Muriella. We are weak and the Campbells are strong. They could—"

"Always too worried about that chit," her sister interrupted. "Have ye forgotten that the Campbells are our enemies, same as the Calders? Sometimes I believe ye actually want them to take her away. Ye don't seem to care if we lose everything, do ye?"

"Ye must forgive me," Isabel snapped, "for thinking more of Muriella than I do of Cawdor. And I'll thank ye to lower your voice. The girl is no' deaf, ye ken."

Another aunt repeated, "She is marked."

From her precarious perch, Muriella wondered over what they said, but she could make no sense of it. What did the Campbells and Calders have to do with her? She had been raised by her mother's family, had always considered herself a Rose, though she bore the name of Calder. Shaking her head, she forced the voices into the background, but she could not make them go away altogether. As she leaned toward the river, her head began to spin with the desire to disappear through the window and reappear at the edge of the water, stretched out on the wet ground. She drew in her breath, straightening one leg, then the other, until both fell beyond the edge of the window. She pressed her hands into the stone and threw back her head when she felt the wind come up beside her.

*"Muriella!"*

She whirled, tangling her legs in her skirts, to stare into her mother's terrified eyes. Isabel Calder stood with her arms outstretched toward her daughter. "Ye could have fallen!" Her voice trailed off at the vision of the girl tumbling from the window to her death on the ground so far beneath.

Muriella sucked in her breath. Her mother and aunts had climbed up from the sewing chamber; now they were ranged before her in various states of disgust and fear. In their faces there lurked a certain harshness; the set of their mouths revealed no sympathy for the girl who stood before them. Only Isabel's face softened when her eyes rested on her daughter, but then the worry lines deepened—those lines that had marked her mother's skin for as long as Muriella could remember. Isabel's eyes swept her daughter up and down, betraying her despair.

Muriella shook the river from her head, obliterated the comfort of the cool, green water, and confronted her stern aunts. "May I go down to the river?" she asked.

Isabel glanced at her sisters, apprehension tingeing the high edges of her cheekbones pink. "Can't ye stay and sew with the women as ye should?"

The girl breathed deeply once, then threw back her head. "Ye must let me go!" she cried. "I can't bear to stay here any longer. 'Tis so warm and close."

Isabel, who still held her sewing in her hand, fluttered it before her daughter's face. "Muriella, my dear, ye must learn that here ye can't simply wander as ye did at Kilravok. Ye have become a woman now. Ye must stay close."

"But if I'm a woman, why am I watched like a bairn? Why can't I do what I wish?"

Isabel shook her head sadly. Taking her daughter's hand, she murmured, "No woman can ever do as she wishes, my dear. Especially ye. Ye have to understand that we don't get to choose our own fate. I'm afraid ye'll learn that for yourself sooner than ye care to."

Muriella saw the hopelessness in her mother's face. All at once her desire to escape from Isabel's fear and dread was overpowering. Her eyes locked with her mother's, and the girl's gaze held the woman immobile; she could not look away. "Please may I go?" Muriella repeated.

Isabel threw up her hands and the white cloth fluttered to the floor. For a full minute she regarded her daughter in indecision, wondering if she should listen to the inner voice that bid her free Muriella from the tower. She knew that by doing so, she was taking the chance of losing the girl to the Campbells, and though the thought brought with it another flash of fear, she knew in her heart that it was time to let her daughter go. She had told her sisters more than once that the Roses could no longer keep her safe.

She remembered vividly the tender look on the Earl of

Argyll's face the night he had come to Kilravok. She remembered the unspoken promise that had passed between them. She had believed him then. She must believe him now.

Her father was making a desperate mistake, and Muriella would pay the price. Isabel could not let it happen. Not when she knew, when she had felt Archibald Campbell's strength of will, his unbending determination. *She'll stay only as long as ye can keep her safe. No' a moment more! Remember, you're sworn,* he had said, and turning to Isabel, added softly, *and now, so are ye.*

As if the words had been wrenched from her, Isabel said, "Go then. But ye must take one of the guards with ye." Her eyes met Lorna's, and she felt a painful band tightening across her forehead. Both women knew that a single guard would never be enough; she might as well send none at all. But she must pretend for the sake of the others who were watching her so warily. "Ye must take care, ye ken?" she added softly, turning at the cry of startled disapproval from her sisters. "Can we keep her bound in the tower forever?" she demanded. "The guard will protect her."

"And *I* will." Lorna touched the dagger in a sheath at her waist.

The aunts shook their heads, but Isabel turned her back to them. For the first time, she would openly defy the men who had ordered her days, her months, her life by their will. She had made her own decision, listened to her own voices. She shivered at the thought, but pushed her doubts aside.

She did not know why she had not explained everything to her daughter sooner. Like Hugh Rose, she had pretended she would never lose Muriella. And in pretending, she had betrayed her daughter, bewildered her, hurt her. She didn't know how to make that right; it was too late. But she *could* save Muriella's life, and hope that someday her daughter would understand and forgive her.

She heard one of the women rush from the room, no doubt to warn the men, but Isabel knew her own orders would be followed. Thank God her father had not yet arrived with her cousins. They would have sided with her sisters, she was sure. "Lorna, will ye take her down?"

Lorna moved forward until her gaze met and held Isabel's for a long moment.

Overcome with a last, sinking feeling of uncertainty, Muriella's mother clutched her skirt in stiff fingers. "I believe 'tis best if we let her go," Isabel murmured to Lorna. "Do ye?"

The other woman glanced once at the girl, long and thoughtfully, then nodded.

As Muriella peered up at her friend's pleasant brown eyes and broad, gentle mouth, she felt a fine, shimmering thread of hope. She took a step forward, unable to stay still a moment longer.

Lorna frowned at Muriella's impatience. Sensing that the girl was poised for flight, she put her hand on Muriella's shoulder.

The girl curtsied, kissing her mother's outstretched hand. "Thank ye, Mother," she said. "I don't know what ye want of me, but I'll try to do as ye say."

"Never mind now. Tomorrow will be soon enough."

Muriella smiled up at her; the girl's face became vivid and at the same time vulnerable. "Good day," she said.

Isabel's heart stilled as she watched the girl turn away to start down the stairs with her companion. Lorna's hand rested on Muriella's shoulder, and Isabel saw that she was at home beneath that hand. As she stared after the stranger who was her daughter, the lines of Isabel's face hardened into panic. Yet she turned away from the stairway, sinking back into what had always been the comforting presence of her sisters. She bent to pick up her sewing with a sigh that was not even noticed amidst the disbelief and consternation that pervaded the room.

Muriella strained under the gentle pressure of Lorna's hand. The sedate pace the woman set was an uncomfortable restraint on the girl's desire to flee. However, she moved forward slowly, because that was what Lorna wanted.

The guard, with his sword at his side and his bow slung

over his shoulder, followed the two unwillingly. He had been awakened from a nap a few minutes before and was less than pleased to discover that he was to accompany the girl down to the river. "'Tis daft, that's what," he muttered under his breath. "Safer in the tower. But then, ye don't care what I think."

Lorna ignored him and Muriella was too caught up in her own excitement to pay the grumbling man any attention. When, having struggled with the rusty bolt, Lorna finally shoved open the heavy oak door, Muriella tumbled outside in a rush despite all her efforts to hold herself still. She ran, stumbling, past Lorna, the guard, and the shadow of the tower, down the steep hill that protected the south side of the castle. Leaves, bushes, and crawling ferns blocked her path, and the bells of the hollyhock brushed her legs, but they did not slow her down. Holding her skirts above her knees, she flew as if wind-borne. Then, as the river appeared from beneath its ceiling of leaves, she let fall the dark hood she had drawn around herself before her relatives; her face became young again and her green eyes glowed. Without glancing backward, she motioned to the other woman.

Muriella did not see that Lorna had paused with the guard beside her. Together they surveyed the trees and thick foliage between the castle and the river. It was several moments before Lorna turned toward the riverbank.

When Muriella reached the bank, she knelt in the damp moss that straggled in and out of the water. She felt the moisture seeping through the cloth at her knees and listened with delight to the marvelous harmony of water and stones and her own desire to escape into the music of the river. She stretched out a hand, placing it just above the water. As she moved it to and fro, she felt the last remains of the weight of the tower leave her. She breathed the air, which was cool under the sheltering trees. At last, she smiled—slowly, triumphantly.

She realized Lorna hovered nearby, watching in silence. Muriella sensed a certain tension that was uncommon in Lorna's easy nature, and she turned to consider the woman inquiringly.

"Muriella, come sit with me in the copse for a while. 'Tis—more comfortable there." Lorna surveyed the landscape once more, then turned to the guard, who stood at her elbow. "Stay here and watch. If ye see anything—"

"Aye," the man mumbled, "if ye say so."

Lorna pulled Muriella away from the river, retreating into a group of trees with thick ferns growing beneath them. As the woman sank gratefully into the safety of the darkness, Muriella lay down beside her. The damp ground, covered by a layer of curling fronds and dead pine needles, was soft against her back.

"Lorna," the girl murmured, "why have we really come here?"

Lorna paused for a moment, then murmured, "For your wedding."

Muriella frowned in confusion as she stared up at the shadows overhead. She knew everyone around her was tense and excited, but she also knew it had nothing to do with her marriage to her cousin Hugh. She had grown up with Hugh, after all, had always known she would wed him one day, although the two young people had not been officially betrothed until her twelfth birthday. Besides, as far as she knew, few preparations had been made for the impending ceremony. No, it was something else that was disturbing her family. "'Tis what the others told me, but 'tis no' the truth, is it?" She knew her companion from childhood was the only one who would not lie to her.

Lorna took a deep breath, considering Muriella through half-closed lids. "You're right, 'tis no' all the truth." With a sigh she continued, "Ye know Cawdor Castle has belonged to ye since your father's death?"

Muriella nodded.

"Ye never knew your father," Lorna observed. "I wonder if 'twould have been different if ye had."

The girl wrinkled her forehead as she tried to build a picture of her father in her mind. He had died of consumption just before she was born, and though she had seen a small portrait of him once, she could not remember his face at all.

"I don't believe he really existed," she said. "I can't see him."

"But he did," Lorna assured her. "He had a troubled life, your father, and ye have inherited so much that was his."

"I don't understand."

"No, I don't suppose ye do."

A long silence followed while Muriella lay still, her gaze wandering beyond the copse toward the castle. She could barely see the south wall of the tower from where she sat, but she had seen the rest the day before. It stood tall and severe behind the thick stone that circled it on three sides, dominating the hilly ground on which it sat, dwarfing the trees and the river that curled at its back. Staring steadily at the dull, weather-beaten stone of its walls, Muriella felt ill at ease. This was not her home. Her gaze moved back to the river.

Above her, Lorna tore at a leaf until it lay in tatters on her skirt. Then she said suddenly, "Muriella!"

The girl sat up at the note of alarm in her friend's voice. "What is it?"

Lorna glanced toward the riverbank, then toward the castle. She plucked at the bracken beside her, but when she caught a glimpse of the guard beyond the trees, her hand grew still. "'Tis nothing. Do ye know the history of the castle? Ye should, since 'tis yours."

Muriella bit her lip while she tried to follow Lorna's thoughts. Something of great significance was amiss, she was more and more certain of that, but just now she could not untangle her confusion; instead she lay back and listened.

"Your great-grandfather built the castle here," Lorna began. "There's a story that a large bird spoke to him one day, telling him to strap all his gold into a trunk and place it on his mule's back. Then he was to follow the animal wherever it might choose to go. 'And,' the bird said, 'when the mule lies down to rest, there ye should build your castle.' So your great-grandfather followed the animal up and down the Highlands 'til the mule fell down beneath a hawthorn tree and went to sleep.

"There your relative began to build. Since he didn't want

to destroy the tree, he built the castle around it. Ye were just in the room with the tree growing through its center. 'Tis the very same one.

"When he died, your grandfather was very wealthy and a friend to James, the King. Both his son and his grandson added land and money to his original possessions, and when the land came to your father, it included a vast fortune. Vast enough to make more than one man covet the power and wealth Cawdor would bring him."

Before Muriella could respond to the warning in her voice, Lorna continued, "John Calder married your mother in order to end the feud between the Calders and Roses that had disrupted the lives of everyone in Nairnshire for many years. I suppose he hoped that together the two families would be strong enough to hold Cawdor in peace. But the bitterness had gone too deep. A single marriage couldn't heal it."

The girl braided her fingers together, then held them over her eyes, looking up at Lorna through the broken pattern the shadow of her fingers made on her face. She knew about the feud between the two families; she could not help but know. She had grown up hearing about the Calder raids, the thefts, the animosity that had plagued the Roses for so long. It seemed to her that the hostility had intensified in the past two years. There had been more frequent raids with more than a few cattle and sheep taken, and men had lost their lives—both Calders and Roses. "Why didn't we stay here after my father died?" she asked at last.

"Your mother was lonely and missed her sisters, so she took ye home to Kilravok."

The girl bent her head back so she could look into Lorna's face. "I think she was unhappy here. That's why she wanted to go away." A memory flickered at the back of her mind—something her cousin had told her once. "Hugh says the Calders didn't like my mother, that my Calder uncles didn't want her here."

It was not a question and Lorna did not deny it.

"But," Muriella continued before her friend could speak, "why have we come back now?"

Lorna looked away from the girl's puzzled face and up toward the leaves overhead. She was troubled and did not wish Muriella to see. "Your grandfather Rose made a promise, and now he has no wish to keep it."

"What did he promise? And *why* must he send me away?"

"He believes ye will be safer here."

At the slight hesitation in Lorna's voice, Muriella turned, leaning her hands on the woman's knees. "But *ye* don't think 'tis safer? Can't ye tell me what you're trying to protect me from?"

Lorna closed her eyes, placing her hands on top of Muriella's with a sigh. "I don't know what to think. But your mother and I can't help believing ye'd be better off away from the Roses and Calders. They're greedy, ye see, and ye have so much that they desire. It keeps them always bickering and makes them unwise at times. Yet I couldn't bear to see ye taken from me." She pulled the girl to her breast and held her tightly.

When she felt the tension in Lorna's body, Muriella remembered a conversation she had overheard once between her mother and her grandfather Calder. He came so rarely to Kilravok that she had been curious, and at Hugh's urging, the two children had knelt in the hallway to listen.

"Will ye never leave us in peace, old man?" her mother had said. Muriella had been shocked at the tone of disrespect in Isabel's voice; old William Calder had once been Thane of Cawdor.

"I'll leave ye in peace when I have what's mine returned to me."

"'Tis yours no longer and well ye know it. 'Twas your own choice to give your title to your son. Ye can't berate us for that."

"I can and I do, woman. Ye're all a pack of fools and I shall regret 'til I die that I married John to one such as ye. No doubt ye drove him to his early grave merely to spite me."

Her mother's voice was bitter when she replied, "My husband is dead. We can't change that, nor can your false accusations reclaim what you've lost."

"I *will* have Cawdor back! I will not stand by and watch a bairn—and what's worse, a daughter of Rose—take it from me. I'll have it no matter how I have to get it. Ye are the last who should stand before me and cry 'Fair play!' Ye—"

Hugh had dragged Muriella away then and she had clung to him, asking him to explain what she could not understand. For a while he had refused, but then, at last, he had given in to her entreaties. He told her that many years ago old William Calder had stepped down as Thane of Cawdor in favor of his young and vigorous son John, despite the grumblings of his three younger sons. But then John had died of consumption, leaving only a daughter to inherit Cawdor, and that had destroyed William Cawdor's plans. He and his three living sons were left with next to nothing, while the entire Calder fortune had gone to Isabel's tiny daughter.

"But what did he mean when he said he would get it back?" Muriella had demanded, perplexed.

Hugh had shaken his head, but Muriella had seen the flicker of unease that crossed his face; he had been afraid. She remembered, too, that her mother had wept that night, and refused to let her daughter out of her sight for many days thereafter. Now, as she lay with her head on her friend's breast, Muriella realized that Hugh's unease had grown until it had engulfed every person at Kilravok—even Lorna.

All at once, the woman rose and began to pace in agitation. "They're all very much afraid."

Muriella stood to face her, eyes bright. "Are they afraid of losing Cawdor?"

Lorna saw an awful intelligence in the green eyes that held her own. "They're afraid," she repeated, "but 'tis no' just for the land that they fear."

The girl's eyes froze. "Afraid for me?"

Lorna moved away, pressing her hands against her mouth.

Muriella saw that she wished she had never voiced her apprehension. The girl began to speak but found she could not form the words. They were choked off by a low humming in her ears that made her head begin to spin. She gasped at the chill that spread through her body, making her hands shake uncontrollably. The sheltering pines blurred before her eyes, dissolving into the image of a huge, shimmering loch. The water was black and still, except where the moonlight reached across in a wide gleaming path, and the trees scattered along its shore were tipped with silver leaves. Beneath the placid surface of the moonstruck water, shadows moved darkly, threateningly; then the water stirred, scattering the silver light into glittering fragments that shone for a moment, then faded into the blackness.

Muriella thought she might fall to her knees when the humming in her ears grew louder, then began at last to subside. As the trees gradually ceased their spinning, she fought for breath, clasping her chilled hands together in an attempt to still their trembling. She didn't know what the vision meant, but she knew how it made her feel. "I think they're right to fear," she whispered.

Her voice slipped up to Lorna and alarmed her. The woman caught Muriella by the shoulders, turned the girl's face up to her own, staring into her still, dark eyes. She knew what those blank eyes and the cold, clammy feel of her shaking hands meant; Muriella had had one of her visions. Once, when her face had clouded over this way, she had foretold Lorna's own mother's death.

Lorna believed in Muriella's gift. There was more to her than just a wild girl with strange green eyes. The aunts called her a witch, but that was because they were afraid, and Lorna ignored them. They did not want to believe in the Sight, but there were many in the Highlands who did. She felt the girl slipping from her grasp and shook her firmly. "Muriella!"

"Aye," she responded as her eyes began to clear.

Lorna attempted to divert her by pulling her back down into the bracken. She did not know how to comfort Muriella because she was so uneasy herself. She began to talk randomly, chanting old legends, hoping to settle the girl's mind on the past.

Muriella listened, leaning forward slightly, but the words

fluttered past; she heard only the sounds, the inflections. They had no meaning for her and began to mingle with the pulse of the river beyond. She rose, wandering from the voice, the trouble of trying to make sense of the words. She moved out of Lorna's reach, toward the water. The girl glanced around, but could not see the guard anywhere. Shrugging her shoulders, she knelt on the bank.

Lorna's voice had flickered out at last. Gazing at her distorted reflection in a small pool, Muriella thought she heard a new sound flowing through the water. She turned her head, closed her eyes, and, wrapped within herself, she listened. Her eyebrows came together and her hair fell unheeded into the river as she tried to identify the source of the sound. It began to beat against her in heavy rhythm and the rhythm rose out from the water. Finally her eyes flew open when she recognized the thud of horse hooves splashing through the river. They had begun far in the distance but now they were quite near. Muriella fell into the musical pulse while the blood pounded in her ears.

Something made her turn to look over her shoulder. A single rider sat several yards away from her, watching. He held a bloody sword in his hand and his eyes glittered, even in the long shadows beneath the leaves. As she stared at him, horrified, he grinned. It was then that she saw the guard lying half-concealed by the bushes, crumpled in a spreading pool of his own blood. She opened her mouth to scream, but no sound came; fear lodged in her throat, choking off her voice as she stood helpless, her heart pounding erratically. Before she could force her frozen limbs to move, a dozen horses came at her from the heart of the river.

The thundering of hooves through the water made her turn, her mouth still open in a silent scream. Suddenly the river was crowded with steaming animals and strange men; the sight freed her voice at last and she cried out in terror—a long, high wail of warning that echoed upward through the trees. Muriella did not need her Sight to tell her there was danger here. The faces of the men who glowered down at her from the safety of their horses showed her that. She shuddered at the bleakness that moved through her blood, encircling her, crawling behind her neck in a chill that set her body trembling.

In desperation, she whirled toward the copse where she had left Lorna. She saw her friend running, trying to get to her before the men and horses. Muriella reached out, but as she did so, she felt a sickening coldness in her chest and knew that Lorna could not help her.

Chilled and unthinking, she tried to run, but the man with the bloody sword blocked her path while the other riders moved forward threateningly. Finally one clear thought penetrated the fog of fear in which she moved; she could not escape them. They were everywhere, surrounding her in a circle of gleaming swords. Struggling to breathe around the constriction in her throat, she turned at last to confront the strangers. Another scream welled up from the hollow in the pit of her belly, but her tongue was swollen, useless, and once again no sound escaped her.

"'Tis a bonnie lass she is," said one man, who sat easily on his horse before the others. Rob Campbell of Inverliver peered down at the girl, the patchwork of crisscrossed lines on his face crinkling as he gave her a reassuring smile. Despite her fear, Muriella saw that his thick, speckled beard lent softness to his leathery skin. There was kindness in his eyes, but she recognized in the blunt strength of his mouth a determination beyond her own. When he motioned behind him, a younger man rode forward.

John Campbell leaned down, examining Muriella's face with care, surprised that she seemed so young. As his uncle had said, the lass was bonnie, but his blue eyes betrayed nothing as they lingered on the lush auburn hair that fell in disarray half across her face and behind to her knees. Then he turned to Rob. "So," he said, "this is John Calder's heir?"

Rob Campbell nodded. "'Twould be wise—"

He was interrupted by a quick movement from Lorna that drew one man out of his saddle. He did not touch her, but stood watching, arms crossed. Lorna paused.

The coldness in Muriella's chest expanded to her shaking limbs. Hardly aware of what she was doing, she stepped back instinctively into the river. Lorna saw the girl retreat, saw her shiver up and down as the water slapped at her legs beneath her sodden skirt. Breaking through the ring of horses, the woman flung herself toward Muriella and felt the girl clinging wildly to her neck.

Lorna glanced once toward the castle, but she knew these men had been too wise. They had chosen the only path by which they could approach the tower without being seen by the guards: the river. The trees effectively hid them from sight.

Both John and Rob dismounted, pausing beside their horses in water that came to their knees. Lorna took the girl's hands from around her neck, cupping them in her own. "Muriella," she whispered, "this is what they feared. Ye'll be taken from here. Perhaps that is even best, though ye may not believe it now." She stopped, glancing up at the waiting men. "It may be many years before we see ye again, and things change so quickly." Her words came faster and faster, as if she sensed that the men's patience would wear thin soon. "The time will come when ye return to claim your heritage. When ye do, we must be certain 'tis ye who comes and no imposter. Take care." Her voice broke, but she steadied it resolutely and raised the girl's left hand to her lips.

Muriella's eyes were luminous; they mesmerized Lorna with their steadfast gaze.

"I must mark ye so we can always be sure." With a silent plea for understanding in her eyes, Lorna tore her dagger from the sheath and brought it sharply, unerringly, downward, slicing Muriella's little finger deep and to the bone.

Muriella wrenched back in disbelief at the searing pain. For a moment, she saw only blackness. Far away she heard an aunt say coldly, *She is marked.* She shuddered, the blackness cleared, and she saw Lorna with blood on her hand. Muriella screamed once, wildly, then again and again until the pain leapt up her arm, silencing her at last. "Lorna!" she gasped out the name as if its owner were already far away—too far for her to reach. The men and horses began to circle before her eyes.

She sank to her knees, looking up at her friend one last

time. Lorna reached for her, but Muriella shrank back just as John Campbell stomped forward through the water, drenching Lorna when he came up beside her.

"What in God's name have ye done to the lass?" he bellowed.

Muriella did not understand what he said. In that moment, she heard only the angry rasp of his voice; the wavering image of Lorna's face was replaced by the unfamiliar features of the man who stood above her threateningly. He would drown her with the weight of his body, push her beneath the water until the blood that flowed from her finger had disappeared into the rushing river. Muriella froze where she crouched, half-covered by water, praying that the spinning would stop and the man above her fade into the moving shadows.

John reached for Lorna, grasping her arm in an unrelenting grip, but then he felt Rob's hand on his shoulder.

The older man nodded toward the castle meaningfully. "We must go before they send more men from the tower. We have the girl and 'tis all we came for. Leave her, Johnnie. She only sought to protect her charge."

John hesitated while Rob bent to scoop up Muriella. Without once looking at her face, he lifted her from the water, swinging her up to his waiting horse. John glanced at Lorna once more, his fingers tightening on her shoulder, but when Rob shouted, "Johnnie!" he turned away and mounted his own horse.

As the men turned to go, the rider who had dismounted stood watching Lorna, a question gathered across his brow. John shook his head, calling down to him, "Come, Jemmie. We've no' got the time!"

Only then did the last man leap on his horse to follow the Campbells away.

Lorna climbed out of the water and stood unmoving for a long time; then she lurched toward the nearest tree and clung to it. She could still see the look in Muriella's eyes, and the bloody image of the girl's hand would not leave her. She turned and retched into the bushes. She had lost Muriella, hurt her, and she was afraid for her. But she was afraid of the Roses and Calders as well. She could not think clearly. There was no answer.

At last she made her way up the hill to pound on the unyielding door. As a stiff aunt pulled it open, the hinges screamed and Lorna panted into the stifling air, "Muriella is gone!"

# 2

Muriella sat tensely in front of Rob Campbell while his arm circled her like an iron band, protecting her from the tumult of men and horses all around. The girl watched the green world fly past and tried to keep from clutching Rob's arm each time the horses thundered down a hill. The throbbing pain in her left hand weakened all her senses until she was aware of little besides the blood spreading across her gown and the agony that pulsed up her arm. She pressed her lacerated finger against her bodice, hoping to stop the bleeding.

Behind her, Rob sat taut, driving his horse forward. Once he leaned down to say, "I'll see to the finger as soon as I can. A piece of the kirtle might help. Do ye think ye can tear it?"

Muriella bit her lip; she did not wish to help him. She wanted him to be aware of her torment. Had it not been for him, her finger would be unmarred. But the stabs of pain were becoming more intense and she knew she must bind the wound before she lost much more blood. With an awkward movement, she lifted her sodden skirts and worked at the kirtle until she ripped a piece free.

Just then the horse swerved to avoid some roots that straggled across the path. Rob crushed the girl against his chest so tightly that she thought her ribs had given way. When the animal was under control, Rob shifted his weight, loosening his grip to assure her as much comfort as possible.

With one hand on the reins, he took the scrap of cloth from her and began to wind it around her finger. The movement of the horse made his task more difficult, but he dared not slow down so close to Cawdor. After struggling for a moment with the wet cloth, he grasped one end with his right hand and leaned down to catch the other in his teeth. Then he pulled sharply.

Muriella sat still, closing her eyes against the spasm that nearly left her senseless. She looked away, unable to watch as Rob swathed the finger.

"I'm sorry to have hurt ye, lass, but the bleeding must be stopped."

The girl did not respond, but held her hand against her chest, praying that the throbbing would cease. At last she opened her eyes and forced herself to watch the gentle hills covered with groves of oak and pine and hawthorn, hoping to distract herself from the pain. Still, every inch of her body was aware of the arm that circled her.

Once John Campbell rode up beside his uncle. As he passed, he considered Muriella's face for a moment. She was uncomfortably aware of the intensity of his cool blue gaze. His eyes seemed startlingly light compared to his tanned skin, dark hair, and full beard. She saw again the menace that had radiated from those silver-bright eyes beneath their bushy brows when he had come crashing toward her through the water. Muriella shivered, sinking her nails into Rob's arm as John moved on ahead.

"There now, lass, he won't be hurting ye, that I guarantee."

The girl heard the kindness in Rob's voice and traced with regret the marks her fingers had made in his flesh. She passed her hand over the five crescents, hoping to make them disappear, but when she caught sight of the bandaged finger, her hand stopped in midair. Already the blood was seeping through the cloth, dripping down onto Rob's arm. Muriella felt a wave of nausea overcome her, and when she saw Lorna kneeling before her, raising her hand to kiss it, she turned to retch over the horse's neck.

Rob removed his arm from around her waist and began to stroke her hair. The girl heard noises in his throat that she did not recognize as words, yet she understood the comfort he offered. She stared at the ground and conjured the image of his face before her: gray and marvelously wrinkled was all she remembered, but the eyes had been soft. The vision smiled up at her, and against her will, she felt herself responding, yearning toward those eyes, when all at once a dark mask fell across the image, blocking it from her sight. Muriella's heart slowed as she shivered and leaned against Rob's chest for support. She felt a shadow coming to this man and she could not fight it off.

As Rob Campbell looked down, he felt a rush of compassion for the girl. "Do ye know who we are, lass?" he asked.

"No." Her voice was small and distant, weakened by the premonition that would not leave her.

"I'm Rob Campbell of Inverliver, and these"—he motioned toward the rest of the riders—"are mostly my brother's men. My brother is the Earl of Argyll. Have ye heard the name?"

When Muriella shook her head, Rob's eyebrows came together in a frown. The girl had led a more sheltered life than he had supposed. The second Earl of Argyll, Lord High Chancellor and Master of the Royal Household, was a man known from one end of Scotland to the other. But then, no doubt the Roses had their reasons for keeping Muriella ignorant. He was afraid that ignorance would only make things harder for her now. "Then ye truly don't know why we've come for ye?"

"Because ye want Cawdor, like the others."

Rob was silent for a moment. So there were some things the girl had learned, after all. "Well," he said at last, "'tis partly true. But 'tis no' the only reason. We came because we believed ye were in danger."

Twisting in the saddle, Muriella peered up at him. "I'm not in danger now?"

Rob's gaze met hers as he asserted quietly, "No' from me."

The girl sensed that it was true but turned her back to him just the same, remembering that she had trusted Lorna, too. What was it her friend had said? *Perhaps ye would be better off away from the Roses and Calders.*

Suddenly Muriella felt very cold. The throbbing in her hand was a constant reminder of the terrible thing Lorna had done to her. Maybe her friend had betrayed her to these men as well. Maybe she had told them to come and take her away. How else could they have known to come straight down the river? How could they have guessed that was the only safe approach? Like a far distant memory, the sound of her mother's voice came back to her. *I believe 'tis best if we let her go. Do ye?* "Dear God," she whispered.

"Do ye believe ye were in danger?" Rob asked.

"Aye, I believe it."

"Do ye know," he continued, "that we have the right of it?"

"They're my family!"

"'Tis true enough, but when your father died, King Jamie gave your wardship to the Earl of Argyll, Johnnie's father." He nodded toward John. "The Earl has been your guardian since ye were a few months old."

Muriella stiffened. Her mother had never told her. Surely she must have known. And Lorna also had said nothing. She wondered what else they had kept from her.

"We came, lass, because we've heard that the Calders mean ye harm. And no matter how much they wish it otherwise, the Roses simply aren't strong enough to keep ye safe."

That was just what Isabel had told her doubting sisters, and though they had not wanted to listen, they *had* been afraid. Even Hugh had been afraid. But only this stranger had bothered to explain why.

Muriella's thoughts were interrupted when Rob gripped her roughly. He looked up, his hand clenched on the handle of his sword; he heard horses coming at them from out of the forest. As the riders emerged from the bushes, he recognized the Campbell plaid and smiled in relief. "'Tis glad to see ye, I am," he called to his eldest son, who led the horsemen onto the narrow path. "We'll be needing your help, if I'm not mistaken. Did ye bring the horses?"

His son nodded and Muriella saw that each of the new men held a fresh animal by the reins.

"You're just in time, lad. This one can't last much longer." Lifting the girl down after him, Rob changed horses as swiftly as possible, as did the others who had come from Cawdor. In a few moments, the men who were staying behind disappeared back into the trees, taking the exhausted horses with them.

Muriella realized there must be forty Campbells now. And they were ready to fight should any man, Rose or Calder, come to hinder them. All because of Cawdor.

As the men made their way down the sloping path, Rob's son guided his animal up close beside his father's. Leaning forward, he eyed Muriella, frowning when she moved away. The light was murky by now, but he was surprised to see that her hair fell below the horse's neck in a tangled mass of red gold that glimmered, catching what light was left. Her eyes were deep green and, like her hair, they caught the fading light and held it fast.

"Here, David Campbell!" Rob bellowed above Muriella's head. "Leave the lass alone! She's seen enough of our ugly Campbell faces today."

"So she's a beauty as well as an heiress. Johnnie's a lucky man."

Muriella stared at the ground, wondering what made John lucky.

"Did ye have any trouble?" David asked. "Or did Hugh Rose decide to keep his bargain after all?"

"Och, no! The old man's a fool, right enough. He took the girl to Cawdor, thinking he could hold us off from there. He should've known better than that. But there's something that's been nagging at me, just the same." Running his hand through his hair, Rob glowered at his son. "'Twas a mite too easy, ye ken? There was only a single guard waiting for us, and him quickly overpowered. Then 'twas just the child and one woman. But," he snorted in disgust, "the Roses were always foolish and oversure of themselves. Ye'd think they'd have the brains to see the Calders were more of a threat to the lass than we were."

Muriella felt as if she might be sick again. Her palms were icy with sweat. Maybe it had been easy because Lorna had intended that it should be so.

"Where's the woman who was with her? Did ye take her?"

"No. Left her behind. Didn't want to give the Roses time to gather their men."

"She'll warn them then. We'd best hurry."

"We've been hurrying, man! Can't ye see that? Ye won't find Campbells creeping through the brush when 'tis time to run. Besides, I've a suspicion we've got nothing to fear from the Roses. 'Tis the Calders I'm thinking about."

David nodded, glanced once over his shoulder, and kicked his horse forward.

Muriella swayed, then leaned back, closing her eyes, and gave herself up to the clamor of the horses and Rob's soothing voice above her. She tried to make her thoughts grow still, and at last her fear began to ebb and she almost slept.

Four hours later, Rob rode up beside his nephew. "There's a glen no more than a mile from here. 'Tis a safe enough spot to camp for a few hours, and easily defended."

John peered at his uncle through half-closed eyes. His face had settled into weary lines and his shoulders drooped with fatigue. "'Tis no' wise to stop, Uncle Rob. We'd be inviting the Calders to catch us. We'd best go on for a bit."

"No," Rob protested. "The girl is weary, and she's losing blood from that finger. We've got to stop the bleeding and give her some rest."

John glanced at Muriella's pale, shuttered face, then back down the forest the way they had come. He shook his head in distraction.

David Campbell, who had been riding close by, called out, "Ye wouldn't want her to die, would ye?"

One of the other men replied before John could open his mouth, "She won't die so long as there's a red-haired lassie on the banks of Loch Awe willing to win the prize of Cawdor."

Rob dismissed the man with an angry glare and turned back to John. "She's weak and frightened, Johnnie. Let her rest. I could use a bit of supper myself."

John considered Muriella's slumping form. Her hand and arm were dark with blood, her head seemed too heavy to hold upright. Exhaustion and cold had tinged her skin slightly blue. He sighed, giving the signal to stop.

A few minutes later, the horses filtered into a glen with a burn running across one corner. The thick trees offered the men a sense of protection, and Rob nodded in approval. Slipping from his horse, he caught Muriella around the waist, then lifted her to the ground. "David," he ordered, "ye take Jemmie and watch the north. Simon, ye take the east, Archie, the south. They won't be coming from the west, that's certain."

The guards trudged off to take their positions while Rob carried the girl into the shadows, away from the curious eyes of the men. Sitting wearily on a boulder, he seated her on the ground at his feet. Without speaking, she watched as the men laid a fire and placed the cooking kettle above it to heat their dinner. They crouched around the brilliant flames that rose up to warm the chilled, misty air, each man huddling close to the fire, drawing his plaid tight against the cold.

As the sounds of movement began to fade into the low murmur of voices, Muriella found herself staring at John again and again. He stalked around the circle of men, stamping his feet against the ground as if the raw leather boots laced up his calves were not warm enough to keep out the chill. His heavy cloak swung out when he walked, revealing the gray padded doublet and tight-fitting trews beneath before he drew the wool closed with his fist. The glow from the fire altered his rugged face, emphasizing the heavy dark brows and giving his skin a gray translucence as he moved through the wavering shadows. In Muriella's mind it lent him an air of unreality. The only reality she recognized was Rob's legs against her sides and his warm cloak about her shoulders.

Rob felt her drawing closer, as if by doing so she could escape the threatening darkness; he saw that she was watching his nephew—and wondering. "Johnnie's to be your husband, lass," he explained. "Argyll has decided. That's why my brother sent him to fetch ye. I thought he might run into trouble on the way, so I came along."

Muriella heard nothing beyond *Johnnie's to be your husband.* "But that can't be. I'm betrothed to my cousin Hugh. I must marry *him.* They always told me—"

Rob shook his head. "They had no right to tell ye that. Your guardian must be the one to pick your husband. Surely ye know that." But then he remembered how little this girl's family had seen fit to tell her.

She stared at him in disbelief. "But Hugh—"

"Hugh was in the past," Rob said. "Things have changed and ye must learn to accept that. The Campbells will see that you're happy now."

Her heart sank at his decisive tone. "I was happy at home."

"Were ye indeed?" Rob sounded doubtful, but before Muriella could say more, he added, "Ye were a child at Kilravok, protected mayhap, and secure, but we left that child behind when we took ye from Cawdor. Ye're thirteen—a woman. And that means ye must marry the man the Earl has chosen."

*Ye have to understand that women never get to choose their own fate,* her mother had told her. *I'm afraid ye'll learn that for yourself sooner than ye care to.* Only now, as her own stomach knotted in despair, did Muriella understand the resentment with which Isabel had spoken. Unable to force words past her stiff, cold lips, she pulled her feet in tight against her body, wrapping Rob's cloak about her neck as she attempted to steady her uneven breathing.

Rob slipped down beside her to put his arm around her

shoulders. "He's a good man, is Johnnie. Ye'll see. 'Tis no' such a terrible thing to be wed to him. And he'll be good to ye, I promise that, or by God, he'll be hearing from me!"

Unaware of his uncle's conversation with the girl, John Campbell paced the boundary of the glen several times, flinging his cloak restlessly over his shoulders. Despite the cold, sweat stood on his forehead. Finally, he strode toward the fire and, glowering into the shadows, called, "Uncle Rob, do ye have her?"

Rob stood up to draw Muriella to her feet. He waited a moment to be certain she could stand alone, then pushed her gently into the circle.

The men gasped as the firelight struck the girl mercilessly. The light from the torch someone had thrust into Rob's hand encircled her with an unnatural glow. Her matted and windblown hair fell in disorder to her knees; the flickering light crawled down the auburn curls, giving them a deep radiance. Her eyes were distant and leaden, but as the firelight moved, they changed to flashing green.

Even more disturbing was the stain that had seeped into her gown from just below the neck. The blood covered her in a swanlike pattern; when she moved, the pattern shifted and lived in the fingers of light and shadow that played over the heavy folds of her gown. As one, the men crossed themselves, certain they were in the presence of a witch. Their apprehension hung in the air, holding Muriella apart from them. She would have laughed at their superstition but she was too tired. The last hours had drained her of the spark that made her whole.

Keeping his hand on her shoulder, Rob nodded at his nephew. John hesitated, then came forward, but he paused as his gaze met the girl's. Green, then gray, then black, her eyes glistened in the firelight. Somehow they seemed to weaken his will; he found he could not look away. Her luminous, frightening stare held him prisoner. He could feel the unease all around him and thought of the men who watched in silence, waiting for him to move. Abruptly, he came closer.

When he took Muriella's hand, she wanted to pull away, but she would not let the men see her retreat, not even now, when she could barely stand. Instead, she allowed him to draw her nearer the warmth of the fire.

"'Tis only her finger that's been hurt. The blood is from her finger," John announced. His voice was strong and deep, but even so, it could not quite break the spell Muriella had cast over the waiting men. They shifted uncomfortably, watching her with narrowed eyes. "Archie, will ye clean and bind this for her? I wouldn't know how myself and it looks none too good."

Archie came forward reluctantly and knelt to examine the finger. "She's bled a great deal," he said. "She'll be needin' some rest before she rides again. I wouldn't be knowin' how well 'twill mend."

Shaking his head, Archie began to work, bathing the finger in the warm water John brought, before wrapping it with the wild grasses and herbs he carried in a leather pouch at his belt.

As Archie covered the jagged wound with a piece of clean cloth, Muriella looked up at him in gratitude. She did not wish to see what Lorna had done to her. Even the thought left her feeling faint. When someone offered her a bowl, she took it without a word and stepped back out of the circle, seeking a tree or boulder to lean against. She felt her strength disintegrating and knew she had to be alone for a few moments. Hardly aware of what she was doing, she sank down beside a bent oak, cradling the bowl of food in her chilled hands.

As she ate, she tried to shut out the sight of the men gathered around the campfire—these strangers who watched her warily and murmured in discontent beneath their breath. She felt completely isolated, utterly alone amidst the hostility all around her. In that instant, her longing for Lorna, her mother, even her unpleasant aunts was so intense that she ached with it. Fighting back tears, she chewed fiercely on a piece of dried venison.

John had watched the girl slip away but did not try to stop

her. He could see that she was too weak to flee just now. Besides, her presence and the strange glow of her eyes reminded him too forcefully of the restless mood of his men. He shook his head in impatience when he realized he shared their feelings. There was something disturbing about the intensity of that girl's gaze.

He looked up to find his uncle watching. Rob's forehead was furrowed in concern, and he glanced often toward the tree where Muriella sat. "She's your responsibility now," Rob's gray eyes seemed to say. John took a bite of his bread, chewing it with unnecessary vigor. Uncle Rob was right, but that did not mean his nephew had to like it.

He resented Muriella, he admitted to himself, because without her his future held little. As a second son, he could look forward to next to nothing from his father's vast holdings. Everything would go to his older brother, Colin. But then King Jamie had given this girl to Argyll as a ward. Because of her, John would be wealthy and powerful; without her he would be impotent—no man at all—and that made him furious. He owed his entire future to a girl he didn't even want. And yet he had to have her. His only other choice was to take his brother's charity, and that would be even more galling.

Abruptly, he tossed his bowl aside and made his way to Muriella where she crouched stiff and silent beneath the oak. He could not see her face, but could hear her shallow breathing. He knelt beside the girl, his cloak brushing the damp grass at his feet.

She did not look up. After a long silence that began to thunder in John's ears, he said, "I'm sorry it had to be this way. But there was naught else we could do."

Muriella raised her head. "Ye could have left me with my family, where I belong."

Her voice vibrated with bitterness and John drew back a little, struggling to suppress his own anger. "'Twas no' safe," he said stiffly.

"They all tell me that," she replied as she looked up at the blur of his face in the darkness. "And mayhap they're right.

But the danger was mine to face, not yours. Besides, I know it wasn't really for my sake ye came."

John blinked at her in astonishment. He had not expected this kind of response from the girl who had seemed so weak a few moments before.

When he did not answer at once, Muriella plunged on. "But then I forgot, *ye* were in danger of losing Cawdor. And ye couldn't let that happen, could ye?"

She made it sound so mercenary. Without thinking, John took her hand roughly, as if the pressure of his fingers could make her understand. "We would have been foolish to risk a loss like that, don't ye agree?"

Muriella felt his anger in the careless touch of his hand when she met his eyes fully for the first time—blue eyes chilly as the night. She caught her breath and her hands grew clammy with sweat. She closed her eyes to shut out the image forming in her mind, but in the darkness behind her lids a torrent of water rose, swirling furiously about her waist. She tried to fight against the white, rushing foam, but it was sucking her under; she could not breathe. Muriella opened her eyes, gasping, and turned away as the image disintegrated and the roar of the water stopped pounding in her ears. She was not even aware that John had risen and returned to the circle of firelight.

In the unnerving stillness he left behind, Muriella tried to fight off the chill that crept over her quaking body. It was not a true vision, she told herself; it was only a waking nightmare caused by her weariness. But she could not quite make herself believe it. She knew then that she had to get away. Somehow she had to flee these men and find her way back to Kilravok. As for Cawdor, she never wanted to see it again.

Her heart beat faster at the thought of escape. Bunching her damp skirts in her hands, she rose carefully to her knees. She did not dare stand or they would certainly see her. Her mouth dry with the fear that someone would look her way, Muriella held her breath as she moved awkwardly, trying not to make a sound. She had covered no more than a few inches, however, when her head began to spin and her body to sway. She gasped and turned back to grasp the tree in both hands, resting her forehead against the rough bark. She was too weak, she realized, and the pain in her finger too intense. Even if she could get away without the Campbells' knowledge, she could not crawl all the way to Kilravok. She was trapped, just as Rob had said.

A weight like lead settled in her chest as she sank back against the support the tree offered. Her gaze was drawn reluctantly to John. She watched, shivering, as he paced the glen in agitation, unable to stay still even for a moment.

Then Rob began to sing softly.

> She hadna ridden a league, a league,
> Ne'er a league but ane,
> When she was 'ware o' a tall young mon
> Riding slowly o'er the plain.

One by one, the other men joined in. Even John paused, listening.

> But nothing did the tall knight say,
> And nothing did he blin,
> Still slowly rade he on befar,
> And fast she rade behind.

At last the voices seemed to draw John in, and he crouched beside his men to take up the verse.

> "This river is verra deep," he said,
> "As it is wondrous dun;
> But 'tis sich as a saikless maid,
> And a leal true knight can swim."

As the mournful tune, the quiet drone of the voices, crept into Muriella's cold heart, she shivered, closing her eyes to the dark circle of heads burnished golden by the firelight. A chill ran down her spine that had nothing to do with the cold night. Still the voices crooned their song, weaving about her an invisible web of melancholy.

"But ride on, ride on, proud Margaret
Till the water cooms o'er yer bree:
For the bride maun ride deep and deeper yet
Who rides this ford wi' me."

The last note quavered, then faded away. In the lingering silence, the girl heard the gurgle of a nearby burn, which slowly began to soothe her until her exhaustion overcame her and she slept.

Muriella awoke and sat up, listening. It was still deep night and she was thankful for the wolf pelts someone had tucked around her. Aside from the snoring of the men who crowded the tiny glen, the night was silent. Yet something had awakened her. Leaning back, she closed her eyes and wondered what it could have been. She recognized the soft rumble of the burn nearby, but knew it was not that which had shaken her from her sleep. Then she heard it—the thrumming of hooves in the darkness.

She dug her fingers into the earth and tried to feel relief. These men were coming to take her home. Home? That meant Cawdor, she reminded herself, and Cawdor was not where she wished to be. She wanted to be back at Kilravok where she and Hugh had played as children, where she had been happy. Before she'd begun to recognize the brutal world that existed beyond the soft, curving hills of her home.

She sensed movement nearby, and her breath escaped in a rush when she heard the warning shout reverberate through the trees.

"Ware! Arms!"

Shadows leapt into men all around her. John Campbell appeared from beneath a fur on one side, his uncle from the other. Both men struggled to shake away the webs of sleep.

"Take the lass and go," Rob commanded at last. "My sons and I will hold them off 'til ye get clear away."

John looked down at Muriella. "No," he said. "I'll stay to face the Calders with ye."

"Get ye gone!" his uncle said gruffly. "I know ye can't bear the thought of missing a chance to cut down a few more men, but ye'll just have to swallow your disappointment this time. The girl is more important than a single sword against this enemy. 'Tis her safety ye must think of, Johnnie. And once you're back at Inveraray, take care of the girl. She's a canny lass, is that one."

John looked unconvinced, but at the adamant expression on Rob's face, he nodded reluctantly. Leaning forward, he grasped his uncle's hand. "Take care." Then he turned away and called for his horse. Kicking the pelts from around Muriella, he pulled her to her feet. The unexpected motion broke the spell that had held her in its grasp. With little effort, she shook her hand free.

Her head was spinning at the confusion of sounds that assaulted her ears—the clanging of swords, the muttered oaths, the terrible cries of death that shattered the darkness. But no, that was not yet. Later it would come; just now she heard only the labored beating of her own heart. She turned toward Rob and reached out blindly. "I won't go unless ye come too."

He smiled while he adjusted his sword at his hip. "There now, lassie, you've no cause to worry for me. I'm a clever old man, am I, and no' afraid of any Roses or Calders, ye can bet."

In Muriella's inner sight, his body turned and turned again in the stiff white folds of a winding sheet, and she knew his faith was foolish. He would die, and soon. The sounds in her head spun faster and faster. She covered her ears with her hands, but the screams only grew louder. She fought to stop the spinning, to regain control of her body, but she was powerless.

She felt John pulling on her hand and resisted. Perhaps if she stayed, if she refused to leave Rob's side, she could change the future and banish this feeling of helplessness. Why had the vision come to her if not as a warning? "I won't go!" she cried. "He was kind to me."

"Come, we've no' much time," John insisted. "Ye can see him at Inveraray."

"No!" she repeated in desperation. "If ye leave him now, ye won't ever see him alive again!"

Shaking his head with exasperation, John lifted her off the ground to place her, protesting, on his waiting horse. He leapt up behind her; then, without a backward glance, he and a few of his men left the clearing.

Muriella fought the dizziness that overwhelmed her at the sudden motion of the war-trained animal. The horses were fleeing from the dim light of the fire and she yearned toward it. Once again, fear touched her as they rode into the starless night. Hearing the tumult begin in the glen they had left behind, she sat motionless in the saddle and fought the sense of desperation that was closing around her. Rob would certainly die, and the others, perhaps all of them—because of her. No matter what they had done to her, that knowledge was a weight too heavy to bear.

Oblivious of the girl who sat silently in their midst, the men rode hard mile after mile. The rocking of the horse was like a drug to Muriella, lulling her body into painful weariness, but John seemed unaffected. He held her tightly and did not relax his grip. She perched in discomfort for a long time before she heard a cry from up ahead.

"Loch Awe, Sir John. We're nearly home now!"

Muriella felt John heave a sigh of relief, then lean forward eagerly. As they paused at the top of a ridge, she realized why. The loch spread below them, wide, rippled and dark, while the moon swept a silver path across its heart. Along the bank, the trees shimmered with leaves that appeared silver white in the moonlight, making the shadows beyond seem even darker. The scene was beautiful in a ghostly way—so beautiful that it made her ache.

The other horses had clattered down the hill and were beginning to pick their way toward the shallow water where they could cross with ease. The men, excited by the prospect of reaching home, urged their animals forward incautiously. Just as John's horse stepped into the water, the animal in front stumbled, dumping his rider into the icy loch. The path of the moonlight seemed to break into fragments that glimmered for a moment in the darkness, then disappeared.

Muriella had seen it all before. She stiffened as the water splashed over her ankles and John leaned forward in irritation. "Are ye daft, man? 'Tis black night out and the horses can't see their way. Ye might have broken your neck!"

Shaking himself, the man lunged for the horse's bridle. As he got the animal under control, he laughed, calling over his shoulder, "Aye, I might have done it at that. Mayhap I'll tell my Flora she nearly lost me. That would warm her up, sure enough."

John was silent, but the other men chuckled. Their journey was finally over.

Muriella could just discern the outline of a range of mountains to the left. They looked huge and bleak in the darkness, and their presence sent a shiver down her back. She was somewhat comforted by the sound of a rushing river nearby, and the scent of the sea in the damp, clinging air. When John tightened his arm around her waist, she saw that they were starting up the last hill.

Some of the tension left his body as the castle loomed before them. It sat at the top of a gentle slope, its walls rising steeply into the night.

"'Tis Inveraray," John whispered. "We're home."

To Muriella it looked dark and gloomy—a cold prison. The chill reached out to enfold her; for the second time that night, she had to fight back tears of hopelessness. "*Your* home," she said, "not mine. You've taken that away from me and well ye know it."

She felt him stiffen as if she had struck him. He removed his arm from around her waist, slapping his horse's side as he did so. She could feel his anger in the labored rise and fall of his breath, but he did not answer her. There was nothing he could say.

They moved in silence over the drawbridge and into the still courtyard.

The men who sprawled on piles of hay at the edges of the courtyard heard a shout that woke them from their sleep. Then the gate began to rise, squealing and scraping as it hit the stone walls. The men shook their heads to clear the drowsiness away and stumbled through the darkness, groping for torches. As the clatter of hooves on cobbles filled the enclosure, each man lit his torch and, holding it high over his head, moved to take the reins that were tossed in all directions from the necks of panting horses.

In contrast to the men who had just awakened, who moved numbly about their tasks, the ones who rode under the gate laughed and called noisy salutations. Except for John. As he slid from his horse, peering through the melee of foaming, stamping animals and exhausted men, he remained grimly silent. The first person he recognized in the fitful light of the torches was Duncan, his squire.

"M'lord?" The young man glanced at the girl still huddled on the horse's back. "Is that her?"

John waved the question away. Turning his back on Duncan's curiosity, the older man continued searching for a particular face. "Is Richard Campbell here?"

"Aye. He couldn't sleep, he said. Thought ye might need him, though I couldn't see why ye should."

Duncan realized that his cousin was not listening. The young squire noticed for the first time that John's shoulders sagged and his face was haggard. "M'lord—"

"Richard!" John shouted.

Responding to the cry, a tall man with dark red hair shoved a sleepy groom aside. He was followed by a younger version of himself, except the hair was brighter and the face covered with freckles.

"Was there trouble?" Richard asked. "I told Andrew here 'twouldn't go well, but he only laughed."

"Aye, well I'm glad to see you're awake." John grasped Richard's hand in relief. "I need ye to go back. Uncle Rob is still there with most of the men. I wouldn't even be knowing how many of the enemy there were. But I want ye to take as many men as ye can gather. Donald will tell ye where."

"Aye, m'lord. We'll be gone before ye look behind ye." Dragging his brother by the arm, Richard moved away. "What did I tell ye?" he called. "Didn't I say there'd be trouble?"

"So ye did," Andrew grumbled sleepily. "But ye need no' shout in m'ear. I can hear ye well enough, man. See to your men instead o' your gloatin'."

John watched them go, then turned to consider Muriella where she sat unmoving on his horse's back. He noticed that a groom hovered at the animal's head, grasping the reins uncertainly; even Duncan seemed to be waiting. He felt a sudden impulse to simply turn and leave her, but his common sense won out over his weary frustration. He reached for the girl to lift her from the saddle and set her on the ground, where she swayed for a moment, then drew herself upright.

Muriella looked up at him, her eyes glassy green, but behind the surface he saw a violent spark of fear—or was it fury? At the moment, he was too weary to care which. Besides, his mind was back in that glen with his uncle and the other men. "Duncan," he called, motioning the squire forward. "See to the girl while I collect my wits." He started away, then added as an afterthought, "Don't let her out of your sight, ye ken?"

"Aye." As his cousin turned to go, Duncan touched his arm. "Colin's here. He rode in this morning. Told us to wake him as soon as ye returned."

John shook his head at the thought of facing his older brother now. At the best of times, Colin and he were no more than uneasy allies, and tonight John was not in the mood to swallow his brother's bitter humor. He moved toward the hall with reluctance, but the thought of meat and ale was too great a temptation to ignore.

Duncan watched his cousin go with concern. This will not be a pleasant night, he thought, remembering Colin's annoyance at having missed the chance to join the long ride to Cawdor. "The hunt," he had called it. Not until John disappeared into the hall did the squire turn to Muriella.

Her shoulders were drooping and she seemed small and frail in the unflattering light of the torches. His eyes narrowed against the yellow glare, Duncan lifted her chin with his forefinger so he could see her more clearly. Her skin was pale and there were shadows under her eyes and along her cheeks. Her lids were lowered, but as he stared down at her, she glanced up. He saw weariness and a kind of hopeless resignation in her gaze that tore at his heart.

Duncan took a deep breath, released it slowly. For a moment he was silent, held by her gaze; then she looked away. "So you're the Calder girl," he mumbled, turning her in the direction John had taken.

"Aye."

"They didn't say ye were so bonnie," he told her.

Muriella was grateful he could not see the grief that welled within her at those words. Hugh had said the same thing the first time they met. Just now the memory was painfully vivid.

Her silence made Duncan uneasy. "I suppose your uncles will be coming to Inveraray soon to try to take ye back."

She whirled, crying bitterly, "They won't. They're too afraid of the Campbells. Mayhap not a few in the woods, but they won't dare to come here." As she said it, she realized it was true and her despair deepened. Without another word, she turned to step through the blackened hole of the doorway and into the vast hall.

A fire burned in the fireplace along the far wall, and several torches guttered in their sconces against the rough-hewn stone, but the light was too dim to destroy the shadows that played about the vaulted, cavelike room. Most of the men were already seated around the rows of trestle tables strung across the uneven stone floor.

Muriella's gaze swept over the Campbells. The heavily armed military force had melted into weak and haggard puppets with their heads cradled against the tables on which they rested; their exhaustion had finally overtaken them. Even John.

He was leaning forward, elbows resting on the table, his face white except where the shadows had settled around his eyes and between his nose and mouth; even his heavy beard could not disguise his pallor. His dark hair was in disarray where he had pushed it back from his forehead, and his eyes were cloudy gray. He sat glowering at the pitted tabletop in silence.

As Muriella paused in the doorway, apparently unnoticed, young women began to appear from the kitchens with thick slabs of bread, cold meat and ale. Nudged out of their lethargy, the men ignored their aching muscles and concentrated instead on filling their stomachs. No one glanced at Muriella or spoke to her or asked her to sit down. For the first time, her weariness retreated behind a wave of anger. It was followed by the same intense loneliness that had overwhelmed her earlier. The Campbells had taken her but did not want to care for her; they made no offer of food or shelter or even a tankard of mulled wine.

A commotion at the top of the stairs drew Muriella's attention away from her own numb misery. A tall man stood laughing, a servant girl fluttering about him. He was fastening his robe, and his blue eyes glimmered when they rested on the girl at his side. Slapping her on the behind, he called, "Get me some ale, lass. 'Tis time to celebrate!"

The girl scurried down the stairs and off to the kitchen while the man followed more slowly. Considering the occupants of the hall with interest, he located John, who stood up. "Ho! Johnnie! Ye've got the lass then?" Running his hand through his sandy hair, he strode forward. "Well, bring her!" he demanded. "Let's have a look."

John squinted across the room at Duncan and the girl. When his cousin nodded, Duncan took Muriella's arm gingerly, as if he were afraid of hurting her. She wanted to shake herself free of his grasp, but wasn't certain she could move without his support. Her attention focused on Colin's flushed face, she managed to cross the hall without stumbling. When she stood before the brothers, Duncan released her. Muriella thought she would fall, but Colin caught both her hands in one of his while accepting a tankard of ale with the other.

"So," he muttered, lifting the tankard to his lips. Above the rim, he looked the girl up and down. He grimaced at the sight of her pallid face, untidy hair, and bloody, rumpled gown. "You're a bit of a mess, gurrl. Johnnie, didn't ye take care of her?" He swung the tankard up again, tilting it so the ale streamed into his mouth, then released Muriella without another glance.

Her stomach churned with fury at his careless treatment, at the way John looked away as if she were merely a shadow in the background. But she swore she would maintain her dignity; she would not let them know they had upset her. She pressed her lips together and made no sound as Colin turned to his brother to ask, "Where are Uncle Rob and the others?"

John sank back onto his bench. "There was trouble," he muttered. "Uncle Rob sent us away, the girl and me. He stayed to keep the Calders back. Or mayhap 'twas the Roses. I don't know which. I can't even tell ye how many there were. I've sent Richard and Andrew to gather some men and go back, though 'tis probably too late." He scrutinized with great concentration the half-empty tankard on the table before him.

"'Twould have been wiser to stay and fight the bastards," a man near John mumbled. "Och, but then, 'twas safer to slip away in the night, wasn't it? Or mayhap ye were just afraid—"

Before anyone could stop him, John rose abruptly and, dragging the man up by the collar, struck him across the jaw with a clenched fist.

"Leave him be," Colin shouted as he pulled his brother away from the stunned man. "We don't need any more trouble tonight."

John faced his brother furiously. "No man calls *me* a coward!"

"How about a fool?" Colin suggested. "The Calders are a cheatin' bunch of bastards and likely to be swarming over the hills to Inveraray any minute now. We need every man we can get to hold them off, little brother, yet ye knock one about as if he were of no use at all. *Think* before ye act, why don't ye?"

John felt the rage flaring within him and struggled to regain control. Then he looked up to see Muriella watching him coldly, her expression an accusation without words. He felt a flash of guilt for having left his uncle, and that only made his anger worse. He had had no choice; it was for her sake he had agreed to go at all. So why did she stand there looking at him that way?

At last Muriella dropped her gaze when she began to shake with spasms of freezing numbness and fatigue. She grasped the back of a chair, standing upright with difficulty, her face rigid with the effort to disguise her trembling.

Duncan tapped his cousin on the shoulder. "The girl is cold," he said.

John took a deep, shuddering breath. He was so weary, so concerned about his uncle's fate, that he had actually forgotten Muriella's needs. He saw that she was shivering. It seemed he could do nothing right tonight, not even care for his future bride. He frowned, motioning over his shoulder to a servant. When the girl approached, he told her, "Megan, take her to Elizabeth's old room. Give her clothes—Elizabeth's will do 'til tomorrow—and a hot bath if ye can manage it. I don't want to see her again tonight. And Megan"—he paused—"don't hurt her, but watch her close. Ye understand?"

"Aye, m'lord."

In silence, Megan led Muriella along the rows of men, who kept their gazes fixed on their food. As the girls mounted the stairs, the servant called for hot water and a tub to be brought. Several others scattered to arrange it.

Muriella followed the servant, but a thick fog had invaded her mind and she functioned only well enough to force herself upward, one worn stone step at a time. The fog chilled her into numbness and she was grateful.

She was not aware of Megan stripping her soiled dress from her, nor of the fire that leapt up the blackened stone in an attempt to warm the cold room in which she stood. But consciousness crept back as she sank into a wooden tub and the heat crawled up and down her body with sharply probing fingers. Pains began to run over her back and thighs, but she preferred the physical discomfort to her memories of the past several hours.

The servant eyed Muriella in concern as she leaned back in the water. "Are ye all right, miss? You're very gray around the edges."

Muriella closed her eyes briefly, saw only blackness there, and opened them. "I'm all right."

"Well, then, 'tis awful glad I am to hear that. For ye ken, I think Sir John means for me to stay with ye. And 'twould be much more pleasant than servin' in the kitchen." As she talked, she rinsed Muriella's shoulders and worked the worst of the soil out of her long, dripping hair. "'Tis a bitter night for a long ride, isn't it? Too cold for the wolves, let alone a poor lassie like ye. I don't know what they're thinkin' of, draggin' ye all over the Highlands without even a cloak. 'Tis disgraceful."

Megan's chatter reawakened Muriella's sleeping senses until she became aware of the touch of the cooling water on her bare skin. She sat up, wondering if she could get out of the tub on her own. But she need not have worried. The servant knelt and lifted her from under the arms. Although Megan was only fourteen and her body was small, she was wiry and quite strong. Muriella felt she could not even lift her hand, but soon she was standing on a soft fur rug beside the tub. She did not move, but stared before her at the shadows that crept up the walls and fluttered in the corners, while Megan threw a linen towel about her body and began to rub vigorously.

When she was dry, the servant handed her a robe. Muriella slipped her arms into the sleeves, surprised to find that they were warm. The robe must have been hanging near the fire. She pulled it close around her, seeking to draw the warmth into her chilled body.

"Ye'd best let me comb out the tangles tonight or we'll be havin' a devil of a time tomorrow," Megan declared. Before Muriella could protest, the servant pulled a low stool forward, motioning her to take a seat.

Muriella was hardly aware of Megan's brisk ministrations. She was conscious only of a deep pain that started in her belly and spread through her body until it reached her throat. She thought of Rob Campbell, saw the glitter of a sword slashing through the darkness, and cried out as she buried her face in her hands.

"Miss?" the servant murmured tremulously.

Muriella shook her head, motioning for Megan to continue. The servant found it difficult to keep her fingers steady as she worked the comb through the tangles; she could not forget that single anguished cry. Yet she dared not ask what it meant. When at last she was finished, she moved away quickly. "There ye are, miss. The bed is all ready for ye. I thought ye might be weary."

Muriella nodded, then rose, turning toward the bed that dominated the room. She pushed the heavy curtains aside and climbed up onto the mattress, moving awkwardly because she could not seem to make her muscles work as they should. At last she crawled under the furs and rough linen sheet and stretched her feet toward the warming pan. Before she closed her eyes, she looked up at Megan, who hovered beside her. Surprisingly, Muriella gave her a half smile. "Thank ye," she said.

The servant blinked. "Och, you're surely welcome, miss. Are ye really all right, then?" When Muriella nodded, Megan crept away to blow out the candles on the rosewood chest in the corner. Moving quietly, she went to a small pallet against the far wall. "Good night, miss."

Muriella closed her eyes with a sigh. Eventually, the pain inside eased a little as the darkness washed over her in waves. At last she slept.

In her dream she was a child again at Kilravok, before the fear had changed her. Her long braids hung over her shoulders, and as she ran, she enjoyed the swinging weight of her hair against her back. She slipped into the woods with the cool breeze on her face, seeking out the shadows where she could conceal herself from Hugh. She heard him coming, heard the low, teasing note in his voice when he called her name. Smiling, she turned away from the overgrown path.

"Ye know I'll find ye," he called. "I always do."

Now he was so close that she could hear his light footfalls and see his flaming red hair. Muriella held her breath. Pressing close to the trunk of a gnarled oak, she watched him duck beneath the trailing leaves, calling softly, "Muriella."

All at once, he was gone, enfolded by the moving shadows. She could no longer hear the crunch of twigs beneath his feet. Muriella waited a moment more, then crept from behind the tree to follow the path Hugh had taken. But before she had gone far, she heard his shout of triumph as he came up behind her and grasped her shoulder. "Ye see," he cried, "ye can't escape me no matter where ye hide." He wound his hands in her hair, tugging so she turned to face him, tangling them both in her heavy braids. They held each other and swayed and laughed until the sound echoed upward through the cool, dark woods.

Muriella awoke smiling and burrowed deeper into the feather mattress. Reluctantly, she opened her eyes to the unfamiliar darkness, unwilling to relinquish the pleasant memory of the dream. For a long time, she lay still, listening, while her smile faded and the night silence took the place of her remembered laughter. She looked around the darkened room, but saw nothing beyond the wavering shadows the fire cast over her bed. After several moments, she realized that a commotion outside had awakened her. She sat up, her mouth suddenly dry, her heart beginning to pound. In an instant, Megan stood beside her, rubbing her eyes with her curled fingers.

"What is it, miss?"

Muriella waited for the servant's dark shape to come into focus, then asked in a trembling whisper, "Could ye go to the hall and see if aught is going on down there? I need to know. I think—could ye?"

"Aye, miss, if ye'd like me to." The servant moved toward the nearest chest, struck a light, and held it to one of the pewter candlesticks. Then she picked up her robe and threw it around her shoulders. With her hand on the latch, she stopped to look at Muriella. Her mistress's eyes glimmered incandescent green in the half darkness, lighting her face with alarm and some terrible knowledge. Megan stood paralyzed.

"Please," Muriella cried.

Forced into motion by the sound of that anguished voice, Megan bent her knees briefly before she turned to go, the candle flame dancing wildly in her hand. She disappeared into the gloom of the hall.

At the top of the stairs she stopped, peering over the balustrade into the Great Hall. It was empty now except for Sir John and Duncan and a bloody stranger, who stood with his back toward the girl. The fire had died down and most of the torches were out, so that the hall was unusually dark. A sputtering oil lamp sat before John, creating an island of wavering light in the midst of the chilly darkness.

His eyes narrowed in concentration, John looked up at the other man, who stood just within the range of the pitiful light. "Well, David?" The pulse in his throat throbbed rhythmically.

Megan shivered as she crept down the stairs. When she reached the foot, she sat behind the heavy carved balustrade, her fingers locked around the cool wood, rubbed smooth by the touch of many hands.

Below her, David Campbell moved forward a few steps

and turned. As he raised his arm, pain whipped his mouth into an ugly scowl. He tried to touch John's hand but could not quite reach it.

"Well?" John demanded again.

"Dead, m'lord," David muttered. "All dead." He sat down abruptly, as if he could no longer stand, while Duncan grasped John's shoulder firmly.

"Jemmie said there were no more than ten, coming from the north, so we were aye certain we could hold them off. But the bastards came from the east and south as well, forty or more altogether. They must have gotten to Sim and Archie before they could warn us.

"My father had to think quickly. He wanted to give ye time to get well away. So he had us turn the cooking pot upside down and form a ring around it." He smiled grimly. "To make them think the lass was inside, ye see, so they'd no' go chasin' after ye." His smile faded. "It worked. They surrounded us, and we protected that burned out pot as if the girl and all our fortunes too were underneath." He choked and struggled to go on.

"When they got to the center, when every man in the ring lay dead, they turned the pot over with a shout of triumph, only to find it empty." In spite of the remembered horror of watching his father and brothers die, in spite of his own pain and weariness and despair, he could not keep a flicker of satisfaction from his voice. "The Calders were fair full of fury, but by then 'twas too late. Ye were far away."

He paused, gasping for breath, his skin deathly pale. "I was only wounded, but I suppose they couldn't see that in the darkness. They left me for dead. After they'd gone, I found a horse they'd left behind and came here." His voice shook more with each word until the last came out as a groan.

"Didn't ye see Richard and the others on the way to Inveraray?"

"I saw no one. But had I seen them, I might have killed two or three before I realized who they were. I'm a bit jumpy." David paused to shake his head. "I've never seen so much blood—my father's, my brothers', everyone's." Laying his head on the table, he clenched his teeth against the pain.

Megan wrapped her arms around her trembling knees, rocking back and forth in her hiding place. She bit her lip in sympathy when she saw David's body twitch.

Duncan left John's side to bend over the wounded man. He considered the bloody plaid before turning back the cloak to reveal an arm cut almost to the bone from shoulder to elbow. The squire glanced at his cousin. "M'lord? He's badly wounded in the arm, and probably the hip, judging from his limp. And he's lost a good deal of blood. We'd best care for him."

John looked up. "Uncle Robbie is dead," he declared in a toneless voice. All at once, he sat up; his mouth fell open, then snapped closed. "She warned me not to go. The girl said, 'If ye leave him now, ye'll never see him alive again.' Do ye think she knew? She couldn't have known."

Duncan did not respond, but drew David Campbell gently to his feet. "The man needs care," he grunted.

John stared at the squire blankly for a moment, then shook himself out of his lethargy. "Aye, we must keep *him* alive, at least." He took David's feet and the three men moved slowly around the table and out of the tiny circle of light.

"Shall we wake Colin?" Duncan asked as they shuffled across the floor with their burden.

"No. Tomorrow will be soon enough. There's naught else can be done tonight."

Megan watched as the shadows closed around them. She was not aware that her candle was leaning precariously until hot wax dripped onto her hand. She jumped at the sharp pain that forced her into motion. After waiting for the flame to stabilize, she turned to make her way up the stairs, shading the candle with one hand. To her, the long, echoing hall seemed very dark and very threatening.

When she stood before the door to Muriella's chamber, the servant paused for a moment, remembering with trepidation her mistress's watchful eyes. *The girl said, "If ye leave him now, ye'll never see him alive again." Do ye think she knew?* Megan said a silent prayer, then pushed the door open.

"Och, miss!" she cried. "'Tis terrible. They've all been killed, every man but David Campbell." Before Muriella could respond, Megan retold the story she had just heard.

Muriella looked away as the servant spoke. So she had been right. She had not wanted to believe it, even though she knew her visions never lied. Not Rob Campbell, she had prayed. And yet she had only met the man this morning. He was little more than a stranger to her. Why then did she feel so achingly hollow at the thought of his death?

Muriella had begged John not to leave his uncle to fight alone, had warned him of what would happen if he did, but he had not listened. She remembered with bitterness that as they fled that ill-fated glen, the young man had not whispered a word of thanks to his uncle, nor had he looked back—not even once.

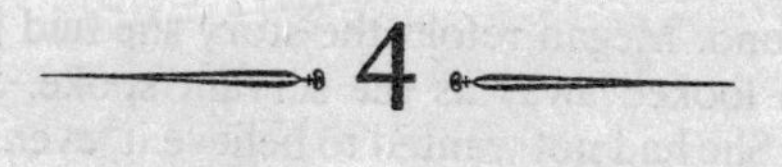

# 4

Muriella awoke the next morning with a start. For a long while she lay still, but in time the early-morning chill touched her nose and cheeks, rousing her more fully. She opened her eyes reluctantly and gazed around her at the unfamiliar room. She saw that the bed in which she lay was huge and bulky. Its oak posts rose menacingly toward the ceiling, disappearing under the brocade canopy, which Muriella decided must be green, although the light was too dusky to tell for certain. She eyed with distaste the bed curtains hanging in dense greenish folds at the corners. At Kilravok, in the tiny chamber she had shared with Lorna, there had been no such luxuries. The plain wooden bedstead had barely raised the mattress from the floor, there had been only a single fur, and the linen had been much less fine. Yet she had felt more at ease there than she did in this dark chamber.

She slid to the edge of the bed, pausing as she stared at the mottled gray stone walls. Nothing moved in the tiny fingers of light that filtered through the closed shutters, yet the empty walls, the oak chest in the corner, even the cold stone floor seemed to call to her out of the silence. Suddenly, the air was full of memories that crowded close, speaking in the voices of the past. She reached out to touch the wall. Through her fingers, she thought she could feel the laughter, the tears, and the pain of one who had abandoned this chamber long since.

When she shook her head, the feeling vanished as quickly as it had come; the room was once again four walls without life or spirit. Muriella pushed a bearskin aside and swung her legs over the edge of the bed. She gasped when her feet touched the floor. The rushes were old and stale; they offered little protection from the cold stone beneath. She shivered as the chill engulfed her bare feet and legs.

In the soft gray light that seemed to swirl around her shoulders, she made her way to the window and knelt before it. She tried to open the shutters, hoping a fresh breeze might dissipate the gloom, but the wood resisted her. After several tugs, she finally drew the shutters open and breathed in the heather-scented air.

With her hands pressed against the wide sill, she leaned out, trying to recognize shapes and colors in the mist. It seemed to her that the air had never smelled like this at Kilravok, nor in the stuffy rooms at Cawdor. But the invigorating scent of morning, lovely as it might be, could not make her any less a prisoner. She wondered if any power on earth could alter the future the Campbells had arranged for her.

She felt a flash of hope when she remembered Hugh. Perhaps her betrothed would come for her and take her back to Kilravok. *Hugh is in the past,* Rob had told her. Muriella shook her head in denial, but when she tried to visualize her cousin's face, she found she could not do it. In that moment, she thought her misery would choke her.

Seeking relief from her thoughts, she peered at the tangled garden appearing from out of the mist. The mountains were still cloaked in clinging white, but the hollyhock and bracken and autumn roses shimmered as the sunlight began to burn away the dew. She listened until she heard the constant crashing of waves against stone—the sea. Although she turned her head in an effort to see the ocean, the heavy stone battlements blocked her view.

"Och, miss! Ye'll be certain to get the ague that way, ye will indeed," Megan spoke unexpectedly from behind her. "Come away and crawl back into bed while I build up the fire again. Ye must come away!" When her mistress did not move at once, Megan put her hands on the other girl's waist and tugged.

Muriella whirled, twisting free of the servant's grasp. Her finger had begun to throb again and the pain swept over her in waves. She started to fall, but Megan caught her. The two girls swayed as the room revolved before Muriella's eyes; when her vision cleared she found herself staring at the servant's troubled face.

"Miss? What is it? Can ye stand now?"

Straightening slowly, Muriella raised her injured hand to find that it was covered with blood. From far away she heard Megan gasp and realized she was being guided toward the bed. Climbing in among the soft, warm furs, she stared blankly at her hand until Megan touched her arm.

"I'll have to change the bandage and try to stop the bleedin', but I'm no' certain I can do it. Sir John brought these last night, but I didn't want to wake ye." The servant dropped a pile of bandages, a dagger and a sack of herbs at Muriella's feet, then with a deep breath, reached for the injured hand. "I'm afraid I'll hurt ye," she murmured.

"Ye will." Muriella's voice sounded overloud in the still room. "But ye must, so ye'd best get on with it."

"Aye, well." Megan bit her lip nervously. "I forgot, Sir John left some wine. Mayhap 'twill help a little."

While Megan poured the wine, Muriella took the dagger in her right hand and cut the old bandage away. She did not look down at the uncovered wound, but turned instead to accept the pewter goblet the servant offered. Muriella swallowed the wine quickly, then stared into the low-burning fire while Megan worked. Twice she thought she would faint as the spasms of pain moved up her arm, but with an effort she kept the blackness at bay.

At last Megan pulled the new bandage tight. While Muriella leaned back, the servant went to revive the fire. Megan dressed quickly when the flames began to creep again up the blackened stones, but the heat did not stop her from shivering as she moved barefoot over the rushes. "Can I get ye some more food, miss? Or more wine?"

"Aye, a little more wine."

After Megan handed her the goblet, Muriella pulled one of the furs from the twisted pile around her and held it toward the servant. Megan gaped at her.

"Ye look cold," Muriella explained. "The fire doesn't seem to warm the room well enough."

Megan's eyes widened in surprise. She smiled shyly as she wrapped the heavy fur around her shoulders. "I never had a mistress do that before."

Muriella frowned. "Do they mistreat ye here?"

"Och, no! 'Tis just that in the kitchen ye don't have much chance to get cold, what with the big ovens and the runnin' back and forth. And even if ye did, no one would care. 'Tis different down below, ye ken. The cooks aren't always in a pleasant frame of mind. They don't ever hurt me—at least, no' very often. But once they threw Davie out on his head. He had a great lump for near a week." Megan chattered until her curiosity overcame her. "They hurt ye yesterday, though, didn't they?"

"I—who?"

Megan lowered her voice as if afraid someone might overhear. "Why, the Campbells, miss. Your finger. What did they do to it?"

Her mistress looked away. "'Twas no' the Campbells. 'Twas my friend, my nurse from when I was a bairn. She—" Muriella choked on the words but forced herself to go on. "She cut it through to the bone."

Megan gaped at her, eyes wide with horror. "But *why?*"

Frowning, Muriella tried to remember through the painful haze that cloaked her thoughts. "She said she had to mark me." Speaking with difficulty, she added, "So the Campbells couldn't bring an imposter to claim Cawdor."

Megan bit her lip until it ached, then murmured, "But miss, just think how much she must have loved ye to do such a thing. It couldn't have been easy for her."

Muriella blinked in surprise. She had never thought of that. With a sigh, she bowed her head. She could not think of it now either; thinking hurt too much.

Unnerved by the despair she saw in her mistress's face, Megan turned away. "Well," she said briskly, "we must find ye something to wear. From what I saw last night, we'll have to get rid of the things ye came in. I'll give the wool to the seamstress to cut up for the servants and we'll burn the others. Do ye mind?"

"No," Muriella whispered. She watched, nodding in approval, as Megan scooped up the tattered clothes and dropped them into the fire. She wished she could as easily destroy everything that reminded her of yesterday. As the flames leapt up the stones, she found herself enthralled by the moving light that reached out for the bed, licked about its heavy legs, then crept away. Muriella felt caught up in the play of light and shadow.

"There!" When the last fragment of cloth had been consumed by the flames, Megan wiped her hands and turned to the chest against the far wall. Lifting the lid, she called over her shoulder, "Mayhap we can find something in here. I know Miss Elizabeth kept her things, even from when she was a bairn. Mary told me she wouldn't throw anythin' away if once she'd loved it. Now, let me see." Megan explored the inside of the chest, talking softly to herself as she pulled the clothing this way and that.

"Who is Elizabeth?" Muriella asked, remembering the overwhelming sense of another presence she had felt there earlier. "This was her room, wasn't it?"

"Aye, it belonged to her before they married her to Lachlan Maclean. She's Sir John's elder sister. They were always close when they were bairns. At least, that's what Mary says. She says Sir John used to play the lute and sing while Miss Elizabeth worked her tapestry. But of course, 'twas a long time ago. They don't speak so much anymore, even when she comes to stay here."

Megan's head disappeared into the chest again and she added another gown to the pile on the floor beside her. "Ah," she said at last, "here." She held up a light blue gown with a square neck and long, full sleeves. "It must have belonged to Miss Elizabeth a long time ago, 'tis so small. But it just might fit ye, miss. I don't want ye bein' tied up in one of those heavy things." She pointed to the gray and black gowns at her feet. "Too dark, with no life in them. But there!

Ye don't need to listen to me. Mary never does, nor does Jenny. That's because Jenny is always listenin' for Colin, ye see. But I listen to them, ye can bet. I've learned a great many things that way."

While Megan talked, Muriella tossed the covers aside and stepped onto the floor. She discarded the gown she had slept in, then stood still while the servant slipped the blue gown over Muriella's head.

Megan fumbled for several moments before she managed to tie the strings. Then she stepped back and smiled. "Ye look much better than ye did last night. Blue suits ye, that it does, though with those eyes, green should be your color, don't ye think?"

Muriella was looking out the window, unaware of Megan's question. "Could ye take me to the garden? 'Tis so cold and dark in here."

Megan considered her mistress in silence. When Sir John had brought the bandages last night, Colin had been close behind him. The older brother had warned Megan that the girl might try to escape. "And if she does, I don't have to be saying what will happen to ye, girl," he had threatened.

But Muriella's expression was so wistful as she looked at the garden. Surely there was no slyness in her eyes. Besides, the servant had always found a perverse delight in upsetting Colin. It was not difficult to make him angry enough that the lump for which he was so well known would rise between his brows. "We couldn't go by the front gate, that's sure," she mused. "The guards won't open for us, and they'd probably call Sir John."

"Is there no other way out?"

"Well . . . " Megan paused. "There is another passageway. But ye mustn't let on that I told ye."

Muriella recognized the servant's hesitation. "Ye needn't fear that I'll run, for no doubt I couldn't get far before they caught me. Besides, I don't think I would be safe at Cawdor now." The sound of those words on her own lips—and the jolt that went through her when she realized they were true—made her shudder with cold. In sudden determination, she started for the door.

Megan stopped her with a gentle tug at her elbow. "Do ye think I might go down to the kitchen first to get some bread and cream? Aren't ye hungry?"

Muriella was not, but she realized she had not eaten much last night. And she had been too restless to eat at Cawdor. She would make herself ill if she wasn't careful, and she sensed that she would need all her strength in the days to come. "Aye," she agreed, "and see if ye can find some meat as well."

Megan smiled with relief. "That I will. Don't worry yourself, I'll be back soon."

Once beyond the door, Megan was swallowed by the gloomy shadows, and her mistress felt intensely alone in the silence left behind.

Several minutes later, with bread and meat in hand, Megan led her mistress to a door a few yards beyond the one to Muriella's chamber. "This is the way. Are ye sure ye want to go down? 'Tis dark and cold in this passage."

"I want to." I need to, she added silently.

Nodding, the servant put the rest of her breakfast into one of her huge pockets and, grasping the heavy iron handle on the door, pulled with all her strength. As the door swung open, Muriella stepped back in surprise; it made no noise, and the hinges at Cawdor always squealed.

Megan glanced over her shoulder, then, taking her mistress's hand, drew her into the passage. Muriella had not thought anything could be darker than the hallway, but this was much worse. The light had never touched these walls that towered damp and forbidding on either side. Here the smell of stale, chilled air that filled the castle was even more intense, and the gray stone was beaded with moisture. There was no noise besides the slapping of their feet against the packed dirt floor to disturb the silence.

The girls twisted around several corners, clutching the damp stone to keep from sliding as the path cut sharply downward, before they came to another door. This one had three bars across it and a rusted bolt at its edge. Megan began to push and shove, panting as she heaved each bar back. She struggled with the bolt for a moment, then at last pushed the door open.

Muriella moved past her to stand in the sunlight, which banished the chill that lingered inside the castle walls. She gazed about her in wonder at the bracken and heather that twisted among the swaying pines and birches. Here and there sprays of white or red broke through the confusion of green and brown and silver, making their own disorderly pattern on the sloping landscape. Muriella thought it wonderful. Even the tall, brooding mountains seemed less threatening in the sunlight. The jagged sides were slashed with rushing streams that glittered silver against the unrelieved blackness. It was beautiful in an unsettling way. With a sigh, she clasped her hands before her and listened; she could hear the pounding of the sea somewhere to her right and the smell and feel of salt was heavy in the air. "'Tis lovely," she mused aloud.

The servant considered for a moment, brow furrowed. "'Tis a bit overgrown, don't ye think? I'm always afraid I'll get lost in the roses and cut myself on the thorns."

Muriella smiled. "Ye need only take your time and learn to know the plants. Then they can't hurt ye." Her eyes darkened as she knelt to touch a cluster of yellow roses.

Megan saw the shadow in Muriella's eyes. It reminded her with sudden clarity of the look she had seen in those eyes the night before. What was it Sir John had said? *Do ye think she knew? She couldn't have known.* The servant shivered and, after a moment's hesitation, touched her mistress on the shoulder.

"Aye?"

Taking a deep breath, Megan said, "Last night, when ye sent me down to the Hall, Sir John said something that made me wonder—" She broke off to swallow dryly. "Ye have the Two Sights, don't ye?"

Muriella wanted to deny it—she had spent her whole life in an effort to do so—but she could not. "Aye," she murmured, "I'm afraid 'tis true."

"Afraid? But why? 'Tis a wondrous gift to know how to

see the future. Ye must be blessed indeed." Megan wanted to reach out to touch Muriella again, as if she might absorb some of the magic, but she withdrew her hand when Muriella tensed and turned away.

"'Tis a curse, not a gift. I don't see joyful things, ye ken, only death and sorrow. And even though I know 'tis coming, I can't stop it." She took a deep breath. "It's never given me pleasure, only pain. Can ye understand that?"

Megan stood with her mouth open, hands buried in the pockets of her plain muslin gown. "No, miss, I can't."

With a sigh, Muriella rose, smoothing out the creases in her skirt. "Have ye ever been swimming in the sea?"

"Aye, as a bairn, but I don't see—"

"Didn't ye ever feel afraid while the waves crashed around ye?"

Megan considered the question; her eyes widened as a memory struck her. "Aye, one day the wind came up and the water rose so high I couldn't even see the shore. I was sore afraid then, I can tell ye."

Muriella nodded. "That's how 'tis when the Sight comes to me. 'Tis as if I'm out there in the sea and the water beats against me 'til I can't stand upright anymore. I can feel the waves pulling at my feet, swirling around my head, choking me, and I have to fight with all my strength to keep from going under. I can kick out and wave my arms, but I can't win, because the sea is stronger. It'll drown me someday, because I have no' the power to stop it."

"Have ye tried?" Megan asked.

"Aye," Muriella replied wearily. "Every day of my life. And until yesterday, I thought I'd learned to shut out the knowledge I didn't want. I hadn't had a vision in a long, long time."

When her voice trailed off, the servant touched her hand, unable to conceal her impatience. "What happened then?"

Muriella crushed the petals of a rose between her fingers without knowing that she did so. "The Campbells came for me."

There was such despair in her voice that Megan knew she could not question her further. But she did not really understand the anguish in those strange green eyes. "Aye, well, things are different for ye now."

With a sigh, Muriella inhaled the fragrance of the garden, the tang of the sea as if they had the power to heal her. When the smell of fear had dissipated a little, she asked, "Can ye take me to the loch? We crossed it in the darkness, but I want to see it now, with the sun upon it."

"'Tis a way down the hill," Megan said, "and too near the gate for my likin'. Ye wouldn't want the watchmen to see ye." At Muriella's look of disappointment, she added, "But I can show ye the sea. 'Tis round the back. The castle sits on a cliff, ye ken. But ye can't reach the water from here. Ye must go round the hillside for that." She took Muriella's hand to draw her forward.

As they passed the end of the weathered battlements, Megan fell silent while Muriella froze beside her. Away from the protective walls of the castle, the wind rose howling and shook her to the bone, twisting her skirt around her ankles. She was not afraid, although she stood at the edge of a steep cliff that terminated in jagged rocks far beneath her. She was fascinated with the deep blue bay, sheltered on both sides by long groves of trees that swayed with the force of the wind. Muriella loved the smell, the feel, the sound of the water, and she smiled with delight at the way the sea reached in from beyond the farthest group of trees, the water changing again and again from ice blue to green to turquoise.

Behind her, the walls of the castle seemed to be a mere continuation of the ground at her feet. Steep castle walls and jagged cliffs towered in sullen contrast to the peaceful heart of the bay. Below, the waves thrummed ceaselessly against the shore and she breathed in the throbbing rhythm.

The scene was frighteningly beautiful. She had never seen anything like it before. She felt a constriction in her chest, a heightening of all her senses, as if the wild beauty of this place were too much for her sight to bear alone. Despite the sorrow within her, she could not help but respond to the exultant cry of the wind above the rising thunder of the waves. She leaned out, wanting to capture the moment in her open palms, but when she drew her hands close, she saw that they were empty. Her heart dragged, her breath became painful, and an unnatural silence locked her in its grasp. "Listen!" she hissed. "They're coming."

"Who's comin'?"

Muriella looked right through the servant. "They're coming."

"Do ye mean the Calders? Och! We'd best get inside!"

"No. 'Tisn't the Calders. Listen."

Megan tried to concentrate so she might understand. She twisted her fingers together, glancing twice toward the path that had brought them here, before she finally heard it. It was not the sound of an invading party. The tread of the horses was too plodding. In fact, the sound was melancholy and echoed the expression on Muriella's face. The servant took her mistress's arm beseechingly. "We must go inside, miss. We must!"

Muriella ignored her. Without waiting for Megan, she left the cliff top and started back around the wall in the direction of the castle gate. Megan followed reluctantly, her heart pounding out a hollow and persistent warning.

"I *will* go, and caution be damned!" John cried, glaring at his brother across the crowded library.

Colin rose from his chair and moved toward the fire. "Johnnie, I've told ye, it wouldn't be wise to go after the Calders now. Wait 'til the Earl gets back from the Isles. We can strike then if we want. But not now."

As he paced back and forth, John cursed under his breath. "I can't stay still. They've killed Uncle Rob and twenty-six others, and who knows what else they have planned for us?" His grief and exhaustion had combined with uneasy dreams of the slaughter, leaving him frantic with his own frustration.

"Haven't ye been responsible for enough death just now, little brother? Or do ye wish to see the entire clan ruined before the week is out?"

John fought down an angry reply, sickened by the nightmarish memory of David Campbell's ghastly tale and gaunt, gray face. He could not quite conquer the thought that it should have been he who sat there, broken and bleeding. He noticed with disgust that his brother appeared to be well rested. The events of the previous night obviously had not disturbed his sleep. "I might be able to make up for yesterday with a surprise attack on the Calders," he said.

"And who would ye take with ye? Tell me that. Would ye gather the men who have not slept for more than three hours and who rode all day and half the night? Or do ye intend to wait 'til Richard comes back, then drag his men out again? I'll tell ye, Johnnie, Inveraray wouldn't be a safe place to be if ye did that. We've lost too many men as it is. Don't be a fool."

With an effort, John kept his fists at his sides. "Then what do ye intend to do?"

Aware of the suppressed fury in his brother's voice, Colin smiled to himself. "I intend to wait, as I told ye, 'til our father returns."

"What if the Calders strike again? Or the Roses? There's nothing to stop the Roses from riding south to attack us."

Collin pressed closer to the fire, stretching his hands toward the flames. "I think I'd best speak to the girl about that. Mayhap she'll know of their plans."

John smiled at Colin's simplicity. "She won't be eager to tell ye anything, even if she knows, which I doubt. Ye'd be wiser to leave her alone for a time."

"She'll tell me," Colin muttered, "whether she wishes to or no'."

"More likely she'll bury a dagger in your chest, nor would I blame her." John remembered her chilling anger the night before, the power he had felt in her gaze. It weakened him somehow, that memory, and his fury grew hotter, more volatile.

With a snort, Colin turned away. "Where would she be getting a dagger, do ye think? And how would she raise it if she had one, with her hands tied behind her back? I'm no' fool like ye, Johnnie. I won't give her a chance to thwart me." Colin moved past his brother and started toward the door. "I'll speak with her now, and we'll see what she has to say."

John shifted uneasily. Did the girl deserve Colin's tactless questions? John shook his head. And yet—if she had once shown a moment of weakness, if she had wept or shivered or turned to him for comfort, he could have borne anything for her sake. But Muriella had made it clear she did not need him—not nearly as much as *he* needed *her*. For a moment he was tempted to let Colin barge into her chamber all unsuspecting, but he decided against it. "Wait," he said. "There's something ye should know."

"What could ye possibly tell me that I wouldn't already know three times over, little brother?"

"I might tell ye," John spat, "that I gave Megan a dagger last night to cut the bandages with."

"Damn ye! Are ye determined to wipe out the Campbells in a single day? Why didn't ye simply give the girl a satchel of poison to kill us with and an escort back to Cawdor?"

For a flicker of an instant, John wondered if he'd done it on purpose—left her a weapon and the chance to slip away. He brushed the thought aside. It was madness, after all she'd cost them in less than a single day. John thought his brother might try to strike him, but Colin only glared furiously, then turned to leave the room. John followed at a distance. He had a feeling he'd better be nearby when his brother confronted the girl face-to-face.

"M'lord?"

John paused, squinting into the shadows where a man stood waiting, while Colin went on ahead. "Richard?"

"Aye." Richard Campbell moved forward into the dim light. His clothing was caked with earth and blood, his arms black to the elbow. "We were too late. They were already dead. All of them."

"I know. David made it back. He told us."

"I'm sorry, m'lord. There have no' been many like Rob Campbell."

John was silent for a moment, fighting off the blackness that took his sight and left him shaking. He clenched his fists until the pain brought him sharply awake. "No," he managed to choke out, "there was not even *one* like him."

Shaking his hair back from his face, Richard sighed

wearily. "We buried most of them in the glen. Rob and his sons we brought back."

"Thank ye, Richard. Ye did what ye could. Ye must rest now. The others will see to the bodies."

"Aye, I sent most of the men off already. I swear Andrew was asleep in the saddle all the way back."

*"Johnnie!* Where the devil are ye?" Colin's bellow echoed through the halls long before he appeared. When he spotted his brother, he stopped still. His breathing was ragged, his jaw set in a dangerous line. "She's gone, do ye hear me? The girl is gone!"

Muriella and Megan rounded the corner, coming upon the front gate just as a shout rose in the courtyard.

"The girl must be found and soon! Every damned one of ye drop what you're doing to look for her. And when ye find her, bring her to me." It was Colin's voice. Already Muriella recognized it.

"Miss." Megan put her hand on her mistress's shoulder. "Won't you come inside before Colin comes out?"

Muriella shook the servant's hand away as she peered over the hill that sloped downward from the gate. A string of horses began at the top, circling to the edge of the loch below. Half the animals carried no riders, but the remaining saddles were filled with long, awkward bundles wrapped in solid blankets. One of those bundles was Rob Campbell; she was sure of it.

As she stood unmoving, the noise from the courtyard seemed to increase tenfold until it shattered the peace of the still morning. Feet clattered across the cobbles, men swore, and swords rattled in their sheaths.

"Miss, they're lookin' for ye, and mighty angry by the sound of it."

Still Muriella did not move, not even when the gate screamed up, setting free the men inside. They swarmed across the hillside, stopping only briefly to gape at the somber line of horses. Soon the landscape was dotted with the blue and green Campbell plaid. Muriella thought that perhaps they would never turn to look at the spot where she stood just below the gate, but her thoughts were interrupted by Colin's triumphant cry.

"Here she is, by God!" His face was flushed, his eyes ice blue. As he came toward her, he clenched and unclenched his fists threateningly.

Attempting to pull Muriella with her, Megan shrank away. Colin reached them before they had taken more than a few steps. Pushing Muriella aside for the moment, he twisted his hand in Megan's hair and dragged her forward. "What have ye done? Are ye such a blithering fool that ye can't see the danger out here? The Calders will come to take her away and no doubt kill her. Then all this"—he motioned toward the waiting horses—"will have been for naught."

As he drew back his hand to strike Megan, Muriella flung herself at him, knocking him off his balance. "Ye won't!" she demanded. "Leave her be!"

Colin turned, startled by her attack. "I'll do as I please. Ye have naught to say about it. Don't forget that I can beat ye too." He leaned forward menacingly. "And I intend to. But not just now." Nodding to a man behind him, he called, "Take her inside!"

"No! I won't go 'til Megan comes with me."

For a long moment, Colin glared at her while the pulse in his throat throbbed. The girl thought to defy him, but she would learn. He took a step forward.

"Ye won't hurt me," she declared, facing him squarely.

"And why, pray tell, won't I?"

"Because I am Cawdor. Ye know ye'll lose it if ye lose me. And if ye hurt me, I swear I'll find a way to go. 'Til Cawdor's safe, *I* am safe."

Colin paused with his hands in midair. The girl was right, damn her. He was powerless for the moment. He could not take the chance that she would carry out her threat. But his arms trembled and he longed to crush her between his palms.

Suddenly John appeared at his brother's side. Taking Muriella's arm in one hand, he motioned Megan forward with the other. He wanted to get away from there as quickly as possible. Suddenly he was appalled by the violence, the rage that simmered always beneath Colin's arrogance. He did not want to be his brother's mirror. "Leave them, Colin. I'll see to them. Ye must take care of Uncle Rob and his sons."

"We must not let this pass, little brother," Colin hissed. "Do ye hear?"

"Don't worry. I'll talk to them." John spoke calmly, adamantly.

Colin, still too angry to breathe evenly, gasped, "Get them away, then. Out of my sight!"

Propelling the two girls before him, John leaned down to mutter in Muriella's ear, "Ye would be wise to leave Colin alone. I wouldn't be surprised if he killed ye."

"Wouldn't ye? Does he care so little for Cawdor?"

John stopped, swinging her to face him. "I'm warning ye. Ye would do well to listen."

His last words were lost beneath the deep, labored tolling of a bell. Muriella looked up, caught by the unexpected volume of sound, and just for a moment her eyes met John's. This must be the ringing of the soul bell for the men killed the night before. The mournful clang, clang, clang bade farewell to the souls of the dead, counting out one ring for each year a man had lived. Judging by the number of horses trailing away from the gate, the tolling would not cease for a long, long time. Muriella felt a strange tightness in her throat. Without thinking, she started toward the burdened animals, but John stopped her.

"Ye'll go inside now. You've been enough trouble for one morning."

Looking up at him coldly, Muriella said, "I want to see Rob Campbell before they bury him. If I don't, he'll surely haunt me."

John too had meant to see and touch his uncle before his burial, so that the dead man would leave him in peace. But he intended to say his farewells later, in a more private place. "'Tis no' the time—"

"I need to say good-bye now," Muriella interrupted. Her jaw was rigid, her gaze unwavering.

Her determination, as well as his own gnawing grief, silenced the objections that rose to his lips. John let her go without further protest.

Muriella did not wait to see what he would do, but turned at once toward the horses. She went by instinct to the first animal and, with her hand on the muddy blanket, took a deep, steadying breath. Then she lifted the dark wool to look for the last time at Rob Campbell's gray, lifeless face. Without hesitation, she reached out to touch the sunken cheek, her eyes moist at the memory of the sound of his voice.

John stood where Muriella had left him, watching her in bewildered surprise. She was so clearly grieving and her expression was full of tenderness. She had known his uncle for only a few hours, yet she seemed to recognize what kind of man he had been. How was it that she had come to understand so much in so little time?

He saw the blanket slide from her fingers, saw her turn back to where he waited. Before his common sense could stop him, he went to meet her. Grasping her arms, he looked down into her grief-darkened face and asked, "If I had stayed with him last night, could I have stopped it?" He nodded toward the horses with their grim burdens.

Muriella blinked up at him in astonishment. She wanted to tell him yes, that Rob would not have died if John had stayed by his side. She wanted to tell him the blame was all his, but she knew she could not lie. Besides, there was something in his face—a kind of desperation that had not been there the night before. "I don't know," she said at last.

John turned away for an instant, trying to hide his disappointment. "So be it," he murmured in a voice that was barely audible. "We'd best go in now."

As he led her toward the open gate, Muriella realized that she had been wrong after all. John might not have said good-bye nor turned his head to see his uncle one last time before he left that glen, but he *had* looked back—and was looking back still.

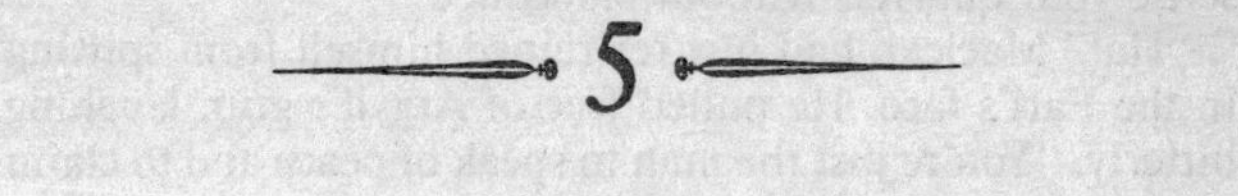

# 5

Archibald, Second Earl of Argyll, stood beside his horse, watching with impatience as the ferryman made his way across Loch Awe. The old man guided the raft with his awkward pole and seemed unconcerned that the Earl had been waiting on the far bank for some time. Argyll, however, was occupied with his own thoughts and cursed with only half his usual vehemence when the man finally pulled the raft up to the rocky shore.

After tying his horse to the edge of the raft, the Earl stepped onto the rocking platform. Although his eyes swept the woody islands scattered across the loch on either side, he was unimpressed by their beauty. His mind was still at Duart Castle, where he had left his daughter, Elizabeth, and Lachlan Maclean. Argyll shook his head, remembering with foreboding that Maclean was too clever by half. The Earl had thought at one time that if he could ever bring himself to side *with* the King rather than against him, Maclean would be a good soldier to fight beside.

But Argyll had never fully trusted the man since the rebellion in 1504 that had threatened to restore the Lordship of the Isles to Donald Dubh. Maclean had been declared a traitor, and although he had since sworn allegiance to the crown, the Earl was aware that the man still cast his gaze hungrily over the lands of others. He remembered all too clearly Maclean's flushed face and clenched fist when he asserted, "I won't rest so long as the Camerons hold the lands of Lochiel. They took them from me, and they shall no' sit peacefully there while I live!"

Argyll had grimaced as he put his hands on his son-in-law's shoulders. "Ye must try to forget. Ye must let the King settle your quarrels without bloodshed."

"Ha!" Maclean had just restrained himself from spitting in the Earl's face. He pulled free of Argyll's grip, laughing bitterly. "You're just the man to speak of peace and to claim your rights without bloodshed—*ye* who have betrayed us more than once! We are no' so foolish as ye might think, my lord."

The Earl reached instinctively for his sword but did not draw it. Instead he stared into Maclean's mocking gaze and tried to conquer his anger.

"Ye play with human lives to achieve your own ends," his son-in-law continued. "We're aware that Donald Dubh was your prisoner and that ye set him free, knowing we would follow him into a revolt. Then ye turned your energy to smashing the rebellion *ye* had created. You're a devious man, Father-in-law, but we aren't blind. My only comfort is that ye follow a king who will destroy ye, just as ye have destroyed us."

Argyll was suddenly aware of Elizabeth, who hovered in the background, watching. She looked up, gasping at her husband's audacity, and her glance went to her father's sword. Her expression was full of pleading.

The Earl loosened his grip on the handle of his broadsword. Maclean was, after all, his daughter's husband. What was worse, he had chosen the man himself. The marriage had been meant to solidify the new bond between King James and his rebellious Highland chiefs. Argyll, as the King's representative, had given up his only daughter. At the time, he had believed it to be an unfortunate necessity, but it had won him the King's favor. Partly because of the peace he had preserved in the Highlands, James IV had appointed the Earl Lord High Chancellor of Scotland as well as Master of the Royal Household. Surely his one small sacrifice had been worth the result.

Elizabeth moved toward Maclean protectively. "Leave him be, Father. Ye know he only speaks the truth."

The Earl stood quite still for a moment, frozen with shock. His daughter's loyalty obviously belonged to Maclean now. His hands trembled with outrage, but he clasped them roughly behind his back. As Elizabeth took her husband's arm, the Earl controlled his voice with an effort. "We won't discuss my business with the King further. If it weren't for my daughter, ye know I'd kill ye."

Shaking his wife's hand away, Maclean stepped forward. "Ye could try, my lord. But you're an old man and I am not. I beg ye, don't think of Elizabeth. Come, try your hand against mine."

It was too much to bear, even for Elizabeth's sake. The Earl went once more for his sword. The metal gleamed as he brought it up and faced Maclean. "As ye wish," he said.

"Father!" Elizabeth threw herself between the two men in an effort to separate them. Maclean lunged forward to push her away, but she stood firm. "Lachlan," she gasped, "how long do ye think ye would live if 'twas known ye'd killed the Earl of Argyll? The Campbells would hunt ye for the rest of your days, and there wouldn't be many. Ye must wait."

Elizabeth looked beseechingly at her father. At the expression in her eyes, he took a deep breath, then shoved his sword back into its sheath. He was not conscious that he did so. *Ye must wait,* his daughter had said. Did she actually wish for his death, then? He looked at the pale oval of her face and for an instant forgot to hide his pain.

"Father, don't make me choose," Elizabeth cried, reaching out to take his hand. "I have loved ye dearly, but Lachlan is my husband. It was ye who bid me marry him. Leave us in peace, please."

Argyll gently withdrew his hand from hers. By now he had reconstructed the mask that covered his weakness and he managed a stiff smile. "I will leave ye in peace," he said. "Take care, Elizabeth."

As he turned to go, the Earl saw Maclean drop his sword to the floor in disgust. Argyll looked back once when he reached the doorway, then, sickened by the scene before him, quickly left the room. Elizabeth knelt at her husband's feet, her hands outstretched toward him. Maclean turned his back on her.

The Earl felt ill, remembering. His fingers closed convulsively on the handle of his sword.

The silent ferryman watched Argyll secretly, wondering what was troubling the Earl. Although his expression was calm, the old man could see his agitation in the whitened knuckles grasping his sword. The man was careful to avoid the Earl's gaze. Everyone knew that his anger was terrible.

"The girl!" Argyll boomed unexpectedly. "Did they take the girl?" Now that he had pushed Duart Castle behind him, he remembered Muriella Calder. He had left word that his brother and his son should take her from Hugh Rose of Kilravok.

The Earl trembled with fury. The man had given his word, and broken it, without a thought. Rose had gladly taken the Campbell's aid and friendship over the years, but in the end, it had meant nothing. The glitter of Muriella Calder's gold had blinded the Laird of the Clan Rose to honor and loyalty, even wisdom.

Argyll should never have trusted him. Indeed, he never really had. Somewhere in the back of his mind, he had always known this moment would come. Enemies once more. It was all he could expect, it seemed. Hugh Rose, Lachlan Maclean—they were all the same. With narrowed eyes, the Earl regarded his companion, who kept his gaze on the end of his steering pole. "Did they bring the girl safely to Inveraray?"

"The lass is at Inveraray, aye," the old man muttered. "Been there a week. And many's the man who won't go near her for fear o' the evil eye."

When the raft scraped against the muddy shore, Argyll stepped off the platform. He paused while the old man untied the horse and brought the animal forward. "Ye say they think she's a witch, do ye? Well then, I must remember to tell the men to keep their thoughts to themselves. But the girl is safe?"

The ferryman nodded. "Aye, *she* is safe enough."

As the Earl mounted his horse, he wondered what the man meant. Had there been trouble? He hoped there had been. It would give him something to occupy his mind—anything to destroy the memory of Elizabeth kneeling with her arms outstretched toward Lachlan Maclean.

Richard Campbell leaned against the wall outside Muriella's door, which was slightly ajar. He shook his head when the regular crunch of rushes inside told him the girl was pacing again.

"Och, does the lass never stay still? She'll drive herself daft at this rate," Andrew said. He crouched a few feet away from his brother, elbows resting on his knees.

"I wouldn't be surprised if she's already daft. Wouldn't ye be if ye were pinned up in a single room for eight days together?"

"Aye, that I would. It doesn't seem like Sir John to keep her locked up this way. Or was it Sir Colin?"

"'Twas Sir Colin, all right." Richard leaned forward and lowered his voice. "And I don't think 'tis either wise or kind."

"Well, ye don't expect him to let her get away, do ye? Seems to me he's bein' most wise."

Richard regarded his brother with troubled eyes. "Aye, mayhap if she was someone else. But no' with that lass. I wouldn't cross her the way Sir Colin has, and I wish Sir John hadn't chosen me to watch her."

Andrew could not restrain a shout of laughter. "You're a fool, sure enough! Don't tell me ye believe the stories the men are whisperin' in the kitchens?" Sitting back on his heels, Andrew chuckled to himself.

With rare patience, Richard waited until his brother was quiet. "Didn't ye hear that she warned Sir John about Rob Campbell?"

"Aye, and so what? 'Tis more likely she knew the Calders' plans than that she's a witch. Have ye never guessed a friend would fall in battle? Come, man, don't let the lass fool ye."

"She didn't tell me, but I believe it just the same."

Andrew shook his head in disbelief. He knew his brother

to be courageous in battle, yet here he was trembling for fear of a young, helpless girl. "Tell me, brother, if she has the power, why hasn't she turned ye to stone? Surely she knows ye to be her jailer."

"Because"—Richard crouched to join his brother on the floor—"I haven't given her the chance. However, I don't think she wishes us all ill. Megan seems to like her well enough, and to tell ye the truth, I pity the lass, witch or no'. She's trapped."

"Aye." The laughter retreated from Andrew's blue eyes. "That she is. But I'll wager Sir Colin hasn't come near her yet, has he?"

"No. And there's a question for ye. Do ye think a normal girl would've had the courage to stand up to him that way?"

"Mayhap." Andrew drummed his fingers on the stone. "But I confess, I haven't seen another do it. 'Twas a marvelous sight, wasn't it? Callen Maellach—old lump-in-brow—with nothin' to say in the face of a lassie's anger. Och! 'twas grand."

"No doubt she stopped his tongue."

"There ye go again with your witches and your spells. You're daft, ye fool."

"Maybe," Richard said, ignoring his brother's skepticism, "But I'll wager ye haven't looked in the lassie's eyes. If ye had, ye wouldn't laugh anymore."

As the Earl stalked into the Great Hall, his two sons rose to meet him. His face wore an ugly scowl and, seeing his expression, the servants hurried to fetch him ale while trying to avoid catching his attention.

"They tell me there was a battle," he called across the tables to John. "Did the Roses come after the girl?"

"No. 'Twas the Calders, and by God, Colin would keep me tied here instead of letting me go after them. The bastards!"

The Earl shook his head at his son's outburst. "Sit down and be calm, boy." Then he turned to Colin. "How many dead?"

"Twenty-seven. Among them were Rob and eight of his sons," he announced baldly.

"Dear God!" Argyll closed his eyes against the too-bright afternoon light.

"I was for going out the next day to even the score," John declared, "but Colin said no, we must wait for ye." He sat up, leaning toward his father. "Will ye let me go now?"

The Earl barely heard. His head was spinning wildly and he did not like the feeling. He had wondered briefly, so many years ago, if leaving Muriella with the Roses was a mistake. Now he knew. He had been wrong, and the error in judgment had cost his brother's life, and his nephews'—too many. He felt physically ill at the thought. Rob and his sons were dead because of Argyll's momentary weakness, because he had seen a mother's love in Isabel Calder's eyes and had not been able to break her heart.

He felt as if a claymore had struck him across the shoulder, as if his knees might buckle at the shaking inside him. He took several deep breaths and, through sheer force of will, remained standing upright, though his eyes burned and his throat felt raw. But none of that showed on his face when he met his son's accusing eyes. He had had no choice. "We must think this out before we do aught. The Calders will be ready and waiting, I guarantee that." Argyll sat back in silence.

Here was Johnnie, ready to wipe out the Calders this very afternoon if only he could get his hands on them. The boy—was he twenty already?—would have to learn about diplomacy. That was one subject on which the Earl was an expert. He had learned a great deal from James IV.

Opening his eyes, he motioned to a servant, who bent to unlace his boots and remove them. He ignored his sons while he downed half the ale he found sitting before him; he would not be hurried. At last he said, "Johnnie, ye'll have to wait for your revenge, I'm afraid. 'Tis too dangerous just now. If we're lucky, the two families will kill each other off and we won't have to lift a finger. But were ye to attack now, I've a suspicion the Roses would side with the Calders against ye. We can't give ye enough men for that kind of battle. No, ye'll just have to wait."

John swept his tankard out of the way, sending it crashing to the floor in the process. "Damn ye and Colin and your waiting. If he'd let me go at first, they wouldn't have been ready. I might have done some damage then. Anyway, the Calders have always hated the Roses, as well ye know. They wouldn't ever fight side by side."

"Men will do many uncommon things for the wealth that girl has. But that's hardly the point. Do ye realize that if ye killed a man each time ye'd a wish to, there wouldn't be a single one left to fight beside ye? You're to be twenty-one soon. Can't ye sit back awhile and allow us the pleasure of seeing ye reach it unharmed? There'll be plenty to do soon enough."

Colin smiled and sat back, propping his booted feet on the edge of the table. "Ye see, little brother, that I know my father's wishes better than ye do."

John raised his foot to the bench Colin occupied and started to push. With a restraining hand on his arm, Argyll stopped him from tipping it backwards.

"Johnnie, I have troubles enough without ye fighting with your brother. Ye remind me of Maclean sometimes, and 'tis no' a comparison I like to make. Sit down now and listen. Protecting the girl is most important." John started to interrupt but the Earl shook his head warningly. "Aye, the girl is more important than your revenge. If ye were to go off to fight the Calders, they'd be just wise enough to send someone to make certain she never reached fourteen. If ye want Cawdor, ye have to wait."

"Can ye wait to get Uncle Rob's murderers? Or don't ye care that he died in your cause? It seems to me that you're more concerned with securing Cawdor for the power it'll bring ye than mourning your brother!"

Argyll rose, placed his hands wide apart on the table, leaned menacingly toward his younger son. "Ye don't care then what securing Cawdor will bring *ye?* I rather thought ye were looking forward to being a rich man."

His son's eyes widened in surprise at the caustic sting in

the Earl's voice. Usually the Laird of the Clan Campbell reserved that biting tone for others.

Sighing, Argyll shook his head. This was getting them nowhere. "As for my brother," he said, "I haven't forgotten him. I won't forget. But neither will I fume and fight and destroy the very thing he died for. Open your eyes for once, Johnnie, and recognize the truth. I *do* care about power. 'Tis the only thing that really matters, and you're a fool if ye believe otherwise. If ye think me hard for speaking this way, then so ye must. I can do naught else."

John shivered at the cold light of determination in his father's eyes.

"I hear the girl speaks of Uncle Rob reverently," Colin interjected.

"Mayhap he deserves our reverence, but he doesn't deserve—and I'll tell ye this just once more, Johnnie—he does *not* deserve for us to lose the girl now, just because ye have neither the strength nor the wisdom to wait." He paused and added, "I've had enough talk and I can see ye don't wish to hear me. I'm weary and need a hot bath and fresh clothes. Then I want ye to bring the girl to me. But just now, let me be."

# 6

Muriella stared out the window at the sweep of garden below, as she had done every day for the past week. From where she sat, she could just see part of the curving shore of Loch Awe, where the water lapped at the bank and swirled among the dappled rocks. Although she had never set foot on the fine-grained earth, she felt she knew the bank intimately. Each morning she rose and went to the window to catch her first glimpse of the water that changed with the passage of the hours from green to gray to shimmering blue. She had come to know all the permutations of those shifting colors, created by the bright sunlight as it crossed the sky. Daily, she waited with anticipation for the occasional eddies of leaves that fell from the branches above to dance in golden patterns over the undulating water. She could not hear the rippling movement of the waves from where she sat, but she could imagine the soft, pulsing sound and it gave her comfort. "The loch is no' pleased today," she said to Megan, who sat sewing on a stool nearby. "Come see."

The servant willingly left the gown she was stitching for Muriella's wardrobe and knelt beside the window. "What do ye mean?" she asked, perplexed, as she often was, by her mistress' strange affinity with the world beyond her window.

Muriella drew Megan forward with a hand on her shoulder, pointing to the spot where the woods retreated from the shore of the loch. "See how the water is tipped with white and how the waves come up so violently against the rocks? Not long ago the surface was clear green, but now 'tis faded to dull gray, as if the joy had left it."

Megan squinted into the afternoon sunlight and saw that the water had indeed begun to roil and spit as if possessed by some unpleasant demon. She had never thought of a loch or a garden having moods as people did, but her mistress had taught her a great deal in the long hours of her confinement. She looked at Muriella and thought she saw a reflection of the restless, gray green movement of the loch in the other girl's eyes.

Muriella leaned out to breathe deeply as the scent of damp heather rose on the wind, intertwined with other fragrances from the garden below. "There's a touch of rosemary in the breeze, I think," she murmured, "and mayhap a little lavender. Can ye tell?"

When the servant sniffed the air, biting her lip in concentration, Muriella smiled. Thank God for Megan, she thought. Once when John had come to check on the girls, he had told the servant she need not stay in the chamber constantly, but she had chosen to do so just the same. The two girls had divided their time between watching the changes beyond their window and working on a new set of clothes for Muriella.

"My mistress can't keep wearin' Elizabeth's ill-fittin' gowns," Megan had declared that first day before John could leave and lock the door behind him. "And if we're to be here with nothin' to do, we could start a gown or two and some chemises, couldn't we?"

John had stared at her in surprise. Megan had never been one to speak out so boldly before. But he had to admit she was right. Within the hour, Mary and Jenny had brought linen and wool, needles and fine thread.

"Thank ye for thinking of such things," Muriella had told her. "And thank ye for staying by me. 'Twould be lonely indeed without ye."

"'Tis only right, miss," Megan had explained matter-of-factly before turning to sort through the fabrics spread over the bed. Muriella had joined her, grateful for the work; it kept her mind busy and did not allow her to dwell on the dull ache that never seemed to leave her. She felt as if she were suspended in time—waiting—though she did not know what she was waiting for.

Megan rose to pick up the simple gray wool gown she had been laboring over so carefully. "Have I done it right this time?" she asked, holding the seam out for inspection. She had never been at her best with needle and thread, but she had learned quickly that Muriella sewed a fine, strong seam.

"Aye, 'tis much better," her mistress observed, running a finger over the tiny stitches. "Even my mother would say so."

Smiling with pleasure, Megan drew her stool closer to the window and settled down to her task once more. "Did your mother teach ye to sew?" she asked.

Muriella nodded. "Aye, and to weave. 'Twas the only time I spent with her, really, when we sat together in the solar." The thought saddened her. She wondered if she would ever see Isabel Calder or Hugh or Lorna again. "She loved to make tapestries, ye see, and it seemed to me that she never left the loom. I couldn't sit still for so long."

"Aye," Megan interjected, "I know just how ye felt. Sometimes I think my back won't ever be straight again."

"Do ye know what my mother told me when I said the same? She said she was doing the work of the fairies, weaving the patterns they'd put in her fingers with their magic. She used to sing a song that matched the rhythm of the loom as she worked the shuttle back and forth. She hypnotized me with her sweet voice, I think, 'til I came to love the weaving as much as she did."

Megan looked up eagerly. "Can ye sing it now?"

Muriella shook her head. "No, I don't remember the words. She made them up as she went along. 'Twas part of the magic."

The servant sighed in disappointment, and Muriella turned her attention back to the half-finished linen chemise in her lap. Thus the two girls had sat for many hours in the past week, while Megan kept boredom at bay with her lively chatter. Day by day, she told her mistress all she knew of the inhabitants of Inveraray Castle.

That was how Muriella had learned of Colin's wife, Janet, who had never set foot here, but stayed in Castle Glamis—Castle Gloom, as Megan called it—outside Edinburgh. "And wise she is, if ye ask me. 'Tis best to stay as far away from Sir Colin as ye can." Then there was the servant Jenny, who fancied herself in love with Colin and followed him about "like a wee, lonely pup." But according to Megan, Colin did not seem to mind.

Muriella had learned too about Elizabeth and her unhappy marriage to Lachlan Maclean. "Though she didn't go willingly, I'll tell ye that. But 'twas nothin' she could do to change her father's mind. They say she wept and refused to eat 'til they feared she'd starve herself to a shadow. Still, in the end, it didn't matter. The Laird had his way and that was that."

It sounded so simple, Muriella thought. A whole life disposed of with a few brisk words. The same, no doubt, that would seal her own fate.

"The Earl's home, I hear," Megan said now. "They say he isn't in a pleasant frame of mind. But no doubt ye'll be seein' that for yourself soon enough. I expect he'll be sendin' for ye."

Muriella considered the information in silence. She felt that Megan was warning her somehow, but before she could ask a question, there was a brief knock, then the door flew open and John entered the chamber.

Glancing up at his noisy entrance, Muriella caught her breath. For some reason, no matter how many times she saw John, a glimpse of his face was a shock to her. It was almost as if, so long as he was out of her sight, she could make herself believe he was no more than a nightmare that had no substance or reality. But once he stood before her, she felt his presence like a blow that knocked the breath from her body. So distressed was she that she did not see him stop still in the middle of the room, staring.

My God, John thought as he caught sight of the slender

girl framed by the light from the window. She looked so slight, ethereal, as if she might blow away at a sudden gust of wind. The sunlight touched her hair and body, emphasizing her fragility and the pale translucence of her skin. She had lost weight during her week of confinement. At the moment, she did not look like an heiress to a large and important fortune. She looked, instead, like a lost child.

John smothered a flicker of pity when he remembered that this child, who was not yet a woman, held his future in her hands. He felt again the resentment that she should have such power over him. "The Earl has called for ye," he said with unusual harshness. "'Tis no' wise to keep him waiting."

Dropping her linen on the stool at her feet, Muriella rose. "Shouldn't ye take the time to bind and gag me? Aren't ye afraid I'll run?"

John took a step forward, his blue eyes glinting a brilliant warning. "Is that what ye intend? Are ye determined to see how far ye can push us before we find it necessary to break ye?"

With an effort, Muriella kept her face expressionless. "I don't—"

"Because we'll do it, I promise ye that. Colin isn't the only one here with a temper, and don't ye forget it. Now come. My father's waiting."

Although she wanted to send him away, to stay where she was until the Earl was forced to come to her, Muriella knew that would be a mistake. She saw with annoyance that John had not even waited to see if she would come; he had already left the room. Biting her lip to quell her anger, Muriella followed him into the hall. Confident that she was behind him, he was leading her beyond the stairway to a part of the castle she had never seen.

The passageway they entered, hung with tapestries and carpeted with fine Persian rugs, was very different from the bleak rooms and endless gloomy corridors she had already passed through. But even here nothing could eradicate the chill that had settled permanently inside the thick stone walls. She noticed that John's leather boots were lined with fur and he'd tossed a wolf pelt over his long saffron shirt to keep out the cold; Muriella was suddenly aware of how inadequate her own linen gown was. Strange, she mused, that these halls should be so damp and uncomfortable when outside the sun was bright. Even the Campbells' wealth could not bring that warmth inside where it was needed.

As she shivered at a sudden draft, she saw a tapestry rippling in the gust of air. The vivid hanging depicted a battle scene in intricate detail. She stopped to examine it more closely. Though she wanted to shut out the sight of the blood and clashing swords, she could not help but marvel at the fine work. Fascinated, she ran her fingers over the fabric, admiring the tight weave.

"I told ye, my father doesn't like to wait," John said impatiently from out of the gloom.

Muriella fought back an angry response and turned away from the hanging. When John disappeared into a strange room, she followed him slowly across the threshold. The chamber was lit by several oil lamps and a roaring fire that seemed to welcome her. She shook her head in disbelief, noticing with growing surprise the patterned blue Persian rug and the carved bookshelves along the walls. So this was the library. Muriella had always loved that room at Kilravok, but it had been small and cold compared to this magnificent chamber.

Muriella forgot the Earl as she glided toward a bookcase and ran her fingers reverently across the leather binding of the nearest manuscript. There were many like it; the browns and tans of the tooled leather books broke up the monotony of gray stone walls that curved up to the vaulted ceiling.

"Can ye read, lass?"

She turned toward the Earl, who sat behind a large oak desk cluttered with parchment and open books. Odd, she thought, but he did not look at all formidable. In fact, more than anything, he looked tired. The light in the room was soft; in the yellow glow of the lamps, the girl could see the resemblance to Rob. The same patchwork of tiny lines crossed the same nose and cheeks, but the eyes were harder blue and the lines of his mouth were sharper. Still, this man was not an ogre as she had made herself believe. Yet he was the one who had given the orders that had changed her life, that would eventually bind her to the stranger beside her now.

"I asked ye if ye know how to read."

Muriella thought his voice was curiously gentle. "Aye. My cousin Hugh taught me. At Kilravok, the library was my favorite room."

The Earl smiled to himself. He had been wary about meeting the girl because of the stories the men were circulating. Having seen her, he wanted to laugh at their simplicity. Muriella seemed normal enough. Her hair was neatly braided and her green eyes sparkled just like any other girl's. "Tell me," he said, "would ye like to read here in the afternoons? As ye can see, there's much ye could look at."

The pleasure drained out of Muriella's face. "I can't. They don't allow me to leave my room."

The Earl frowned as he remembered Colin's account of her first morning at Inveraray. "Aye, they told me. But 'twas your own fault, I hear. Ye shouldn't have tried to run away."

Out of the corner of her eye, Muriella could see John nodding in agreement. For a moment her resentment choked her. "I didn't think 'twould hurt to see the garden. I wanted air, that's all."

Argyll regarded her doubtfully. "Didn't ye wish to flee from us then? I rather thought it might have entered your head a time or two. From what Johnnie tells me, ye weren't too pleased when they took ye from Cawdor."

Muriella felt his cool appraisal, the expectant stillness that characterized his weathered face, and guessed that he was testing her somehow. She decided to tell him the truth. "No, I wasn't pleased. I would have left here at once if there'd been a way. But ye see, I recognized even then that there was nothing—no one—to run to. Surely ye know that."

With a hint of a warning in his voice, the Earl said, "I know it well, lass, and 'tis glad I am to see that ye do too. 'Twill no doubt save a lot of foolishness in the future." He paused to let the message sink in, then, satisfied that he had made his point, added in a kinder tone, "But so long as ye understand, there's nothing to keep ye from roaming the keep and grounds as ye like." He looked up at John, who stood back in the shadows. "What room have ye given her?"

"Elizabeth's."

Argyll tensed at the mention of his daughter's name. Elizabeth's, was it? He would alter that soon enough. "That room was stripped when she married. There's no' a rug on the floor nor hangings on the walls. Have her moved to your mother's chamber." Turning to Muriella, he explained, "Ye'll find it a mite more comfortable there. I see they haven't been treating ye well. But we'll remedy that, ye can be sure. Come here, lass, and show me your skill at reading. There hasn't been a young voice here in a long time." Not since Elizabeth left, he added silently.

Surprised at the change in his tone, Muriella went to stand beside him, reaching for the book he held out to her. She was aware of John's gaze, but did not look up, though she felt his eyes upon her like a heavy hand on her shoulder. The sensation disturbed her and she struggled to keep her voice steady as she read from the yellowed page.

> The bird, the beast, the fish eke in the sea,
> They live in freedom, everyone in his kind,
> And I, a man, and lacketh liberty!
> What shall I say, what reasons may I find
> That fortune should do so?

Muriella lowered the manuscript to look at John. Her eyes blazed and he thought he read an accusation there. He clenched his fists. Must she always be looking at him with her mistrust so clear on her face? After all, he had only done what was best for her. He had saved her from a Calder sword; she must know that. What was it she had said to him? *The danger was mine to face, not yours.* But that was foolish. Surely she did not mean she would have stayed at Cawdor to die if the choice had been hers?

Oblivious of the looks passing between the two young people, the Earl pushed the manuscript away. "Ye have a lovely voice, lass. Do ye know the Gaelic?"

Muriella was still glowering at John, remembering the words of the poem. "I know a little Latin, but no one ever taught me the Gaelic."

"Well then, ye must come here often and begin to learn it. 'Tis your heritage, ye know. Mayhap I'll even teach ye myself. And lass"—he took her by the shoulders, drawing her toward him—"ye must remember that we brought ye here to keep ye safe, but ye shall not be our prisoner." He turned back to his son to add, "See that she has two men to watch her always. We don't want to tempt fate, after all. We've only just found her. 'Twould be a shame if we lost her again so soon."

Was he trying to frighten her? Muriella wondered. Or was this just another warning? She felt the determination in his grip on her shoulders, yet there was tenderness in his eyes. Concentrating on those eyes that revealed so little, she saw that there was pain there too; he was suffering and did not wish to show it.

At her intent perusal, the Earl thought suddenly, vividly of Rob's loss and felt an aching emptiness in his stomach. For the second time, his eyes began to burn, and for the second time, he fought back the bleakness that swept over him. Along with his brother, all that was good in the Earl had gone. Rob had been his other side—the gentleness, the undisguised affection, the unswerving loyalty to all he loved, the simple human understanding. The hole where Rob Campbell had once stood was dark and ugly and cold now—empty.

Argyll was so shaken by the image that his vision blurred. He was surrounded by men, yet completely, inescapably alone, as he had always known one day he would be. Only Muriella's tentative smile and the compassion in her eyes penetrated the fog around him. He focused on her face until the blackness turned to gray.

"Ye must take care," he said at last, with difficulty. "Do ye understand?"

"Aye," she told him softly.

Argyll nodded, pleased, and before he realized what he was doing, reached out to touch her hair with his fingertips. He sighed and just stopped himself from calling her Elizabeth.

"There's trouble!" Colin exclaimed from the doorway.

Argyll let his hand fall to the desktop. "What is it?" he asked wearily. He had had enough trouble for one day.

His son nodded toward Muriella. "Send the girl away."

With a wave of his hand, the Earl murmured, "Ye must go now. We've business to discuss."

For a moment, Muriella had thought he would tell her of his grief, but she saw now how foolish she had been. At the sound of Colin's voice, Argyll had turned toward his son as if Muriella ceased to exist in that moment. Without a word, she did as he had bid her and left the room. Colin glanced after her, waiting until she was lost in the shadows before pulling the heavy door closed behind him.

"Well?" Argyll demanded.

"A messenger just rode in from Nairnshire with news that William Calder and his three sons have filed two legal petitions with the Precentor of Ross. The first claims that inheritance can't be passed through the female line."

"'Tis easy enough to disprove," the Earl interrupted.

Colin shrugged. "The second"—he paused, glancing at John—"the second claims they have evidence proving the girl illegitimate."

"What?" The Earl stood abruptly and brought his fist crashing down on the desktop. "What evidence?"

Smiling with satisfaction at his father's reaction, Colin pulled a chair forward and settled himself on the brocade seat. "The Precentor appears to be in league with the Calders. He won't say what the evidence is."

"Have ye given me a bastard to marry then?" John demanded.

"Quiet, boy! 'Tis some trick they've thought up among them to stop us from getting the girl's fortune. I must think what to do. And I'll need your help, not your anger!"

"Mayhap 'tis no' a trick. Mayhap she *is* a bastard."

Colin's lips twisted slightly upward; the idea seemed to please him.

"Then why have they waited 'til now to show their evidence? They could've done it long ago."

"Mayhap," Colin said skeptically.

"I don't understand," John muttered. "William Calder chose to step down in favor of his son. Why is he fighting to keep Cawdor now?"

"He didn't know that his son would die in less than four years, and that the only child would be a girl. He's regretting his haste, no doubt."

"Then why hasn't he done something before this?"

The Earl leaned back in his chair. "I believe he thought he'd get Cawdor back somehow, so long as the girl was nearby. But he doesn't want to let it fall into Campbell hands. He knows we're too strong for him. He's afraid, that's all, and desperate as well."

John paced the room, brow furrowed.

"Johnnie, do ye really believe I'm so careless? Muriella is the legitimate heiress. I know her history. Don't worry, we'll fight them through the courts."

John swung to face his father. "Why don't we just kill Calder and his three sons? Ye said they're afraid of us. We *are* stronger. Why must we wait?"

Argyll peered at his older son, who sprawled in his chair, smirking. "Leave us, Colin."

"But—"

"Leave us."

Even Colin dared not question the quiet authority in his father's command. He rose, pushed his chair away, and strode out, slamming the heavy door behind him.

"Sit down, Johnnie. There's a thing or two ye must learn."

Unwillingly, John took Colin's chair.

"Ye need to know, boy—"

"I'm no' a boy."

"As ye wish, so long as ye listen to me. There are ways to get what ye want without killing, Johnnie. There's always a bargain of some kind ye can make."

His son glared down at his hands. He knew all about his

father's bargains. "Ye mean like the one ye made with Donald Dubh before ye set him free to start a revolt?" He could not hide the distaste he felt at the memory.

Argyll clenched his teeth in anger. The rebellion of 1504 again. It seemed he could not escape it today. Now even John had become his judge. "I did what I had to do. I thought ye understood that. Or don't ye *wish* to understand political necessity?"

"I don't see why 'twas necessary to trick your enemies into becoming traitors."

"Ye were only a boy then. Ye didn't realize that the Macleans were daily growing stronger, and they'd made it clear how willing they were to ally themselves with Donald Dubh against the crown."

John snorted in disbelief. "I was old enough to fight with the other Campbells," he reminded his father. "And are ye so sure it was King Jamie ye were concerned for? Ye would have lost a great deal if they'd succeeded in establishing Dubh as Lord of the Isles."

Argyll had not realized his son knew so much about those events five years ago. "You're right," the Earl said stiffly, "the Macleans were a threat to my position in the Highlands and I chose to rid myself of that threat. Is that so hard to understand?"

His son regarded him intently. "Mayhap 'tis easier to understand than 'tis to forgive."

Argyll rose, kicking the chair from behind him. "Who are ye to question my methods?" he demanded. "They succeeded, didn't they? We broke the Macleans like a dried-out twig so they couldn't challenge the clan again." He had spoken with more vehemence than he intended and had to fight to regain his composure.

John considered Argyll doubtfully. He had always admired his father—his strength, his cleverness, his wisdom. He had shared an unusual closeness with the Earl, who was often too busy to bother with his children's feelings. But he could not forget how Argyll worshiped power above all else; it made his son uneasy. "Ye may have broken them for a while," John pointed out, "but it doesn't mean they've forgotten. Ye just left Maclean. Ye must know that he hates ye."

"Aye," the Earl agreed reluctantly, "the man's memory is long and vivid. And I suspect he'd do anything to get back at me. I sometimes wonder if he won't use Elizabeth—" He stopped when he realized what he was saying. "You've changed the subject, Johnnie. My sins aren't important. What I want to discuss is your temper. 'Tis that which threatens our welfare just now."

"But ye were the one who taught me how to fight for what I want. Don't ye remember?"

The Earl nodded, seating himself again so he could look his son in the eye. "Aye, that I do." He had known from the beginning that as a second son, John would have to struggle for everything he wanted. Things had come much easier for Colin merely because he was his father's heir. So Argyll had goaded and encouraged and forced his second son to be strong on his own. He had learned early to fight with vigor and determination. It was strange, the Earl mused, that John should also have grown close to his mother and Elizabeth. Perhaps it was their influence that had taught him to feel things as deeply as he did. But now it was time for him to begin to control his wayward emotions and learn wisdom as well. "Just the same, there are times when ye forget yourself, when ye act without thinking."

Leaning forward, John demanded, "Would ye have me be like Colin, then—cold and calculating, with no feelings at all?"

Argyll narrowed his eyes in displeasure. "Colin is what he has to be to survive," he snapped. "There's no room for foolish emotion in a man meant to lead the Clan Campbell. It weakens your judgment when ye need it most, and 'tis no' a risk either your brother or I can afford to take. Ye can't blame Colin for that." Rubbing his forehead to dissipate a persistent pain, the Earl looked away. Argyll was glad his younger son was different. He liked to think John was more like Rob—caring, and strong as iron underneath.

But Rob was dead. The Earl had actually forgotten for a moment. The rush of grief he felt shocked him with its intensity, made him more certain of what he was saying. John had been ruled by his heart long enough. "I wouldn't have ye follow in your brother's footsteps, as well ye know. But nevertheless, ye must begin to control your anger and impatience. Otherwise, they may well be your undoing."

"Mayhap." John was unconvinced. He stood to terminate the conversation before it went any further. He had heard enough lectures for one day. He started to leave the room, aware all the time of his father's disapproving gaze on his back. When he reached the door, the Earl's commanding voice stopped him.

"Don't forget what I've said," the Earl warned. "And one last thing. We need time in order to do this wedding properly. Everyone in the Highlands is waiting for it, and we must show them what we're capable of. The ceremony is set for Muriella's fourteenth birthday in February. You've several months to keep her safe, and I warn ye, 'twill no' be easy. Until then, she's always in danger. Don't forget that, and don't relax, ever."

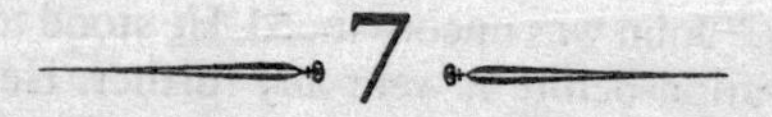

# 7

Lachlan Maclean stared at the letter in his hand. He read the message over a second time before tossing the parchment onto the table, then threw back his head and laughed. The laughter ended too abruptly as Maclean turned toward the fire, running his hand through his thick red curls. "Argyll would have me for a guest when he secures his latest possession."

The men seated around the table shifted uncomfortably, unnerved by Maclean's brief laughter. They knew he was most dangerous when he laughed that way—harshly and without real humor. The clan members looked at the discarded letter in curiosity but no one attempted to pick it up.

Aware of their unease although he could not see their faces, their laird motioned toward the parchment. "Read it. Argyll wouldn't be sending me state secrets. 'Tis only an invitation to John Campbell's wedding."

Maclean's nephew Evan, who sat nearest the head of the table, reached for the letter, then pushed back his bench so he could see his uncle's face. "What will ye do?"

"I don't know." Seating himself in the carved armchair at the head of the table, Maclean looked at the anxious faces of the men who sat before him. "'Twould be a shame to miss a Campbell wedding. If nothing else, the Earl knows how to have a celebration to remember. But"—he paused when a new thought struck him—"I'm no' the man to jump when

Argyll whistles. And I've no wish to see him crow over the wealth that girl brings with her. I'll stay at Duart." With a flourish, he took the parchment from Evan and crumpled it in his fist.

There was silence for a long moment while the men shifted again on their benches. Maclean could see they were not pleased with his decision by the way they turned expectantly toward his nephew.

Finally, Evan spoke. "We think ye should go, Uncle. Ye might be able to do us some good." When Maclean did not respond, his nephew swallowed once, then continued, "Don't ye see? We've spent the morning agreeing that Argyll must no' be allowed to swallow the Highlands whole, but we can't see where 'tis possible to stop him. Yet here's a chance fallen right in your lap."

Eyeing his nephew suspiciously, Maclean muttered, "What are ye thinking, Evan? Make yourself clear, man."

"If ye were there, ye might be able to stop the wedding. There's no surer way of ruining Argyll's plans than that."

In an instant, Maclean was out of his chair. "Are ye daft, the whole lot of ye? Stop a Campbell wedding?" He looked at the ring of faces until he had taken in the expression of every man there. They *were* serious. And they'd obviously talked this over before they came. The idea hadn't sprung into their heads with the arrival of the letter. Well, serious they might be, but that didn't preclude the possibility that they'd lost their wits. When Maclean spoke, his voice was barely controlled. "Ye know I'd like nothing better than to hurt the Earl. But he isn't a man to let a prize like this one slip through his fingers. 'Tis a dangerous thing you're asking of me."

"We know what kind of man Argyll is, Uncle. That's why we can't let him grow any stronger. We also know that the Earl thinks ye a clever man. I've even heard it said that he's afraid of ye. Surely ye can think of a way to outfox him. Likely he'll be drunk every night anyway, so pleased will he be at his good fortune."

Maclean moved toward the fire, turning his back on the clan members who had gathered from all over the western

Highlands to decide what must be done about Argyll. "Not one of ye, not a single one of ye knows the Earl as I do. And I tell ye, he isn't a fool. He knows many would give a great deal to stop this marriage. He knows and he'll be ready. He won't be getting drunk 'til 'tis safe to do so. And he'll have one eye on me, ye can bet on that. That's why I won't be playing your game this time."

He did not turn to see their reactions. Instead he gazed into the flames and wished his men were right, that there was a way to thwart the Earl through this wedding. The idea of hurting Argyll had long been one of his fondest daydreams. But he was wise enough to know his own limitations—most of the time.

Evan's voice broke into his thoughts. "Have ye forgotten Alex so soon?"

Maclean grasped the mantel so tightly that his hands began to ache. "I haven't forgotten my brother. I will no' forget." Unknowingly, he used the Earl's own words. He tried to stop the picture from forming in his mind as it always did at the mention of his brother's name, but he was unsuccessful. Against his will, Maclean stood again amidst the carnage on the battlefield five years ago. He remembered with the same bitter self-recrimination that he had sent Alex and the others there because it would be safe. But he had not reckoned on Argyll's duplicity. Since the rebellion was nearly over, the rebels nearly destroyed, he had thought the Earl would let the Macleans reach home safely. James IV had won, after all; Argyll still held the Lordship of the Isles in his own grasping fist. Alex had led the tail end of a bedraggled and beaten army into that glen without fear, because Maclean had assured him he could do so.

But the Earl had decided the rebels needed one more lesson, and his army had fallen upon them late that night. Not a single Maclean had left that glen walking. They had been slaughtered, every last one—Alex and Evan and David and the others. And Anne.

Maclean knelt before the fire, pushing his hands toward the flames. He must not think of Anne, or he would destroy the Earl and himself along with him, and maybe the whole Clan Maclean as well.

When he saw his uncle's expression, Evan rubbed his hands together nervously. He knew it was not always wise to evoke the past for Maclean. It was a sure way to rouse his anger against the Earl, but that anger was often so intense that it threatened to harm others besides. The servants here had told Evan about Argyll's last visit, when Maclean had nearly taunted the Earl into fighting him. Though he had not seen it, Evan knew what the outcome would have been. Argyll was getting old and was no match for his son-in-law's ability with a sword. The Laird of the Macleans would have killed his father-in-law.

Evan shook his head. His uncle could be a fool when he lost his temper. Had the Earl died that day, Macleans all over the Highlands would be fighting for their own lives now.

"I assume ye have some kind of plan?" Maclean's voice rose hollowly from where he crouched before the fire.

With a start, Evan sat up. Maclean was wavering now and his nephew had to press his advantage, regardless of the consequences. "It seems to us that there's just one way to be certain the marriage never takes place."

Maclean swung around. "You're mad if ye think I'll kill the girl. I won't drag myself down to Argyll's level. If that's your meaning, ye can believe I won't be helping ye."

His nephew stood up, moving to join the laird near the fire. "There are many who would do all in their power to stop this union between the Calders and the Campbells. The Calders themselves are opposed to it. Perhaps there is one who desires the girl's death more than we do. Someone who could do more harm than we could, so the name of Maclean need never be involved at all."

"You're speaking of the outlaw, Andrew Calder, aren't ye?"

"Aye. He's already stolen Campbell cattle and horses and a great deal of Campbell gold. And he makes no secret of his intentions. He wants the lass. Once she's gone, Cawdor would be his."

"He won't be getting her. He can harry the Campbells 'til they snap, kill their men, take their horses, but he won't be able to get the girl."

"No." Evan smiled slightly. "Not without your aid."

"I thought ye were leading to that." Maclean turned to face his nephew. "Do ye really think the Earl would allow it, man?"

"Argyll has a great deal to occupy his mind of late. Besides, he has no wish to antagonize ye just now. What could he do, short of attacking Mull? And ye know as well as I that with Elizabeth here he won't do that."

Eyes narrowed in concentration, Maclean turned to the men who waited in silence. "I believe supper is ready," he said. "Go fill your bellies. I must think." He nodded toward the door, indicating that his nephew was to follow them.

Before he left, Evan placed a hand on his uncle's shoulder. "'Tis our only chance in a long time. We must take them as they come."

"Aye, I'll remember. But I want ye to leave me now."

Evan went, closing the door behind him.

An intense stillness fell upon the room in the absence of the men. Maclean paced before the fire, trying not to listen to the sound of the silence, trying to think of a way to injure Argyll without any risk to himself. But he found he could not plan the future so long as vivid images of the past continued to flash through his mind. For a long time now, he admitted, the present had meant little to him except as an opportunity for vengeance against the man who had ruined his past. Alex had been so young—only seventeen. The scene of the deserted battlefield rose before his eyes once more.

He did not hear Elizabeth enter and was unaware of her presence until she touched his shoulder from behind. "Lachlan?"

He spun to face her, feeling the revulsion her touch sometimes gave him. Somehow, he always hoped she would be Anne. But no, that was absurd. She was Elizabeth, and Argyll's daughter as well. He stepped back until she withdrew her hand.

"What is it?" He tried to control his voice but could not keep the chill from creeping in.

Elizabeth was not blind; she recognized his distaste for her. She could see by his face that he was falling into one of his moods. Presently he would begin to look through her as if she were not there. He would shudder when she touched him, as he had almost done a moment ago. Last time this had happened, he had locked himself in the library for a week, refusing to see anyone.

That had been after her father's last visit. She well knew that her husband's moods were connected with his hatred of the Earl. She looked beyond Maclean, staring into the fire. She would comfort him gladly, she thought, if only he would let her. "Won't ye eat with us?" she asked at last.

"I'm no' hungry and would be alone." Her husband turned his back on her.

"Lachlan—"

"Leave me!"

This time she did not pause. Without another word, she fled.

Damn the woman! Maclean thought when he heard the door slam shut. Couldn't she see that he didn't want her? Couldn't she understand that every time he looked at her, he saw Anne's body covered with blood, her face marred beyond all recognition? He leaned heavily against the mantel. Anne. He still remembered her face as it had been before Argyll's men ruined it. He still longed to touch her Highland red hair and watch her green eyes dance. She would have been his wife if it had not been for the Earl.

Maclean himself had sent his betrothed with his brother because he thought Duart Castle might be threatened, despite the uneasy peace. He had sent her away so she would be safe, and by doing so, had sent her to her death. The now-familiar self-loathing began to tie his stomach in knots. Argyll's men had killed her, but Maclean had given them the chance.

When the Earl had offered his daughter to his enemy as a bond of good faith after the final treaty had been signed, Maclean had laughed. Argyll must be mad, he had thought, to first kill a man's betrothed then offer up his daughter as a sacrifice.

Maclean smiled oddly. He had agreed to the arrangement because he believed he could manipulate the Earl through Elizabeth. He had thought the marriage would give him a convenient means of power. But it had never occurred to him that Elizabeth would love him. He had not realized that every time she looked at him with softness in her eyes, his stomach would tighten in pain. She ought to hate him; he tried to make her do so, but she persisted in loving him, even when he flaunted his whores before her face.

He found, to his dismay, that because she loved him, he could not hurt her. He could not use her against her father as he had planned, yet he could never forgive her because she was not Anne.

Maclean shook his head wearily. He knew he was only destroying himself and getting nowhere. But what could he do?

A spark leapt into the rushes beside him. He watched it glow, then blacken. It seemed that Evan had had an idea. What was it he had said? Oh yes—the outlaw, Andrew Calder. Maclean stood up abruptly and headed for the door, shouting, "Evan! Evan, we have plans to make!" When he pulled the door open, he was laughing.

# 8

The Gypsies! The Gypsies have come!"

Muriella heard the shout above the chatter of the seamstresses who surrounded her. All morning the women had been here, measuring and cutting, pulling her this way and that as they tried one fabric after another against her skin. Through it all, the girl had stared toward the open door as if longing to escape.

The seamstresses were puzzled by her disinterest. Muriella was being given a wedding wardrobe that made their own mouths drop open in wonder. Here in the Highlands, the women rarely touched anything more delicate than rough linen and wool. Yet behind them now stood trunks full of velvets, brocades, satins and even French lace.

The Earl had decreed that Muriella and his son would have a grand wedding. He had gone down to the sea to meet the ships coming in from France and brought back chests full of splendid lengths of cloth. Then he had gathered the seamstresses from all over the Highlands to make Muriella's wedding gown. The women gazed at the rich cloth with reverence, but the girl stood stubbornly silent in their midst.

The instant Megan's cry that the Gypsies had come pierced the circle of bustling women, Muriella moved lithely. Before anyone could protest, she hurried toward the door. She found Megan waiting in the hallway. "Where are they?"

The servant could barely contain her excitement. "At the

foot of the mountains, in the little valley over the hill. Shall we go see them, miss?"

Grasping Megan's hand, Muriella drew her toward the stairs. "Oh, aye!" she said.

"But don't the seamstresses need ye here?"

Muriella smiled over her shoulder as she started down the stairs. "They'll manage without me." When the girls reached the bottom step, she paused. "I'd begun to think I'd go daft with those women always fluttering about. They remind me of my aunts; they don't ever run out of things to say."

"But—"

"Don't worry. They've had me all morning, and ye know the Earl won't mind."

Megan had to admit that was true. Once he'd become convinced that Muriella would not try to flee, the Earl had allowed her more freedom to do as she wished. Each day, following whatever fancy struck her, the two girls walked down by the loch or followed the path of the river or wandered in the garden. Once they had even shared a wild ride along the seashore. Duncan and Adam Campbell, their swords at their sides, were never far behind on these daily expeditions outside the keep; at the Earl's suggestion, John had set them to watch over Muriella until the wedding.

As the girls went through the hall, Muriella saw Duncan rise, motioning to Adam across the room. Though she had become accustomed to their presence long since, at first she had wanted to hide from the curious eyes that followed her everywhere. But gradually she had realized the boys were no threat to her. They left her in peace as much as they could but were always nearby in case she should need them.

She forgot about the guards when she and Megan reached the top of a low hill that sheltered the valley from the west. There Muriella stopped to catch her breath, enchanted by what she saw.

The Gypsy camp spread below her, covering the floor of the valley in an uneven circle. The men were raising striped, multicolored tents, and the women were unpacking dilapidated wagons whose sides were painted with faint but still-discernible symbols in black, red, and gold. Many of the dark-haired women circled the fires dotting the landscape, and the air rang with laughter and the jingle of many bracelets. At the far end of the camp, where the river crossed the valley, a deep purple tent was already standing. From inside it, Muriella could hear the song of a harp. She smiled, shrugging away the gloom of the endless morning.

Megan tugged at her mistress's elbow, and the two girls, Duncan, and Adam started down the gentle slope toward the camp. "Shall we sit by the fire and listen to the women?" Megan asked. "Mary says last time they came they told some wonderful, strange tales."

Muriella was hardly aware the servant had spoken. She was staring at the purple tent as if hypnotized. She felt that the notes of the distant harp had captured her, were drawing her toward the cool, shadowed center of the tent. "We must go," she said. Willingly, she let the music pull her from one end of the camp to the other.

Megan followed at her mistress's heels, intrigued. All at once, Muriella's eyes reminded her of the gray green loch on a day when no breeze stirred its gleaming surface. As they approached the tent, the flap covering the door was thrown back and a man stepped out into the light. In his hands he held an ancient clareschaw—the small Highland harp that minstrels had carried since music first rose from the wild Scottish hills.

Muriella stopped to stare at him, although she was not certain why. What was it that arrested her? His eyes, which were a strange shade of gray that flickered into green when the sunlight struck them? Or was it his thick, silver gray hair that curled down to his shoulders and blended with his full gray beard? His face, she noticed, was weather-beaten; deep lines ran from his nose to his mouth, cutting across his leathery, reddish brown skin. Clearly he was not a stranger to the sun.

While Muriella continued to stand mute, the Gypsy sat cross-legged on a cushion with his harp resting on his knees. When he had settled himself to his satisfaction, he looked up. "So," he said finally, "ye've come."

Megan gaped at him, charmed by his deep, melodic voice, which gave even those simple words a touch of magic.

His gaze locked with Muriella's, the Gypsy smiled and pointed to an embroidered pillow beside him. "I'm Alex," he said. "Will ye sit with me?"

Megan stood undecided for a moment, then backed away. The Gypsy's piercing gaze made her uneasy; she could see the way he seemed to draw her mistress down to the pillow without a word or a touch. The servant shifted from one foot to the other, feeling that she did not belong. She looked over her shoulder and caught sight of Duncan hovering by the nearest campfire. With a last concerned look at her mistress, Megan went to join the squire.

Muriella sat on the soft cushion and found it much more comfortable than the hard chairs and benches at the castle. She did not look up at the Gypsy's face; like Megan, she had been disturbed by the power in his eyes. Instead she studied his clareschaw with interest. It was the music that had brought her here, after all, and she wanted to hear more. But Alex did not move to pick up the instrument. With a slight smile playing about his lips, he watched the girl and waited.

"Isn't there something ye wish to ask me?" he suggested at last.

Muriella considered the question for a moment, then murmured, "Ye seemed to expect me. How did ye know I'd come?"

"I dreamed of ye last night. My dreams speak to me, and I've learned to listen well, for they never lie, as men do."

With a sharp intake of breath, Muriella leaned closer. "Ye have the Sight, then?"

"Aye, since I was a wee bairn." He pushed the hair back from his face as his eyes grew warm with memories. "I recall the very day it first came to me. I was standin' above a river, starin' into a pool of clear water, when I saw the face of a woman I didn't know. At first I thought she'd fallen in, but when I leaned to fetch her out, 'twas no one there at all."

"But ye met her afterwards, didn't ye?"

"That I did. 'Twas no' 'til many years later, but I knew her just the same." The Gypsy's thoughts were drifting away; he brought himself back to the present with an effort. "And what of ye? When did ye first know that ye had the power?"

Muriella's eyes widened in surprise. "I don't remember," she said. "Besides, 'twasn't me who had the power. 'Twas the *power* that had *me*." She stared down at her hands in order to hide her distress, but Alex seemed to sense what she was feeling. He reached out to cover her fingers with his.

"I know," he whispered. "Ye wonder sometimes if your mind and body are your own anymore, but 'tis the price ye have to pay for havin' the gift."

Muriella looked up at him. "How did ye know?"

"'Twasn't hard to guess. I could see it in your face." He ran his fingertip lightly over the corner of her mouth. "Here, where your confusion has changed the curve of your smile. And here"—he traced the slight shadows under her eyes—"where fear has left its mark on many a sleepless night." He touched her cheeks gently. "Here, where the pain has settled in the wee hollows." At last he rested two fingers on her eyelids. "And most of all, here in your eyes, where I see the knowledge that tears at your heart."

As he spoke, Muriella realized that he too bore the signs of suffering from the weight of a burden that was sometimes too heavy to bear. Then he took her hand to place it against his cheek. Without conscious thought, she followed on his face the path he had traced over her own. She touched the grooves and wrinkles and hollows of his leathery skin, and in that moment felt that the strands of their pasts had been woven together because of the grief they'd shared.

"Ye see, lass, that ye aren't alone."

She drew away, bewildered by the lump that had formed in her throat. "Does it ever get any easier? Does the fear go away?"

"No," Alex told her sadly. "But in time, ye learn to make the best of a power ye can't fight." He regarded her for a moment in silence, then added, "You're to be married within the month, isn't that so?"

The question called to mind a vivid memory of John's

bearded face, and Muriella stiffened at the rush of fear the image brought with it. "Aye," she said. "The Earl of Argyll has given his son a gift—me."

The Gypsy sighed. "You're young, lass. Ye must come to accept the bonds ye can't break."

"I can't do it," she cried. "I'm afraid—"

"Of what?" he asked gently.

Muriella shook her head. "I don't know."

His gaze clouded over and he turned away, listening to a sound she could not hear. When he spoke again, his voice was strained. "Ye'll learn things today that ye don't wish to know."

Muriella touched his hand and felt the trembling of his fingers and the chill that had settled on his skin. "Tell me—," she began, but he interrupted her.

"You've come here to forget, no' to remember. Listen to the sound of the river. 'Tis singin' today and won't stand for any sadness." He did not turn to look at her, but picked up his harp and began to strum a tune she had never heard before. His fingers moved lithely over the strings, weaving a pattern of notes that echoed the soft rumbling sound of the river nearby. The leap and swirl of the water sang through the seasoned harp in Alex's hands. In spite of her unanswered questions, Muriella felt herself being drawn into the pleasing rhythm.

The tent blocked the river from her sight, but with his music, Alex re-created the jubilant bright cascade of water over stones. Her heartbeat answered the pulse of the song, the song the pulse of the rushing river. She smiled slowly, with delight.

"I'm thinkin' your friends are wantin' to dance," Alex said, motioning toward Megan and Duncan and Adam.

The three had turned their backs on the fire and were swaying with the music. Only then did Muriella realize that others were playing their harps and the pure sweet notes of a flute rose now and then above the melody. Suddenly, as if beckoned by a silent hand, the Gypsies began to drift away from their tasks toward the glowing bonfire. They paused just beyond the reach of the flames, eyes closed, while the music possessed them. Men and women alike raised their arms until palm met palm; then they began to turn slowly, drawing Megan and the others into the dance with them.

Just when Muriella felt she could not resist the lure of the music any longer, a woman knelt and reached for her hand. "Come," she crooned, "leave your troubles for a time."

Muriella nodded, staring fascinated at the pendant that hung on a chain around the woman's neck—an intricate golden flame with a ruby at its center. The ruby flashed and glimmered when the Gypsy moved, so that the flame itself seemed to flicker.

Alex followed Muriella's gaze. "Lovely, isn't it?"

"'Tis beautiful."

"Come," the woman repeated. "Ye must answer the call of the music before it fades away."

With a last look at Alex, whose head was bent so she could not see his eyes, Muriella rose and moved toward the circle of laughing dancers.

Crouching low in the saddle, Andrew Calder watched and waited, his hand poised above the handle of his sword. Through the pattern of leaves that hid him from view, he could see the blue and green Campbell plaid draped over the shoulders of the men coming toward him. Leaves and plaid shifted, blended, became indistinguishable, then separated once again as the five men on horseback rode ploddingly toward Calder's hiding place.

"Are ye ready?" he hissed to the men who waited with him. "We don't want to miss our chance."

"Aye, we're ready, sir, but—"

Calder turned in irritation at the uncertainty in the man's voice. "Davie?" he rasped. "What's worrying ye now? We've twice as many men and they won't be expecting us."

David Fraser looked unconvinced. "Aye, but 'tis a lot of money, just the same. The Campbells won't soon forget this one, Andrew. Are ye sure ye want to risk it?"

With a snort, Calder looked away. "I intend to risk everything to get back what they stole from me. If you're afraid of trying, ye can leave us now, Davie. But ye knew before we started what we meant to do." He leaned forward to get a better view of the approaching riders. They were Campbells all right, and their saddlebags were fat and heavy, just as his informant had promised. That was good. This little raid might just be worth the effort.

Of course, no matter how much gold was hidden in those bags, it could not compensate him for the loss of Cawdor. Calder glowered through the foliage, remembering that, like a fool, he had felt relief when his oldest brother died so young. It had not occurred to Andrew that as the second son, he would not inherit all his brother John had lost. He had been furious when he learned that Isabel Calder had borne a baby girl who became John Calder's heir.

"Look at those bags," one man whispered reverently. "There must be a fortune on the backs of those nags."

"Money for the big wedding, I'll wager," another sneered. "They tell me the Earl can't spend enough on the girl. But then"—he elbowed Calder roughly—"he's thinkin' to get it back, no doubt, after the ceremony."

"There won't be a wedding if I have aught to do with it," Andrew snapped. "Mayhap this time Argyll will see I'm not boasting when I say so." His fingers closed down on the cool metal of his broadsword. Andrew had been all for seeing that the girl never lived to enjoy her inheritance, but William Calder had advised against it. He had claimed that the clan could not afford the full-scale war with the Roses that the girl's murder would have caused. The old man had even hinted that he had other ways of seeing that Cawdor remained in Calder hands.

He had been wrong. The Campbells had seen to that.

"If ye mean to stop the ceremony, why do ye wait?" Davie demanded. "Why haven't ye tried for the girl yet?"

"Because it may not be necessary. My father has plans of his own. And I must confess, 'twould amuse me no end to see John Campbell of Lorne married to a penniless bastard." In the meantime, he intended to get what he could from the Campbells. He knew it would be impossible to break the clan, but he could certainly make them uncomfortable while his own pockets grew fat with their wealth. Then, if his father's plan failed—

Andrew Calder was no fool. He knew what would happen if Muriella became a Campbell. He and his father and brothers would be left in poverty while their inheritance passed to the coffers of their greatest enemy—Archibald Campbell. Argyll was second only to the King in wealth and power, but King James was busy with his squabbles at court. Here in the Highlands, it was the Earl who ruled. Calder had sworn he would not let Argyll have his way this time. He had had no difficulty finding men willing to join him in this enterprise; his brothers fought for the sake of Cawdor, the others for their hatred and fear of the Earl. They were outlaws now, every last one of them, and desperate enough to do whatever Calder asked of them.

"'Tis time!" someone hissed. "Be sure your aim is true!"

Calder drew his sword, grinning in anticipation of the fight. The riders would be easy prey, but that did not dim his pleasure.

"Now!" he cried as he kicked his horse into action. In an instant, the narrow path was crowded by the outlaws, who screamed their war cry as they hemmed in the five couriers. The Campbells were hardly able to pull up their horses before the attack, let alone draw their own weapons. They gave up the gold, and four of their lives, without a fight.

As Davie started to finish off the last of them, Calder stayed his hand. "Leave him. We want the news back at Inveraray as soon as can be. By the telling of this deed, I'll make certain that from today, the Campbells of Inveraray will never forget the name of Andrew Calder!"

Colin sprawled across the uneven bench, clasping a servant girl with one hand and a tankard of ale with the other. The Earl and John sat nearby. All three looked expectantly toward the man who had just ridden in from Cawdor.

"Well, Richard, what have ye found?" the Earl demanded.

Richard wiped the sweat from his forehead with his shirt sleeve before answering. "M'lord, the Calders have two witnesses who swear Isabel Calder lay with a man besides her husband."

"That doesn't prove the girl is illegitimate!" John exploded.

"They also swear Isabel and her husband kept apart and that he never lay with her at all."

Rising from the bench, John began to pace behind his father's chair. It seemed he had done little but pace the floor in frustration ever since they had taken Muriella from Cawdor.

"Be calm, Johnnie," Argyll demanded. "The witnesses have been paid, that's all. We'll simply have to force them to admit it. Tell me, Richard, do the officials believe these lies?"

"Aye, m'lord. But they've no more desire to see the Campbells at Cawdor than the Calders do."

"Thank ye," the Earl murmured absently. "Ye can go."

Sighing in relief, Richard shambled off to the kitchen to find himself something to drink.

For the first time, Argyll became aware of the girl who sat beside Colin. "Can't ye send her away? We've no need to have the servants knowing our business."

His oldest son smiled, tightening his hold on the girl. "Jenny here won't speak a word, will ye, hinny? She's quiet, is this one, the way I like 'em."

"Forget the girl," John interrupted. "What are ye going to do about this?" He bent down to look into his father's face. "And what if the witnesses aren't being paid? What if they aren't lying?"

"If they aren't, they'll nevertheless swear that they are. I'll see to it. But I tell ye, they're false witnesses. Had they been legitimate, William Calder would have brought them forward a long time ago." He paused, considering his son thoughtfully. "I'll go to Cawdor myself, tomorrow. They all know I speak for the King. They'll listen to me."

Colin chuckled. "They know ye speak for Argyll and they won't listen. Maclean didn't hear ye, and the Calders have far more to gain than he did." He pinched Jenny, sliding his hand along her arm. "But if ye should be successful, I'm sure Johnnie's bastard will be grateful."

John stopped his pacing, clenched his fists, and moved toward his brother.

"Johnnie," Argyll interjected, "the men are in the courtyard preparing for the hunt. Go with them. Don't worry about this. I'll see it comes out all right. We've gone to too much trouble to give up now."

John glared at Colin for a moment longer, then spun on his heel and stalked out of the hall.

The Earl turned to Colin. "As for ye, I suggest ye take your woman and get out of my sight."

His son shrugged. "The boy's a fool. Too sensitive by far. He won't ever make a good fighter; he's all hot blood and no common sense."

"Get out!" Argyll bellowed.

Colin went, pulling Jenny along behind him.

* * *

Several hours later the hunters returned. They burst into the Great Hall, laughing and triumphant. Most of them were streaked with blood; John's saffron shirt was died brown to the elbows, and where he had pushed back his hair, the blood had stiffened the tangles into permanent disorder. One sleeve was torn clear to the shoulder and his knee protruded through his filthy trews. But he was smiling as he had not smiled for many days.

Stumbling with the weight, he lifted a deer carcass into the air and shouted, "A deer! In this season! We shall eat well tonight after all."

The other men slapped him on the back with hands and elbows, applauding his success. "Och, Johnnie! Congratulations!"

With John in the lead, the hunters paraded through the hall to deposit their treasures in the kitchen. When they returned, ale had replaced the day's kill. Joking and shoving, they settled around the tables while John sat on a stool by the fire. He leaned his head against the rough stone and grinned to himself.

There was a brief commotion in the courtyard, then Megan, Muriella, and her two guards came into the hall. Like John, they were pleased with themselves. For once Muriella's eyes were unshadowed. She smiled as she and Megan whirled for a moment in each other's arms. Breathing heavily with the exertion, they swung themselves toward the fire.

"What's this?" John exclaimed as he set his tankard down on the floor. "What's turned ye daft in a single afternoon?"

Muriella did not hear him; she was still under the influence of the Gypsy music. Entranced by the graceful movement of the flames in the fireplace, she watched them leap and twirl like golden dancers.

"Och, Sir John! 'Tis the Gypsies yonder in the valley!" Megan panted. "They're wonderful, m'lord. They sing and dance and their clothes are so bright." Unable to contain her excitement, the servant pirouetted once more.

Her pleasure was contagious. Without a word, Richard rose, smiling, and took her hand. Megan curtsied, then gathered her skirts about her as he twirled her out and back and out again. Then Duncan took up the beat, tapping his foot to the memory of the Gypsy songs, and bowed low before Muriella. She grinned, swaying with the rhythm of the crackling fire, and touched his hands briefly with her palms. Soon they were spinning beside Megan and Richard, tripping over the rushes and kicking them aside. The couples met and parted, met and parted, while Adam and two others joined them, until all were moving in a dance without pattern or partners. They needed no harps to guide their feet; the only music they recognized was their own muted laughter and the enthusiastic stomping of feet that urged them on. Muriella smiled and dipped and spun and curtsied, aware of nothing but her delight in the movement of her own body.

John watched in astonishment, as if this were an apparition created by the too-bright glare of the afternoon sun. His gaze was fixed on Muriella, who seemed to have forgotten, for the moment, the devils that usually haunted her. Why, with color in her cheeks and a little life in her eyes, she's lovely, he thought. Before he could stop to consider, he left his stool and went to take her hand.

Unconscious of the condition he was in or the interested stares of the men, John circled with his betrothed. As they whirled faster and faster he felt a strange stirring inside him. He had never seen her smile before, never seen her face when it was not clouded with accusations or mistrust.

He realized with a start that he was actually enjoying the feel of her body in his arms, the whisper of her hair as it rose and fell with the dance. Although she was to be his wife, he had never thought of her as desirable. But he had never before seen in her the woman she would someday be. John drew her closer until he could smell the scent of her hair and feel the swish of her skirts against his legs.

He smiled and felt the blood running hotly through his veins as she swung toward him so her breasts brushed his chest. God, but she was torturing him without knowing; it had been too long since he'd had a woman, and Muriella was weaving a web of enchantment with her smiles. Overcome by the sudden strength of his need, John buried his hand in her hair and tilted her head up with the pressure of his demanding fingers. Then he lowered his head and kissed her, hard and full on her parted lips.

Just for an instant, still lost in the dream, Muriella felt a tiny flicker of warmth race over her flushed skin. Then the heat of John's mouth on hers shook her violently awake, burning away the music and the magic and the rhythm that had held her in its grasp. She took a step backward. As John's bearded face came into focus, she felt as if the ground had slipped from beneath her. She swayed, her hands clenched into painful fists, as the water rushed about her body and she was sucked into the center of the raging white foam. For an instant she believed the vision was real, that her skirts were sweeping furiously around her ankles and her head was sinking under the waves, but as her body grew still, the image faded. "No!" she gasped, wrenching free of John's arms.

Muriella stood trembling from the vision that had overpowered her so completely that even now she felt her legs might buckle. Her heartbeat slowed, seemed to drag in her chest, and she had to struggle to catch her breath. Frozen with shock, she took in for the first time John's soiled and rent clothing and his face, on which blood and dirt vied for dominance. He was still reaching out, waiting for her to return to him, while the rush of the water pounded in her ears once more.

The Sight had not touched her for many days, and now it would not leave her; her fear was so strong she could smell it in the air like the clinging odor of bitter herbs. She was weak with shaking, and all around the men were watching, staring open-mouthed, not bothering to hide their curiosity. With a strength of will she had not known she possessed, Muriella forced the vision back into darkness, then took another step away from John.

The silence stretched between them—chill and implacable—while he tried to collect his wits. She had bewitched him for a moment, that's what she'd done. He had not even tried to stop her. Now he became aware that the other dancers had stopped and everyone in the hall was watching to see what he would do. "There's work aplenty," he called to the men. "Don't stand about gawking as if ye'd nothing better to do."

One by one they looked away. Finally, John turned back to Muriella. "Ye'd best go to your chamber and rest," he told her. "Ye don't want my father to find ye unpleasant company at dinner."

Although his voice was little more than a whisper, she heard the warning concealed there. "Aye," she breathed, but she did not know what she was saying. She only knew she had to be alone before the illness in her body betrayed her completely.

# 10

Megan closed the chamber door and leaned upon it, her fingers wrapped tightly around the latch. Her gaze swept over the hangings that now covered the gray stone walls, the new curtains gracing the huge oak bed. Her mistress had chosen to remain in Elizabeth's room, though the Earl had tried to change her mind. "I want to be where I can see the loch," she had explained. "'Tis simple enough to move a tapestry or two and make it more comfortable." In the end, Argyll had relented and the two girls had cleaned the room from top to bottom, brought in fresh sheets and furs, and draped the walls with vivid color. But just now, in the hushed stillness, the chamber felt chill and unwelcoming.

Muriella was kneeling by the window, as she so often did, trying to lose herself in the ebb and flow of the distant loch. She was aware of little besides the roughness of the stone beneath her palms. When she heard Megan sigh, she turned.

The servant did not like the shadows in her mistress' eyes. Not long ago the girls had been intimate friends, but now Muriella was far away from her. "What ails ye?" she asked in concern.

The other girl reached out as if groping for words, then whispered hoarsely, "I 'saw' something just now. 'Twas—" She broke off, closed her eyes, and took a deep breath. "'Twas my own death."

Megan gasped, crossing herself protectively, and took a

step backward. For a long moment, she merely stared, eyes wide with horror. "Surely you're mistaken," she whispered finally. "Mayhap ye weren't seein' clearly. Haven't ye ever had a vision that didn't come true?"

Muriella looked away. "Never," she said. "The Sight never lies. This vision will come to pass, just as the others have. I can't stop it and I can't change it. All I can do is wait. 'Tis the waiting that's the worst. Ye don't know when or where or why . . ." Her voice grew more and more ragged as she spoke, until her words were indistinguishable.

"Dear God," Megan groaned. She could find no other words to speak.

"Now that ye know, do ye see that I can't marry John?"

The servant was so surprised by the change of subject that it was a moment before she could find her voice. "Ye can't—? *Why,* miss?"

Without realizing what she was saying, Muriella breathed, "He touched me, and he wanted—more."

Megan heard the panic in those simple words and all at once she thought she understood. She grasped at this new problem eagerly; she did not want to think about the other. "Of course he did. He's to be your husband." When she saw that the blood had drained from Muriella's face, Megan went to stand beside her. "Didn't ye know about that? You're nearly fourteen. Didn't your mother tell ye what a marriage means?"

"No." Muriella saw now that she had been blind and foolish; she had assumed that as her husband, the only things John would take from her were her fortune and her name. Now she realized that she would lose more than that when she wed—much more. They called her a woman, but she was not yet ready for all that that meant.

"But, miss, I don't understand. Ye told me ye were betrothed before."

Muriella stared down at her hands. "I never thought of Hugh that way. We grew up together, ye see. We were companions, friends, that's all."

"He didn't ever touch ye?"

Closing her eyes, Muriella tried to remember. "He held my hand sometimes, but 'twasn't the same. He never looked at me the way John did."

Megan put her hand on her mistress's shoulder. "Marriage would have changed that, ye ken."

"I suppose so, but I didn't realize—"

"'Tis time ye did then, with your weddin' no more than a month away."

Muriella shook her head. Against her will, she felt again the pressure of John's body against hers, the heat of his lips and the momentary desire she had seen in his eyes. She was bewildered when she remembered the warmth that had touched her own skin. Dear God, some night he would reach out to her with his rough, careless hands— "He was filthy with blood," she gasped.

"But I heard them say he's killed a deer. There'll be venison this night instead of mutton. Ye can't hunt without gettin' a mite dirty. Besides, I don't see what it matters."

"Don't ye?" Muriella murmured. She herself had seen it clearly. Only for an instant, it was true, but that had been enough. She felt that she was no longer fighting for her freedom alone; she was fighting for her life. "I can't marry him!"

"The Campbells want ye. They'll have ye, miss."

"They shall *not!* Do ye hear? I won't have John Campbell. I'll think of a way."

Megan took a step backward, stunned by the force of Muriella's declaration. There was no point in arguing with her now; she would not listen. "As ye say, miss." She turned to the carved oak clothes chest in an effort to escape the gleam of her mistress's eyes. "Ye should change before supper," she said as calmly as she could. "Your gown is muddy."

The simple practicality of her request brought Muriella back to earth. Megan was right; there was nothing she could do. She had decided that the first day they brought her here. But the knowledge did not stop the despair from creeping in, coloring her world gray and bleak. Numbly she undressed to slip into the gold kirtle and pale cream gown with fur-lined sleeves that Megan shook out for her. She stood unprotesting while the servant fixed her hair, twining gold ribbons among the long auburn braids. When she was ready, she followed Megan from the room. What other choice did she have?

As they reached the top of the stairs, the two girls stopped. They could hear giggling from the end of the hallway, but it ended abruptly when a low voice interrupted. Megan chewed her lip in indecision. Maybe what her mistress needed was a distraction from her own thoughts. After looking to Muriella for approval, she turned toward the sound of the voice.

Her mistress followed close behind. In Muriella's three months at Inveraray she had discovered that Megan was right. One could learn a great deal listening to the servants' gossip.

"And they said . . ." The speaker, who Muriella recognized as Jenny, paused for effect, then continued, "They said her mother lay with another man. They *swore* it, and—"

After the first few words, Megan attempted to pull her mistress away, but Muriella refused to move.

"They swore her mother and father never lay together at all. The Calders'll get back her fortune if 'tis so. Then Colin laughed and called her a bastard, and Sir John said, 'What if 'tis true—' "

Muriella whirled away into the darkness with Megan at her heels. She was not aware of the direction she took; she only knew she must escape from that voice. She was shocked, therefore, to find herself at the head of the stairs and to hear the Earl's voice calling up to her.

"There she is. Come down and join us, lass. The Gypsies are coming to sing for us, we have venison, and tomorrow I must go away. So tonight we must enjoy ourselves. Come, let's eat!"

As the stairs swayed under Muriella's feet, the flames from the torches leapt across the walls, throwing ghostly shadows over the room below. Laughter, mingled with the din of pewter on wood, assaulted her ears. She saw that John stood at the foot of the stairs, his face clean and his torn garments discarded for whole ones. In the alternating grim light and shadows, his face seemed to stretch and darken, his mouth to twist into a leer. The men glowered up at Muriella, their mouths open and their expressions hostile. Then the girl caught a glimpse of the Earl's face.

"What is it, lass? Are ye ill?"

The steps ceased their movement; the flames crept back into their sconces, leaving the men no more than men. John's face settled into its usual lines and the leer disappeared from his lips. When she felt Megan taking her arm from behind, Muriella forced her body into motion and started down the stairs.

Throughout dinner, the Earl did not allow her to leave his side. He put his arm across her shoulders and examined her face as she seated herself on the bench beside his ornately carved chair. Her skin was pale, he noticed, and her eyes seemed overlarge. "Are ye certain ye aren't ill? Would ye like another cushion to sit on?"

She shook her head, focusing her attention on the salted herring and venison heaped on her platter. She had no real appetite and only chewed absently on a bit of bread covered with sweet butter. She looked up once to find Colin watching her across the table. *And Colin laughed and called her a bastard*— He looked away when she continued to stare at him. Inside, she was trembling.

Concerned by her silence, the Earl offered her a tray of sweetmeats and dried figs. "Ye must eat something or ye'll be ill indeed, and we can't have that."

To please him, she took a fig and put it in her mouth, surprised to find that she liked the sweetness on her tongue. Somehow she had thought every morsel would taste of dust tonight.

"Tell me, little one," Argyll murmured, choosing an iced cake and placing it in her hand, "did ye like the green velvet for your gown?"

She looked up at him, remembering when they had brought the gift to her. She had sat gazing at it for a long time before she ran her fingers over the deep, soft fabric. Green, like her eyes. The kind of velvet she had often wished for at Kilravok, but known that she could never have. Argyll's thoughtfulness had brought tears to her eyes. She had realized, in that moment, that the Earl would give her anything she asked for—anything but her freedom. "'Twas a lovely gift," she told him. "I was surprised that ye went to so much trouble." She smiled with her lips, but her eyes remained dark and still.

Then the Gypsies began to file into the hall. She watched anxiously as the minstrels crossed to the fireplace. Alex was the last.

The Gypsy's gaze met hers at once. *Ye'll learn things today that ye don't wish to know.* He smiled and nodded and Muriella tightened her grip on the Earl's arm. Perhaps, she thought, the music would erase the memory and the word that now echoed inside her head: *Bastard. Bastard. Bastard.*

As the minstrels played reed and harp and lute, the men began to stamp their feet beneath the tables. Alex's voice rang out above the others, deep and sure.

Cauld winter is awa', my luve,
And spring is in her prime,
The breath o' God stirs all to life,
The grasshoppers to chime.

The buds canna contain themsel's
Upon the sproutin' tree,
But loudlie, loudlie sing o' luve,
A theme which pleaseth me.

With their bellies full and their tankards thrice emptied, the men laughed and joined in the singing. Then one or two rose, grasping passing servant girls, and began to dance. The Earl turned to Muriella with a smile. "Ye should dance too, lass. 'Tis a celebration."

Muriella shook her head. "I'm a little weary."

"Surely not so weary that ye can't dance with the man who's to be your husband?" Colin asked with mock chagrin.

Muriella wondered if he had heard about her earlier encounter with John; by the challenging gleam in Colin's eye, she guessed he had. But she would not play his game. "I said I don't wish to." She looked up to find John watching her. What was he thinking, she wondered, with his frosty blue eyes and his unsmiling mouth?

"Can't ye learn to enjoy yourself?" he asked. "Or don't ye dare?"

Did he think she would enjoy being held in his arms? She took a deep breath. "I told ye—"

"Aye, so ye did." As he watched the play of the torchlight over Muriella's face, John leaned forward unwillingly; her strange green eyes drew him to her when he wanted to turn away. But as he struggled to pull himself out of her gaze, he came to a decision. He would not let her make a fool of him again. He blinked twice, then rose and, turning his back on his betrothed, sauntered toward the musicians and picked up a clareschaw. He began to play softly.

O Lassie, is thy heart mair hard
Than mavis from the bough;
Say must the whole creation wed,
And ye remain to woo?
Say has the holy lowe o' love
Ne'er lighten'd in your eye?
O, if thou canst not feel for pain,
Thou art no theme for me!

He was singing to Muriella, gazing at her mournfully, but his eyes belied the solemn droop of his mouth. Some of the men began to laugh.

Muriella clenched her fists. Rising slowly, she faced him across the crowded expanse of the hall. "Don't mock me!" Her voice rose high and piercing; she was certain everyone could hear the pounding of her heart as it spelled out the word *bastard* again and again.

Perplexed by the anguish in her tone, John took a step forward. "I didn't mean—"

"Ye did!" she cried. "I know what ye meant."

They stood immobile, staring at each other, while an uncomfortable silence settled over the hall. Then, abruptly, the musicians began to play and the sound of the deep Gypsy voices shattered the waiting stillness. Muriella's heartbeat slowed as the pounding in her ears diminished. Hiding her trembling hands in the folds of her gown, she took a deep breath and turned back to her place at the table.

Much later, when most of the men had gone up to bed, the Earl found her in the library, curled on the rug with her face toward the fire. He pulled up a chair and sat down, looking beyond her into the flames. "What is it, girl? Why do ye speak to Johnnie so?"

Her only answer was a tremor that began at her feet and ran through her body once, then twice, before she was still.

"Listen to me, Muriella. Has he harmed ye? Is that why?" His tone held a threat to his son that the girl recognized, even in her own shadowed mind.

"No, he hasn't."

Running both hands through his thinning hair, the Earl frowned. "Then why? All the men were watching."

Muriella sat up to face him. "I don't care!"

"Ye must care!" he insisted. "He'll be your husband. Ye must learn to respect him and obey him."

"I can't." She rose, moving off into the shadows.

His voice followed her, taut with anger. "Ye can and ye will." When she did not reply at once, he snapped, "Muriella? Do ye hear? Ye'll do as I say!"

His harsh command struck her like a blow across the face and her control finally snapped. "Who gave ye the right to decide what I should do? Ye don't even ask what *I* want, what *I* feel. To ye I'm just a gamepiece to be moved about at your will."

Muriella knew she should stop herself, but just now that was beyond her power. "Tell me," she demanded, "why I should give up everything just to swell the Campbell coffers! It makes no matter to me that the King made ye my guardian. I don't owe ye anything."

"Only your life," Argyll said, his face flushed with rage

that this girl should challenge him so. "But you're right, your feelings about this marriage mean nothing to me. Quite simply, ye have no choice."

The cold finality of his tone chilled Muriella, but she would not retreat. "You've said ye care for me. Then why won't ye listen to what I say?"

"I've heard enough." He gripped the arms of his chair roughly, but his voice did not waver for even an instant. "The good of the clan comes first. 'Tis time ye learned that. All the weeping in the world won't change a fact so fundamental."

Muriella took a step backward, shocked by the grim implacability of the Earl's expression.

Argyll saw her retreat and regretted briefly the despair he saw reflected in her eyes, but he would not withdraw a word. She had to learn to accept the truth just as Elizabeth had once done; the sooner she did so, the easier it would be for her. He released the chair arms, surprised at the ache that spread through his hands. He hadn't been aware of how tightly he was gripping the polished wood.

Muriella did not move. She stared at him while the shadows played across her face like fleeting ghosts. She looked pale suddenly, and fragile. The Earl sighed and spoke more quietly. "Johnnie's a good man, though a bit young. He's never hurt ye, ye say so yourself. Ye'll marry him in less than a month, and ye'll obey him, do ye hear? Ye won't be a girl any longer."

*Ye have become a woman now,* her mother had whispered. But that was before Muriella knew that Isabel had betrayed her unforgivably. Muriella spoke from the protection of the shadows. "A bastard needn't follow your rules. Mayhap your son won't want to wed me."

The Earl slumped forward, burying his head in his hands. The last of his anger faded when he heard the pain in her voice. "Dear God, what have they told ye?" When she did not respond, he murmured, "Lass, come here."

Muriella went to him slowly, trying to fashion an expression less tinged with bitterness than the one she now wore.

Taking her hands, he examined them in the firelight. He

noted the crippled finger, healed now but still bent and rigid and scarred. For some reason, he did not wish to look at her face. "Ye must no' listen to servants' gossip. Ye aren't a bastard. 'Tis just that your grandfather Calder wants Cawdor back. He'd say anything to make certain he gets it."

"They swore."

"They lied."

"Will ye look at me and say so?" She knew he could not lie to her if he once looked in her eyes.

His head came up and his grip on her fingers tightened. "I swear to ye."

Brow furrowed, Muriella started to reply, but before she could do so, the door swung open. Richard Campbell crossed the threshold and stood gasping just out of the reach of the firelight.

The Earl looked at him sharply. "What is it?"

"Andrew Calder struck the men coming from Edinburgh." Richard tried to steady his harsh breathing, then added, "Seems he escaped to Mull."

Argyll rose. "Is Maclean sheltering him at Duart?"

"'Tis what we suspect, though we can't be sure. But there's something else." In his agitation, Richard did not see Muriella, who had slipped back into the shadows.

"Well, man? Out with it!"

"He murdered four of our men and he swore—"

Argyll took a step forward. "He swore what?"

"That he'll kill every Campbell he meets 'til ye give up the girl."

# 11

As she had every night since she'd come to Inveraray, Muriella slept uneasily. The Earl had been gone for a week now, and she had heard nothing from him. If John and Colin had received word, they did not tell her so; but then, they spoke to her as little as possible. John was away most of the time, and when he was there, he quarreled with anyone who had the misfortune to come upon him. Muriella stayed out of his way; she remembered all too clearly how he had stopped the Earl as he left the keep, heading for Cawdor.

"Let me go after Andrew Calder. He's in our territory and his kinsmen are far away. I could take him with little trouble."

Argyll had answered in exasperation, "I see ye haven't learned a thing. If Maclean is protecting the man, ye can be sure 'twill no' be easy to take him. And we can't risk antagonizing your brother-in-law just now. Suppose he *isn't* aiding Calder? If ye attack Mull with a force, ye'll make him an enemy. And don't forget, he has your sister. Ye must wait 'til Calder comes into the open."

"If I meet him, I'll kill him!"

The Earl had swung himself onto his horse. As he joined the dozen men who waited at the gate, he had called, "So long as ye see him away from Mull. But I warn ye, don't go to find him!"

Tonight Muriella could not escape the memory. The scene played itself over and over in her mind, like a distant threat—or a warning. Eventually, when the darkness became so deep that it clung even behind her closed eyelids, she fell asleep. In her dream she heard her mother's voice: *Will ye never leave us in peace, old man?* And her grandfather's reply: *I will have Cawdor back! I won't stand by and watch a child—and what's worse—a daughter of Rose, take it from me. I'll have it back no matter how I have to get it.*

Then her mother was floating down the aisle of the church near Cawdor. The room was alight with hundreds of candles, and wild roses decked the walls and benches. Near the altar stood a man whom Muriella recognized as John Calder. He gave his hand to Isabel and the two repeated their vows while the candles cast flickering shadows over their bent heads.

When the couple rose from their knees, Isabel Calder dropped her husband's hand to turn toward the gloom at the left of the altar. A man stepped from the shadows, taking her in his arms. She offered her lips to him while the congregation gasped. When she stepped back, everyone saw the man lift his hand in salute. It was too dark and his figure too indistinct for anyone to recognize him, but they saw quite clearly that the little finger on his left hand was crippled and scarred.

Isabel turned, kneeling again at the altar. The church was filled with shadows that danced over her face before melting into leaves overhead. The altar became the moss on the riverbank, and Isabel became Lorna, kneeling in the water with blood on her hand. Her mouth was moving, forming the words "We must always be certain we know who ye are."

Muriella stared down at her hand, which was covered with blood. She could still see the blurred shape of the man in the church with his bent finger outstretched. When Muriella looked at Lorna, she was Isabel, and she was weeping. "Forgive me! Forgive me!"

Muriella sat bolt upright in bed. Pulling her knees up to her chest, she rocked in silence. She dug her fingernails into her legs through the soft wool of her nightrail, hoping the pain would bring her back into the present, away from the influence of the dream.

In a moment, Megan appeared at the bedside, her brown hair loose around her shoulders. "Have ye been dreamin' again?"

Muriella nodded, fumbling for the servant's hand. Megan locked her warm fingers with her mistress's cold ones, trying to force the heat from her body into Muriella's.

The servant asked no more questions and Muriella clung tightly to her hand until she fell asleep again. Even then, she did not loosen her grip.

Megan stayed where she was, brow furrowed, until she sensed that dawn had broken.

Muriella awoke with a feverish glow in her eyes. "Megan, I must go to the Gypsies. There are things I must know."

"But miss, 'tis just past dawn. 'Twill no' be safe to leave the keep yet. Wait 'til we've broken our fast. Then Duncan and Adam can come with us."

Throwing off her nightrail, Muriella bent to pick up her gray kirtle where it lay near the dying embers of the fire. "I must go *now*. I *can't* stay still." As she spoke, she pulled her cloak from the peg beside the door and tossed it over her shoulders. "And I must go alone."

Megan had her gown half over her head in an instant. "No. 'Tis too risky. At least let me go with ye."

Muriella stopped her in the middle of tying the strings of her gown. "Ye can't go with me. I'll be safe, I know that much. I'm not in danger today."

Megan saw the certainty in Muriella's gaze and found it oddly reassuring. "You're sure?"

"Aye. Ye must wait for me here. And don't tell them. Please."

Twisting her fingers together, Megan berated herself for her foolishness a moment longer before the determination in Muriella's face dispelled her doubts. "If ye must. But take care."

Nodding once, her mistress turned to disappear through the door.

* * *

"Where is she? Christ! Have ye let her go again?"

Megan heard the suppressed fury in Colin's voice and clasped her hands behind her nervously, trying to still their trembling. She looked up into his face, distorted by his anger so the lump between his brows swelled and pulsed. "I don't know, m'lord. She was gone when I woke."

"She was, was she?" Colin pounded his fist on the table standing between them. "Isn't it your duty to care for her, to keep watch over her? Do ye let her wander about on her own?"

"I can't stop her, m'lord."

"Damn ye, girl! Don't ye know that Andrew Calder seeks her day and night?"

"Aye."

"Do ye know *why* he seeks her? Do ye think 'tis to take her home to her mother?"

Megan shook her head.

"Well then, ye know he wants her life. Do ye hear? Her life! And if she were to lose that, *we* would lose Cawdor. That must not happen."

Megan continued to stare at him but said nothing. She was thinking of her mistress alone in the Gypsy camp. Suddenly, Muriella's belief in her own safety seemed absurd.

"She isn't in the castle." John and several other men joined Colin in the Great Hall, where he stood over Megan. "Where the devil has she gone? I won't ask ye again."

When the servant remained stubbornly silent, Colin brought his palm down hard across her cheek. "Speak!"

Grasping the tabletop, she was just able to catch her balance when he swung from the other side. This time she fell, hitting her head on the bench. When she looked up, Duncan was standing over her. He offered his hand and she took it; her own was shaking now so that she could not stop it.

"Leave the girl alone." Duncan's voice was soft compared to Colin's growl, but he caught the men's attention. "I think Muriella might have gone to the Gypsies."

"Why in the name of all that's holy would she do that when 'tis barely light out?" Pushing past Colin, John confronted his squire.

"She seems to find comfort there. She's visited them many times in the past week. I suggest ye search the camp first."

John considered for only a moment before signaling to the other men to follow. "The camp it is, then. Colin? Are ye coming?"

With a last glowering look, Colin left Megan to join the others. "Ye're damned right I'm coming. I want to be there when we find her," he hissed. "Whether she lives or no'."

Muriella moved slowly, feeling her way through the fog. She had come to know this path well in the past week, but the mist-shrouded landscape that shimmered around her was one she had never seen before. It was as if the fairies had touched the morning with their cool, billowing breath and made a new world for their pleasure. Muriella felt isolated, cast adrift in a sea of swirling moisture that clung to her hair and face, pressing closer and closer, leaving her alone with the scent of heather and the memory of her dream. When she stumbled over a root, she paused to peer into the enfolding whiteness. It was so quiet, so achingly still, that even the sound of her breathing seemed to cease. But there was something—some distant music that penetrated the silence. Was it the rumble of the river? All at once, she was suffocating in the damp stillness. Desperately, she pressed outward with her palms to break through the mist and reach the distant healing murmur. The movement seemed to free her from the cloud of silence. With a sigh of relief, she started forward again, following her instincts toward the Gypsy camp.

Alex was waiting in the purple tent, as she had known he would be, sitting on the cushions scattered along one wall. As her eyes adjusted to the light, she saw the single room was rich in hangings. Like the cushions, they were worked in deep colors and designs that were strange and fascinating to her.

"What's troublin' ye, lass?"

In the somber light, Muriella could not see his face, so she moved closer. "I've come to ask ye if I'm a bastard."

Alex remained silent for a long time. Finally, he motioned to a cushion beside him. Muriella sat down with reluctance, because from there she could not read his expression.

He took her hand, holding it loosely, running his fingers over her palm as if seeking the answer she needed. "You're the legal daughter of Isabel Rose and John Calder. Ye are *not* a bastard."

She thought his voice quavered slightly, but she couldn't be certain. "How do ye know?"

"Ye came to me, didn't ye, because ye trust me more than those at the castle? Because ye know I have knowledge that others don't have? Then ye must listen to what I tell ye. Ye are legitimate."

She leaned forward, seeking reassurance. "They say my mother had a lover."

Alex shook his head. "I don't know everything about your past. I can't tell ye whether 'tis true or no'."

Muriella was not satisfied. There was something that was bothering her, some uneasiness she could not quite understand. "Why have ye come here?" she demanded without warning.

He did not seem surprised by the question. "We always camp in this valley in the winter. The Earl makes us welcome when others don't—mayhap because we bring him news he would no' get else—so we come back year after year."

"But there's something more than that, isn't there?"

Alex sighed in resignation. "Aye, there's another reason. We were in the north last, in Nairnshire."

"Near Kilravok?" All at once Muriella thought she understood.

"Aye. There's trouble brewin' there, as you've no doubt guessed, especially between the Roses and Calders. People in trouble sometimes seek out the Gypsies, so your mother came to me."

"She told ye about me?"

"That she did. Ye see, people tell me things they wouldn't or can't—even tell their own families. Ye make them believe in ye and they find relief in speakin' of their problems to a stranger. When she told me of her fears for ye, I promised I'd watch over ye 'til your marriage, since 'twas already our plan to come to Inveraray."

"She didn't forget me then? I thought, somehow—" Muriella found that she could not go on.

"How could ye believe such a thing?" Alex asked gently. "A mother doesn't so easily forget her bairn."

The girl felt her heart contract with an ache that spread through her chest and slowly outward to her limbs. Forcing herself to stand, she said, "She sent me away, ye know. She knew the Campbells were coming and didn't even try to stop them." She was shocked at the ragged hurt in her own voice.

"Have a wee bit of faith," the Gypsy murmured. "She must have had her reasons."

Turning away to hide the tears that burned behind her eyes, Muriella pressed her hands against the wall of the tent, seeking support. Only then did she realize how much she missed Isabel. She wanted to sit at her mother's side, to hear her soft voice, feel her gentle but firm hand. She wanted to look into Isabel's blue eyes and ask, "Why? *Why* did ye send me away? Why didn't ye tell me the truth, a lie, *anything* to help me understand? And why can't ye hold me and help me forget?" But her longings were hopeless, the answers to her questions bleak silence. The knowledge brought her a loneliness as intense as she had felt, for a moment, when the mist closed around her. She swallowed dryly, helplessly.

While she struggled to catch her breath in the suddenly stifling air, a flash of anger flared within her. She whirled to face Alex again. "If she fears for me, why don't ye take me away from here, back to Kilravok?"

"Because ye belong here."

"Why? Because the King chose to give my fortune to a favorite? Because the Campbells are the only ones strong enough to hold me? Or is it because my own family doesn't care enough to get me back?"

Alex rose to grasp her shoulders in both hands. "'Tis for none of those reasons. 'Tis simply right that ye should be here. Ye don't understand that yet, and I can't make ye do so. But 'tis true just the same. Ye'll save yourself a great deal of pain by learnin' to accept it."

When Muriella shook her head, the Gypsy released her. "You're too stubborn by half, lass. Mayhap ye'll learn that in time. But ye'd best go now. I'm weary, and no doubt the men at the keep have missed ye."

"But—"

"Go! I've nothin' more to say."

Muriella balked. She did not want to go, to leave this place where she felt a vague and tenuous bond with the mother she had lost. Here, in the shadows, with Alex nearby, she could almost believe she was not estranged, abandoned, forgotten.

The Gypsy stood, arms crossed, unrelenting. He gave her no choice. Muriella stifled a sigh, turned and ducked beneath the tent door. The flap fell closed behind her, shutting away the soft, kind shadows, the fleeting memories she had tried so hard to grasp and hold. But her hands were empty now. She felt numb, as if she walked in a dream.

Slowly, the sun had begun to burn away the mist. The rising light destroyed even the dream, and Muriella stood alone and unprotected in the sun. She squinted at the line of horses along the rise that overlooked the Gypsy camp. Some of the riders had seen her. She drew herself upright and waited for them to come. There was nothing else she could do.

As the horses approached, she saw that John's face was distorted with anger and a kind of fear. Beside him, Duncan was smiling at her with relief. Bracing herself against the onslaught of John's fury, she held her hand up to him. She had no other choice.

Lifting her onto his saddle with one hand, John waved over his shoulder with the other. The riders who had reached the bottom of the hill paused, then stopped to await him.

"Are ye some kind of lunatic?" John hissed in Muriella's ear. "Do ye wish to die, is that it?"

"Perhaps," she said.

He brought his horse to an abrupt halt. "Do ye truly want such a thing?"

When she turned to look at him, her eyes were as hard as clear stones. "I'm your prisoner, nothing more and nothing less. I wish only to be set free."

"That's impossible," John snarled, setting his horse in motion with more energy than necessary.

At that moment, Colin rode up beside his brother to glower at Muriella. "So ye found her." He leaned forward. "I'd like to whip the skin off your back for the trouble ye've caused us today." He reached over to grasp her chin in rough fingers. "Do ye hear, girl?"

"I'm no' afraid of ye," Muriella spat.

"Ye should be. Ye will be after today. There's been nothing but trouble since Johnnie brought ye to Inveraray. Thirty men dead, the Earl on a hopeless errand among his enemies, and Andrew Calder threatening to attack us. All for your sake."

Muriella twisted free of his grip. "All for the sake of Cawdor," she said.

"Be quiet, Colin," John demanded in fury. "'Tis not the girl's doing. She can't stop this any more than ye can."

"'Tis for her sake nonetheless," his brother repeated obdurately. "And mayhap it's all been for naught. Mayhap she's no more than a—"

"Quiet! Ye fool!"

When John felt Muriella stiffen, he glared at Colin. She had behaved unwisely, even dangerously, in coming to this valley alone, but she did not deserve his brother's vicious attack. To stop himself from blackening at least one of Colin's eyes, he dug his heels into his horse so it shot ahead of the others. When he stopped at the gate, John saw that Richard Campbell was waiting for him.

"M'lord—"

"Is something amiss?"

"Aye," Richard answered grimly. "Andrew Calder struck on the other side of the keep while ye were away. He had about thirty men."

Colin came up beside them, jerking his horse to a standstill. "I heard," he said. "Did they try for the castle?"

"No, m'lord. But they took a great many of the cattle grazin' on the hill. Slaughtered the others. With most of the men yonder in the Gypsy valley, we couldn't stop 'em."

John did not need to hear any more. He lifted Muriella from the saddle and set her on the ground. Turning to Duncan, he called, "We'll get him this time. They can't have been gone long. Watch the girl, and whatever ye do, make certain she doesn't leave the keep again, ye hear?"

Duncan nodded as Colin leaned from his horse's back to take the quiver of arrows a groom offered him. When he sat up, he looked directly at Muriella. "For your sake," he said.

Muriella winced and clenched her teeth, watching the riders hurry away. By the time she and the squire turned toward the keep, she had forced the sound of Colin's voice into the back of her mind where it could not hurt her. But when she ducked beneath the gate, Muriella felt her head begin to spin. She stopped with her hand at her throat. For an instant she thought she was lost in the mist again, that the world was retreating behind the concealing drifts of moisture. An unnatural stillness settled around her and she felt that she was falling; she would fall until the silence closed around her forever.

Then, out of the mist, she saw a small, moving light. It faded, flared, and leapt as other flames appeared around it. Muriella gasped and found she could not move her feet. She wanted to close her eyes and blot the image from her sight, but knew it was stronger than she. In the darkness behind her lids the vision would only glow brighter, and with it, the knowledge that death was coming to this place—again. Not just one death, but many. Would it be Colin or John or the others, whose names she did not even know? From the number of flickering lights, she knew it might well be all of them.

"Miss Muriella?" Duncan cried, alarmed by the pallid color of her skin and the way she trembled, as if she had to fight to remain standing.

The mist retreated at last, burned away by the sound of a human voice. Muriella stared at the squire, trying to anchor herself to reality with the sight of his face. "Colin's right, 'tis my fault!" she cried.

"No," Duncan said, taking her arm. He was frightened by the blank look in her eyes and did not know how to help her. "He's only angry that ye slipped away again. He said it to hurt ye, that's all."

Muriella shook her head. "Ye don't understand. I know they'll die, but I can't change it."

It came to Duncan then that what the men whispered about her power was true. Instinctively, he recoiled from her. "Ye don't mean—" He choked on his own words and could not go on.

Muriella gripped his doublet in stiff fingers, hardly aware of what she was doing. "There's nothing I can do, don't ye see that?" Her voice came out a ragged whisper. "Why can't I stop it? Dear God, why?"

The moment John and Colin and the others rode into the woods north of the keep, they found evidence that the outlaw had passed there before them. They plunged into pursuit without further thought. Believing that Calder was running in fear, rather than with a purpose, John and Colin were too intent on catching their foe to notice that the trail was too clearly marked.

They rode up hills and made their way along paths choked with underbrush but never met a single enemy. Several times they were forced to stop to rest their horses, but each time the men were ready to move again, they found a fresh trail.

Finally, near noon, Colin reined in his animal and turned to his brother. "I think the outlaw's playing with us. The trail is always clear, but we never seem to get closer. I smell another Calder rat."

"And mayhap the rat wears Maclean's cloak." John's eyes

blazed with a light that had burned out hours ago in the eyes of his comrades. Raking his fingers through his heavy beard, he considered the path before them.

He knew that, like Colin, the men had begun to be suspicious. They had not eaten yet that day, they were tired, and although none of them would have faltered had they met Calder with thrice their own number in straightforward combat, they were uneasy about the sense of deception that had begun to gnaw at their nerves.

Grasping the handle of his sword, John looked directly at his brother. "Ye may want to turn tail and run, but I won't do it."

"If he's waiting for us—," Colin began in a harsh whisper.

"Then so be it," John hissed back. "If Calder thinks he can beat us so easily, he has a thing or two to learn about the Campbells. He's laid down a challenge, and I intend to meet it, whatever the consequences." He paused when he realized his voice was shaking with the force of his anger. "Besides," he said more calmly, "don't ye see what will happen if we turn back now? Calder will have provided for just such a move and they'll be waiting for us, that I guarantee."

Colin glanced back at the men, who were watching the brothers with close attention. He could see that the horses were tired and the men almost equally so. But Johnnie was right; should they retreat, Calder was certain to jump them. "Well then, I suppose we must go forward for a bit. But I warn ye, be ready for anything."

In a few minutes, the Campbells reached a clearing in the trees. On all sides of the tiny glen, the oaks grew thick and the underbrush was heavy, so that John and Colin could not see ahead or behind. The smell of the sea was strong in the air. For a long moment, there was complete silence; then Andrew Calder struck.

The men seemed to fall from the branches of the trees—men who wore the Fraser plaid, the Rose, the Calder, and the Maclean. While the Campbells scrambled from their horses, the enemy abandoned their bows to a man, drawing their broadswords instead. It was not long before the glen was in complete confusion.

John took a single deep breath, his eyes glowing with excitement. He saw at once that his men were outnumbered, but that only made him more determined. An easy victory meant nothing to him. Facing an enemy who was stronger gave spice to the game.

Before he had slid from his horse's back, he struck a man down with one blow of his dagger. When his feet touched the ground, he grasped his heavy broadsword in the other hand and swung it from side to side, slashing indiscriminately at the red-and-green Maclean plaid. As he lunged and retreated and lunged again, his gaze swept the glen, seeking a man who might be Calder. He knew the others would fall into confusion once their leader was down, but the swords were closing in around him and he could not stop to find the outlaw in the blur of blood and plaid and sweat-soaked skin.

Glancing to his right, he leapt out of the way an instant before a heavy blade came slashing down in the spot where he had just been standing. He brought his weapon up, then down, and another Maclean fell beneath it. Somewhere to his left, he heard Colin cursing violently and his own eyes told him that the Campbell's situation was far from promising.

John's exhilaration turned to dismay when he saw that he and his men had been forced into a knot at the center of the glen, with the Macleans pressing in on all sides. "Damn!" he swore. A challenge was one thing, but this could well be a slaughter. The ground at his feet was covered with blood; he did not know how much of it belonged to his companions. He and Colin exchanged a telling look as they were thrown together and paused to catch their breath. They were losing, that much was clear. More than half the men who had followed them into the glen now lay dead outside the circle of their enemies.

John clenched his hand around his blade until his fingers ached and a strange stillness seemed to enfold him. The ring of clashing blades, the harsh cries of triumph, even the groans of pain faded into the background and he felt, all at once, that he was completely alone with the smell of death. He raised his sword, swinging it wildly to ward off the silence threatening to choke him. He struck a man with the side of his blade, forcing him to his knees in the grass. Thus the two men remained, frozen in time, until the enemy's death cry tore from his throat, waking John from the trance that had gripped him.

It was then that a bellowed order to retreat sliced through the glen. Incredibly, the Macleans fell away and began to back toward the sea. The Campbells watched in silence, their stained swords poised in the air before them. For an instant, they were too stunned to move; then they raced after the men who had slipped beyond the trees and away.

As he followed the path they had taken, John saw that the woods opened onto a rocky beach. The Macleans had sheathed their weapons and were hurrying over the sand toward several boats waiting to take them to Mull.

"After them!" John shouted, slashing at a wild myrtle in his path.

"No," Colin said. "We've lost too many men already. We wouldn't catch them anyway, and I wouldn't be surprised if they had more men waiting on Mull. Mayhap they *want* to lure us to the island, then claim we attacked them on their own land. I don't know for certain, but I do know I won't be a fool twice in one day."

John cursed under his breath. "I didn't even see Calder. How do we know he was here?"

"He was here. And no doubt he'll be back. Come." Colin nodded toward the shadowed glen beyond the trees. "We must see to our dead and go home."

When Colin, John and the other survivors drew near the castle, they met the Earl and his escort returning from Cawdor.

"What the devil!" Argyll exploded. Both his sons were streaked with blood and dirt, and they led a string of riderless horses. Behind them came a group of tattered, weary men who seemed barely able to stay on their animals. "Was it Calder?"

"Aye," Colin answered. "And ye needn't be wondering whether or no' Maclean is protecting the outlaw. That glen was so crowded with red-and-green plaid that ye couldn't tell the enemy from the bloody grass. And there's something that puzzles me still. Calder had us. We couldn't move at all, yet he retreated. I don't like it."

The Earl regarded his eldest son with a troubled frown. "Ye can bet he means to strike again. Now he'll have even more reason to try to get the girl."

John, who had been thinking back to the moment of stillness in the midst of the battle, looked up, suddenly alert. "What do ye mean?"

With a grim attempt at a smile, Argyll pulled a piece of parchment out of his doublet. "This document declares Muriella Calder to be sole legal heir to the Thanedom of Cawdor. Ye'll note that the witnesses against her mother have sworn they were paid by Calder to lie. Even William Calder himself has signed."

"I don't believe it!" Colin cried.

"Believe," Argyll said. "Don't ye see what it means?" Nodding toward the empty horses, he smiled bitterly and declared, "We have won."

Listen," Muriella said. "'Tis so lovely."

"What is, miss?" Brow furrowed, Megan leaned forward to concentrate more intently.

Spreading her arms to encompass the narrow strip of shore, the placid loch and the pines and larches that crowded in toward the water, Muriella whispered, "The stillness. 'Tis for that I came." She tilted her face toward the sun, the first they had seen in days. It shone wanly overhead, barely able to warm the cold air, but Muriella welcomed it like an unexpected blessing.

For five days she had not been out of the castle. The rain had beat ceaselessly against the walls and turned the river outside into a torrent. Nevertheless, the preparations for the wedding moved forward. Although Muriella was not allowed to go out, the seamstresses came in. With them came the first of the wedding guests, who had begun to arrive from all over Scotland. The castle had rung with the sound of unfamiliar voices for many days now.

This morning, when the lowering clouds had parted at last to reveal a pale blue sky, the waters of Loch Awe had seemed to call to her from her tiny window. It had not taken her long to convince Megan of her need to escape. "But without Duncan and Adam," Muriella had insisted. "We'll go no farther than the loch, and just this once I don't want their watching eyes to follow me."

Megan had hesitated, remembering all too well the morning a month ago when her mistress had gone to the Gypsy camp. She would have refused at once, except for the look of pleading on Muriella's face and the chill that had settled into her own bones in the past few days. She too wanted to breathe fresh air, free of the musty dampness that had invaded every part of the keep.

Besides, Andrew Calder had been quiet for a month, since the disastrous battle in the glen, and with the number of armed men who had arrived, the castle was well fortified; it was not likely Calder would strike now, when the Campbells were strongest. So the two girls had slipped on dark cloaks and made their way through the courtyard and under the heavy iron portcullis that was raised in welcome to arriving guests.

"Aye, I see what ye mean," the servant agreed as the warmth of the sun at last began to dissipate the chill in her body.

Muriella leaned against the boulder at her back, breathing in the peace of the moment. Loch Awe spread out before her, its surface woven of shifting shades of blue and gray in the pale February light. The fine-grained earth clung to her hands, clasped about her knees, and the water lapped softly on the shore, swirling pale changing patterns in the sand as it retreated. Smiling at Megan, who sat with her eyes closed in contentment, Muriella said, "I haven't felt this way in a long time. Not since I left Kilravok."

Megan opened her eyes. Muriella did not talk much about her past. "Was it as lovely there as 'tis here?"

"In a way, though we didn't have a loch—only a bubbling burn with a little pool. 'Twas no' as beautiful as Loch Awe. And it had no secrets." She leaned her head on her knees and added thoughtfully, "Everything seems bigger at Inveraray and more impressive somehow." From here the far bank of the loch was not even visible, obscured as it was by the tree-heavy islands scattered across its surface. "But I loved that wee pool just the same."

Closing her eyes, she tried to bring her memory of the burn into sharper focus. "The only one who knew of it besides me was my cousin Hugh, and he didn't go there often."

The servant leaned closer, chin resting on her cupped hands. "But sometimes he did? Ye weren't alone always, surely."

"No, I was often with Hugh," Muriella mused. "Most days we played together in the afternoons. We used to chase each other into the woods, then hide among the trees. But Hugh always found me before long, and then we'd start again. When we were too hot and tired to run anymore, we'd go to the burn and cool our feet in the pool."

She looked out at the loch and saw her memories reflected in the silver green water. The rhythmic lap of the waves was soothing, lulling her into dreamy tranquillity. For the moment, she could forget the feeling of dread that had haunted her like an accusation since the day when she'd seen those flames glimmering from the center of a chilling mist. It was not over yet.

It would not be over until she became John's wife. Until she took the Campbell name, and in doing so, proclaimed that the Earl's right to Cawdor could no longer be questioned. "Muriella Campbell," she repeated under her breath. The name sounded strange and remote, as if it could never really belong to her.

"Just think, in four days ye'll be a married woman," Megan whispered, echoing her mistress's thoughts. "Aren't ye excited?"

That was not the word for the distress that flared in her many times each day as she wondered what her life would be like after the wedding. Because the Earl's wife was dead and Colin's Janet never came to the Highlands, Muriella would be mistress of Inveraray. The thought only added to her trepidation. She sensed that Argyll would expect a great deal of her. But first would come the ceremony—and then the wedding night. She remembered, suddenly, John's urgent kiss on that long-ago afternoon; she could not quell a shudder at the thought of his body stretched out beside hers in a huge, fur-strewn bed.

Choking back the lump in her throat, she concentrated

more fiercely on the beauty of the loch. The waves reached for her, retreated, reached out again with clear fingers, then retreated once more. She could hear the wind sighing in the treetops overhead, then dropping down to touch the still water. She felt that it was calling her closer, drawing her away from the cold, damp reality of the keep beyond the trees. For the moment, the clouds had scattered and there was no hint of a shadow on the loch. There was nothing but the sound and sense of the wind on the water.

She rose to make her way toward the rocks tumbled along the shore as a seabird flew past, its image reflected like a streak of silver on the loch. She followed its path with her eyes, kneeling on a large, flat boulder, trying to settle her heavy skirts behind her without dipping them into the chilly water. With her palms pressed against the stone, she looked down at the bottom of the loch. "Megan!" she cried. "Look! I've found a magic castle."

The servant came at once to kneel beside her mistress. There was barely room for the two girls on the boulder. Megan would have tumbled into the water if Muriella had not caught her with both hands. Leaving one arm across the servant's shoulders, she pointed through the water at an overgrown rock thick with moss and waving grass. With its fissures and crevices and tall, carved spires, it did resemble a keep, though Megan herself would never have seen a castle in the shaded gray stone.

"Mayhap 'tis a home for the Kelpies. Ye know how they love the water."

Muriella tilted her head, considering. "Aye," she murmured at last, "maybe 'tis." She leaned closer, suddenly intent. "Or mayhap 'tis no' the Kelpies at all. 'Tis something different."

Smiling, Megan pointed at a reflection on the water. "'Tis your own face, miss, with the darkness of your braid over your shoulder."

Muriella nodded, aware that her face had been captured for a moment on the surface. Then a breeze touched the loch and the image rippled, blurred and slowly, subtly, began to change. Now the face was that of a stranger—a lovely woman with pale blue eyes. She combed her long blond hair as it twined itself among the rocks, then set a ring of bright flowers on her head. Above the lap and swell of the water, Muriella heard a keening cry that vibrated through her body. She reached out to touch the enchanted face, but it was gone.

She felt a vague stirring in her heart that she did not understand. Perhaps it was only an echo of the longing she had seen, for an instant, in the woman's eyes, or perhaps it was an answer to the sigh of the wind as it rippled over the water. Was it fear or joy or something beyond either? She did not know, but it fluttered inside her, restless and warm, and she felt suddenly alone, though Megan knelt beside her.

"Miss," the servant said, shivering at the rising breeze, "'tis colder altogether than I thought." She noticed that a shadow had fallen upon the water and looked up to see the clouds gathering across the sky, dark and threatening. "Look! The rain's comin' again! We'd best get back or we'll be wet to the skin."

"Aye," Muriella murmured. She too noticed the change in the air—the heavy dampness that clung as she moved, the swelling of the clouds that only emphasized the shimmering movement of the loch between the shadows.

Megan shivered but Muriella welcomed the turbulence that filled the air while the storm clouds gathered. The water rose in whitecapped waves as the wind blew more and more fiercely, churning the loch to a caldron of silver-gray that leapt and spat at the darkening shore. Interwoven with the black lacery of winter branches, the wind moaned with a voice as compelling as the beat of an ancient, frenzied song.

Muriella paused, her face raised to the sky, and felt her heart beating in time to the primitive music of the tempest. When the first drops of rain began to fall, she let them run down her cheeks, sharp and clean and stingingly cold. The clouds grew heavier, the loch ever darker, and Muriella shivered with a kind of fearful rapture at the wild beauty of the rising storm.

Swiftly, the two girls started toward the sheltering trees. The servant drew her hood over her head and stared at the ground, but Muriella did not try to keep out the rain that streamed down over her face and hair.

"'Tis too dark!" Megan cried suddenly, her voice full of fear. "I can't see the way!"

Muriella stood for a moment getting her bearings. The trees took shape before her—oak and pine and silver birch—until she saw the place where human feet had worn a path through the bracken. She smiled, put her hand on Megan's shoulder, and pointed. "Don't fash yourself," she murmured. "We'll find the way." Then she leaned close to add,

> And see ye not that bonnie road
> That winds aboot the fernie brae?
> That is the road to fair Elfland,
> Where thou and I this night must gae.

Megan gaped at her mistress in astonishment, but Muriella was already drawing her forward into the protection of the trees.

# 13

Come in, Colin, and close the door behind ye," the Earl commanded tersely.

Colin obliged, pushing the heavy oak door closed with one foot. "Well?"

In a glance, the Earl took in his eldest son's confident stance—his legs spread in their raw leather boots, the way he hooked his thumbs negligently into the belt that gathered his knee-length saffron shirt at the waist, the knowing smile that curved his lips. Colin breathed arrogance from every pore, and that was as it should be. "Where's Johnnie?" Argyll asked, disguising his approval beneath hooked gray brows.

"Ye needn't worry that he'll disturb us. The men were frustrated, what with all the rain, and they've started a fight to keep themselves occupied."

"Your brother's in the thick of it, I suppose?"

Colin nodded and his father sighed. "'Tis just as well. He doesn't need to hear this. 'Twas ye I wanted to talk to." The Earl indicated a chair, where his son seated himself.

"What's bothering ye?"

The Earl spread his hands on the desk and leaned forward. "As ye know, Maclean will soon be here. When he comes, we must be ready."

Frowning, Colin shook his head. "Why did ye ask him to the wedding? Ye know he's our enemy. Ye should be plotting how to take Duart, not welcoming him to Inveraray as your guest."

"Doesn't it occur to ye that I want the man close by, where I can see him? I feel safer with him under my roof than out there where he can do as he likes."

Colin narrowed his eyes in doubt. "Have ye forgotten his connection with Andrew Calder? Just because he's been quiet for so long doesn't mean he's given up."

"No, I haven't forgotten," Argyll snarled with sudden fury. "And I'm sure he hasn't given up." The color crept into his cheeks as he spoke. "He made fools of the Campbells last time. I don't intend to let that happen again." He leaned forward, his hands clenched into fists. "Not ever. He's left a stain on the name of our clan that I'll wash clean if it's the last thing I do. That's why I want Maclean here."

His son did not like to be reminded of the massacre in the glen by the sea, and his father's tone told him the Earl liked it even less. He too was eager to even the score with the men who had trapped him so easily. "What do ye mean to do?"

"Bring my son-in-law here, trailing Calder behind him in the shadows, no doubt, and force him to make a mistake."

When Colin spoke, it was with more violence than he had intended. "Why don't ye just send someone out to kill him? 'Twould be simple enough to arrange and not nearly so dangerous."

"Because"—here the Earl smiled grimly—"'twould be too easy. I don't want him to die in a dark passageway with no one to see him suffer. No, I want to humiliate him in front of everyone, as he humiliated us. I want people to watch his disgrace and see for themselves how unwise it is to challenge the Campbells. We'll bring Andrew Calder crashing down, I promise ye that, and when we do, Maclean will go down with him."

Colin considered Argyll thoughtfully, wondering if for once Johnnie didn't have the right idea—kill their enemies and get it over with. Besides, he doubted that even Maclean would be foolish enough to risk betraying the Earl in his own castle. "Ye'll need a kind of bait that he can't resist."

"We have what he wants. Use your head, Colin."

His son looked up in surprise. "Ye mean to use the girl?" Everyone at the keep knew how close Muriella had grown to the Earl in the past month.

"She's the prize we all seek, isn't she?" The Earl paused and his blue eyes gleamed. "Don't misunderstand me; I don't intend to let him hurt her. If the Campbells aren't strong enough to protect their own, then woe to us, my son." His voice trembled ominously and he raised a hand as if to ward off a horror too unthinkable to consider. "But she's the only one likely to lure our enemies into the open. We have no choice."

Nodding, Colin admitted that his father was thinking clearly after all. "Well then, when he does get here, I'll see that Maclean is watched."

"Not too closely," Argyll warned. "He'll be wary enough as it is. Ye must give him room to dig his own grave."

"Aye," Colin said, smiling with anticipation. "A spectacle I long to see fulfilled. I do believe I'll enjoy this wedding after all."

It was late afternoon. Though the rain lashed against the walls of the keep with fury, inside the cavernous Great Hall the guests huddled by the fire, feeling safe and protected from the storm. The brawl had ended earlier with some bruised faces and fists and a great many roars of good-natured laughter. The men had slapped each other on shoulders and backs to show that no ill will lingered, then settled happily over their tankards of ale.

Muriella sat near the hearth, her hair braided to hide any remaining dampness, her mauve kirtle and gown fresh and unwrinkled. No one would guess now that she had been away. She looked around at the flushed faces, most of which belonged to strangers, and noticed how the huge fire gave a golden glow to their skin and a glitter to their eyes. Everywhere she turned there was noise and laughter; at last the chill in this room had been destroyed.

Bending forward, she drew her thread taut and pushed the needle through the linen shirt she was embroidering for

John's groom gift. Despite her mistress's reluctance, Megan had insisted that she do this small thing for her husband-to-be. It was not long before Muriella's delight in the pattern she created with her needle made her forget, for a while, the one for whom it was intended.

She heard a commotion nearby and looked up to find Alex weaving his way across the room. The Earl was in a generous mood these days, so he had invited the Gypsies in out of the rain. The ones who chose to accept showed their gratitude by diverting the Campbells' guests from their boredom and frustration at the weather that made them prisoners.

Alex found a spot on the hearth next to Muriella and began to strum his harp. She leaned her head against the rough stone, blackened by years of roaring fires, and closed her eyes.

Megan, who sat beside her mistress, smiled at the Gypsy. "Will ye tell us a story?" she asked.

"Aye, if ye like." His fingers continued their dance on the strings as he spoke. "Have ye heard the tale of the makin' of Loch Awe?"

Megan knew the local legend, as did many of the guests, but the fire was warm, the sound of the Highland harp pleasant, and Alex's voice melodic, so they did not object to hearing it again. As he began his story, many of the women crept closer to listen.

Alex cleared his throat. "'Twas a time when Loch Awe was a wide, lovely valley ruled by a bonnie lass with pale golden hair and eyes as blue as a summer sky. Each day, she hunted with her friends, and rare was the time when they weren't blessed with game enough to feed them and sport enough to please them. But the Kelpies in the valley were sore jealous of the lassie's beauty and her pleasant life, which they determined to end.

"One day, as she knelt beside a burn to take a drink, the vengeful Kelpies cast their spell over the lady like a net. The while she was under their power, they made her promise to place a stone over the mouth of the spring each evenin' at twilight. If she didn't do so, they warned, they would swell the burn into a torrent that would flood the valley to its very top.

"So 'twas that every evenin' the lady knelt by the burn, callin' the Kelpies to watch as she placed the stone. Each evenin' they watched her in the twilight, golden hair glimmerin' and blue eyes bright, and wished that someday she'd forget her promise."

By now Muriella had dropped her needle. The harp held her spellbound, unmoving, and she was strongly aware of the warmth of the fire at her back.

"It happened that one day," Alex continued, "the lassie and her friends had hunted for long hours and were sore weary. Her companions begged her no' to stop at the spring as she usually did, but to return with them to the castle to eat and drink the night away. She told them sadly that she must stop, if only for a moment. They rode on without her.

"She was thirsty, and the lady stopped to drink at the mouth of the burn. As she splashed the water over her face, swallowin' the cool liquid gratefully, she was drawn to her own reflection in a puddle nearby. Smilin' to herself, she drew her fingers through her hair and watched it fall in soft curls along her cheeks. She saw that her head was bare, and noticin' some flowers that grew along the way, she began to weave a wreath for her hair.

"As soon as she placed the flowers on her head, she began to feel drowsy. So drowsy that she didn't notice the sun was slippin' behind the rim of the valley. Layin' her head on a soft bed of moss, she fell fast asleep.

"When she awoke, 'twas dark and the tiny burn had swollen into a river. She stood watchin' helplessly, the wreath askew on her golden hair, as the water gushed from the ground and swept through the valley. Fallin' to her knees, she pleaded with the Kelpies to free her from her promise. But they only laughed.

"She died there when the river filled the valley to the top in a single night. At last the Kelpies had gotten their wish. But in the end, they couldn't rid themselves of the memory of the lady, for she gave her beauty to the loch she left behind. On many a night, ye can see the fall of her golden hair in the path of the moonlight over the heart of Loch Awe."

Although the story was common in the Highlands, Alex had given it a kind of magic. Perhaps it was the song of his clareschaw, which gurgled like a tiny burn, then swept through the room like a torrent; or perhaps it was his musical voice. Whatever the reason, his audience was pleased. They applauded him with fervor and a few threw him coins.

Muriella could not move; she was lost in the valley Alex had just described. She remembered the wavering image of the woman with the flowers around her head, the woman whose hair had spread through the water, twining itself among the rocks. She remembered too the strange, keening lament she had heard, and knew that Alex had put her vision into words. She shivered at the thought. In her memory, the caressing waters of Loch Awe became cold and unfriendly and they seemed to close around her, swirling before her eyes until she was blind.

Glancing at Muriella's troubled face, Alex waved the other Gypsies over. They began to play together, encouraging the ladies to sing with them. Some of the Gypsy girls began to sway, their red, green and blue skirts swinging in the firelight. The guests clapped their hands, laughed, and were not aware that Alex had put down his instrument.

The Gypsy leaned back until his head rested on the stone next to Muriella's. "Ye'll always create your own nightmares, lass. Ye and no one else are at the heart of all your terror."

How had he known what she was thinking? she wondered. Could he really believe that there was nothing here for her to fear? She looked away from him, following the dips and swirls of a Gypsy woman in blue who danced nearby. Once when the woman bowed low, Muriella caught the flicker of a golden flame against her chest. She stared, hypnotized by the dark red ruby.

"Ye aren't so wise as ye might believe. And ye'll always

reject that which ye most desire. But at least ye won't be able to lie to yourself."

She looked up, but before she could ask any questions, the Gypsy smiled once, briefly, and was gone.

Just then the squealing of the gate outside announced more visitors. A few minutes later the door swung open and a man and woman came into the hall, bringing the rain with them. By the time the door had been secured, there was a large puddle on the stone floor at their feet. The pair stood uncertainly, as if unsure of their welcome.

"Elizabeth!" the Earl's voice boomed from the top of the stairs. In spite of himself, he could not disguise his pleasure. He had not seen her for many months—not since his last disturbing visit to Duart Castle. Hurrying down the steps, he swept his dripping daughter into his arms to kiss her on both cheeks. Then he backed away, nodding coolly at his son-in-law. "Maclean." Argyll scowled as he guided the couple toward the fire. When he caught sight of Muriella at the hearth, he called, "Come, lass. Ye must meet my daughter."

Muriella came forward, curtsying to the new arrivals. She surveyed with interest the wet and bedraggled woman who gazed longingly at the fire. Elizabeth was not beautiful, nor was she plain. She had Colin's sandy hair and her eyes were an indeterminate gray. Argyll had said his daughter was twenty-two, but just now she looked older. Her eyes were dark with what Muriella guessed was constant suffering. The girl did not have to look far to find the source of Elizabeth's pain.

While she had been watching the other woman, Muriella was aware that Maclean had been looking *her* up and down appraisingly. She reminded him of someone, but he could not remember who. When he took her hand, he squeezed her fingers and seemed reluctant to let her go.

When the Laird of the Clan Maclean bowed and smiled, Muriella's heart turned cold. It was not that his features were unpleasant. His red hair and beard were thick and full and his gray eyes clear, but even as he smiled, she could feel the bitterness beneath that smile.

Withdrawing her hand quickly, Muriella turned to Elizabeth. "Come sit by the fire. 'Tis much warmer there. Ye can dry out a little and have a cup of wine to chase the chill away."

The Earl looked at Muriella in surprise, then smiled in approval. "'Tis a good idea," he said.

Maclean was not listening. "So you're the heiress," he muttered. Drawing the girl away from his wife, he lifted her chin with one finger. "You've no idea how lucky ye are to be marrying into the Campbell family. But then, they've always had an eye for the pretty ones. So long as they're rich as well." Smiling unpleasantly, he brushed her cheek, then let his hand slide over her shoulder and down her arm.

"Maclean!" The Earl stepped in front of his son-in-law, separating him from Muriella. "I think we can leave your wife in Muriella's care. There are matters we must discuss."

The two men moved away, holding themselves apart with care. As they started up the stairs, the Earl hissed, "Leave her be, Maclean! She has no part in your grudge against me."

Muriella watched them go, wondering if, once they were married, John would treat her as Maclean treated his wife. She shivered and turned back to Elizabeth, who was stretching her chilled hands toward the fire. It seemed to Muriella that she had not noticed her husband's indiscretion. Taking Elizabeth's arm, Muriella murmured, "Come, we'll go to my room and dry ye out. I see your servants have brought in your chest of clothes, so ye can change."

Elizabeth straightened and when Muriella saw her face, she realized the woman *had* noticed. Her cheeks were tinged with red, her lips pressed together as if she were willing herself to remain silent. Placing her hand on Muriella's shoulder, she spoke for the first time. "Ye are kind."

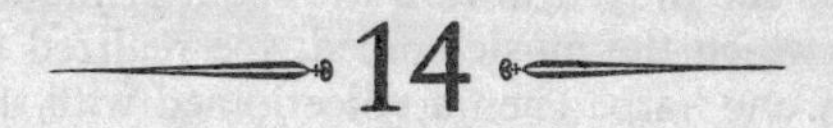

# 14

Elizabeth had fallen asleep with the fur tucked in close to her chin. Even after discarding her wet clothes, she had found it difficult to stop shivering. Finally, Megan had filled the warming pan with hot coals, insisting that Elizabeth get into bed. Then servant and mistress sat watching in silence until she fell asleep.

"She can't have a very pleasant life with that man," Megan murmured.

"No," her mistress agreed. "I only wish there was some way to help her, but 'tis too late for that, I'm afraid." Restless, frustrated by her own helplessness, Muriella rose to wander across the room, searching the empty corners with impatience. "Megan, can ye stay with Elizabeth in case she should wake?"

"Aye, miss, but where're ye goin'?"

"I don't know."

Muriella's expression was distant, her eyes dark and feverish. The servant nodded. "I'll stay by her."

"Thank ye. I just can't stay still, ye ken?" Without waiting for an answer, Muriella left the room.

Outside the door, she stood uncertainly for a moment. The narrow hall with its curved ceiling was lit by many torches, but they seemed to multiply the shadows rather than eliminate them. She surveyed the empty passageway from end to end, then turned left, creeping by instinct down what seemed like endless stone corridors. There was something she needed to find, some force that was pulling her away from the safety of her darkened room.

All at once she heard it clearly—the music that had drawn her here. The harp had captured her, as always, in its melody. As she moved toward the room at the end of the hall from which the music spilled, she realized there was more than one harp. Then a voice joined with the instruments.

> An thou were my own thing,
> I would love thee, I would love thee;
> An thou were my own thing,
> How dearly would I love thee.

Muriella paused. The voice was familiar. She leaned against the cold stone, listening.

> To merit I no claim can make,
> But that I love; and for your sake,
> What man can, more I'll undertake,
> So dearly do I love thee.

The voice was deep and so incredibly sweet that the softly sung words mesmerized her. The girl smiled in the darkness as two more voices joined in for the chorus.

> An thou were my own thing,
> I would love thee . . .

One of the voices belonged to Alex, that much she knew, but she couldn't identify the other two. Now the first singer began again, alone. Muriella was surprised to hear a harpsichord in the background. She had not known there were so many musical instruments at Inveraray.

> My passion, constant as the sun,
> Flames stronger still, will ne'er have done,
> 'Til Fate my threads of life have spun,
> Which breathing out, I'll love thee.

The words drew shivers up along her neck and arms. Pulling her skirts close about her legs, Muriella slipped down the hall until she could look in the door of the chamber. It was a small music room hung with exquisite tapestries and flooded with candlelight. The harpsichord was in the far corner; Alex sat behind it, running his fingers over the keys as he sang the chorus. The other two voices belonged to Duncan and John, who sat with their backs to the girl, strumming their harps. Muriella caught her breath.

How dearly would I love thee.

As the chorus ended, she twined her fingers together, waiting to see which one had been singing so beautifully a moment before.

While love does at his altar stand,
Have thee my heart, give me thy hand,
And with this smile thou shalt command
The will of him who loves thee.

It was John. Looking up, Muriella found Alex watching her. She felt the color drain from her cheeks; she did not want him to see her confusion. Moving out of sight beyond the door, she prayed he would not speak. For a long moment the silence closed around her, suffocating in its intensity; then at last she heard the three men repeating the chorus once more.

Apparently, Alex had decided to keep her secret. John would never know that she had heard him sing and that it had shaken her deeply.

Swinging the study door closed, the Earl turned to face Maclean. "You're no' a wise man, Son-in-law. Ye push me and push me and presently ye'll learn that I'll take only so much for my daughter's sake."

Maclean threw himself into a chair before the fire. Placing his hands together fingertip to fingertip, he smiled. "I don't know what ye mean, my lord. All this talk is beyond me."

Argyll clutched the back of a chair to keep himself from exploding in the man's face. "Keep your filthy hands to yourself when you're in my keep," he said. "Ye may consort with outlaws on Mull, but at Inveraray ye'll behave like a gentleman, difficult as it may be for ye."

Maclean looked up in mock surprise. "'Consort with outlaws'? Whatever do ye mean by that? I'm sure I can't guess at the workings of your mind."

"You're a liar, and not even a very good one. We've seen Andrew Calder cross to Mull twice now. No one stays on that island without your consent. And how do ye explain the Maclean plaid on the men who attacked my sons last month? Do ye take me for a fool?"

Tapping his fingers against each other, the Earl's son-in-law replied, "No, ye aren't that. If ye were, we might have a defense against ye. As it is, we have none."

Argyll turned his back on the man. "We were speaking of Calder."

"It seems to me he's only trying to get back what you've taken from him," Maclean said.

"Ye know the girl is rightfully mine."

"Aye, we know King Jamie gave her to ye. He's given ye a great deal that belonged to others. The question I have is, who did ye betray this time, that he should grant ye such a favor?"

The Earl came to stand before his son-in-law. His fists were clenched and the firelight flickered over his face, deepening the hollows and increasing the glitter in his eyes. "I won't be badgered into killing ye, Maclean. But I'll tell ye this, and ye'd do well to listen. Stay away from Muriella—far away. If I find ye near her again, I promise ye'll regret it. She may no' be a bride yet, but she belongs to the Campbells just the same. Don't ye forget that. Now get out of my sight, and I suggest ye refrain from exchanging pleasantries with my sons and me until this wedding is over."

Maclean stood, kicking the chair away as he did so. "'Twill give me great pleasure to avoid ye, Argyll. Ye make my stomach turn each time I see ye." He pushed past the

Earl, but when he reached the door, he turned. "As for the wedding, well, we shall see about that."

When the door was closed behind him, Argyll drew his sword and sank it into the chair where Maclean had been sitting. With a muffled curse, he slit the brocade from edge to edge.

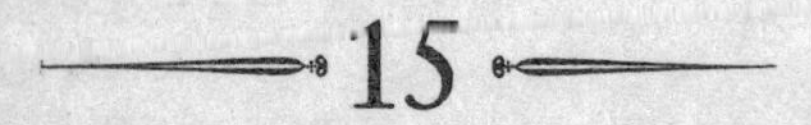

# 15

Muriella started back down the hall, but the music followed her along the passageway. In her agitation, she turned down a strange corridor. She did not realize for some time that she was lost. The music had long since disappeared into the shadows she had left behind. Now she looked about her and tried to catch her breath. These must be the rooms where the guests were staying; she could see a trunk sitting just inside a doorway. Here there were no candles, only an occasional torch, and the passage was long and dark. She was trying to decide in what direction her room might lie when she heard someone approaching.

"So, little one, I find ye at last. Were ye coming to see me?"

Muriella turned to find Maclean smiling down at her. With a little cry, she backed away. "I have better things to do than spend my time visiting unpleasant guests. Excuse me."

As she moved, he caught her arm. "I won't excuse ye. There are things I wish to say." Leaning down, he examined her face for the second time; there was something about her that drew him but at the same time, made him uneasy. Not that Argyll's warning had frightened him. If anything, it only made him more determined. His hand closed tighter around her arm as he dragged her toward the open door through which she had seen the trunk.

"No!" she cried. "I must go!"

He leaned closer, tangling his fingers in her hair. "Ye won't. Not 'til I've finished with ye."

"You're mad!" Pushing against his chest with all her strength, she tried to duck under his grasping hands. But he was too quick for her.

"No' at all. I've just been thinking 'twould be a shame if John Campbell were to get a damaged bride." He raised her chin with two fingers until his lips were just above hers. "'Twould be most sad, don't ye agree?"

She looked directly into his eyes for the first time. What she saw there made her insides raw with fear. She shivered and her throat closed until she could not breathe. Her hands were cold and shaking, but she struggled to force them upward. When he loosened his hold on her arm and tried to take her by the shoulders, she took a deep breath and dragged her nails across his neck from ear to collarbone.

For a moment he was too surprised to respond, but then, swinging her against the wall, he attempted to pin her hands behind her. "Damn ye. Ye'll be sorry for that." With one hand he ripped open her gown and kirtle, leaving only her chemise to cover her chest. With a guttural curse, he kissed her brutally, grinding his mouth against hers until she tasted blood. She shuddered and retched with dry, heaving sobs, but he did not notice. Her body felt soiled, like an alien things that she could not—did not wish to—call her own. Just when she thought the sickness would choke her, he backed away. Sharply, he hit her across the face, knocking her off balance.

She grabbed a chair to right herself just as he swung again. This time she hit the wall with a crash and her head began to throb.

But as Maclean moved toward her where she huddled against the stone, the sneer on his face changed to a frown and his hard, cold gaze softened. The girl's hair was auburn, he thought, the color of Anne's hair. And the eyes were the same green. His heart wrenched in sudden pain. "Anne," he whispered, "I won't hurt ye. Only don't leave me again."

Muriella gaped at him in disbelief. All at once, his face

was very young and vulnerable. He reached for her, drawing her toward him gently. Though she turned her head, he kissed her face again and again until he found her lips with his. His fingers ran over her bare shoulders, and she shuddered at the cool, damp touch of his hands on her skin. When he released her for a moment to run his forefinger down her cheek, she drew herself upright and sank her teeth into his hand. He leapt back, roaring, as she slipped under his arm and ran. Though she looked back several times, ready to scream if he should pursue her, she realized at last that he was not going to follow.

She did not know how she reached her own room, for she was running blindly. When she came to her chamber, she could not make her clumsy fingers open the latch. It took three tries before the cold metal moved in her hand. She shuddered as she slammed the door behind her and leaned against it, gasping. Megan was beside her in a moment, staring in horror at the torn gown and deep red marks on her mistress's face. "Dear God, miss, what's happened? Ye must come and sit down. Who did this to ye? Was it Colin?"

Muriella began shaking her head and found that she could not stop. She stared before her, unseeing, as Megan pulled off her gown and guided her to a chair.

Kneeling at her mistress' feet, Megan whispered, "Ye must tell me, miss. Who did it?"

At last Muriella found her voice. "I'll tell ye, but ye must swear ye won't repeat it. Above all, ye must *not* tell the Earl, do ye understand?" She was not certain why this was so important; she only knew she could not discuss the attack, not even with Argyll. To say the words aloud would somehow make the whole thing real, and she did not think she was strong enough, yet, to face the full horror of what Maclean had tried to do.

The servant sat back on her heels, regarding Muriella doubtfully. Then her expression hardened. "'Twas Maclean, wasn't it? I saw how he looked at ye in the Great Hall."

Muriella closed her eyes. "Swear ye won't tell."

"But miss, he's a dangerous man. He must be watched."

"The Earl is watching him already, don't worry." Suddenly she remembered Elizabeth and looked up, appalled.

Catching her thought, Megan assured her, "She's gone. 'Tis nearly time for dinner."

Muriella exhaled in relief. "Megan, ye must swear to me, please!"

Reluctantly, the servant agreed. "If 'tis what ye really wish, I swear."

"Then come, we must ready ourselves for the meal."

By the time the two girls made their way down to the Great Hall, half of Muriella's face was swollen and purple. Together, the two had concocted a story to explain the marks away.

As the Earl took Muriella's hands in his, he asked, "What have ye done, lass? Your face!" He leaned down to examine the bruises more closely.

"My gown wasn't even," she explained. "I stood on a stool so Megan might straighten it, but one of the legs broke and I fell. The rushes were gone, ye see, for they meant to change them today." Over the Earl's shoulder, she saw Maclean, his red curls combed carefully down to cover the scratches on his neck. He was staring at her, trying to pretend he had nothing to hide, but Muriella could see the cold fear in his eyes. For a moment, she wanted to tell Argyll the truth, but Elizabeth was beside her husband, her hand resting on his arm, and Muriella knew that, for the other woman's sake, she would not say a word. She would not add to Elizabeth's humiliation.

When Elizabeth saw the bruises on Muriella's face, she glanced from her husband to the girl and back again. Her eyes grew shadowed and she seemed to retreat inside herself. She had not been fooled.

Argyll would have questioned Muriella further, but his mind was on other things. By now his anger at Maclean had abated somewhat and he'd had time to think. He was as bad as Johnnie, he cursed himself again and again, the way he'd let his fury get the better of him when he faced his son-in-law in the library an hour since. He would have to be certain it did not happen again. "Shall we sit down?" he said.

Just then John came up beside his future bride. Tilting her chin upward, he considered her face and frowned. "So, little one, ye'll be damaged for our wedding. Are ye sure ye haven't done it on purpose?"

His touch made Muriella wince. She could not help but remember how Maclean had spoken the same words, called her by the same name—"little one." She tried to move away, but John did not seem to notice. As he directed her toward the table, she saw she was to sit beside him. Although she wanted to refuse, she felt the Earl's gaze upon her and knew it would not be wise.

John settled onto the bench, his thigh touching Muriella's, and wondered why he had spoken as he had a few moments before. He had regretted the words the instant they were out of his mouth, but it had already been too late. He did not understand why he wanted to hurt her. "Muriella—," he began.

She turned unwillingly, he thought, and waited. Now, with her gaze upon him, expectant and a little hostile, his remorse evaporated. "This marriage wasn't my choice," he said. "I don't like it any better than ye do."

"No," Muriella murmured, "I don't suppose ye do."

For a moment, John was too taken aback to respond. Without thinking, he took her hand. "Then since we can't stop it, can't we try to make it easier?"

She opened her mouth to reply, but before she could utter a word, his fingers closed more tightly around hers and the room began to sway. She could hear the water rushing in her ears, but this time she would not succumb. With every last ounce of her strength, she fought the coming of the Sight, clenching her teeth and closing her mind to all thought. Sweat broke out on her forehead, and her breathing became more and more labored, but at last the humming ceased and the room came back into focus. She closed her eyes with a sigh of relief.

John stared at the girl as the color drained from her face

and she withdrew her hand abruptly from his grasp. "Ye don't want to make it easier," he said. "Ye still blame me for bringing ye here."

"No, not for that—" Muriella stopped, her hand at her throat.

"For what then?" John asked, cupping her chin and forcing her to look at him.

She took a deep breath, struggling against the fear she could not express. "For the men who are dead. For the ones still to die."

He released her, drawing back as if she had struck him. So she had not forgotten Rob. Or was she thinking of the battle with Andrew Calder? He grasped his dagger, speared a piece of eel, and began to chew it with unnecessary violence. He had tried to eradicate the memory of that day, the awareness that it was he who, in his eagerness to best the outlaw, had urged the men forward instead of back. He who had led them headlong toward the slaughter in the glen. His dreams had been peopled with the ghosts of the dead men ever since.

But Muriella could not know that. Or could she? He met her eyes for an instant—those mysterious eyes dark with the knowledge of death to come. He shuddered and looked away.

Muriella felt him recoil from her, just as Duncan had done, as if she were diseased. It had happened before. All her life people had shunned her, fearing the power of her Two Sights, but the hurt their rejection caused had never eased. Before she could stop to think, she touched John's shoulder. "I didn't mean that," she told him. "No' the way it sounded."

When he stiffened, her hand fell away. "I don't think ye know *what* ye meant," he muttered.

Mary, the serving girl who had slowly made her way around the long table, leaned down next to John with a platter of fish. "Will ye have some salmon?" He nodded, grateful for the interruption. She used a thick knife to push some of the salmon onto his pewter plate. "And ye, miss?" she asked Muriella.

Aware that the Earl was watching, Muriella allowed Mary to serve her, but shook her head when the eel floating in a clear sauce was offered. John did not speak to her again, and for a time, she ate in silence.

"There are sweetmeats from France, Lachlan," she heard Elizabeth say. "Won't ye have some?"

Muriella looked up to find the Earl's daughter holding a tray of nuts and dried fruit for her husband's inspection. She saw how Maclean grunted and continued to eat his salted herring as if his wife had not spoken, and she trembled with anger for the woman's sake.

Elizabeth was not aware of Muriella's sympathetic gaze. She looked pleadingly at her husband, touching him often, to assure herself that he was still beside her. Once or twice she opened her mouth to speak to him, then seemed to think better of it. Through the rest of the meal, her gaze never left his face nor her hand his arm.

Muriella choked down a piece of bread that was suddenly dry, though it was covered with thick, sweet butter. It was evident that Elizabeth loved Maclean. So much so, that when she recognized the marks of his hand on another, she sought not to berate him, but to win him back.

"Have ye heard?" Colin said from the end of the table. "Old William Calder is dead. Brokenhearted by his recent failures, no doubt."

Frowning, Muriella tried to conjure an image of her grandfather, the man who had caused her so much sorrow. All she could remember was the bitterness and rage she had heard once in his voice, the way he had made her mother cry. She had never known him and he had never wanted to know her. He was her grandfather, yet she could not grieve for him. She shivered at a sudden draft.

Argyll grinned, clapping his hand on Muriella's shoulder. "Aye, our troubles are over. Ye'll be safe enough now, lass." Raising his tankard, he beamed at his guests. "A toast to the bride-to-be!" As everyone raised their cups and saluted, the Earl noted Maclean's complacent smile. The man believed it, then. That was just as it should be. None of the guests seemed to recognize the hard gleam buried just beneath the laughter in Argyll's eyes.

"And since 'tis safe now, we must carry on in the Campbell tradition and make our journey to the shore of Loch Awe before the wedding." He leaned over to explain to Muriella, "The entire party, guests and all, ride to the loch, where the bride and groom are blessed." He took another swig from his tankard, then announced, "We shall go the day after tomorrow, the day before the ceremony. You're all invited. But for now, let us eat!" Argyll smiled at the girl and carefully avoided glancing at Maclean.

When the meal was over and the women had retreated toward the warmth of the fire, Muriella took the Earl's arm to draw him aside.

"What is it?" he asked, his voice low-pitched.

"We mustn't go to Loch Awe."

He looked at her more closely, noting the blank expression in her eyes. "What do ye mean? Of course we'll go."

"We mustn't. There'll be trouble there."

He took her hands and was shocked at the clamminess of her skin. He had not reckoned with this. Perhaps the girl could sense danger as easily as he did. But she must not be allowed to ruin his plans. "Lass, I'm well aware that ye don't desire this marriage. Nevertheless it will take place. Don't try to stop it with your foolishness and talk of trouble. The men may think ye a witch and tremble in fear of meeting your eyes, but I don't. You're my ward still and must do as I say. We *will* ride to Loch Awe."

"No."

When he felt her hands tremble, his resolution wavered. Staring down at her bruised face, he realized it would mean a great deal to him if he were to lose her. "Lass," he said gently, "ye must learn to trust me. I'll keep ye safe."

She shook her head in mute denial.

"I'll listen to no more," he declared. "'Tis settled." He stalked away, leaving Muriella to stand alone, her eyes gray with foreboding.

* * *

The hall had been long empty and the castle long silent when Lachlan Maclean crept down the stairs and into the courtyard. The man who awaited him stepped from the shadows, directing Maclean toward a niche in the wall where they could talk without being seen.

"Well? Have ye any news?"

"Aye," Maclean muttered, "they've done half your work for ye. They ride to Loch Awe day after tomorrow. The guests will be along and 'twill be difficult to keep order."

"The girl will be there?"

"Riding at the front of the pack with her bridegroom. They couldn't have given ye a better target if they tried."

The other man laughed but Maclean warned him to silence. "Don't be oversure of yourself. Ye weren't so successful last time."

"I would have been if ye hadn't called me away at the last moment. The Campbells were at my mercy, man!"

"'Tis lucky for us both that one of my men recognized ye held both Argyll's sons in that glen. Had ye killed them, ye wouldn't have lived out the week, nor would I. I hate the Earl, but I'm no' a complete fool. Ye must tread carefully with that man."

Andrew Calder smiled in the darkness. "I'll tread so carefully that he won't even know I'm near, except that the girl will fall dead in his son's arms."

# 16

Muriella kept Megan close to her as much as possible on the ride from the castle to Loch Awe. She had come to know the twists and turns of this shoreline well since her arrival at Inveraray, but today it was somehow different. The water looked dull and lifeless, despite the tiny whitecaps that stirred in the rising breeze. The loch was like a stranger whose unfathomable gray depths were beyond her reach or knowledge.

As the horses crowded onto the hilltop that looked down on the loch, the Earl rode up between his son and Muriella. He glanced around for a long moment, then looked back at the guests who followed. He was uneasy. Maclean had chosen to stay behind today and Argyll did not quite know what to make of it. Perhaps, he thought, his son-in-law believed he would not be implicated if he waited at Inveraray. Perhaps he thought the Earl foolish enough that he did not know the man's intentions. Argyll smiled sourly. He'd have to be blind and an idiot besides if he failed to realize what Maclean desired. The man might as well have proclaimed it aloud.

Turning to the girl at his side, the Earl considered what he could see of Muriella's face beneath her hood. She was pale, and held her lip between her teeth as if trying to keep herself from crying out. "Ye see," he murmured, "there's no danger here."

"What do ye mean, no danger?" John looked past his father at Muriella.

"Your betrothed tried to tell me we shouldn't come today. She said 'twould be dangerous."

"Ye didn't believe her?"

"Of course I didn't! She's a nervous lass, that's all."

John grasped his father's arm. "Ye should have listened. She knows."

"Johnnie," Argyll snapped, "don't be a fool."

"I tell ye, she knows! She warned me about Uncle Rob. And she told Duncan that men would die in that glen."

The Earl shook his head as he urged his horse forward. "Enough of this nonsense. I must see to my guests."

John knew it was not nonsense. Cursing under his breath, he took hold of Muriella's bridle. "Stay close to me."

As the horses picked their way along the hillside, Muriella pulled her cloak tighter around her neck. When the animals stopped at the edge of the water, she sat stiffly in her saddle. Something was amiss; she could feel it like a heavy weight bearing down on her slender shoulders. She peered over the water, seeking the source of her unease, following the shore from tree to tree until her attention was caught by a group of pines separated from the riders by a shallow arm of water.

Unexpectedly, her voice pierced the silence. "Megan!" she screamed.

The servant leaned forward, and as she did so an arrow flew past the spot where she had been a moment before.

In an instant, John had dragged Muriella from her horse. He looked about for Duncan and was relieved to see the squire appear at his side. John lifted the girl across his saddle, depositing her in Duncan's arms. Nodding toward the castle, he commanded, "Take her home!" Then he dug his heels into his horse's sides and moved down the bank and into the water.

Duncan watched his cousin disappear into the group of men who were crossing the narrow arm of the loch, then turned his horse back in the direction they had come. He pulled up short when Muriella's fingers closed around his in a punishing grip.

"Megan!" she gasped.

The boy squinted into the sun, trying to locate the servant. As he wheeled his horse, he saw that complete confusion reigned on the shore of the loch. Many of the guests were not certain what had happened, but they sensed fear in the air and seemed to be possessed of an urgent desire to flee. One of the animals had stumbled in the mud and his rider scrambled from his back to cling to the stirrup of another horse and rider, begging to be carried back to Inveraray. Only Megan sat absolutely still in the center of all the turmoil. She had not moved since Muriella screamed. Her face pale and bloodless, the servant leaned forward, listening but hearing nothing. Duncan called but Megan did not move.

When the squire's horse was near enough, Muriella placed her hand on Megan's arm. "Megan," she whispered. "'Tis all right now. We must get away, back to the castle."

The girl turned to stare blankly at her mistress.

"Come," Duncan urged. "Do ye want to give them another target?"

The threat awakened Megan from her stupor. She shook her head to clear it, glancing at Muriella to make certain she was all right. Then the servant guided her horse up the hill and the three rode after the other guests.

When the Earl saw Duncan and Muriella pass, he nodded. He cupped his hand above his eyes, turning to watch John and Colin lead the men across the lake. Argyll was undecided. Should he follow his sons or go back to the keep? He sought out Duncan's galloping horse once more among the confused group spread out along the rise above him. The squire would see that Muriella got back safely, he thought. Then he raised his head, frowning. Duncan was taking the lass to Inveraray. And Inveraray was where Maclean waited. Without a backward glance, he fell in behind the ring of strangers who sheltered Muriella.

Nearly a dozen men began the chase after the unknown antagonists who had hidden themselves in the trees across the shallow water. At first, the riders could see only one man fleeing before them. Although they circled the area again and again, it soon became clear that there had been no others. One man had attacked a group of more than a dozen men and twenty women. It was insane.

John, who rode near the front, believed he knew why. The man was Andrew Calder and he had come alone because he had only one end in mind—to kill Muriella before she became a Campbell. A single man could easily conceal himself in the trees to await his opportunity. He need have only one arrow if his shot were true. Alone, he could elude his pursuers with little trouble, particularly in the confusion caused by a group of frightened guests.

However—and John smiled grimly to himself at the thought—the outlaw had reckoned without the fact that two girls, heavily cloaked, with faces effectively concealed, would be riding with John. Then again, Calder had not known about Muriella's strong sense of her own danger and the strange power that somehow kept her safe.

The chase was a long one. As the men pushed their animals beyond the limits of their endurance, they began to fall back one by one. There was, after all, only a single man to pursue. They had all heard John Campbell declare he would not let Calder escape this time, and both horses and men were exhausted and thirsty. There was little more they could do, so they turned their horses toward home.

But the two brothers did not give in. When their animals seemed ready to collapse beneath them, they stopped at a nearby manor house, exchanging the horses for fresh ones. The owner was only too glad to give up his horses for the fine-blooded Campbell animals.

After two hours of furious riding, Calder had abandoned his mount to lose himself among the craggy rocks scattered along the foot of the mountains. At that point, John dismounted. Turning to Colin, he said, "Go back. I want to be the one to take him."

Colin shook his head. "You're a fool, Johnnie. Two men are always better. Calder's an outlaw, remember. Running is his trade. He'll outfox ye yet."

"He won't," John declared with complete conviction.

"We're only wasting time arguing. I want the man and I intend to get him, do ye hear?"

Running his hand along his horse's damp neck, Colin considered. He was tired, after all. And Johnnie was stubborn. Besides, he had grown up playing among these rocks. It should not be difficult for him to trap a single man here, especially a stranger running scared like Calder. "Aye, well, I'll leave him to ye, then. But remember, tomorrow is to be your wedding day. Ye'd best be back well before dawn, or there'll be the devil to pay."

John smiled at his small victory as he slung his bow across his shoulder. Without another word to his brother, he adjusted his quiver and walked away.

Lifting his shoulders in a shrug, Colin turned toward home.

John crept among the boulders with great care, for he was determined not to let Calder escape him. Although he knew the outlaw would be tired, like himself, John also knew that he had the advantage. He had learned long ago the secrets and surprises of these tumbled stones. Calder would find it difficult to make his way through the bizarre outcroppings that protruded at odd angles, blocking clear pathways unexpectedly.

For some time, John crouched, listening, until he heard the splattering of pebbles overhead, which indicated the direction Calder had taken. Readjusting his bow so it would not swing out and betray him, he placed his sword on the rocks at his feet. It was too bulky and he did not intend to use it anyway: he had other plans for Calder. He could hear by an occasional scraping noise that the outlaw had not rid himself of his own weapon.

John began his climb slowly and patiently. For once, he knew he had the advantage, and he did not mean to lose it by acting in haste. As he moved along behind Calder, the sun began to set. Already the shadows were long and the light dusky. So much the better, he thought.

For a long time the outlaw stayed well ahead of him, but John was unconcerned. He could see where the man was heading. In his ignorance, Calder would back himself into a corner; then he'd be right where John wanted him. It was quite dark by the time the outlaw pulled himself over a final ridge and dropped down under an outcropping of rock that sheltered him from the back.

Above him, John smiled as he watched Calder gazing around, his inspection only gradually assuring him of what he had done. At his back, the face of the rock jutted out, curving over his head to form a solid wall. The wall was joined on two sides by slabs that stood so close there was no room for a man to squeeze through. Before him stood a huge, flat rock that both protected him from the front and blocked his escape. The only way out was the way he had come, and he was sure John Campbell was waiting there.

Crouching in the darkness, John waited for over an hour, until the moon should rise above the trees, giving him the light he needed to finish off Calder. For the time being, the outlaw huddled behind the flat rock so John could not see him. Minute by minute, the moon filled the rocks with bleak shadows, but still Calder did not move. When he did, however, John would be ready. Taking his bow from his shoulder, he drew an arrow from the quiver and stretched the bowstring taut.

Calder, having heard no sound, no breath of life, for over an hour, decided he could wait no longer. He had to see what was happening out there. Moving as quietly as possible, he pulled himself up so he could peer over the rock face and try to discern, in the added light of the moon, what his enemy's position might be.

As the outlaw's forehead appeared above the boulder, John drew back the arrow until the bowstring reached its full length. Then, screaming the Campbell war cry, "Cruachan!" he let the arrow fly.

Muriella sat up in bed as the familiar coldness swept through her body. She had been dreaming of Hugh again, running from him in the woods and laughing, when the trembling awakened her. She clutched frantically at the warm, tangled furs in an effort to assure herself of the firm reality of the bed, but the spinning had already begun in her head and she could not stop it. She felt the shadows closing around her and shivered violently. The air was still and heavy with darkness until a triumphant voice pierced the silence. "Cruachan!" An arrow sped through the night, then blood spouted up and out, spilling over the face of a huge, flat rock.

The smell of blood was everywhere; Muriella was choking on it. The world tilted and swayed around her before the spinning ceased at last. But the coldness lingered; it simply would not go. Covering her mouth with her hands, she bit her palm to keep from crying out.

Across the room, Megan sat up sleepily and called, "What is it, miss?"

Muriella had to struggle to force her vision into words. When she finally answered, her voice was hollow. "Andrew Calder is dead."

# 17

Megan woke Muriella before the sun had risen. "Come, we must begin early or we won't be ready in time. Och! Miss, there's so much to be done!"

Her mistress sat up, making an effort to control the trembling in her limbs. For an instant, when her feet touched the floor, she thought her legs would not support her, and the humming inside her head made her press her hands against her ears. She felt that she was spinning in a whirlpool, and no matter how she struggled, she could not stop herself from falling.

"So it's come," she whispered in a voice so strained it did not sound like her own. "There's nothing I can do."

"No, miss, nothin'," Megan said firmly. "But come, we must bathe ye while the water is warm. Miss Elizabeth brought ye some of her special scent. She makes it herself." She knelt at the edge of the rough wooden tub and sniffed. "'Tis heavenly."

Muriella stood beside the tub, watching the steam rise in clouds that drifted through the cold morning air. Her nightrail lay in a heap at her feet, and the light from the torches danced over her naked body, painting it with an orange glow.

Megan contemplated her mistress in surprise. She had changed in the past few months; her breasts were fuller, her waist more slender. She looked, just now, more like a woman than a girl. And tonight that transformation would be complete. In order to hide the concern mixed with fear in her eyes, Megan bent her head, concentrating on the task of running the sponge over Muriella's shoulders.

Washed, dried, scented, and creamed, Muriella stood before Megan, Mary and Elizabeth. The three women surveyed with alarm the bruises that discolored the bride's face.

"Isn't there anythin' we can do?" Megan asked, biting her fingernail in distress.

Elizabeth came forward. "Aye, there's a way." She looked at Muriella's face, and her eyes darkened with shame at her husband's cruelty to such a young girl. "I went to the Gypsies and they gave me a cream to cover the bruises and a powder to smooth over the cream. The old woman swore they would hide the marks."

"I've never heard of such a thing," Megan whispered, gazing in wonder at the heavy white cream in Elizabeth's palm. Tentatively, she touched it, circling her fingertip through the thick, cool mixture that clung to her hand when she drew it away. "Do ye really think 'twill work?" she asked.

"The Gypsies can do a great many strange and wonderful things," Mary said. "They have the magic touch."

"I only hope it hasn't left them today when we need it most." Turning to Elizabeth, Megan added, "Can ye do her face while I work on her hair?"

Elizabeth nodded and Muriella was guided to a low wooden stool where she sat staring into the empty air before her. She avoided meeting Elizabeth's gaze just as Elizabeth avoided hers. The older woman spread the cream with slow, gentle motions, and Muriella found it soothing, despite her inner turmoil. Behind her, Megan tugged a comb through her hair and began to separate the strands into sections. Mary helped, giggling when they dropped a braid or hopelessly tangled the interlaced strands. Soon, even Megan was laughing as they looped and wove and arranged Muriella's thick auburn hair.

At last both Megan and Elizabeth declared their work

done. "Och, Miss Elizabeth," Megan cried, "ye've done it right enough! Ye can barely see the bruises. In the dark chapel, ye won't be able to see 'em at all."

Now the dressing began. First, Muriella stepped into the chemise and Mary held her breath, marveling at the fine linen edged with tiny lace. It had obviously been made in France; the Highlands could boast nothing so delicate. As Mary deftly tied the laces, Megan shook out the kirtle made of pale cream satin.

When the simple shift with long fitted sleeves was in place, Elizabeth knelt at Muriella's feet, straightening the hem. The girl looked down when she felt Elizabeth's hand tremble. Her own sense of hopelessness was only intensified by the sight of the tears that fell down Elizabeth's cheeks. Her face looked furrowed with care in the light of the torches, and behind the tears, Muriella sensed a desolation that outweighed her own. She looked away.

Finally, Megan lifted the green velvet from the bed. Standing on a chair, she lowered the gown over her mistress's head with great care. It slid easily over the satin.

The velvet was warm, and Muriella realized she had been cold for some time, although Megan's face was flushed from the heat of the fire. Muriella curled her fingers within the wide sleeves, trying to spark some feeling in the numb shell of her body, but it was useless.

At last Mary placed a wreath of wild roses on the girl's head and the two servants stepped back to admire their handiwork. The flowers rested among the many tiny braids surrounding Muriella's face, while the rest of her hair fell down her back to her knees. The deep green of the low-cut velvet gown tied with sea-green ribbons made Muriella's eyes seem wide, though the usual fire that kept them bright burned low. The broad green sleeves were folded back to reveal the tight satin sleeves of the kirtle; below her elbow, the sleeves fell almost to her hips. The skirt was so voluminous that the green satin slippers were not even visible.

As the three women stood staring, there was a knock on the door. Mary pulled it open a crack to peer out. "What is it?"

"I wish to see Elizabeth, if ye please." It was Duncan's voice.

Elizabeth went out into the hall, and when she returned, she held a carved wooden box. Standing in front of Muriella with the box in her hands, Elizabeth felt she should kneel to the strength that kept the girl's eyes still and her small hands steady. "Your bride gift from the groom," she said.

Muriella stared at the box in silence. The top was intricately carved with gryphons, dragons and winged horses that cavorted on their dark rosewood background until one was nearly indistinguishable from the others. Muriella felt herself begin to sway again. She had, of course, sent the embroidered linen shirt to John quite early that morning. She had known he would send her a gift as well, but was reluctant to see what it was.

Elizabeth did not move. She waited patiently, holding the box while Muriella fought to make herself reach toward the gift. She touched it first with her left hand, letting her fingers trace the raised design. Her scarred finger looked pale and unnatural against the dark wood; with sudden resolution, she lifted the lid and took out what lay inside. Again she paused, struggling for breath, as she gaped at the object in her palm. It was a pendant on a thick gold chain: a carved golden flame with a ruby at its heart. As the torch light moved above her, the flame seemed to leap in her hand.

So, she thought, Alex had told him. The Gypsy had seen her look at the pendant and had told John she desired it. She began to breathe again, irregularly. She could not understand the ache that began deep in her chest and spread throughout her body.

Peering into her mistress' cupped palm, Megan took the pendant to fasten it about Muriella's neck. It fell against the kirtle, glimmering. The flame never seemed to lie still, but danced and flickered constantly. "Miss." Megan's voice was low with admiration. "I haven't ever seen anyone so lovely."

The chapel at Inveraray was seldom used, Muriella guessed. As she stood in the courtyard, clinging to the Earl's arm, she could smell the damp, stagnant air pushed out the door in the wake of the skirts that swept inside. By now, she was surrounded by a thick mist that cut her off from the rest of the world, yet she was aware of the flame on her chest as if it were a real one. Even the Earl's presence could not comfort her.

Argyll was resplendent in a blue velvet doublet and jacket, and he wore a fine linen shirt tucked into his trews instead of the usual belted saffron garment. This was a celebration indeed, and he intended to make the most of it. His pleasure was only slightly dimmed by the knowledge that Maclean had not suffered a disgrace after all, but at least Andrew Calder was dead. The Earl would have to be content with that for the moment.

Although he was aware of Muriella's dumb misery, the Earl chose to ignore it. He loved her dearly, but she was young and obstinate. She would learn in time to accept her marriage and all it meant. He would see to it. As he squeezed her hand, her cold fingers closed more tightly around his.

He heard the signal he had been waiting for and started toward the open chapel doors. The ceremony had begun. Argyll and Muriella walked down the narrow aisle to the strumming of harps from the gallery above, but the girl did not hear the music. She could see John waiting with Colin at his side. The silver decoration on the wooden altar gleamed behind him, making a glittering backdrop for his thick, dark hair. His roughly carved features were softened by the light; even his heavy beard seemed less wild. For the first time, he actually looked handsome. As she came up beside him, she saw that beneath his dress plaid and velvet doublet he wore the shirt she had made for him.

Bride and groom turned to the altar in silence, without meeting each other's eyes. Each gazed fixedly at the priest as he raised his hands and began to intone the traditional Latin phrases. They listened with heads bent, repeated the words he told them to speak, knelt and rose at the right moments, leaned down to kiss the cross of his ruby-and-pearl rosary. But the words were strangely empty, the gestures stiff and unnatural.

When at last John took her hand, Muriella was shocked at how cold his fingers were—as cold and rigid as her own. The knowledge made her look up to meet his gaze for the first time. She had expected to find him grinning in triumph because he had finally won Cawdor for his own, but his lips were no more than a thin line, and his eyes were dark and empty. She realized then that he'd meant it when he said he wanted this marriage no more than she did. For an instant, the bleakness of his expression touched her and she felt a flash of something she had never thought to feel again—pity.

Then the priest spoke, raising his voice as he lifted his hands in benediction. "Go from me in peace as man and wife, never by others to be parted again."

It was over.

With her husband's arm linked through hers, Muriella left the altar. Her skin was pale, almost transparent, and the bruises had begun to show again, dark and ugly, from temple to chin. Her nostrils flared, quivering, and she held her lips in a forced smile. But it was her eyes that shocked the guests to stillness; they glowed with a despair so plain that those who saw it felt the need to look away. John saw it too, and he too turned away.

Suddenly the Earl was upon them, kissing his son on both cheeks and clasping his daughter-in-law in his arms. He alone, of all who had stood in the chapel, had not seen the look in the girl's eyes. He alone appeared to be unconcernedly happy. Grinning, he escorted the couple to the Great Hall and up to the dais. For the occasion, the table had been covered by a linen cloth and set with the finest silver and pewter.

"A toast!" Argyll called, lifting his tooled silver goblet from among the wreaths of white winter blossoms that decked the table. "To this day and all the blessings it has brought us. To the bride and groom!"

Obediently, Muriella touched the rim of her goblet to John's. For a moment, their gazes met and held. He swallowed once, then forced a smile that she answered with one of her own, but the chill in their fingers as they brushed told their own story. When the Earl drew his son and daughter-in-law closer, Muriella bent her head to take a sip of her sweetened wine.

She knew when the servants approached with the first platters of meat; the heavy smell of spice-laden beef and mutton rose in the air and clung around her shoulders. At Argyll's enthusiastic gesture toward the heaping platters, John chose the first morsel of beef, then leaned toward Muriella. She chose another, larger piece and held it up to her husband's parted lips. They ate together, accompanied by roars of approval from the crowd, but they were hardly aware of the sound. It was as if they stood alone: two strangers who shared a meal, but nothing more.

"Come!" the Earl said. "Sit! Enjoy!"

With a sigh of relief, John did as his father had bid him. As the endless meal progressed, he spoke to his new wife now and again to ask if she cared for salmon or sweetmeats or bread, and she saw that he had enough ale and meat to satisfy him. But as congratulations flowed into tankard after tankard of choice ale and course after course of rich food, John's senses began to dull and he did not turn to Muriella again. Instinctively he did not touch her, not even to place his hand on her arm, not even when he was so drunk he could not stand. He would never be drunk enough to forget the way she had shuddered when he put his arm around her waist to lead her to the seat of honor. He would never be drunk enough to forget the look in her eyes.

# 18

The banquet had gone on for too long. The musicians, gathered from all over Scotland, had played too many lilting ballads on their Highland harps. Too many tankards had been refilled again and again with the thick ale, too many platters of beef and lamb and poultry had circulated through the room. The men, drunk as they always were at weddings, had begun to pull the women out to the center of the floor to dance, kicking the rushes aside as they moved. Both men and women had forgotten the bride's face in the midst of their drunkenness and flushed laughter. They clasped hands and circled the floor, their brightly colored plaids flowing behind them, their satin and velvet and brocade gowns swirling about their ankles.

The Earl was pleased. He could see that his guests were impressed by the splendor of the occasion, perhaps even a little intimidated. That was as it should be. He had given them a taste of the wealth and power at his command; he knew the memory of this day would linger, serving as a reminder that the Campbells were worthy friends—and dangerous enemies. He speared a piece of lamb with his dagger and watched the juice run down the blade. Things were going very well.

When Muriella saw Argyll's satisfied smile, she looked away. She thought he had forgotten her, as the others seemed to have done. She realized then that although this was a wedding feast, no one was really celebrating her marriage. They were celebrating the Campbell victory over their enemies, the acquisition of one more piece of valuable land and one more stack of golden coins. She might as well have been an ornament on the wall for all the attention they paid her. Only Elizabeth seemed aware of her new sister-in-law's distress.

Muriella could not help wondering if her marriage to Hugh would not have been different, if, on that occasion, someone—her mother or Lorna or Hugh himself—might not have smiled at her and meant it.

She raised her head when a drunken man stumbled up to the far end of the dais, where John was speaking to a friend. "Johnnie, m'laddie," the man called, "tonight's the night and no mistake. No more serving wenches in the stableyard for ye."

He lurched forward, grinning, and cupped his hands in the unmistakable shape of a woman's body. "Looks to be a ripe one, doesn't she?" the man whispered loudly enough for all to hear.

Muriella's gaze was caught by the sight of John's hand clenched around the handle of his tankard. The fingers were clutching the pewter so tightly that the knuckles appeared unnaturally white, the rest of the skin unnaturally red.

His wife could not look away. She stared in fascination at the hair that grew in tufts on those strong fingers. The skin of his palms would be rough from the swords he had wielded, the leather belts he had beaten to softness, the arrows he had let fly.

Those hands, clutching the pewter in a fierce grip, would later touch her in the same way, possessively, hungrily, just as Maclean had touched her once. The veins on John's hands seemed to throb beneath the sun-toughened skin. All at once she knew she was going to be ill.

Muriella glanced at the Earl, but he was nodding in his chair, his head resting on his hand. As she rose abruptly, Elizabeth looked up at her, taking her hand for a moment. The older woman smiled in understanding of her sister-in-law's need to escape. Squeezing Elizabeth's hand in gratitude, Muriella turned and slipped around the end of the high table and out of the hall.

The fresh, cold air outside struck her brutally after the cloying heat in the hall, but the chill made the sickness retreat. Muriella closed her eyes as the pounding of her heart slowed to normal and the blood began to move through her veins once again. She kept to the shadows, in case anyone should follow, but by the time she crept beneath the gate, she realized only Elizabeth had seen her go.

She moved away from the towering walls of the keep, taking huge gulps of the crisp air. Then she caught a glimpse of the light from the Gypsy bonfires over the hill and heard their gay music. She could not resist. Without looking back, she found her way through the darkness toward the Gypsy camp.

When she reached the ridge, she stopped, taking in the glorious scene before her. The circle of tents was outlined sharply by the glow from the two bonfires that burned at either end. Where the tents did not block the light, figures danced with abandon around the leaping flames. The women's skirts swung out almost straight from their bodies as they spun and dipped in the quivering firelight.

Near the dancers were the musicians—the flutist, the lutist, one man blowing on the pipes. Several men with deep bass voices sang enthusiastically, but the words were indistinguishable. Those Gypsies who stood between the girl and the fire were no more than silhouettes against the brilliant flames, but now and then she would catch a glimpse of a ruddy face lit by the orange glow, or a cascade of dark hair against pale, gleaming skin.

Muriella was entranced. The Gypsies, she thought, did not need wine and ale to help them find their pleasure. Back in the Great Hall, the couples staggered in broken circles, oblivious to their surroundings. But the Gypsies circled their bonfires in fluid motion, dipping and revolving with infinite grace. Neither were they aware of their surroundings, but that was because they were caught up in their private frenzy, sheltered by their strange magic. To them, the world was no more than the fire, the music, and their own bodies, awake to every flicker of flame and song.

Muriella scrambled down the hill, her sleeves billowing behind her. She ran toward the center of the camp and the Gypsy men turned to stare as if she were an apparition. The firelight moved across her face, catching the gleam of her eyes and outlining the bruises along her cheek, but even that could not spoil the beauty of her face in that moment. One man reached out to pull her down next to him, but she slipped away before he could catch her. She was looking for Alex.

She found him sprawled on the ground beside the musicians, his clareschaw lying at his side. His gaze was fixed on the dancers and his voice rose and fell in time to the pulsing music. As she came near, Muriella saw that his hair looked even grayer in the fitful light; despite the elation all around, his expression was full of sorrow.

The girl knelt, taking his hand in hers. "You're grieving," she whispered.

He turned to look at her, then did not move for some time, slowly absorbing the sight of her face. At last he slid his hand from between her fingers and nodded. "I should send ye back," he murmured, "but I find that this time I can't do it."

"Why can't ye?" Muriella asked, locking her arms around her legs.

The Gypsy looked beyond her into the light of the fire. "Just now, ye can only think of those who might comfort ye. But ye'll learn, in time, that ye have a great ability to comfort others. There are depths in ye that ye don't yet comprehend."

While Muriella considered this in silence, Alex looked with concern at the bruises along her cheek. Now and then, a wisp of auburn hair trailed over the discolored skin; somehow it made her seem terribly fragile. Yet for once the shadows were gone from her face and she looked peaceful, even relaxed. In that moment, she reminded him of a woman long dreamt of but never seen. A woman who would haunt him indefinitely, leaving him always unfulfilled. The girl would find a difficult path ahead of her, he knew, and tonight was her last night of freedom—if indeed she had ever known freedom at all. "Ye must dance, lass!" Alex cried.

Muriella nodded, then smiled in delight. "Aye, to dance!" She rose, stood nearby for a moment, watching the dancers rotate; then she bent to touch his cheek. By the time he reached up to the place where her hand had rested, she was gone, a part of the glittering circle made fantastic by the firelight.

The velvet swirled about her legs, and she was drawn into the dance regardless of her will. She circled slowly at first, aware of her own strangeness in the face of the lighthearted Gypsy girls, but as the song swept her up, she lost all sense of those around her. The music rushed through her blood and she moved without thinking, in perfect time. She could do nothing else; she was wrapped in the spell of the light and the songs. Her wedding night might have been many miles away, her bridegroom a nightmare she had created. Only the dance was real. Only the sensations that shook her body from head to toe and left her laughing.

When Megan broke into the circle, interrupting the flow of the music, Muriella refused to answer the call of responsibility or the reality of the keep just over the hill. Grasping the servant's hand, she drew her along in the dance.

Eyes wide with concern, Megan found herself whirling with her mistress through the firelight. Somehow, she could not pull away. When she saw the exaltation on Muriella's face, she forgot, for the moment, the turmoil at the castle, the drunken search for the bride who had disappeared. She forgot the Earl, bellowing that Muriella must be found, his voice louder with each word, as if by increasing the volume he would increase the chances of finding the girl. She forgot Colin with his crude jokes, laughing at his brother's misfortune. But she did not forget John, standing like stone at the head of the table, his face stricken, repeating again and again, "She's gone. I knew she must go."

Megan, suspecting where her mistress might have gone, had crept into the courtyard, determined that she would be the one to bring Muriella back, not those reeling men. She found Duncan already there, and in silent assent they left the castle and went to the Gypsy camp.

Now, with the music pounding against her ears and the incandescent green of Muriella's eyes to reassure her, Megan danced, losing herself in the rhythmic pulse. Then she caught sight of Duncan, waiting patiently at the edge of the circle. With desperate energy, she pulled her mistress from among the dancers, breaking the pattern that had held her in its grasp.

The shock was severe. Muriella stood, breathless, and gaped at the servant in astonishment. For a full minute she did not recognize her. Then, as the music died down and her skirts ceased swinging around her legs, she remembered. The knowledge of her wedding, of what was to come, made her shudder violently. She grabbed Megan by the shoulders and her eyes filled with misery.

The look on her face was more than the servant could bear. Her determination wavered and she wrapped her arms around Muriella's waist, weeping. The girls rocked there, lost in their sorrow, clinging together because there was no other comfort but each other.

Duncan waited, clutching his sword. That he did not understand the source of the girls' grief did not stop him from feeling it throughout his body. But then his senses began to return. Resolutely, he moved forward. Placing one hand on Megan's shoulder, he said, "We must get back."

The girls steadied themselves but continued to cling together, unwilling to part.

"They'll send the men out soon. We mustn't let that happen." With one hand on each girl, he drew them apart.

At last Megan nodded. Without another word she took Muriella's hand and began to shove her way through the watching Gypsies. Duncan followed and the three moved out of the reach of the firelight and into the starless night.

Muriella paused in the doorway, staring at the wreckage strewn about the Great Hall. Empty dishes covered the tables and the dogs roamed the floor, sniffing among the rushes for discarded bones and meat. Only a few men still sprawled across the benches. The rest of the guests swarmed through the hall and up the stairs, searching for the missing bride. No one looked up at the girl framed in the doorway.

It was the Earl who discovered her. Staggering down the stairs, he caught sight of the green velvet gown. "Aha!" he exclaimed as he pulled her into the light. "So you're found at last!" His fingers dug into her arm and he leaned down, speaking into her ear, "Did ye mean to frighten us half out of our minds? If so, ye did a pretty thorough job of it. I promise ye, I'll not forget that."

She did not have time to respond before the guests gathered around her. The women were giggling now, all except Megan and Elizabeth.

Taking possession of John, the men moved off to allow the women to precede them up the stairs. With Megan and Elizabeth close behind her, Muriella was propelled upward, her heart pounding against her ribs. As she climbed the stairs one by one, fear lodged itself in her throat and throbbed there dully.

She saw that they were leading her to a huge bedchamber hung all in crimson. The women crowded into the room, laughing and blushing, while Megan began to remove her mistress's clothes. The green velvet fell to the floor, and next came the kirtle; it fell at Muriella's feet in a gleaming pile. Megan's expression was rigid as she began to untie the strings of the chemise. Men shouted in the hallway, chanting obscenities, pounding on the door.

Muriella heard the voices—echoing harsh and crude against the stone—which threatened to force the door inward. She imagined the smell of drunken breath and nausea rose in her throat. When the door began to creak open, she choked back the sickness time and again.

"Let us in!" the men roared. They no longer cared about propriety; they were Scotsmen, Highlanders, many of them, and all they wanted, just now, was one more bit of fun to remember.

Though only a man or two managed to get a glimpse inside the room, Muriella saw the avid glitter in their eyes. Behind them would come John, her husband. No door would be strong enough to keep him out. Nothing could have prepared her for this moment, for the laughter, the lewd remarks, the cruel leers that penetrated the heavy wood, stripping her of the last of her pride. Her marriage had left her with nothing—not even her self-respect.

All at once, a man forced his way into the chamber. Before anyone could stop him, he pushed Megan aside and, turning Muriella with one hand, slapped her soundly on the behind.

It was too much. The terror and helpless fury that had been building inside Muriella erupted in a moment of madness. Naked, face white with rage, she whirled and struck the man hard across the face. Surprisingly, she heard shouts of approval from the onlookers.

John, who had been forced to the front of the crowd, lunged for the man as he fled the chamber, but Colin caught his brother in a close grip, pinning his arms to his sides. "Ye wouldn't want to ruin your wedding night, now, would ye, little brother? Besides, your wife has done your work for ye."

The offending guest had disappeared, and the crowd had grown quiet, stunned, for the moment, into sobriety. Clenching his teeth in fury, John wrenched himself free of his brother's grasp. His clothing had disappeared along the way and the candlelight fluttered over the sweat glistening on his chest. Muriella swallowed convulsively and stood frozen with fear.

Elizabeth and Megan touched her gently. "Come to bed. 'Tis warm there, and safe from prying eyes." Rigidly, she allowed them to lead her toward the high curtained bed, to help her up, to draw the linen sheets and furs beneath her chin.

John stood facing the dwindling crowd until most of them had crept away in shame. Only then did he climb up beside his wife.

Megan and Elizabeth slipped out of the chamber quietly, trying to erase the image of Muriella's gray, drawn face, just as the Earl entered. His drunkenness seemed to have dissipated in all the excitement.

"Ye see, Johnnie," he said, "if ye just wait, ye'll eventually get what ye want." He nodded toward Muriella. "There was no' any need to hunt the Calders down 'til ye'd killed every last one. Simply by marrying the girl, you've struck them a blow from which they may never recover. Don't ye forget it." Glancing at Muriella, he tried to smile, but even he could not keep up the pretense that for her this was a celebration. With a sympathetic shake of his head, he left the room, pulling the heavy door closed behind him.

Muriella sat very still. She was determined not to betray her inner torment, and so twined her fingers together and fixed her gaze on the shadows at the foot of the bed.

"I couldn't stop it, ye know," John said at last.

The sound of his voice made her shiver. "Ye could have refused to marry me. Then 'twould never have happened."

"You're a fool if ye believe that. 'Twould have happened sooner or later. If no' with me, then with someone else."

Muriella turned to look at him for the first time. "But it had to be ye, didn't it? It had to be, because ye couldn't bear to lose Cawdor. Ye didn't care what *I* thought. Ye didn't even ask."

"Ye made your feelings clear enough." He remembered with a fresh wave of anger how Colin and the guests had laughed into their tankards when Muriella's absence was discovered. They had been laughing at him. As he turned to his bride, his hands clenched into fists, the fur slipped down, revealing his bare chest.

With a stifled cry, Muriella shrank away from him.

"I'm not a monster," he cried, struggling to keep his voice steady, "no matter how much ye might want to believe it."

His eyes glittered icy silver blue, like the sea before a winter storm, and Muriella could not suppress a shiver of apprehension. "I believe only what I see," she told him.

John swung around, leaning on the carved headboard so he held her imprisoned between his two hands. "I don't think ye understand. You're my wife."

As he spoke, he moved closer until she could feel his

breath like a warning on her cheek. She stared at him, wide-eyed, painfully aware of his naked body so close to hers, of the strength of his arms on either side of her head. Nevertheless, she was wholly unprepared when he tangled his fingers in her hair and forced her head upward to meet his fierce kiss.

His lips pressed against hers with the heat of his anger, and though she tried to break away, he held her too tightly. She shuddered, gasping for breath, and pushed frantically at his chest until her fingers curled inward and she sank her nails into his flesh.

At the sudden pain, John raised his head, staring down at her through the flickering light of the torches. "It doesn't have to be this way," he said. "If ye didn't fight me at every turn—"

Muriella felt the pressure of his fingers ease a little while he hovered above her, waiting for an answer. She twisted out of his grasp, scrambling for the other side of the bed. "No!" she cried, when his fingers closed around her arm.

"Aye," he muttered, pinning her down with his callused palms on her bare shoulders. He raised his head to gaze at her white slender body, freed at last from the hindrance of furs and sheets. She had ceased her struggles, and lay rigid and unresponsive beneath his hands. This was not what he wanted, but he knew she would give him nothing more. Infuriated by the cold, blank expression in her eyes, he kissed her again, bruisingly.

Muriella's vision blurred; she felt that the blood in her throat would choke her. He drew her beneath him so the weight of his body pressed her down and down into the mattress where she could not escape from the touch of his skin or the harsh demands of his mouth on hers. From somewhere deep within, the water began to hiss and churn until it rose inside her head, white, cold, and furious, drowning out everything but the sound of her fear. She tried to cry out, but he swallowed her cries with his hungry lips.

A fine sheen of sweat covered his body. She felt its clammy coolness on her skin, penetrating her pores so even her insides were tainted by his touch. Then, with a groan, he entered her, pausing for an instant when she gasped in pain.

He looked up, and Muriella, released at last from the pressure of his lips, turned her head away as she fought back the illness that rose in her throat. He rocked against her, his hands buried in her thick, tangled hair. With each thrust, the pain became greater, until it merged with the rushing water to swamp her senses. Just when she was certain she could bear no more, he ceased his assault and collapsed beside her.

Her heart dragged, as if it could not bear the strain of her terror anymore. Quivering, her palms cold with sweat, her head spinning into the unfriendly darkness, Muriella rolled over and, drawing her knees to her chest, retreated to the farthest corner of the bed.

When his breath began to come more easily, John turned to look at his wife. She lay curled at the edge of the bed, so near that he thought she might tumble to the floor at any minute. She was shivering, her arms wrapped protectively over her breasts. "Muriella—"

He reached for her but she shuddered and pulled away. She was cold, as cold as the gray stone walls around them. He could not bear the sight of her small trembling body. He shut his eyes and turned away.

Muriella did not move, but lay as she would lie for many hours, staring blindly at the blank face of the door.

When she awoke, the torches had burned themselves out and the morning light was just beginning to push its way through the shutters. Someone had covered her with a heavy fur and she huddled beneath it, unwilling to turn and face her husband. When at last she glanced up, she found that the bed was empty. Her racing heart slowed to normal. As she looked over the remnants of the night before—her gown on the chest, her kirtle glimmering among the rushes, her chemise flung onto the back of a chair—she knew she had to get away. Groping through the half darkness, she picked up the kirtle and threw it over her head. Then she went to the door to look outside. She guessed that because of the celebration the night before, the guests would sleep until late in the morning. She did not know where John might be, but prayed she would not meet him.

Muriella slipped through the sleeping castle like a wraith, her bare feet making no sound on the stone floors. When she reached the Great Hall, she was surprised to discover that the door hung open, forgotten in the excitement. Gathering her skirt about her, she stepped out into the dawn.

It did not take long to reach the hill behind which the Gypsy camp was hidden. Arriving at the top, breathless and exhausted, she stared in disbelief at the scene before her. The Gypsies had gone. The tents had been pulled down during the night, the wagons packed and the fires put out. The only sign that they had ever been there was the two blackened holes where the bonfires had burned.

Muriella was stunned. She looked up and down the valley again, hoping for a sign that the Gypsies would return, but there was none. They had gone, every one of them, and Alex had gone with them, leaving her behind. While back at the castle, her husband was waiting. Muriella sat down on the barren hilltop and wept.

# PART II

## 1513–1514

# 19

The shutters had been thrown back to admit the breeze, and the scent of summer flowers drifted through the wide windows of the solar. Muriella looked up from the loom to breathe deeply, enjoying the fragrance of lavender and roses that wafted up from the garden.

"The loch should be lovely today," Megan observed. She knelt beside a finished tapestry, binding the last of the dark silken threads. "Shall we ride to the shore when ye've done with this?"

"Aye," her mistress agreed, turning her attention back to her task. The Earl had hired an artist the winter before to paint the sketch of this new tapestry. Now, with the huge piece of painted linen secured from behind, Muriella was transferring the design to the vertical threads of the loom with charcoal. That way, when she and Mary began the weaving, they would have a pattern to follow.

Muriella gazed through the tightly secured wool threads, which could not obscure the bright colors of the painting. She was pleased with the first panel in a tapestry that, when finished, would tell the story of the legend of Loch Awe. She had wanted to capture the magic in color and thread ever since she first heard Alex tell the story nearly four years before, and now, at last, it was becoming a reality. Bending closer, she traced the outline of a tumble of rocks at the edge of a stream.

"M'lady?"

She turned to the servant Jenny, who had been working beside Megan on the hanging they had cut from the loom that morning. "The edges are bound. Must we start with the finishin' now?"

Muriella shook her head. She could see that Jenny was bored with the work, and her needlework suffered when she grew restless. "No. 'Tis enough for today. We'll all begin sewing the slits between the colors tomorrow. 'Twill go faster with many hands."

"Then may I go?" Jenny's eyes brightened at the prospect of escape. She rose, straightening her stiff knees with difficulty.

"Aye, for the moment."

Without bothering to curtsy, the servant left the room. Before the door had closed behind her, Mary stepped over the threshold. "The Laird is askin' for ye, m'lady," she said.

"Thank ye, Mary." Muriella put down her charcoal. Turning to Megan, she said, "Ye can do what ye like for a time. I'm only grateful that you're more patient than Jenny."

"Och!" Megan scoffed. "A mad dog is more patient than that one. 'Tis no' such a virtue, after all."

"Mayhap not when ye put it that way, but I thank ye just the same."

A flush of color crept up Megan's cheeks. She bent to busy herself with the loom to hide her pleasure. "Ye don't want to keep the Earl waitin'," she said.

"No." Muriella smoothed out her rose silk gown and kirtle, which had become crumpled as she knelt before the loom. Then she crossed the room and stepped into the hall. She moved through the curving stone passageways toward the library, noting with pleasure that the narrow corridors were almost warm; summer had finally made its way inside the thick stone walls of the keep. Even the walls themselves were vibrant with color, so that the empty hall seemed less grim and forbidding. The hangings she and the servants had woven in the past four years kept out some of the chill and disguised the unevenness of the rough stone beneath. With the two looms the Earl had had built soon after her wedding, she had created several tapestries that hid the mottled stone behind brightly woven scenes from the poems and legends she loved.

Muriella stopped on the threshold of the library to smooth back the few curling red hairs that had come loose from her heavy braid. She frowned when she saw that the Earl was seated before the empty fireplace, eyes closed, head resting against the back of his carved chair. His face was deeply lined and his thick beard seemed grayer than she remembered. His expression was grim, almost despondent. He had been away only three months, but he looked much older, as if years had passed since he'd last closed his eyes in his own keep.

"Is there trouble at court?" she asked softly as she came into the room.

Argyll opened his eyes with a start. "Ah, Muriella. 'Tis glad to see ye, I am, lass. I swear ye grow lovelier every time." Smiling with pleasure, he took her hands and held them tightly.

She noticed that he had not answered her question. "We missed ye while ye were away."

His grip on her hands increased for a moment before he released her. "And I ye." He sighed, then shook his head to clear it of the lingering chill of a bad dream. "Ye'll not be surprised to know that I brought ye something from Edinburgh. 'Tis in the little chest by the hearth."

Muriella left him reluctantly and went to kneel beside the carved oak chest. Lifting the lid, she found several huge spools of silver and gold thread. "Oh!" she breathed. "They're lovely."

The Earl looked over her shoulder as she took a strand of fine thread and rubbed it reverently between her thumb and forefinger. "I thought ye could use it in your hanging of Loch Awe. Silver for the moon and gold for the path of the light across the water."

Muriella's eyes filled with tears at his thoughtfulness. She had worked with the dyes for many days, trying to create just the right color for the moon and the radiant water, but she had never been quite satisfied. For this tapestry especially, she wanted everything to be perfect. "How did ye know?"

Argyll smiled at her obvious delight. "I watched ye as ye worked at choosing the colors. And I've come to know ye well enough to see when ye aren't happy."

He put his hand on her shoulder and she turned to smile up at him. "Thank ye," she murmured.

"You're welcome, lass. 'Tis the least I can do to help ye make this keep more of a home. I didn't realize how cold and empty the castle had become 'til ye changed it with your woman's touch. I'm grateful for that, ye ken." His fingers tightened briefly on her shoulder before he moved away. "Besides the thread, I brought some cakes of dye that Queen Margaret sent ye from her own stores. She was sore disappointed that I didn't bring ye with me this time."

Muriella unwrapped one of the cakes, exclaiming over the deep blue color. "The Queen is kind to remember me."

"No," the Earl murmured, "she's wise to recognize a true friend when she has so few."

There was a hint of something in his voice that Muriella found disturbing. "'Twas a difficult trip, wasn't it?" she asked.

Argyll ran his hand through his heavy gray beard. "Aye, but I don't wish to think of that right now. Give me a little time to enjoy being safely home." He leaned a hand against the wall, staring moodily into the lifeless ashes of the fire.

He looked so weary, so burdened by his own unhappy thoughts, that Muriella's heart went out to him. Argyll rarely allowed her to see his sorrow, but now she could read it in every line of his face. "Shall I recite to ye?" she asked, closing the chest with care.

Without looking up, the Earl nodded. "Aye, I'd like that. Mayhap John Barbour can keep my attention today. Naught else can."

"'Tis to be *The Bruce,* then?" The epic poem told the story of one of Scotland's first true heroes, Robert the Bruce, and Argyll loved it above all others. Muriella had spent so many hours reading and then reciting it with him that she knew it by heart.

"Ye know the part I like to hear, don't ye?"

"Aye, I know." Muriella sat on a low stool and clasped her hands together, summoning up the familiar words and lines like old friends.

> Alas that folk who e'er were free,
> And in freedom wont for to be,
> Through their great mischance and folly
> Were treated then so wickedly
> That their foes their judges were.
> What wretchedness may man have more?

"'Tis good to hear your sweet voice again," the Earl murmured. "I only wish ye could do it in the Gaelic. Och, what a spell ye could weave then. But don't let me stop ye."

Muriella drew a deep breath, then continued.

> Ah! freedom is a noble thing!
> Freedom makes a man to his liking.
> Freedom all solace to man gives.
> He lives at ease that freely lives!

"'Tis true, ye know," Argyll murmured more to himself than to her, "though some don't choose to understand that." Before she could begin again, he picked up the lines where she had left off.

> A noble heart may have none else,
> No other thing that may him please.
> But freedom only; for free liking
> Is yearned for o'er all other things.

His voice faded and Muriella saw that he had forgotten her for the moment. His brow was furrowed with thought, and he stared at the ashes at his feet as if they held some meaning only he could see. In the sudden stillness, she could hear his heavy breathing and her heart began to beat unsteadily.

She was feeling oppressed by the silence when Argyll turned unexpectedly.

"Tell me how you're getting on with Johnnie," he said.

She looked down, spreading her fingers across the silk covering her knees. So it was to be her husband again. That was the only subject about which she and the Earl had quarreled over the years. He was watching her closely; when she met his gaze, she noticed a hard gleam in his eyes. "We manage well enough," she said at last. "Things don't change much."

The Earl left the fireplace to seat himself across from her. "'Tis just as I thought." With his feet planted firmly on the floor and his hands gripping the carved armrests of his chair, he ceased to resemble the man she had come to love and became instead the unbending Laird of the Clan Campbell.

"Don't ye realize how quickly the days are slipping through our fingers? You're seventeen, Muriella. 'Tis long past time ye bore my son a child."

Muriella bit her lip as she thought of Colin's wife, shut away in Castle Glamis with only her sons and daughters to keep her company. "If 'tis grandchildren ye want, Colin's Janet has given ye those."

"Aye," Argyll agreed. "But none who can inherit Cawdor."

Rising abruptly, Muriella turned away. So it was Cawdor he was thinking of. Always it was Cawdor. But this time he was helpless; even her father-in-law's unbounded ambition could not force her to conceive a child.

He must know that John had not come to her bed for a long time now, but he could not know why. He could not know that, after the wedding, she had tried to accustom herself to her husband's occasional visits to her chamber, but she had never succeeded. Always, when his naked body lay next to hers, the fear came, holding her in its grip. Megan had told her it got easier with time, but she had not found it so. Then her sixteenth birthday had arrived and with it the second anniversary of their wedding. John had come to her late that night. She remembered so clearly how he had put out the torches as he entered the room, how loud his footsteps had seemed to her sensitive ears.

He had said nothing as he climbed into bed beside her, but she knew he had been drinking; she could smell the wine on his breath. Without a word, he had buried his face in her hair, drawing the furs away from her body so it was exposed to his hungry gaze. Even in the darkness she could see the burning blue of his eyes, and the fear had moved like flame through her body.

John bent to kiss her, his mouth hard and insistent on hers, as if he could force her to respond with the mere strength of his own need. "Muriella!" he growled. The single word demanded all she had to give—her attention, her acquiescence, the secrets of her body.

She felt his rough beard scratching her face, her throat and breasts as he moved down, claiming every inch of her with his mouth and hands. She held her breath, praying that this time his assault would not bring with it the vision that had become her nightmare. But when he entered her, the darkness blurred and the humming in her ears began. Then the water rose, cold and threatening, closing around her, filling her mouth and lungs as the waves dragged her under. She was fighting for air, clawing her way through the choking water, but she knew she would never reach the light. Mindlessly, she cried out once, then raised her hands before her to ward off the rushing white foam.

Because the fear still clutched at her throat, she was hardly aware that John had forced her hands apart and was looking down at her through the darkness. Her heart thudded and her skin grew clammy with sweat as her husband's face came into focus. John stared at her for a moment, his eyes cutting away the protective darkness like a bright, sharp blade, then he cursed violently and swung himself off her.

He had left the chamber without a word and had not come again to her bed. She was not quite sure why that was so, but she was grateful, for she had not seen the vision since that night. Almost, she could convince herself that it was no more than an unpleasant memory.

"Muriella, are ye listening to me?" Argyll demanded.

With an effort, she forced her thoughts back to the reality of the crowded library and the warning in the Earl's voice.

"Aye," she said, "I'm listening." But she did not turn to face him.

"Johnnie must have children," her father-in-law repeated.

"I haven't stopped him from doing so."

The Earl regarded her through narrowed eyes. "Mayhap not, but ye also haven't encouraged him. The time has come to stop your games and grow up. I know ye hold yourself apart from him, as if ye were made of ice and stone instead of flesh and blood. But that will have to change. Ye must be a real wife to him."

She whirled on one slippered foot. "I've told ye—"

"Aye, you've told me more than once. But I'm not willing to listen anymore." He saw how she retreated from him, how she struggled to control the trembling of her hands. "'Tis not only for the sake of the Campbells, lass," he added more gently. "'Tis for your sake as well. Ye don't realize it, but ye need Johnnie by ye. Ye need to depend on someone besides yourself."

"But I have ye!"

The Earl sighed, sinking deeper into his chair. This was partly his fault, he knew. He had taken Muriella away from Inveraray too often, but he had wanted her with him when he made the long, lonely trip to Edinburgh. She had been the only light on an increasingly dark horizon. The distance between himself and Elizabeth had grown greater over the years as the Macleans became more hostile to the Campbells, and John and Colin were men with their own concerns. Only Muriella seemed to need him. Only she brought him joy. Because of that he had selfishly kept her by him, even though he knew it was not wise. "I won't be here always," he told her. "I've been lucky so far in my career as a soldier, but—"

"No! I won't listen to that kind of talk."

"Ye'd best get used to the idea," Argyll snapped, "because we go to war with England within the month. I've only come home to gather the men and see that my affairs are in order."

"War?" she gasped. "But why? Have the English attacked the borders again?"

"No," he said wearily. He had not meant to tell her this way, but perhaps it was best after all. "There are many reasons. King Henry has never taken Jamie seriously and our king's vanity has been battered once too often, it seems." He shook his head, releasing his grip on the arms of his chair. "Ye won't believe what decided him in the end. 'Twas a love letter from the French queen." He glared at Muriella as if she might try to deny it. "She fears that Henry will attack France soon, and she told King Jamie 'twould no' be chivalrous to leave her at England's mercy. So, we go to battle."

"For a woman's pride? Only that?"

"I advised the King against it, and others with me, but he won't be swayed."

Muriella's heart began to pound. "If ye think he's wrong, why can't ye refuse to join him?"

"Don't ever suggest such a thing to me!" Argyll cried. "'Tis not only a woman's pride that's at stake now. 'Tis Scotland's pride. And that I'll fight for. I wouldn't ever stain the name of Campbell by hiding like a coward in my keep. What I do, I do because I must—for honor. If the clan loses that, they lose everything I've fought for."

He paused to take a long, deep breath. "In a week we leave to join the King. 'Tis likely I'll be away a long time, and ye'll have to turn to Johnnie when I'm gone."

"He isn't going with ye?"

"No," the Earl told her, leaning back in his chair, eyes closed. He had no strength left to argue or explain. "This time when I go to war, I go alone."

"Why?" John demanded furiously. "Surely you've lost your mind!"

The Earl, who sat where Muriella had left him two hours since, schooled his features with difficulty. "Because I want ye here. Ye and Colin can help gather the men, but neither one of ye will go with the army this time."

His son was staggered by the Earl's calm announcement. Ever since he was thirteen years old he had been at his father's side in battle. "Do ye think we've grown lazy in the use of our swords? That we aren't skilled enough—"

"Don't be a fool, Johnnie!" Argyll snapped in annoyance. "I know full well that ye and Colin are two of the best fighters in Scotland. Ye wouldn't be my sons else. But nevertheless, ye'll stay behind."

John ran his hand through his hair in agitation. "I don't understand."

"No, nor can I expect ye to. But the fact remains that I've a feeling about this war. The King isn't always as wise as he should be, and 'tis simply not the time to pick a quarrel."

He could not argue with the Earl's knowledge of politics, but John knew a thing or two about tactics. "If the time is wrong, isn't that all the more reason to make our army as strong as possible? Shouldn't we bring all the men we can?"

Argyll shook his head. John had grown up a great deal in the past four years, but he was still overeager to get himself killed. "Johnnie, ye must trust me. I won't be shorting the King, ye can bet on that, but I want my sons at Inveraray. Think about this, for example. Would it be wise just now to leave the castle at Maclean's mercy without protection from either ye or Colin?"

It was true that the Macleans had been restless of late, but that was not reason enough for Argyll's reluctance.

"Besides," the Earl added softly, "there's your wife to consider."

John rose, suddenly uncomfortable under his father's probing gaze. Planting himself before the cold hearth, he stared at the blackened stones. "I don't see what Muriella has to do—"

"Don't ye? *Think* for a minute. What if ye went off heedlessly and were killed fighting the King's cause? What do ye suppose would happen to Cawdor?"

"I hadn't considered that."

"Well, mayhap 'tis time ye did. Old William Calder still

has two sons living, and then there's Muriella's cousin, Hugh Rose. He hasn't married yet, I hear. No doubt he'd be happy to take Muriella back, so long as her dowry was Cawdor."

"The Campbells are strong enough to protect her," John muttered.

The Earl shook his head in despair. It seemed his son was as blind as his young wife. "Without an heir, Johnnie, they'd have no right. Ye'd do well to remember that before ye rush off to war. The Campbells come before your pride or your lust for battle."

John clenched and unclenched his hands until his fingers began to ache. His father did not know what he was asking. He did not know about the night when John had last gone to his wife's bed. It had been nearly two years ago, but the memory was still painfully vivid. He had been drunk, John remembered, and Colin had been taunting him, as he so often did, about how little John would be without Muriella's inheritance. Like a fool, he had let his brother's gibes rankle, and had gone to his wife in anger.

He had put out the torch before joining her, because he did not want to see the fear she could never quite hide at his approach. She was more withdrawn than usual that night, and her silence only fueled his rage. He kissed her harshly, and though the warmth of her body teased him—just out of reach—her lips remained as cool as the night air.

"Muriella!" he growled, demanding what he knew she could not give. Then he felt her stiffen beneath him. The cold rigidity of her body at last penetrated his wine-fogged brain and he paused. He saw her raise her hands before her face as if to ward off the devil himself. For a moment the rage rushed through his body, blinding him to everything but his own frustration. Roughly, he forced her hands apart. "Look at me!" he wanted to cry. "I'm a man, not a monster!"

But the words never left his mouth. As the pale blur of her face came into focus, he saw that her eyes were blank and still and her skin was covered with a fine sheen of sweat. She stared through him as if he were not even there, as if the sudden trembling of her body came, not from the pressure of his naked skin on hers, but from the presence of a force he could neither see nor understand. The Sight was with her, he realized, and more real to her, just then, than his fury or his pain or his hungry body.

He froze at the realization while an unnatural stillness wrapped him in its grasp. Muriella began to shudder violently. As the blankness left her eyes, they were filled with an expression of such terror that it burned his desire to ashes in an instant. Too appalled to speak, he pulled away from her and left without a word.

He had not been to Muriella's bed since. There were women enough who welcomed his caresses, who did not shudder at his touch. He had never had joy of his wife, nor she of him. In the end her fear had proved stronger than his need. Yet, though he no longer lay with her, sometimes she flitted through his dreams, strange and wraithlike, beckoning, luring him toward disaster. But he could tell his father none of these things.

The Earl watched his son as he struggled with his thoughts. Something was wrong, but he sensed that John would not tell him what it was. For the first time in his life, the Earl of Argyll felt helpless. "Muriella needs ye, Johnnie," he said at last, "whether she admits it or no'."

"Ye don't know her as well as ye think if ye believe that."

"But *ye* don't know her at all," Argyll murmured.

"Aye, well, she seems happy enough as she is."

"Mayhap, and mayhap not. But this ye cannot argue. I'm going off to war within the week. She's come to depend on me, Johnnie. Now it will have to be ye she turns to. I know I can count on ye to keep her safe, but will ye see, too, that she's cared for?"

John looked up. "She's my wife," he said. "I haven't any choice."

It was not exactly the answer the Earl had been hoping for. "Colin has a wife too, but that doesn't seem to concern him overmuch."

"I've told ye before, I'm not like Colin."

Argyll leaned forward, hands braced on his knees. "Ye

say that as if you're proud of the fact, but 'tis not always such a good thing. As I've told *ye* before, Colin is the kind of leader this clan needs."

"The men don't like him," John pointed out obstinately.

"But they fear him, and 'tis that very fear which gives him his greatest strength." As he considered the rigid line of John's back and the angle of his head, framed by gray, lifeless stone, Argyll inhaled sharply. He realized with a shock that though John was still guided by his heart and his rage instead of his head—or perhaps it was because of that—this son had come to mean a great deal to him. For some strange reason, John had given him hope. But that did not—could not—change the facts. "And ye might think of this, Johnnie," he added quietly. "Colin is no doubt much happier than ye, because he doesn't rage at things he cannot change."

John turned to face his father, fingers hooked in the wide leather of his belt. "I'd rather rage than feel my blood turn slowly and surely to ice, and no matter how often ye call me a fool, *that* won't change."

Shrugging in defeat, the Earl rose from his chair. "I didn't call ye here to discuss the flaws in your character, nor your intention to cling to them, even knowing they might destroy ye one day. 'Tis your choice, after all. But losing Cawdor is *not* your choice. I want your word that ye'll do something about securing Muriella's inheritance while there's still time."

John knew his father was right, but the knowledge could not erase the memory of the horror he'd seen one night in his wife's eyes. "I'll think," he said, "but—"

"'Tis no' good enough, Johnnie, and well ye know it. You've a responsibility to the Campbells. 'Tis that which must guide ye, just as certainly as it's always guided me." Argyll regarded his son closely. He wondered if all the arguments, demands and logic in the world could alter John's course once he had chosen it. A deep, aching sadness settled in the Earl's bones at the thought. He waved his hand toward his son in dismissal, and his shoulders sagged with a weariness so great that it seemed, almost, like hopelessness.

# 20

"Och, m'lady! I've tangled the thread again," Mary cried in dismay. "I don't think I'll ever learn to do the faces."

Muriella sat at the second loom, the shuttle idle in her hand. She was glad for the distraction. Abandoning her own weaving, she crossed the room to Mary's side. As she bent to examine the first panel of the tapestry, she saw with pleasure that the design was beginning to take shape. Mary, Megan and she had been working on it for nearly two months, ever since the Earl's brief visit home in July. "You're doing a fine job," she assured the servant, running her hand over the forming image of a bubbling burn in a lush green valley. In the background, men and women rode to the hunt, their plaids streaming behind them in the wind.

"But look, I've woven her hair over part of her face and now we'll have to pick it free again." The servant sighed, shaking her dark head woefully.

Muriella knelt and took the shuttle from Mary's hand, carefully guiding the weft thread back through the warp until the outline of the woman's face was free of yellow silk strands. "There! 'Tis no trouble, ye see. This time, try to go more slowly. The smallest areas take the most time, ye ken."

"But my fingers go faster than I tell them to and the weave gets bigger, though I try to keep it small."

Muriella tapped down the threads with the comb, then leaned closer so her auburn braid fell over Mary's shoulder. "Mayhap 'twould help if ye did as my mother used to do. Ye find the rhythm ye need for the shuttle as it passes back and forth, and then ye sing a little song in time."

Mary wrinkled her forehead as her eyes followed Muriella's quick movements. Soon she began to feel the regular sweep and weave and tightening of the threads, but no words came to her. "What should I sing?"

Muriella tapped her foot, seeking the words that would flow with the sound of the clacking loom. Then she began to chant softly,

> Still on my wayis as I went
> Out through a land beside a lea.
> I met a bairn upon the bent
> Methought him seemly for to see.

"Aye, I know that one!" Mary cried. "The men sing it in the Great Hall when they can find naught else to keep them busy." She took the shuttle from Muriella's flying fingers and sang softly,

> I asked him wholly his intent—
> Good sir, if yer will be,
> Since that ye bide upon the bent
> Some uncouth tidings tell ye me.

Her pale, smooth face grew flushed with pleasure and her sweet voice rose and fell in time with the moving shuttle.

> When shall these wars be gone
> That loyal men may live in lee?
> Or when shall falsehood go from home
> And Lawtie blow his horn on hie?

When Muriella saw that Mary was working almost as deftly as her mistress, she blessed the memory of the hours spent in her mother's solar. Isabel had taught her daughter well—not only the many skills it took to create beautiful hangings, but also the patience needed during endless hours of weaving. "Remember, lass," her mother had said more than once, "the boredom only lasts for the moment, but the magic of the scene ye create is forever."

Overcome with a wave of sadness she had thought never to feel again, Muriella rose, leaving the servant to her task. The silent loom across the chamber no longer called to her. She went instead to stand at one of the wide windows, missing Isabel, feeling empty, bereft. Why, in all this time, had she heard nothing from her mother? Why had her own letters never been answered? And why, today, did Isabel's silence hurt so much? Why was she so desperately alone?

Muriella rubbed her arms vigorously, but they were cold and stiff.

She was restless, and though she was not certain what she sought, she gazed out the window as if the view of the turbulent loch beneath held the answer to her question. She tapped her fingers on the edge of the stone sill. Friday, September 9, she repeated silently for the fifth time. There was something about today, but what was it? She shivered when she noticed the rain was falling again. It had rained off and on for three weeks now.

"'Tis too quiet today," Jenny complained from the bench where she sat sewing on a shirt for one of the men. "I don't think there'll ever be news of the war. We'll be locked away here 'til we starve, no doubt, and never know what happened to the army."

"The rain's keepin' the messengers overlong on their travels, I'll wager," Megan interjected.

"Mayhap." Muriella leaned out toward the falling rain and wondered if Megan were right. It had been too long since they'd heard from the Earl about the progress of the war with England. The clack clack of the loom and the rise and fall of Mary's voice made a pleasant contrast to the stormy loch below, but today Muriella did not find comfort in these things.

She glanced at Megan as the servant bent to stir the fire back to life. The room, with its huge windows facing the loch, was thoroughly chilled. When it wasn't raining, the sun was lost behind the dark clouds that never seemed to leave the sky. Despite the lowering weather, Muriella had ridden out every day to escape the somber mood that hovered over the keep, but today the violence of the storm had defeated her; she had had no choice but to remain inside. Fingering the intricate embroidery on her silk shawl—a gift from the Earl—Muriella turned suddenly. "I'm going down to the hall," she told the servant. "If the light fades much more, ye and Jenny and Mary might as well stop your work and get warm by the fire below."

"Aye, m'lady," Megan murmured. Her mistress crossed the room, her green velvet gown rustling about her legs. Megan watched her go with concern. She had seen that look of unease on Muriella's face before, but she could not remember when. All she knew was that it made her heart beat faster.

Muriella moved quickly along the passageway. She was possessed of a sudden urgency she did not understand. When she reached the gallery above the Great Hall, she heard the crash of swords below and hurried to the head of the stairs.

She paused with her hand at her throat when she saw John and Colin facing one another, booted feet spread wide on the bare stone floor, broadswords in their hands. The blades met with a clash so loud it vibrated through her body while the two men stood frozen for a moment, stunned by the impact of metal on metal. Muriella gasped as John lunged expertly toward his opponent and Colin stepped back, then swung his own weapon in a wide arc. Dear God, the inactivity and boredom had finally overcome them. They would kill each other out of pure frustration.

Muriella had opened her mouth to call out when Duncan came to the foot of the stairs to smile up at her. "Ye needn't worry, m'lady. They're only practicing to keep themselves busy."

John heard and turned abruptly, dropping his blade to his side. "Aye," he snapped, "here we are playing games when out there the real war is going on." He waved toward the barred doors that opened onto the courtyard. "'Tis madness!" He forced his sword into its sheath and tossed it toward the hearth with such violence that it rang against the stone. The sound echoed through the vaulted, cavelike room like a fierce lament without words.

Muriella moved down the stairs as the flickering torchlight closed around her. "There's still no news, then?" she asked her husband.

Pushing the tangled hair back from his forehead, he regarded her through clear blue eyes. "None," he said, "but ye know that. 'Tis three times you've asked me just today."

"Have I? I don't remember." Muriella's eyes grew clouded; she looked around the room as if she could not recall what had brought her here.

"Ah!" Colin called jovially, tossing his own sword away. "Here's Jenny, freed from her loom at last. I missed ye, girl." As the servant approached, he flung his arm around her shoulders and guided her back up the stairs she had just descended.

Muriella was hardly aware they had gone. There was something she should know—something that hovered in the back of her mind, just out of reach. She saw that her hands were trembling and her skin was suddenly cold. She felt her head begin to spin and knew the Sight was with her again. Straightening her shoulders, she took a deep breath and closed her mind against the blackness that was coming. For a moment, she shivered uncontrollably; then, as the haze cleared, she saw John leaning toward her. "I think I'll go read for a bit before supper," she told him, amazed that she could speak at all. "'Tis warmer in the library."

Without another word, she turned to leave him. A chill of unease ran up John's back as he watched Muriella go. He saw how she paused at the foot of the worn stone stairs, then started laboriously upward, as if the weight of her body were too heavy to bear. He did not like it.

When she had disappeared from view, he swore silently, turned and started toward the door. "I'm going for a ride," he called to Duncan, "and the weather be damned!"

"But, m'lord," the squire objected, "your horse won't be able to find his way through the rain."

John did not pause as he shouted over his shoulder, "That animal could find his way over these hills blind, and well ye know it. But don't worry, ye needn't come with me this time. I'll go alone."

The squire hurried over the rushes, blond hair flying. "What if he loses his footing in the mud and throws ye? We wouldn't be able to find ye in this downpour."

"Leave off!" John roared. "I've heard enough. I have to get away from here before I go mad." Ignoring Duncan's restraining hand on his arm, he lifted the heavy bolt and wrenched the doors open. The cold, damp air rushed in with a force that stopped him in his tracks. He could only stand and stare at the rain falling in slashing silver sheets across the courtyard. Even he could not penetrate that wall of fury. It would be madness to try. Once again he was a prisoner in his own castle, held captive by the malevolence of the weather.

He swung the doors closed, cursing under his breath. It seemed he had done little else since his father had left with the Campbell army. John waited for news and heard none, longed for the release of battle and found only boredom and frustration. "This can't go on," he said to no one in particular. "Something has to happen soon." The memory of Muriella's pallid face came back, wavering in the air before him like the shadow from his dreams. There had been something in her eyes today—something dark and threatening that lingered even after she had gone.

Without conscious thought, he kicked aside the rushes in his way and started up the stairs after his wife.

The hallway was dark, and much colder than the hall, Muriella discovered. She felt the chill penetrating her skin, seeping into her blood as she hurried toward the library. Pausing for a moment on the threshold, she pressed her hands lovingly against the heavy oak door. In the maze of rooms and galleries and passageways at Inveraray, this alone was her haven. Here she felt safe, protected, among the leather-bound manuscripts she loved. She pushed the door open and was relieved to find a huge fire burning in the fireplace. Someone had already lit the lamps, though it was still the middle of the day. But the Earl was not here.

It seemed like years since she had seen him, though she remembered clearly the brief moment before he left when he had pulled her to him. She could have sworn she felt him shiver, even through his cloak. "Take care, lass," was all he had said.

Drawing the chair close to the desk, she ran her hands over the manuscripts scattered before her. She sat for a moment, undecided, then reached for the large book in the new leather binding. She opened the cover reverently. The Earl had given it to her before he left, encouraging her to continue with her reading. Scanning the brightly painted title page, she read it for the hundredth time: *"Lancelot of the Laik*—for Muriella, the last of my children and before God, the dearest. I believed I had nothing left to teach, but ye have proved me wrong. God bless ye. Archibald Campbell, Second Earl of Argyll."

She lowered her head when the words began to blur. She could see the other works they had read together: *Alexander the Grate, The Three Priests of Peebles,* and the first printed book the Earl had owned, *The Morale Fabillis of Esope,* by Robert Henryson. Muriella smiled, remembering when he had brought that one home with him. He had come to her laughing and pulled the book from its canvas shield as if it were a great treasure. When she stared at it, shaking her head, he had laughed again, explaining, "'Tis printed on a press, lass. They can make many at a time. There are already two hundred of these." She had been delighted, as he had known she would be. They'd begun reading it then and there, huddled in their chairs before the fire with the book open between them.

Muriella closed the manuscript, rubbing her fingers over the soft leather. Why was she thinking back, remembering so much today? It was a habit she had overcome soon after her wedding when she realized it only caused her pain. But now she could not seem to avoid images of the past.

All at once she became aware of the shadows the lamp cast over the desk. She watched as they danced across the books; she stared until the books became indistinct, the shadows hard reality. Her head began to hum with strange, discordant notes and she swayed forward, driven by a force beyond her will. She held her head in her hands, breathing raggedly, and fought against the trembling that possessed her, but it would not go. With a gasp, she leapt up from the chair, hoping to shake herself free of the premonition.

For a second, her mind grew black as she grasped the edge of the desk in a painful grip. Then the blackness cleared and a red mist took its place. There was confusion while men scrambled blindly through the red fog. Flying mud filled the air, turning from brown to crimson as down the hill the men came racing, but few reached the bottom. Dead, dead, one after the other, until they lay like deep snow covering the earth, soaking it with their blood. The pipes were wailing, wailing, screaming, pleading. . . .

"Holy Mother of God!" Muriella gasped.

John stood outside the library with his fingers spread on the cold stone. He had been there long enough to see his wife take the book from the desk to look at the title page. He'd had the odd sensation that for the first time, he could read her thoughts as if they were written out before him. She was remembering her reading sessions with the Earl, missing him. John was surprised when she closed the book to lean back, staring, her eyes dark and wide.

It was happening again; even as he watched, the Sight had come upon her. He saw how she trembled, how her breath came in painful gasps as the vision transformed her. He could feel the little hairs along his neck standing on end and he wanted to turn away. He could understand battles and death and war, and so, did not fear them. But this—

Muriella rose abruptly, clutching the edge of the desk to keep herself from falling. She turned her back to him until she faced the fire. Her body tensed and she cried, "Holy Mother of God!"

He realized then that he could not leave her. She was swaying forward; he knew he must catch her before she fell. John crossed the room quickly and, with his hands at her waist, turned his wife to face him. He swallowed dryly when he saw her expression.

Her eyes were pitch black—dark and empty—and the blood had drained from her cheeks, leaving them chalk white. Near her temple and down the center of her forehead two purple veins stood out, pulsing rapidly. But none of these things disturbed him as much as the way she stared at him as if he did not even exist.

When Muriella began to shake, he pulled her closer, circling her with his arms. All at once the tension left her. She grew slack and heavy, nearly slipping to the floor, but he held her more tightly, bracing her body with his. For a long time she continued to shake uncontrollably.

When the trembling began to subside at last, he guided her to a chair near the fire. She seemed oblivious of his presence. She was like a carved doll without life or warmth. He did not know how to bring her back. Perhaps some wine would help.

Having placed her in the chair, he went to pour a glass of the dark liquid. Then he knelt, closing her fingers around the glass. His wife hesitated for a moment longer, then raised the glass and began to drink. After a few sips, she closed her eyes. Taking both her hands in his, John spoke for the first time. "What is it?"

Muriella felt her head grow lighter as the wine moved down her throat, burning a warm path to her stomach. She was vaguely aware that someone was nearby, but she was still under the influence of the images of blood and death, and could not focus her thoughts enough to discover who it might be. As the wine began to stir her awake, she realized her hands were cupped by other hands, and she heard a voice. Whose?

"Muriella, what is it?"

Carefully, she opened her eyes, squinting through the red haze that clouded her sight. As she blinked, the face in front of her began to come into focus. John.

"Tell me," he insisted, "what have ye seen?"

She sat rigid, leaning forward slightly, her face gray and haggard. Unaware of what she was doing, she reached out to put her hands on her husband's shoulders and draw him toward her. When she spoke, her voice seemed to come from somewhere outside herself. "'Twas a terrible slaughter," she said. "The English destroyed everything—King Jamie, the army, Scotland's honor and her pride. Your father couldn't save those things." She faltered, then forced herself to go on.

"He couldn't even save himself. He's dead."

# 21

The bell rang through the castle, echoing upward, slow and mournful, counting off the years of the dead men's lives. So many had died at the battle of Flodden Field that the bell had not been silent for many hours. Muriella had listened to the hollow tolling for so long that it had become one with the pulse of her blood, drowning out even the clack of the loom. Within the mesh of wool and silk beneath her busy fingers, the burn flowed through the valley, lovely and tranquil under the Kelpies' watching eyes, but its beauty did not touch her.

"M'lady, ye must come away from there!" Megan pleaded. "Ye'll make yourself ill if ye don't eat."

"I'm not hungry," her mistress replied, her hands never faltering in their task.

"But it's been near two days that ye haven't left this room. Ye can't stay hidden away here forever." Megan's voice rose shrilly on the last few words; she was frightened by the unnatural pallor of Muriella's skin and the blank look in her eyes. Since the news of the Earl's death had come, Muriella had not wept or cried out once. Instead she sat hour by hour at her loom, retreating within herself until Megan could no longer reach her.

"Please," the servant began again, but when the door to the solar opened, she paused to look up in relief. "Sir John," she cried, "will ye talk to her? She won't leave the loom."

John frowned when he saw the shadows under his wife's eyes. So she had had no more rest than he in the past few days. Then her flying fingers caught his attention and he stared, momentarily mesmerized by the lacework of silver and blue that shimmered under her skilled hands. He wished, for an instant, that he could lose himself in the soothing rhythm as Muriella seemed to have done. "'Tis time," he said at last.

His wife concentrated more fiercely on sliding the shuttle between the threads. "Time for what?"

"To see my father."

She flinched; then her hands grew still.

"The hall is quiet now," he continued, "but, 'twill no' be for long. I thought ye'd rather go down when no one else was by."

Muriella let the shuttle fall from her fingers to dangle against the brightly colored fabric. "Have ye—" She stopped, unable to say the words.

"No. I didn't want their eyes upon me when I said good-bye."

She looked away. "I don't think I can do it."

"If ye don't," Megan interjected, "the Earl will surely haunt ye."

"He'll haunt me anyway," her mistress whispered. He was with her now, this moment, in the thin red mist that cloaked her thoughts, in the memory of his voice that echoed through the emptiness inside her.

John moved closer, resting his hand on his wife's shoulder. "Come," he said. "There isn't much time."

She had no strength to resist his command, no desire to draw away from the pressure of his fingers on her shoulder. She knew John was right; she had to see the Earl's body. It was the only way to bar his bloody specter from her dreams. Leaving the shuttle swinging free, she rose to follow her husband from the room.

They moved in silence through the narrow passageway while the torches leapt and wavered above them. They had nearly reached the top of the stairs when Mary met them on her way to the upper keep. She stopped as if turned to stone, her eyes wide with fear, when Muriella met her gaze. With a cry of alarm, the servant crossed herself and fled.

"Damn!" John cursed, glaring at the servant's retreating back. "'Twill no' happen again," he added. "I'll speak to her later."

"No. Leave her be." It was not the first time a servant had shrunk from meeting Muriella's eyes in the past few days. They had heard, no doubt, of her vision of the slaughter of the Scottish army, and their fear of her power had flared again. Even Mary could not face her. It seemed that, of the servants, only Megan had that kind of courage. When Muriella swayed on her feet, John took her arm. She welcomed his support as they continued down the corridor.

At last, the stone walls seemed to fall back and with them the enveloping darkness. Narrowing her eyes against the light, Muriella stood with her husband at the top of the stairs. The worn stone steps led directly to the bier resting on trestles in the center of the Great Hall. John's grip on her elbow increased, and slowly, on feet made of lead, they started downward.

The silence, broken only by the ringing of the soul bell, swelled until it filled John's head. He stood for a long time with his hands on the lid of the plain wooden coffin. *I've a feeling about this war,* the Earl had told his son in despair. Argyll had known the cause was hopeless, had guessed before it even began what the outcome of this conflict would be. John clenched his fists impotently against the unyielding wood. He simply could not believe that his father had chosen to die alone.

Closing his eyes, he summoned the rage that had burned in him for so long, but now that it would have brought him relief, he found that it was gone. In its place there was only his grief, which ate at him constantly, leaving his insides hollow and raw. With sudden resolution, he pushed the lid aside.

Muriella hung back when she saw John grip the wood in rigid fingers, then shudder, breathing with difficulty, as if he could not get enough air. His face was haggard in the unkind light of the many torches, and his eyes revealed an agony so great it made her shiver. Then he reached out to touch the Earl's cheek. Muriella turned away from the sight of his pain.

When John looked up, she moved closer to the bier, willing the numbness to protect her. Her heart pounded dully in her chest and, for a moment, her eyes refused to focus. Then, gradually and with painful clarity, her sight returned. She saw before her the corpse of a man who had died a violent death from the blow of an English bill, but it was not the Earl. This gray and rigid death mask belonged to a stranger, not the man she had grown to love. Her throat felt tight with unshed tears as she reached out to touch Argyll's sunken cheek, as she had once touched Rob Campbell's. In that moment, the chill seemed to move from the Earl's body into hers. She thought she might be ill, but then she realized that John was pulling her away. Without a word, he replaced the lid.

"Johnnie, where the devil have ye been? We're gathered in the library to discuss what's to be done about the Macleans. David Campbell is asking for ye."

Colin's voice rang out, competing with the tolling of the bell. John stiffened as he turned toward his brother. Colin seemed unaware of the coffin and its burden; his attention was occupied with the heavily carved silver brooch he was polishing with a corner of his plaid.

John caught a glimpse of the familiar brooch that bore the Campbell arms and the wild myrtle that was their badge. For all the years of his life, his father had worn that symbol of the Laird of the Clan Campbell. To him it was obscene that Colin should flaunt it so openly when the Earl was not yet buried. "The Macleans are always speaking out against us. Now isn't the time—"

"But that's where you're wrong. Ye see, Johnnie, I've men watching and listening on Mull, and they tell me Maclean is ready to strike soon. I told David we didn't need ye, but he wouldn't listen." Leaving his brooch for the moment, he added, "What I want to know, little brother, is if you're still a member of this clan or no'? I'm sure we could manage quite well without ye."

John fought back the angry response that rose to his lips. He would not fight with Colin while his father's corpse lay a few feet away. "Ye won't rid yourself of me so easily. I'm coming." While his brother started up the stairs, he turned back to Muriella. "Rest," he told her. "'Twill be a long night."

As Muriella watched her husband climb the stairs behind his brother, shoulders bowed under the weight of his sorrow, she thought it might well be the longest night she had ever spent.

The men and women had come by the dozens for the feast on the eve of the funeral. They had consumed so much ale and wine that the stores in the keep were badly depleted, yet the salmon and mutton, salted herring, sweetmeats and bread they ate by the platterful did not seem to satisfy their insatiable appetites. At the end of the evening, the clansmen reeled around drunkenly, forming the patterns for the funeral dance, while the pipers blew their wailing lament. When it seemed to Muriella that she would choke on the odor of stale food and the sound of their harsh laughter, they began to filter out into the courtyard. Those who could not move lay where they fell among the rushes, snoring from the effects of too much ale. Gradually, the last of the voices faded out and the silent vigil for the dead Earl began.

John, Muriella, Duncan and Megan seated themselves on benches around the bier to watch and see that no evil befell Argyll in these final hours before his interment. At first Colin was there, sprawled across a bench, half-sitting, half-prone. But presently he fell asleep. When he began to snore, John nudged him rudely awake. The third Earl of Argyll went up to bed.

No one spoke as they sat waiting for the night to pass. The soul bell had ceased its ringing at last; Muriella found the stillness oppressive. With her arms crossed over her chest, she stared at the coffin, swaying a little on her hard bench, fighting to keep her thoughts unformed so that they could not hurt her.

Her head rang with the sound of the others' breathing, overly loud in a room wrapped in silence, and she thought she might scream. Then John began to speak, softly at first, so that the words were indistinguishable, but with a slow, measured cadence that matched the labored beating of her heart.

His voice grew louder, stronger, and Muriella raised her head in blank astonishment as the meaning penetrated the fog of her unconsciousness.

> Ah! Freedom is a noble thing!
> Freedom makes a man to his liking.
> Freedom all solace to man gives.
> He lives at ease that freely lives.

The last time she had heard those words, she had been sitting in the library, watching the Earl struggle with a burden of hopelessness she had not understood. Then it had been her own voice that had caressed the familiar lines as John's was doing now—rhythmically, as if they came, not from memory, but from the heart. Muriella felt her husband's gaze upon her and she huddled forward, bowing her head in protection against the pain that flared within her. She tried to close her ears to the sound of his voice, but could not shut it out.

> A noble heart may have none else,
> No other thing that may him please,
> But freedom only; for free liking
> Is yearned for o'er all other things.

Drawn by the rise and fall of the poetry, Muriella looked up until her eyes met John's. She opened her mouth to speak, but could not find the words. Her husband's bright blue gaze was holding her, probing beyond her mask of indifference to the agony underneath, and against her volition, her lips began to move in silent time to his voice.

> Now he that aye has liv-èd free
> May not know well the property,
> The grief, nor the wretchedness
> That is coupled with foul thralldom.

Slowly, she began to whisper the words, prompted by an instinct deeper than fear, until her voice mingled with her husband's as they recited the poem the Earl had loved above all others.

> But if by heart he should know it
> Then all the more he should it wit,
> And should think freedom more to prize,
> Than all the gold in the world that is.

Muriella rocked on her bench, her fingers digging painfully into her arms. When a drop of moisture fell on her gown, she realized she was weeping. Closing her eyes against a wash of pain too fierce to bear, she willed the numbness to cloak her feelings once more. But then John's fingers met hers, burning away her protective veil with a single touch, and she gripped his hand tightly—in gratitude, in grief, and in compassion.

# 22

Dawn brought the men from the courtyard and the guests from their beds. They began to file into the hall, taking their places for the funeral procession. John rose from his chair as Colin appeared at the top of the staircase. Despite all the drinking his elder brother had done the night before, his eyes were clear and unmarked by the heavy shadows that had settled under John's own eyes. Colin descended the stairs with regal calm, surveying with satisfaction the preparations going on below him. His dark cloak was trimmed with expensive fur, his black doublet velvet with carved silver buttons. Beneath his cloak, the wool plaid was draped across his shoulder and fastened with the Campbell brooch. Colin's expression was correctly solemn, but there was no flicker of grief in his eyes as he glanced at the coffin. He nodded once to his brother, then left the hall to head toward the kitchen.

Probably for some ale, John thought bitterly as he turned to help Muriella to her feet.

Her legs were numb from sitting for so long without moving; she swayed for a moment before her husband caught her around the waist. She blinked as the doors swung open and the sunlight—the first in weeks—assaulted her eyes unexpectedly.

"No! Leave me be!"

Muriella looked up at the sound of that voice to see a

woman hovering in the doorway. She was bent forward, her plain cloak wrapped close around her body, the hood pulled low so her face was barely visible. The men watching the door tried to block her path, but she pushed them aside. Before they could stop her, she crossed the hall until she stood in front of John and Muriella. "I came!" she cried in a voice not at all like her own. Her shoulders were hunched forward and her hands shook.

"Elizabeth!" John stood unmoving, appalled at the sight of his sister dressed as a peasant and nearly hysterical.

Muriella saw at once that Elizabeth would not be able to stand much longer. She slipped out of John's grasp to take his sister's arm, drawing the woman closer to the fire.

Elizabeth trembled, speaking brokenly. "He told me I must not come. He told me . . . I thought . . . he left me alone." She pulled the hood farther over her face and stared blankly into the flames.

Muriella drew a bench forward and pressed her sister-in-law onto it. She had moved by instinct when she saw Elizabeth's pallid face. The woman was frightened, that much was clear, even to Muriella's clouded brain.

John, who had also recognized Elizabeth's agitation, brought two goblets of wine. One he gave to his sister, who took it without looking at him. The other he handed to his wife. "Drink it," he told her.

Muriella swallowed the liquid rapidly, surprised to feel it burning down her throat, awakening her insides from their numb sleep. When she was finished, she gave the goblet to John and knelt next to Elizabeth. "Tell me," she said.

Elizabeth ran her tongue across her lips and struggled to find the words she wanted. With a sigh, she reached out to touch Muriella's shoulder. "Lachlan forbade me to come to my father's funeral," she said at last.

"What!" John exclaimed.

" 'He was my father,' I told him. 'And my enemy,' he said. I told him I must go and he . . . he . . ."

"Did he threaten ye?" John leaned toward his sister, lifting her chin with one finger. "Did he?"

"No, he simply forbade me. Then he left." She shook her

brother's hand away. "I believe he thought I wouldn't ever disobey him."

John snorted with disgust. "Aye, Elizabeth. Ye made him believe it."

She glared at him, her eyes bright with anger. "He's my husband."

Muriella put a restraining hand on John's arm. "Please," she said.

Her husband opened his mouth to object, but when he saw Muriella's expression, he decided to leave her to deal with Elizabeth. He was not in a tolerant mood just now. Without another word, he left the two women alone.

Elizabeth was glad her brother had gone. Staring at her feet, she continued in a low voice, "After he went away, I sat before the fire with my sewing. 'I must do as he bids me,' I told myself. Yet I am twenty-five years old, and no longer a young bride who cannot think on her own." She paused, stricken with sudden remorse. "I haven't ever done this to Lachlan before. My father and I haven't been close for a long time now, ye ken, and it doesn't seem right to hurt my husband for him. Mayhap I shouldn't have come."

Muriella covered Elizabeth's cold hand with her own. "Ye did the right thing."

"'Tis not right to disobey your husband," the other woman said, half to herself.

Muriella looked away. "Lachlan was wrong to try to keep ye at Duart," she insisted.

Elizabeth did not appear to be listening. "But as I sat there staring into the fire, I saw my father's face among the flames. It hovered there and I thought, He will burn. He is burning. The flames . . ." She raised her head to meet Muriella's compassionate gaze. "They hated each other, did ye know that? My father made me choose, ye see, and it had to be Lachlan. He couldn't ever accept that. After your wedding he told me my husband was an enemy to the clan and that I should leave him. He said I could live here just as I used to, that he'd protect me. I think he really believed I'd stay with him, but I couldn't do it." She looked up at Muriella, seeking her approval. "He didn't understand. Do ye know, he hasn't spoken kindly to me since then? But I *had* to choose my husband."

"Not this time," her sister-in-law said softly.

Elizabeth looked up in surprise; the thought had not occurred to her before. "No," she said. "Not this time." She held her hands palms upward, examining her fingers as if she could not decide what to do with them.

Muriella threw her arms around her sister-in-law and felt Elizabeth's shoulders tremble. "The Earl spoke of ye often," she said at last. "He loved ye very much, Elizabeth. He would have wanted ye here."

Elizabeth considered her doubtfully. "Would he really?"

"Aye, I know it. I know too that ye wouldn't have been able to forgive yourself if ye'd abandoned the Earl at the end."

The two women clung together for a moment; then Elizabeth said shakily, "I had to come, no matter what, didn't I?"

"Ye did," Muriella assured her.

"Aye." At that, Elizabeth stood, throwing her hood back from her face. She was no longer afraid to be recognized. Then for the first time she saw the bier in the center of the room. The color drained from her cheeks and she found she could not breathe properly.

Muriella slipped her arm through Elizabeth's when she realized the procession was ready to leave. "'Tis time," she whispered.

Six men stood grasping the poles on which the coffin rested, while the priest stood near the door with his brass bell in his hand. Behind him were the five who carried the Earl's armor—his helmet, gauntlets, sword, spurs and shield. Then came the man who bore the Campbell arms. Last, there was Colin, standing at the foot of the stairs with John beside him. When the new Earl tossed his cloak over his shoulder and nodded, the funeral procession began.

Muriella stood rigid, frozen next to the fire. She heard the ringing of the bell in the courtyard but suddenly she could not move. She looked away as the coffin passed. When she glanced up again, John was with her, placing her hand in the crook of his elbow. Behind him the torchbearers began to move. The hundred lights dipped and swayed as each man passed, bowing toward the new Earl. At the end of the line came the pipers.

Just before John guided her into place, Muriella saw that Elizabeth's eyes glittered unnaturally and her face was white, as she bowed her head and stepped into the morning sunlight.

The gate screamed on its hinges and croaked upward, allowing the procession to file out onto the hillside. The hundreds of Campbells who lined the road joined the entourage as it wound its way toward the church where the second Earl of Argyll would lie from this day forward.

Each man was intent on his own sorrow, and no one seemed to notice that some of those who wore the Campbell plaid had unfamiliar faces. No one was aware that these men did not look at the bier as it was carried down the hill; instead, they glanced furtively over their shoulders, seeking a single man.

That man smiled at the backs of those who preceded him. Beneath his cloak, he checked his sword again, pleased to feel the icy metal in his hand. He was near the end of the procession that coiled for nearly a mile through the September hills. The wailing of the pipes seemed to rise from the very ground, skirling around his shoulders. To him the music did not weep; it sang, it promised victory. He was swept up for a moment in the sheer jubilation of his inevitable triumph. This time he would not fail.

He kept his head lowered so no one would see his face and recognize that he did not belong here. That was why, though she passed within three feet of where he stood, Lachlan Maclean did not see his wife move along the road with Colin at her side.

The interior of the church was murky. The torchbearers stood at intervals along the walls, with one man on either side of the gaping hole in the stone where the Earl's coffin would rest. Unconsciously, Muriella clung to her husband's arm. She thought she would fall; her knees felt weak, but somehow she remained standing. As her eyes began to adjust to the gloom, she heard the tolling of the bell overhead: ponderous and grim, it intoned its own monotonous rhythm.

The six men set the coffin on the cold stone floor, then moved to the rear of the church while Muriella, John, Colin and Elizabeth knelt in a semicircle, waiting for the priest to begin. Outside, the pipes still raged through the still air. Then the priest spoke.

Elizabeth was silent while he chanted over the coffin, first in Latin, then in the Gaelic. She was silent when the men on either side of the bier snuffed their torches so the light from behind cast wavering shadows over the mourners' heads. She was silent when the women placed white roses on the lid—white roses in autumn, the sign of early death. She was silent and still while Colin knelt beside the priest, repeating the melancholy Gaelic phrases. But when the men began to lift her father's body and place it inside the hollow stone tunnel at their feet, Elizabeth lunged forward. Falling to her knees, she laid her head against the wood that separated her from the Earl. She screamed once, "Papa!" and clung to the coffin, refusing to move when the men tried to lift her away. The tears came coursing down her cheeks, gathering in a puddle on the lid above her father's feet.

Releasing her husband's arm, Muriella turned to flee.

The Campbells who were unable to squeeze into the crowded church waited outside, listening to the squeal of the pipes and the tolling of the bell. Some knelt, closing their eyes, while some remained standing, their faces wooden with grief. They did not see that their numbers had dwindled and that slowly, slowly, church and mourners alike were being closed inside a ring of strangers.

Lachlan Maclean watched his men as they crept from among the Campbells, moving back until they stood side by side, hands poised above their swords. They only waited for his signal. He smiled. Colin Campbell had thought himself clever, no doubt, sending those men to watch Duart and inform him of Maclean's actions. They were dead now, every one of them. Colin must think him a fool, Maclean thought bitterly. Aye, well, he'd learn the truth soon enough. It had occurred to him that he ought to feel guilt at playing this kind of trick on the Campbells. They were helpless, after all, unprepared for anything but grief.

Grief for the Earl of Argyll—a man who deserved only hatred and derision. He felt again the rush of desperate frustration that had shaken him at the news of the old Earl's death. He had felt cheated; the English had taken Argyll's life and Maclean had had nothing to do with it. Now he would never get his revenge against the man who had figured in his nightmares for so long. But if he could not make the Earl pay for what he had done, then his family would have to pay for him. A tiny voice inside warned him that it was not the same, but he did not listen.

Despite his doubts, Maclean had carefully planned the attack. So long as he knew Elizabeth was safe at Duart, he would feel no twinge of conscience. He still could not bring himself to hurt her, though since her father's death he found her more and more a burden. He shook his head, trying to dislodge thoughts of his wife, but as he raised his hand, ready to give the sign for which his men were watching, he heard a commotion at the door of the church. Squinting through the sunlight, he saw Muriella step outside and stand for a moment looking frantically about her. Then John pushed through the crowd. He was holding a woman who slumped beside him, her head bent.

Maclean paused with his hand in midair. There was something familiar about the woman, though her face was covered. She looked up and he moaned, choking on his own voice. By God, it was Elizabeth. He glanced at the circle of men who stood waiting. The Campbells would look up and see them in a moment; then it would be hopeless.

Elizabeth was weeping, pounding her fists against her brother's chest as the wrenching sobs tore at her throat. Damn ye! Maclean wanted to scream. Damn ye to hell! Turning away, he gave the signal for retreat.

# 23

M'lady! What is it?" Megan whispered faintly.

Muriella stood in her chamber one week after the burial, her eyes moving ceaselessly from one object to another, unable to stay still. Her hands were poised at her throat, her fingers pressing into the tender skin. She had wept no more tears since the eve of the funeral, but now, though she fought against it, the protective numbness had began at last to slip away, leaving her grief exposed to the bright, cold light of day. Her imagination created grisly portraits of the Earl, his chest a mass of wounds, his skull split down the center. Dead at Flodden Field. She had lost him. He had known the cause was hopeless, yet he had followed the King just the same. The Earl had turned his back on Muriella as surely as Lorna and Isabel had done on that long-ago day at Cawdor.

"Please," Megan cried, "tell me what ails ye."

Muriella peered at her friend's familiar face and did not know it. The red mist would not leave her; it lingered, shrouding everything with the same scarlet haze. Her mind was full of images of the past: She was kneeling in the river, staring at the crimson that covered Lorna's hand. She was standing in the wedding chamber with its deep red hangings. There was blood everywhere—her own blood gushing from her finger, Andrew Calder's blood spilled over the rock, the Earl's blood soaking into the swampy ground. She was falling. She would fall until the earth closed around her and she could fall no more.

"I can't bear it!" she moaned, covering her ears to shut out the memory of a mournfully tolling bell. She gazed around her at the gold-and-crimson bed curtains, the walls hung with tapestries shot with scarlet threads. She shuddered from head to foot, then went to the nearest hanging, ripping it from the wall. Blindly, she tore down the next and the next. When all were on the floor, she turned to the bed and began gathering the curtains in her arms.

Megan stood motionless, so frightened by the look in her mistress' eyes that she could not move. For a moment she could not find her voice. "What are ye doin'? What is it?"

Muriella laughed without mirth. The Earl had chosen to die for his King and now she was alone. The swirling red mist obsessed her. She must destroy it. Burn it. She dragged the curtains toward the fire.

Megan stood staring, her hand pressed to her mouth; then she hurried from the chamber, calling for help as she went.

At the foot of the stairs, John caught her as she started past him. "Megan?"

She gaped at him, then gasped, "Your wife! I can't stop her!"

He asked nothing more, but headed at once for Muriella's room. He had never seen Megan so shaken and it made his own heart beat with dread. When he came to his wife's chamber, he stopped abruptly on the threshold. The tapestries lay among the rushes, some of them torn down the center; the bed curtains were piled near the hearth quite close to the flames, and Muriella stood in the middle of the floor, a red gown in shreds at her feet. "Are ye mad?"

"Aye, I'm mad," she chanted. "Mad, mad, mad!" She twirled away from him, wrapping her arms about her waist, and watched him as he stepped back, unable to take his eyes from her.

Then the muscles in his face tensed as his eyes glinted gray blue. "I won't believe it," he declared.

She could hear the anger in his voice, see it in the way he leaned against a chest, crossing his arms before him. She straightened her body slowly, swinging her auburn hair over her shoulders. She was aware of the way the firelight altered her face, increasing its pale sheen. She could feel his penetrating gaze upon her.

Muriella leaned forward, her body stiff and unbending. She leaned out so far that John thought she would fall into the tapestries at her feet. But she remained upright, swaying, her green eyes flicking from the fire to his face and back again.

"What if I lifted my torch from the wall and carried it through the castle, setting all your tapestries afire, dropping the flames into the rushes? Would ye believe it then?"

"I'd most certainly beat ye senseless, but I wouldn't believe you're mad. Do ye intend to try it?" He moved toward her menacingly.

She stepped back, glowering. She had not frightened him. That was strange. Anyone else would have shrunk away from her, but there he stood, unmoved, looking at her with cold blue eyes. As he took another step forward, she drew herself upright.

The madness, he noted, had disappeared. Now he saw for the first time how pale she was, how dark were the shadows beneath her eyes. Her face was covered with a fine film of sweat, though the afternoon was chilly. And her eyes glittered with a light he had never seen there before. "Why have ye done this?" he asked, indicating the chaos on the floor between them.

"They displease me."

Her tone was cool and imperious, but this time he was not fooled. "Why?"

"The crimson." She waved her hand toward the scattered fabrics. "It sickens me." She pressed her palm to her forehead as the haze began to cloud her thoughts once more.

He could see that she was sincere. It did sicken her; her eyes were hollow and her cheeks deathly pale. "But why?" he repeated.

Muriella turned away. "It reminds me of Flodden. There was so much death, so much blood. By the end even the mud was red. Oh, God!" she cried, covering her mouth with her hands.

"But ye weren't even there!"

Whirling, Muriella cried, "Don't ye understand yet? I *was* there! I am still there. The men who died are gone and don't remember, but I can't escape the battlefield. I live the slaughter over and over, every minute of the day, and even in my dreams at night."

For a moment, John was too shocked to respond, then he made himself speak calmly. "Ye need to be busy, to keep your thoughts occupied with other things. 'Twould help ye forget."

Muriella shook her head in despair. "No," she said. "Mayhap ye can hunt and ride to get away from your grief and your anger, but I can't." She closed her eyes, but the mist grew darker, more threatening, and she opened them again. "Don't ye see? That won't work for me, because the horror is here, inside my own head." With a shaking finger, she pointed to her damp forehead. "I can't close my eyes and make it go away; the images only become clearer. I can't run, because they follow." She swallowed with difficulty, then ran her hand down the column of her throat. "And I can't bear it anymore. I can't!"

Before he could stop himself, John took a step backward, to keep her anguish from touching him. For the first time, he began to understand the shadowed world in which his wife lived, and he was appalled. He wanted to turn from her, to make himself forget the tortured look in her eyes, but as his father had pointed out, he had a responsibility to fulfill. *Muriella needs ye, whether she admits it or not.* Slowly, he forced himself to approach her. Grasping her shoulders, he shook her slightly. "Muriella!"

She leaned toward him, and in that instant there was no past, no bitterness, no fear. There was only the blinding scarlet mist that was closing more and more closely around her. "Please," she whispered.

But John did not know what his wife was asking for. He released her while he tried to think.

"M'lord?"

John turned to find Megan standing timidly in the doorway, her brown eyes full of concern. "Is she—," the servant began.

He shook his head. "I think she needs some air. Mayhap a walk in the garden?"

Megan nodded eagerly. "Aye, I'll go with her."

Muriella watched the others from the end of a long, silent tunnel. They spoke of her as if she were not there, as if she were an invalid too frail to make her own decisions. Just now she did not have the strength to tell them differently. She was so weary that her bones ached and the thought of the clear air of the garden brought with it a kind of relief. She had told John she could not escape her inner sight, but that would never stop her from trying.

"M'lady?" Megan said tentatively.

"Aye." Muriella did not look at her husband as she turned to go. She did not wish to see the same aversion on his face that she had once seen on Mary's. Quickly, lifting her gown above the scattered rushes, she left the room.

John stood where she had left him; he was not yet able to move. Running his hand through his hair, he gazed blankly at the cluttered floor.

"M'lord?"

John turned to find Duncan standing with his mouth hanging open in astonishment at the sight of the torn gown and tapestries. "What do ye want?" the older man asked sharply.

Duncan looked up. "What?" The squire's mind refused to function for several seconds; then he remembered why the new Earl had sent him here. "There's trouble brewing. The clans are rising in favor of Donald of Lachalsh. They've proclaimed him Lord of the Isles, though the title is rightfully Colin's."

John considered his squire in silence. He believed there was some question he should ask, but he didn't know what it was. "Proclaimed him Lord of the Isles?" he repeated. Then he realized what Duncan was saying. "A rebellion? Now?"

"Aye. They couldn't have chosen a worse time. We're still weak from our losses at Flodden."

"Ye can bet they know that. They move quickly, I'll give them that. What have they done?"

"Taken Urquart and the Castle of Carneburgh."

John paced the floor, kicking the fabric from under his feet. "Huntly will have to go to Urquart, but Carneburgh—we may be able to gather enough men. Do ye know who holds it now?"

"Aye, 'tis Lachlan Maclean."

John stopped his pacing. "Are ye certain?"

"'Tis certain Maclean holds Carneburgh, and he's had himself named Master of Dunskaich in Sleat as well."

"Where's Elizabeth? Is she all right?"

"We don't know, but Colin believes Maclean left her at Duart. Likely she'll be safe enough."

"She'd best be safe," John hissed, "or by God, this time I'll cut his throat. Do ye hear?"

"M'lord," Duncan said softly. "Colin awaits ye below. We must move as soon as possible."

John massaged his forehead absently. "Aye, that we must." This time his voice was calmer. As he started to follow his squire from the room, he stumbled over a tapestry and his expression clouded. Shaking his head, he closed the chamber door behind him.

When he saw Mary hurrying past, John called her to him and spoke in a low-pitched voice. As she nodded, he heard Colin calling from below and turned to start down the stairs.

Later, Muriella climbed to her chamber, pausing for a moment outside the door. She and Megan had wandered from the garden down to the loch. In the freshening afternoon breeze, the color had gradually returned to Muriella's cheeks. She had stared into the water lapping against the shore and willed the haze of fear and grief to leave her; she had fought against the pain she saw reflected in the green-gray water. With Megan's chatter to help her, she had somehow managed to keep the despair at bay. But now her stomach twisted and her hands tightened on the latch.

She didn't want to enter this room. She remembered the afternoon too clearly and did not wish to see what she had done. At last, however, she pushed the door open, then stood rigid, the breath gone from her body.

The floor was covered with fresh rushes. The shredded gown had disappeared, as had the bed curtains and tapestries. She looked up, expecting to find bare walls, but someone had replaced the old hangings with new ones. Her gaze traveled over them in disbelief. They were all worked in yellows and browns and greens. She turned to the bed, where the curtains had been replaced with gold and green ones. She swallowed with difficulty.

Too stunned to think clearly, she went to the chest that held her gowns. Lifting the lid, she saw that the kirtle for the scarlet gown was gone. She shifted the dresses one at a time, searching through layer after layer, but there was no doubt. She let the lid slip from nerveless fingers, sank onto the chest, her fingers curled like claws on the carved rosewood. She had learned to live with the pain and the emptiness and the fear in the eyes of others when they looked at her, but this single act of kindness was more than she could bear.

The walls that had kept her safe since the Earl's death came crashing down around her and she gave a strangled moan as her body folded inward upon itself. She began to weep with wrenching sobs that tore from her throat and left her shuddering. Rocking wildly, her arms locked over her chest, she sobbed at the pain that washed through her in waves. Then the waves became real ones and she was lost in an angry sea, fighting for breath while the water surged around her, drawing her deeper and deeper into the suffocating darkness, until she could no longer see the light.

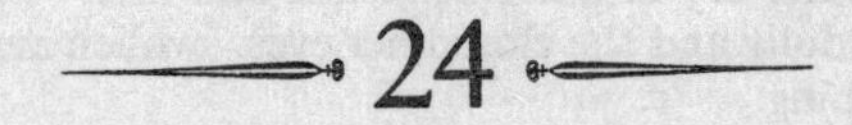

# 24

Muriella struggled upward through the shadows toward a wavering brightness that beckoned like the touch of a human hand. Slowly, as the blackness dissolved, freeing her from the web of sleep, she opened her eyes. The first thing she became aware of was the weight of a cool cloth on her forehead. She was lying on the bed with the heavy furs beneath her, but she could not remember how she'd gotten there. On the far wall burned the torch whose light had lured her out of the darkness. She focused on the gold-and-orange flame, hoping its warmth would chase the chill from her body. Her breath seemed to come and go in time with the movement of the flame, but the heat could not reach her. Turning her head, she peered into the gloomy interior of the room where she saw movement, heard a sharp intake of breath.

"She's awake. Ye'd best go now."

Megan. But there was someone else who murmured something she could not understand before slipping from the room. "Who—" Muriella began, but she could not force the words past the raw pain in her throat.

"'Twas Duncan," the servant told her, approaching the bed on silent feet. "He helped me lift ye from the floor. I couldn't do it on my own." When her mistress started to rise, Megan laid a restraining hand on her shoulder. "Lie still. Ye aren't well."

It was true. Muriella felt weak and faintly dizzy; the slightest movement of her head set the room spinning around her. Her heartbeat was uneven, but when she saw the gold-and-green curtain that swayed as the servant came closer, her pulse increased. She remembered now—the new hangings, her cry of pain, her tears, and then— Her head pounded dully and she closed her eyes, swollen and painful with weeping.

"What ails ye?" Megan asked as she adjusted the cloth on her mistress's forehead. "Ye don't seem to have a fever, but your face is so pale."

Muriella took a deep breath. "I'm not ill," she said. "'Twas only the Sight."

The servant's eyes widened. "But we found ye on the floor. Ye didn't even know we were there."

Muriella found it difficult to speak around the lump that had lodged itself in her throat, but she saw that Megan too was afraid and knew she had to calm her. "I think 'twas because the vision was too strong. It overwhelmed me so completely that I had to fall beneath its weight."

The servant did not understand, but she touched her mistress' hand in compassion, hoping Muriella would not feel how erratically her heart was fluttering. "Was it the battle again?"

"No. 'Twas something I first saw long ago. I thought I was free of it, but . . ." Her voice trailed off as the memory of her own words echoed in her head. *The Sight never lies. The vision will come to pass, just as all the others have. I can't stop it and I can't change it. All I can do is wait.* Her mouth was dry and her hands damp with sweat.

"Well," the servant murmured, "I think 'twould be best if ye closed your eyes and tried to sleep. I'll tell Sir John ye won't be down for supper." She could not quite banish the quaver from her voice. When she turned to go, Muriella put out a hand to stop her.

"I have to go down."

"Why?" the servant demanded. "Ye don't even look like ye could stand."

"Because," Muriella said, "I don't want to be trapped

here among the shadows all evening. Just now my thoughts aren't very good company, ye ken." She paused while Megan regarded her doubtfully.

"Don't worry," Muriella added. "The weakness will go soon. 'Tis always the way. I'll rest for a while, then join the others in the hall."

The servant narrowed her lips into a thin line of disapproval, but she did not argue. She had learned long ago that once Muriella had made a choice, she would not be swayed. Perhaps she should slip away and tell Sir John how she had found her mistress sprawled unconscious among the rushes. Surely he would make her stay in bed where she belonged. Muriella's grip on her arm increased and Megan leaned closer.

"Don't do it," Muriella said. "Swear to me ye won't tell him."

The servant could not look away from those strange green eyes that saw so much. With a shiver of apprehension, she whispered, "I swear."

In a brocade gown of many colors, with her braid wound tightly around her head, Muriella stood looking down into the Great Hall. She saw that John was not at the high table with Colin and it took her a moment to locate him, seated at one of the trestle tables with his men. He was using a thick slice of bread for a plate, just as they were, and seemed perfectly at home on the rough plank bench they all shared. Duncan was beside him, but Muriella could see the squire was not as comfortable as his master. The sight of John's dark, bearded face brought the fluttering wings of fear back to life within her. She wanted to turn in the other direction and make her way to the high table, but the thought of the walls of her chamber made her turn toward her husband.

As she passed, the men fell silent one after another, their knives clutched in their hands, their bearded faces lit by the yellow glare of the torches. The stillness rang in her ears, louder by far than their raucous laughter, and though she looked neither to the right nor left, she felt their wary eyes upon her. The heavy fabric of her skirt gripped tightly in her fingers, Muriella approached the table where John sat. The men around him began to shift uncomfortably.

When he realized how quiet the others had become, John looked up, smiling, and saw his wife, who had stopped at the end of the table. The laughter died on his lips. What was she doing here, waiting expectantly, destroying, with one look from her disturbing green eyes, the easy camaraderie he and the men had shared?

Beside him, Richard Campbell took his slab of meat-soaked bread and, swinging his leg over the bench, made his way to another table. His brother Andrew did the same. One by one the others followed, until only John and Duncan were left.

As Muriella came closer, John leaned forward to speak in a whisper rough with impatience. "Mayhap 'twould be better if ye sat at the high table where ye belong."

The men were watching and listening, waiting for her to turn away, but she could not do it. She could not let them see how much their apprehension hurt her. "'Tis where ye belong as well, but that doesn't seem to worry ye. So," she added, "I'll stay." Without waiting for his response, she seated herself on the bench.

John's fingers tightened around the handle of his dagger, which still held a piece of dripping mutton he had speared before he noticed Muriella. He should have ordered her to leave and been done with it, but it was too late for that. They would both look like fools if he sent her away now. "So long as ye don't linger," he said.

"I'll get her something to eat," Duncan declared, rising from his own bench with alacrity.

Muriella watched the squire go, certain he was grateful for the excuse to slip away, even for a moment. Placing her hands on the rough plank table, she traced the furrows and pits in the wood with apparent concentration.

"Well?" her husband demanded. "What's so important that it couldn't wait?"

She was no longer certain what instinct had drawn her here instead of toward the relative safety of her usual place; she only knew that she had had to come. She wondered why, when she looked up at her husband's frowning face. His brown hair was tumbled in disorder, mingling with the curling confusion of his beard, emphasizing the displeasure she read in his eyes. Muriella forced herself to meet John's gaze. "I came to say that my chamber is lovely." To her the words were an agony that he would never understand; since the Earl's death, John had twice touched feelings she had willed into darkness. Twice he had moved her and made her weep. That frightened her as even his anger had never done, as deeply as the terror that whirled within her at the vision of the rising water.

John stared at his wife in surprise. He had forgotten, in the turmoil of preparing for battle, about the scene in her room that afternoon and the instructions he had given Mary. He had wanted to forget, had welcomed the coming conflict because it kept his thoughts occupied. Even had he remembered, he would not have expected Muriella to acknowledge his gesture. For the first time he noticed that the glitter had left her eyes. Her cheeks were pale, touched slightly with pink, and her face had an uncharacteristic softness tonight. Without conscious thought, he reached out to cover her hand with his. "Ye seem better. Has the vision left ye?"

Muriella shook her head in confusion. She had thought it gone, but now it was back. As John's fingers closed around hers, the image became stronger, more vivid. Or was it something else? Her head began to swim with the image of falling shadows streaked with red and her ears to ring with the clashing of many blades. She saw the struggle, the battle, the death, but it was not the same. It was— Her heart began to pound. "You're going to war, aren't ye?"

John released her hand abruptly. "Who told ye that?" He'd given strict orders that his wife was not to be told until the last minute.

Muriella kept her eyes lowered. "I overheard it in the halls," she lied. "Is't true?"

John sighed. He should have known something like that could not be kept secret. "Aye," he told her. "We leave before first light tomorrow."

Muriella felt a rush of relief. He was going away. She would be safe. Then her throat constricted with a new kind of fear. She'd be out of danger, but he would not. "'Tis the Macleans, isn't it?" she asked unsteadily.

"They aren't the only ones, but they're involved, aye."

"And Elizabeth?"

"We don't know for certain, but we think she's at Duart, away from the center of the rebellion. If she stays there she should be all right."

When he saw that Muriella was not reassured, John squeezed her hand. "Don't worry. Maclean is a fool, but he isn't a madman. He'll see that Elizabeth is safe."

It was not really her sister-in-law Muriella was thinking of; it was John. Instinctively, she closed her fingers tighter around her husband's, asking a silent question of the Sight she had never before summoned of her own free will. For a moment, the warmth of his touch shook her; then the coldness seemed to settle over her skin and the room began to sway.

When John felt his wife squeeze his hand spasmodically, he looked down at her in confusion. She had never done that before. Then he saw the gray cast of her face and the strange darkness in her eyes.

"No!" he shouted, springing up and away from her in one swift movement. "Ye could curse a man that way, don't ye know that?"

His voice rang through the hall, and the men, who had begun to talk among themselves again, fell silent, staring from John to Muriella and back again.

Muriella's eyes cleared, the room ceased its spinning, but her heartbeat dragged and her hands trembled. John glared down at her, his face white with rage or fear, she could not decide which, and she felt inexplicably bereft. Around her the men were staring, their eyes full of silent accusations that echoed John's own. She was alone in a room full of strangers, a world full of strangers who could never understand—and did not wish to.

John heard a movement beside him and glanced up to see Duncan with Muriella's supper in his hands. The older man welcomed the interruption. Motioning for the squire to pass, he said in a voice that carried to other listening ears, "Eat. 'Twill make ye feel better."

Muriella looked away, but not before he caught a hint of the pain on her face.

"Damn!" Turning on his heel, John called, "I'm going for a ride. 'Tis far too close in here for my taste."

"But m'lord, ye'll be riding all day tomorrow," Duncan protested.

John glowered at the squire. "Since when are ye my nursemaid? 'Tis a ride I want and a ride I'll have." Carelessly, he kicked his bench aside and strode across the hall.

When he had gone, Duncan set the platter before Muriella, then sat nearby.

"Ye saw?" she asked, her gazed fixed on the plate of mutton.

"Aye." The squire frowned. "He doesn't mean to be cruel, ye ken."

"No," she said tonelessly.

"'Tis just that a warrior's skill and confidence are all he has to keep him safe. If ye make him doubt those things, if the thought of your premonition makes him hesitate, even for an instant, it could cost him his life and those of his men."

"Aye," Muriella murmured as she toyed with a thick piece of bread. "I suppose you're right." But the knowledge did not ease the ache inside her.

The squire watched her anxiously. He could not forget how lost she had looked this afternoon, lying in the rushes, her face swollen and red from weeping. He had felt as helpless then as he had on her wedding night when he'd watched her tear herself away from the magic of the Gypsy bonfires. He wanted to console her, but knew that there was nothing he could do. No matter how much he might wish to, he could not change the fact that tomorrow, before the sun had risen, the Campbell men would take their broadswords in hand and ride determinedly, even eagerly, into battle.

# 25

In her dream, Muriella wandered through the lower tunnels of the castle where the torches filled the rough stone passageways with an unnatural light. The sound of her footfalls on the packed dirt floor did not disturb the stillness, but seemed instead to meld with the flickering shadows that closed around her.

She paused, listening, when a low moan of fear escaped from the chamber at the end of the hall. Suddenly it was very cold and the torches were painting grotesque patterns on the gray stone all around. She did not want to move forward—in a few steps she would be able to look into the chamber—yet her feet seemed to have a will of their own that carried her closer and closer to the half-open door. Instinctively, she hung back in the shadows, then leaned forward so she could look without being seen.

John was kneeling in the chamber with a dark shape at his feet. It looked like a body, but she couldn't be certain; the shadows were too deep. Then the wind stirred the branches of the tree outside the window and daylight crept between the fluttering leaves. The light played across John where he knelt beside the figure. Laughing, his teeth glittering, he raised his hands above his head. The sound of his laughter chilled Muriella. Then the light struck him fully. His wife screamed, but no sound escaped her. His arms were covered with blood to the elbow. It dripped slowly between his fingers, staining with vivid red the motionless figure at his feet.

Muriella awoke with a start. She lay for a long time, waiting for the frantic beating of her heart to ease and the cold fear to dissipate. As the ceiling of shadows shifted and changed in the firelight, she forced her eyes to focus on the muted patterns above her. She would not let the panic overcome her, she swore silently. Not this time.

It was not so strange that her husband should have blood on his hands; the Campbells were at war, after all. The dream was not a warning, only a nightmare that lingered when the sound of John's laughter and the image of his blood-soaked hands had faded away.

Muriella lay still, willing herself to believe it, until eventually her heartbeat slowed to normal and the heat of her body destroyed the chill the dream had left behind. She fell back asleep while the ghosts of forgotten shadows whispered above her.

The leaves parted in the breeze, fluttered, then came back together with a sigh while their shadows moved over the damp ground beneath. John tensed, reached for his bow and fitted an arrow into place. He did not trust the sudden stillness, broken only by the murmur of the leaves. Eyes narrowed, he leaned forward, his hand on his horse's neck to keep the animal from moving. The men who followed faded into a blur; for him there was only the feel of his bow in his callused palm, the reality of the trees ahead and the awareness of an enemy concealed by the shifting gloom.

A twig snapped. His eyes glinted with anticipation as he raised his head like a wolf scenting its prey. Knees pressed tight to his horse's sides, he drew back the string of his bow, sighted down the shaft of the arrow, released it with a shout of triumph. He knew, even before the man crashed headfirst through the underbrush, that he had hit his target. The pounding of his heart told him he could not have done otherwise.

John swung his leg over the saddle and jumped to the

ground, heading for the man who lay unmoving in the bracken. Richard Campbell was there before him.

"Is it Hugh Rose?" John called.

"No," Richard told him. "'Tis black hair he's havin' and he's too old by half, but he's a Rose, just the same."

John bent to examine the dead man. "Well then, Hugh must be nearby." Frowning at the impenetrable tangle of the forest, he glared through the trees as if determination alone could make them give up their secrets. Turning back to Richard, he added, "This time I mean to catch him."

Richard shook his head. "He's kept ahead of ye for near a week. What makes ye think ye'll find him now?"

"My instincts. He's within our grasp. I can feel it."

"I don't understand why you're so determined to bring him down. You've already scattered most of the rebels, and Hugh's no more than a petty outlaw who can't hurt the Campbells now."

John leaned down to cover the dead man's face with a dry corner of his plaid. What Richard said was true. The rebels had given up the fight a week ago and Colin was on his way to Edinburgh to settle the terms of surrender with the regents. The new Earl had made his peace with the vanquished rebels, but John had not. He had far more at stake, this time, than did his brother. "Hugh Rose is more dangerous than ye realize," he said as the two men started back toward their restive horses. "The people fear him when they hear the tales of the money he's stolen and the murder he's done; but they also admire him for the fearless devil he is. If we don't stop him soon, they'll make him a hero, and then we won't be able to touch him. Besides, there are other reasons. I can't let him go on this way. Ye must know that."

Richard did know it. He had heard the rumors the young Rose was spreading and realized that, sooner or later, Sir John would have to stop the man's tongue. He only wished it did not have to be now, when the men were already so tired. "Aye, but the chase might last forever at this rate, and the men are eager to go home."

"Soon," John promised. "But for now, the hunt goes on."

Bracken and pine needles muffled the footfalls of the

horses as he led the weary men through the forest of hawthorns, oaks and pines, his senses alert for the slightest irregularity. Just when he'd begun to think that night would fall while the forest still sheltered the outlaw in its murky depths, he saw a trampled patch of bracken where several horses had passed recently. His exhaustion left him in an instant when he scented the danger that vibrated through the cool air around him. Raising a hand to warn the men to silence, he swung himself down from his horse and crept forward on foot.

The last of the light filtered through the trees, revealing the group of men sprawled on the ground in the tiny clearing. They were talking among themselves and sharing a skin full of wine, their plaids tossed carelessly over their shoulders, their bows forgotten at their sides. The leaves whispered, brushing John's cheek in the gust of a breeze as he peered through the changing patterns of green and gray to locate the man who must be Hugh Rose. Even in the fading light, he could see the blaze of wild red hair that, along with the outlaw's fierce war cry and his uncontrolled lust for the kill, had earned him the nickname The Devil Afire.

Hugh was laughing as he leaned back on his elbow, his hazel eyes blurred with the effects of the wine. John took in the scene in disbelief. These men knew the Campbells were close behind them—they had led their enemies in a game of cat and mouse for many days—yet now they seemed oblivious of any danger. The sound of Hugh's laughter came to John on the back of the wind, full of self-confidence and the supreme arrogance of the fearless. Clearly the thought of death held no terror for the outlaw. That made him a dangerous adversary indeed. With a wordless curse, John turned away to return to where the men waited.

Motioning silently for Richard, Andrew, Duncan and Adam to follow, he took his bow from the saddlehorn and moved back through the soft bracken toward the clearing. The men understood his intention without words. They circled behind the concealing trees, moving inexorably forward until only the descending darkness and moving leaves held them apart from their enemies. Each Campbell drew his sword, positioning himself near one of the outlaws; then, at John's signal, they screamed the Campbell war cry, "Cruachan!" and rushed from the protection of the trees.

The men in the clearing did not have time to take a breath before they found themselves lying in the grass with the Campbell blades pressing into their throats.

John knocked the wineskin from Hugh Rose's hand, forcing the young man to his back in the same moment. His blood was singing with the scent of victory; it had been so easy, after all. Then Hugh smiled crookedly.

"Ye must be John Campbell," the outlaw observed in a voice laced with secret amusement. "No doubt ye finally got tired of the game." His eyes glinted bright and clear, with no trace of drunkenness to dim them. "Or mayhap ye realized that the only way to best us is to creep up in the darkness and strike before we have a chance to defend ourselves. That seems to be how the Campbells win most of their victories." He could feel the anger radiating from John's body and he smiled again. "Only, when ye took Muriella Calder that way, ye didn't get such a good bargain, did ye?"

The rage that had been building inside John for the past week fed upon itself, growing more powerful with each ragged breath. He pressed the point of his blade deeper into the outlaw's chest until he heard the slight explosion of breath that told him he had broken through Hugh's plaid and doublet to the vulnerable skin underneath. For a moment, his fury blinded him, but something kept him from ramming his sword home. Was it the watching eyes of the men—his own and Hugh's—or the sudden memory of his father's voice? *Think before ye act, Johnnie. Think!*

"Well?" Hugh cried, unnerved by his captor's restraint as he had not been by the sight of the gleaming blade. "What are ye waitin' for? Don't tell me you're a coward as well as a thief!"

John's hand trembled with the force of his anger, but still he did not move. His father's words came back to him like a warning. *There's no room for foolish emotion in a man meant to lead the Clan Campbell. It weakens your judgment when ye need it most.* John fought against his fury with the tiny whisper of reason that still remained in the back of his mind. "I'm not the one who steals from the crofters and lairds alike, burning his way across the north and killing any man who gets in his way," he said at last.

Hugh curled his lip in disdain. "What else would ye have me do? When ye took Muriella from me, ye took Cawdor too, leaving me and the whole Clan Rose with nothing but my sword arm to keep us alive."

"There are other ways to survive, and well ye know it."

"For a Campbell mayhap, who has the King and the Earl of Argyll on his side," the outlaw snapped, "but no' for a Rose without money or power." Despite the pressure of John's blade against his chest, Hugh rose on one elbow. "I won't sit quietly in my crumbling keep watching my family slip away one by one. I may not have the King's ear, but I promise ye this: I'll make such a noise in these glens that the Campbells won't forget the sound of my voice for a long, long time to come. Even though ye kill me now."

*There are ways to get what ye want without killing,* the Earl had told John once. Maybe his father was right. Death was too good for Hugh Rose; it would transform the reckless outlaw into legend for the Highlanders to worship, and John did not want that. "No," he said softly. "I think I'll let ye live." He was aware that Hugh's mocking smile had faded and that his eyes were dark with something that might have been fear. He could feel the curiosity of the other outlaws like a cold hand at the back of his neck. "But I'm telling ye, ye'd best stop your killing and stealing or I'll make ye regret it." Hugh was staring up at him now, jaw clenched and nostrils flared. "And just so ye see that I mean what I say, I'll leave behind a little warning."

The young man winced as John raised his weapon to bring it down with devastating accuracy along Hugh's sword arm, cutting deep and to the bone. The blood poured out, clear and red, staining the saffron shirt, dark doublet and bright plaid that lay crumpled on the ground. John heard the gasp of disbelief from the other outlaws; they did not fear death, but this was humiliation. He also saw the hatred in Hugh's eyes beneath the glaze of pain, but that he chose to ignore. "Take their weapons and leave them," he ordered his men. Then, slowly and quite deliberately, John turned his back on Hugh Rose.

# 26

Muriella leaned forward, pleased that some of her hair had begun to escape from her crown of braids to whip about her face. The smell of the sea was heavy in the air as her horse carried her closer and closer to the silver blue waves whose rhythmic crashing called to her. The moisture clung to her cheeks, cool and invigorating, completely unlike the musty chill inside the walls of the keep. She knew Megan was close behind her, but the sound of the other animal's hoofbeats was lost in the enchanting rush and thunder of the sea. Throwing back her head in pure enjoyment, she urged her horse to greater speed.

As the thrumming of hoofbeats grew louder, Muriella pressed her knees into her animal's sides until he flew over the sand, outdistancing Megan's horse with ease. But no, Muriella could hear the other animal gaining on her after all. She smiled. If the servant wanted a race, a race she would have. Muriella's heart pounded in time with the motion of the horse beneath her, and the wind threw her breath back into her face. She was mesmerized by the speed and the breeze and the hypnotic voice of the sea.

As she approached the cliff that jutted into the water, she realized that the other horse had come up beside her. Then a hand reached out to grasp her reins and she looked up in astonishment at John's sun-browned face. All at once, she found it difficult to breathe. She had not seen her husband in three months. For an instant, the sight of his blue eyes and wildly curling beard caused an ache in her chest and she could not seem to find her voice. "Where—when did ye get back?" she asked at last. Without being aware of it, she smiled.

John caught his breath and leaned toward her, drawn by the momentary warmth of that smile. "Just now. I haven't yet been inside the keep." He and his men had been riding for many hours, exhausted by their efforts against the rebels and the long trip back to Inveraray. He'd been looking forward to settling himself in front of the fire in the Great Hall with a tankard of ale in his hand. But when he saw his wife riding recklessly along the shore, some instinct he could not explain had made him follow. "Tell me what you're running from," he said.

Muriella shook her head. The two horses circled, heading back the way they had come, and she saw Megan waiting farther down the beach. "Not from—to. The sea brought me here." Brushing a damp strand of hair from her forehead, she turned toward the iced blue waves that turned to furious white as they exploded on the sand. "Can't ye hear it calling?" She closed her eyes, conscious that John's callused hand still clasped the reins so that his fingers curled next to hers. "Listen," she murmured softly. "'Come,' they say, 'now. Come to me now.'"

John considered his wife in silence, surprised by her carefree manner and whimsical expression. While he was away, he had remembered only the blank, shuttered look he had come to dread. That disturbing memory was one of the things that had driven him on, made him hesitate to return to Inveraray, long after his allies had turned for home.

But now Muriella's eyes were clear and sparkling, her cheeks rosy from the touch of the wind, her lips curved in a secret smile. She swayed gently, echoing the undulation of the lapping waves.

John sat upright, startled by the frisian of pleasure that shook him. He was glad to be home, surrounded by the familiar safety of the keep where he had grown up, glad to be riding along the beach with Muriella beside him. There was something about the ineffable simplicity of her pleasure which drew him as strongly as her fear held him away. "Muriella," he murmured.

She opened her eyes, at ease with the sight of his darkly bearded face, and surprised that she should feel such calm. "Are ye back to stay?"

"Aye, the rebels have been subdued at last."

Muriella felt a flicker of apprehension. She leaned toward John, her knees pressed tight against her horse's sides. "What of Maclean?"

"He fled to Duart when he saw he couldn't win," John declared in disgust. "No doubt he's still hiding there, hoping we'll forget." He released his wife's horse and touched the battered hilt of his sword. "But we won't forget. He'll learn that in time."

Muriella thought of Elizabeth and her heart sank. "Will ye attack Mull, then?"

"No." John's jaw tightened while he glared at the wind-whipped sand as if he regretted the fact. "'Tis over—for now. We've won this time, and we lost only twenty men."

"Only twenty," his wife repeated hollowly.

"War always means death for some," John said. "'Tis the way it must be. Ye'd best learn to accept that as the men have. They aren't afraid, so long as they die with honor."

"No," Muriella mused, "but then, they aren't the ones left behind." She thought of the last three lonely months, of the long, dim corridors of the keep, emptier by far without the voices of the men to fill them. While the warriors were away, the women had been subdued, going about their chores ploddingly and without laughter. Often, seeking companionship, they had huddled together in the solar to sew and weave the yawning days away. Only the colors and patterns beneath their hands grew and changed; all else remained the same—hushed and expectant, waiting for the men to return. *If* they returned.

Muriella pushed the thought to the back of her mind. The waiting was over; the men were home. Yet, inexplicably, the loneliness lingered. And somehow, the sight of John's face, softened by his disheveled hair and framed by the drifting clouds all around, only made the ache deeper.

Later that evening Megan and Muriella joined the women grouped around the fire, listening while the men told stories of their adventures in the north of Scotland. The warriors did not seem at all dangerous now, perched as they were on benches or the floor, their tankards beside them, the firelight softening their rough-hewn faces. The keep rang once again with the triumphant laughter of men and women alike, so that the huge, vaulted room seemed a little warmer and the stone walls a little less forbidding.

"Besides," Andrew Campbell was saying, "once we saw the back of the Macleans, we didn't get another glimpse of their faces. Turned tail like a pack of crazed hounds, they did."

"What did ye do then?" Jenny asked.

"Well"—Andrew rubbed his chin thoughtfully—"we went to Urquart for a day or two. Sir John wanted to see for himself that all was quiet there."

Jenny sighed with disappointment. "Wasn't there anything more excitin' to keep ye busy?"

Andrew beamed at her. It was just the question he had been hoping for. "We did search the north for rebels who weren't wise enough to go home, and caught some, too. Sir John seems to smell 'em out, even when *we're* certain there're no more to be found." He leaned forward so his bright red hair fell into his eyes. He pushed it back impatiently. "But 'twas no' long before we saw that he was really lookin' for one man." Pausing dramatically, he took a large drink of ale and wiped his lips with the back of his hand.

"Don't play with us, Andrew. Who was it?"

Andrew grinned, whispering loudly enough for everyone to hear, "The outlaw, Hugh Rose."

At the sound of that familiar name, Muriella straightened. Surely she had misunderstood. Hugh—an outlaw? Hugh, who had been her only childhood friend? She realized with a stab of dismay that she had not even thought of him for many months. She turned, suddenly intent, as Jenny spoke again.

"Ye mean the one they call The Devil Afire?" she asked, barely able to contain her excitement.

"The very same."

"I hear he's gey handsome," the servant Mary observed from the corner where she crouched near the fire.

Frowning, Andrew shook his head. "I wouldn't be knowin' about that. But I know the man's been makin' trouble with the Calders for a long time and he couldn't seem to decide who his friends were in this war. One day he and his men would attack a band of Campbells and the next he'd swoop down on the Macleans. It didn't seem to matter to him."

"Andrew!" his brother Richard said warningly, "didn't ye ever learn when to shut your mouth before it gets ye in trouble?" He glanced in Muriella's direction.

"Don't be such a worrier, lad. Can't ye see the ladies're hangin' on every word?"

"Aye," Jenny said. "We want to hear more. Though I'll wager ye didn't catch *that* Devil. I hear he can vanish into the air with a wave of his hand."

"But that's where you're wrong. Sir John tracked him for near a week before he trapped Rose and his men in a wee clearin'. He surrounded the place and, with only four men, he had the outlaws cryin' for mercy. So what do ye think about that?"

"I think ye should learn when to hold your tongue."

John spoke from outside the circle of men and women, his voice rough with anger. Muriella looked up to find her husband regarding Andrew with displeasure. He must have arrived near the end of the story; he had certainly not been there before.

"But m'lord," Andrew objected, "ye didn't say—"

"I expected ye to use your wits, man. But no matter. 'Tis done now. Only remember in the future, what ye do under my command is my business and no one else's."

Muriella was hardly aware of Andrew's grumbling as she watched the light play over her husband's face. Had he really made Hugh cry for mercy? She could not imagine such a thing. At the moment, all she could remember was Hugh's shock of bright hair and his warm, comforting laughter. A feeling of dread settled like a weight in her chest and, with sudden resolution, she rose to follow her husband when he turned away.

John started up the stairs, trying without success to still his unreasonable fury. He paused with his hand on the balustrade when he realized someone was coming. Turning, he found his wife looking up at him. "Aye?" he said, more brusquely than he intended.

"I want to know what happened in that clearing. I want to know if Hugh—if my cousin is dead." Her green eyes were tinged with gray, her cheeks pale in the flickering light of the torches.

Damn Andrew Campbell! John had hoped to prolong the fragile sense of peace he had shared with his wife on the beach earlier. But he guessed from the shadows in her eyes that the momentary calm had fled. God, how he wished there was nothing to tell her, that he could laugh off Andrew's story and make Muriella smile again. But he would not lie.

John drew a deep breath and said carefully, "Hugh Rose lives."

"But Andrew said—"

"I've told ye Hugh Rose is alive," her husband interrupted, "and 'tis the truth."

His lids were half-lowered so she could not see the expression in his eyes, but she noticed how his fingers tightened on the worn oak balustrade. It might be the truth, but it was not everything. Twining her fingers together within in the heavy damask folds of her gown, she murmured, "Andrew called him an outlaw. Why? What has he done that ye should hunt him down that way?"

John ran his hand through his hair again and again, searching for the words to answer her. The moment when she had faced him across a room full of torn, red tapestries, he'd caught his first glimpse of the horror she lived with day and night. He had been stunned at the revelation. If Hugh's violent deeds were not already inside her head among the other visions of blood and death, then John would not be the one to put them there. "It doesn't matter what he's done. I warned him, ye see, and no doubt he'll change his ways soon enough. Ye needn't concern yourself with such things."

"But—"

"No," he said, cutting her off with a wave of his hand. He would not let her push him to anger this time, for her sake as well as his own. "We won't discuss it further." Before she could object, he turned on his heel and left her standing alone at the foot of the wide stone stairs.

# 27

Muriella had been wandering through the keep for a long time. She felt unsettled and could not stay still; she had not been able to rest since her husband had turned away from her last evening. She could not escape the memory of Hugh's laughter, cut off again and again by a careless wave of John's hand. Her head echoed with the sound until she thought she would go mad.

Without quite knowing how she had gotten there, she found herself in the lower passageways. As she felt the damp mustiness of the abandoned corridors close around her, she became aware of an uneasy tension that urged her on. Peering through the dimness, she listened to the hollow thud of the packed dirt floor as she moved down unfamiliar tunnels, lit by a few torches set in the walls at random intervals. Muriella felt the shadows move around her; her hands grew clammy and her stomach tight. The walls fell back and back and she was closed tighter and tighter into her purpose, though she did not know what that was.

As she approached the end of the corridor, she heard a sigh that penetrated the stillness like a flare of light. Stopping with her back to the wall, she crept up to a door that hung half-open. Carefully, she leaned forward to look inside the tiny chamber. Then she sucked in her breath so she would not gasp and betray her presence.

John crouched before the window, naked, with a woman at his feet. His form loomed tall and dark, framed by the speckled light that filtered through the leaves outside the window. In her astonishment, Muriella studied his body, from his broad shoulders to his chest to his muscled thighs. She wanted to look away but could not; she was mesmerized by the hungry glitter in his eyes. It reminded her too vividly of the way he had looked the last time he came to her bed, when, for an instant, he had let fall the cloak that usually hid his desire from view. His face was shaded so his hair and beard blended with the shadows; only his eyes were clear and bright. But it was enough. In those eyes he had bared his passion—like his body—for Muriella to see.

The woman lay gazing up at him, the light playing softly along her breasts and face. Muriella recognized the servant, Mary. Her black hair half covered her body to her knees and spilled over onto the floor beside her. John's shadow touched her skin, holding back the light from her thighs and stomach. Muriella sensed the tension in Mary from her ragged breathing, though she lay absolutely still. She was waiting.

As Muriella watched, John laughed and his eyes glistened. Then he leaned down and, gathering the woman's hair in his hands, raised his arms before him. Her hair fell over his arms to the elbow to slip between his fingers, settling like falling feathers on Mary's skin.

Muriella shivered. She had seen it before, but could not remember when. She shrank back farther into the shadows as her husband leaned down to nibble at Mary's earlobe, then swung his leg over to cover her trembling body with his own. The servant moaned, fastening her arms about his neck, and pulled him to her. Their legs intertwined and their lips met and clung, fierce and demanding.

Muriella felt the coldness of the stone penetrate her skin in waves that left her shivering. Shock had forced the breath from her body and she had to struggle to get air. She should not have been surprised; she had suspected that her husband, like Colin, used other women to fulfill his physical needs. She had even been grateful. It had allowed her to forget what she did not wish to remember. But now the knowledge of the desire that drove John was with her again, so near that she could feel the heat rising from the two bodies, and she had to get away.

She ran, finding her way blindly through the curving passageways. Gasping for air, she left the castle behind, seeking the refuge of the forest. The patterns of the leaves fell on her face; they brought to her again a sense of the moving light on Mary's body. Muriella tried to clear her mind, to soak in the green and gray of the trees and bushes until the colors obliterated the image of the little room with the speckled image of muted light.

The sound of the rushing river intruded on her visions, urging her to follow the soothing rumble to the shore of the loch. Here the bushes were heavy with moisture and she lost herself in their leafy protection. At the edge of the water, where the trees held back the light, Muriella breathed in the fragrant darkness. Kneeling among the wild grasses, she leaned out over the loch. Its movement calmed her, seemed to run through her head, flooding away all traces of violence. She swallowed the sound of the lapping water and felt it slide down her throat to dampen her parched insides.

Then she saw, captured on the undulating surface, the image of John's body merging with Mary's. She would not think of that, she told herself. She would not remember the pain of seeing her husband's hands on that woman's skin. She would not think of the rippling of his muscles, which had seemed to absorb the light all around him. She would not—dared not—recall the feeling of despair that had spiraled through her body at the sight of two people filling that tiny chamber with their hunger and their need.

Sitting up abruptly, Muriella saw that her hair had fallen over her shoulder and into the loch. She watched it float, spreading gracefully over the clear, rippled surface. Leaning forward, she shook out the auburn waves and fed them into the water. As they danced among the stones, she began to breathe in rhythm with the current. Closing her eyes, she bent down until her cheek brushed the fusion of liquid hair beneath her.

"Kelpie."

The voice intruded, breaking the fragile mood of the moment.

Muriella felt someone behind her. Gingerly, she turned her head.

"You're a Kelpie who's come from the water."

As she looked up, Duncan knelt beside her. A few minutes ago he had seen her running from the castle. A single glimpse of her face had told him how distressed she was. He had not planned to follow her, but the memory of her haunted eyes had drawn him here against his will. He had stopped when he saw how she swayed toward the loch as if communicating with the spirits that dwelled there. The woven web of her hair across the water had hypnotized him, catching him up in a spell he could not resist. Unable to stop himself, he bent down. Gathering her hair in his hands, he buried his face in the dripping tendrils.

She sprang up and away from him. "Go!" her voice rose shrilly. "Don't!"

"Muriella." When Duncan's brown eyes met and held hers, she felt that he was looking beyond her to the little room with the light across two bodies. She stepped backward.

"Forgive me," he murmured. "I shouldn't have done that." Staring at Muriella's closed and wary expression, he wanted to reassure her, to tell her he had only come to see that she was all right, but he sensed that she would not hear him. Yet he had seen enough to know that the loch could hold her, soothe her as he had not succeeded in doing. He sat in the grass where she had been a moment before and whispered, "Listen to the stillness."

Muriella stood where she was, uncertain. Sensing her reluctance, the squire turned away to look into the water. "Don't go. I won't disturb ye."

She wanted to believe him. His presence was somehow reassuring. Without another word, she sat on the bank, the wild grasses brushing her legs. The two were silent, letting the water enchant them. After a while, Duncan felt some of the tension flow out of her and knew that her agitation had begun to pass.

Muriella studied the squire thoughtfully as he shook the shoulder-length blond hair away from his face and moved his thin, lanky body to a more comfortable position. Duncan looked frail, she thought, compared to her husband's large stature, almost as if he did not belong in the same world with John. Just as she did not. She trailed her fingers in the water, welcoming the chill.

Slowly, so gradually that neither was really aware of it, they moved closer until their hands met. Duncan twined his fingers with hers, willing his own warmth into her cold skin. Overhead the clouds grew dark and threatening and the wind rose, stirring the loch into whitecapped silver waves. The leaden sky seemed to sink lower and lower, until the clouds, heavy with moisture, rested on the choppy surface of the water. When Muriella shivered, Duncan rose reluctantly. "We'd best get back before the storm breaks."

She nodded but did not move at once. "I'll come soon. Ye go ahead."

She looked up, her eyes reflecting the turbulence of the gray green loch, and the squire knew it would do no good to argue. "'Til later then," he murmured.

"Aye," she answered softly, before she turned back to the loch whose fierce beauty made her tremble with fear and admiration. She rose to her feet, drawn toward the image of a lovely face surrounded by tendrils of blond hair that curled and leapt with the movement of the water—the woman of the loch, who had once ruled this valley, whose lament for her lost happiness rose, high and piercing, from the heart of the storm.

When the rain broke through the leaves overhead, Muriella tore herself away from the hypnotic call of Loch Awe. She had brought no cloak and was reluctant to leave the shelter of the trees, but knew she had to get back. She turned toward the castle as the rain began to fall more heavily. She hurried her step, noticing as she went the brilliant green of the dripping trees and bushes all around her.

Finally she arrived at the courtyard and slipped beneath the creaking gate. There was no one about, so she lost no time in reaching the gaping doorway that opened onto the Great Hall.

She saw that the men sat around the tables engaged in noisy conversation. They had turned their backs on the huge double doors and slitted windows high in the walls, hoping to shut out thoughts of the chilling rain. Torches burned on every wall, attempting to push the darkness away. The men, who had discarded their doublets and cloaks, sat in their shirts and trews, drinking ale and shaking the stray drops from their beards. Their rumbling laughter rose, dissipating as it approached the vaulted ceiling.

Watching as they attacked the bread and meat on the platters before them, Muriella was suddenly aware of her drenched hair and clothing. The green world fled behind her, and she jumped when someone slammed the door and barred it at her back. She wished now that she had gone to the entrance on the other side of the castle and found the way to her room in solitude.

Unexpectedly, John loomed above her, scrutinizing the wet clothing that clung to her arms and legs, leaving puddles in the hollowed stones of the floor.

"You've been caught in the rain," he observed. "Mayhap ye should go and change. Ye'll catch the ague in this drafty room."

As she looked up at him, her stomach wrenched. "I sought the big fire," she said, turning toward the stone fireplace that swallowed up one wall of the room. John followed her—she could feel him at her back—and she wished that she had stayed in the rain. The heat of the crowded room oppressed her; she felt more of a chill in the uncomfortable curiosity of the men than in the storm outside. When she paused at last, John stopped beside her. What was he waiting for? she wondered. She was afraid he might touch her and then she would scream.

Platters and tankards were suddenly still. She could hear the dogs digging for scraps in the rushes beneath the tables. One by one, the men had abandoned their supper to stare at Muriella's long, dripping hair. Auburn in the sunlight, it now hung limp and dark to her knees. Near her face, where a few short hairs had begun to dry, the curls strayed across her forehead and fell along her cheeks.

The men began to shuffle their feet under the tables. The mutton sat cooling before them, but they continued to watch Muriella. The flames framed her body in brilliance; they could not pull themselves away from the sight.

When she looked up at John, a vision of him and Mary, very bright, flashed through her mind. She stared at his bearded face, her eyes pale gray.

John froze. Muriella was lovely and frightening, dripping, dark and flushed, and her eyes were full of some emotion he could not fathom. His wife bent toward the fire, rubbing her hands together near the flames. Her hair fell down her back in twisted tendrils that dripped rhythmically against the rushes.

Someone whispered, "Witch—she's come from the water."

No one moved. She held them all in a chimerical web; they worshiped her and wished her gone. Some of them remembered the sight of her four years ago by the terrible campfire, with her bloodied gown and flickering eyes. They believed, in that moment, that she was not human.

Leaning close, John touched her shoulder. He held his breath, letting his fingers stray against her hair while he searched her face. He felt an uncomfortable tightening in his chest and found it difficult to breathe. All at once he became aware of the hush that had fallen over the hall. It was as if his wife had crushed the everyday sounds beneath her feet, replacing them with a thin shroud of silence. It was too quiet.

"I shall starve," he bellowed, "if I don't eat soon!"

As his voice rang through the room, the men looked away from Muriella and back to their meal. Someone belched and laughter followed. A tankard clattered on the table, then another and another. Satisfied, John turned back to his wife. She stood unmoving while the firelight enwrapped her, wavering within her eyes. Mesmerized by her gaze, he reached out to wrap his hand in her hair. The strands were cold and wet against his palm. He turned his hand upward, letting the hair spread over his callused skin.

The water dripped from the strands, slipping between his fingers, tinged golden, then orange, then red with the reflection of the firelight. Almost like blood, Muriella thought. Then her body grew rigid. In that instant, the dream came back to her, so vivid that the colors swam before her eyes—John's laughter, the shifting sunlight, the blood that had run down his arms to the elbow. Only it had not boon blood. She remembered Mary lying at her husband's feet, the way her hair had settled onto her body, falling through John's fingers with a whisper of longing. Suddenly the fear was with her again, clutching at her throat. Obsessed by the sun-striped room where Mary waited, Muriella seized her husband's free hand.

"Let me go!" she shrieked, though it was she who held him now.

John released her. "Muriella," he said sharply with a sidelong warning glance at the men.

Under his warning gaze, Muriella's fear gave way to anger. "Would ye have me be silent? Do ye think ye can command me so easily? Don't ye know it doesn't take words to curse ye? I can do it with my eyes alone. Look at me!" she cried. "Look at me while ye fall—ye and your women and all your men with ye!"

A hush fell over the hall as her words echoed against the stone, then faded into silence. This time she had gone too far. In the suffocating stillness left behind, John raised his hand and struck his wife full across the face. He acted without thinking, from a deeply engrained instinct for self-preservation that had taken root in him at birth.

Muriella's knees threatened to give way beneath her. Her head rang with the force of the blow while the pain burned over her cheek, freeing her from the madness that had overwhelmed her for a moment.

"Go," John said with dangerous calm.

The rage hovered, glittering, in his eyes, daring her to defy him. She did not speak again, but turned, hands clenched in the folds of her skirt, and crossed the endless hall while a hundred watching eyes bored into her. She stared at the rush-strewn floor beneath her feet, knowing that if she once looked up to meet those gleaming eyes, she would not find compassion or even pity in their depths, but only a grim and chilly triumph.

# 28

Elizabeth Campbell Maclean listened as the last sounds of the night crept through Duart Castle. Pulling the furs over her lap, she settled against the headboard. She was waiting. She sensed that her husband would come to her soon, although he had not done so for a long time.

She believed Lachlan needed her tonight. For the past month she had watched as he paced before the fire in the library, trying to pretend he was not waiting for Evan to return from Edinburgh. But Elizabeth had known. She knew, although he had not told her so, that her husband's nephew had gone to treat with the new regents to settle the terms of the peace between rebels and crown. Once again the Macleans had fought a losing battle to restore the Lordship of the Isles to their own, and once again they were suing for peace.

It had been a hopeless cause from the beginning; even Elizabeth had known that. She also knew that her husband had insisted upon sending a list of demands to Huntly, Angus and Arran, the Queen Mother's new advisors. The Macleans were the vanquished in this rebellion, yet at Lachlan's instigation, they were demanding reparation from the crown.

Elizabeth reached for the wine on the chest beside the bed. She swallowed slowly, feeling the liquid slide down her throat. She hoped it would still the rapid beating of her heart. Evan had come back today. Lachlan and his nephew had disappeared into the library while Elizabeth waited in the hall. Neither had noticed her; it would have made no difference if they had. What they had to discuss was meant only for the ears of men.

Inside the library, Maclean had faced his nephew warily, waiting with ill-concealed impatience for Evan to speak. "Well, what's the news, man? What said Huntly to my demands?"

Evan was silent for several moments. He had been dreading this interview since the day he left Edinburgh. No, it had been long before that, on the day he left Duart with Maclean's preposterous list in his pocket. "What do ye think he said? He laughed and threw them in the fire."

"What? Did he dare? He won't laugh again, I'll tell ye that," Maclean grunted.

"Uncle, ye must stop pretending now. 'Tis over. There's naught we can do. With the others, Arran and Huntly were generous. But from the Macleans they required submission without condition."

"Are they mad?" Maclean stalked up and down, trying to control his rage. "Did ye kill them where they stood?"

Evan shook his head. "No. Nor did I want to. Don't ye see that we've lost everything? With Argyll hovering at our backs, we're helpless. Ye'll have to admit it sometime."

"No!" His uncle stood perfectly still in the center of the room. "I won't admit that ever, do ye hear? How could ye give them what they want without a fight?"

"Because we've nothing left to fight with," Evan snapped. "Can't ye see that? 'Tis over, Uncle. The Campbells have finally beaten us for good."

Maclean's eyes were smoldering, his face flushed with anger. "You're wrong, ye traitor. You've dishonored the Macleans."

"Have I? Is it so despicable to admit defeat when it stares ye in the face? To keep two hundred men alive when they could be slaughtered? Ye know as well as I that we had our chance to beat the Campbells and we lost it. If we'd struck at the funeral as we planned, we could've won. We could've caught them unaware and dragged them down. But we didn't. Ye called us away. Are ye sure ye want to accuse *me* of dishonor? Are ye certain 'tis not *ye* who is the traitor?" He did not wait for an answer but turned on his heel and left the room.

Maclean clenched his fists convulsively. He knew Evan was not the only one who thought that way; the others were simply too afraid to say it aloud. His clan believed he had betrayed them. Failed them miserably at the very least. His nephew was right; the funeral had been their only chance and they had lost it. Running his hand through his hair, he tried to force down the nausea that climbed up his throat. Lost it because of Elizabeth. The blood pounded in his ears, deafening him.

Elizabeth had stood in the hallway, transfixed by Maclean's expression. His face had been pallid, his cheeks sunken, except where the red flamed high on his cheekbones. He had stared unseeing before him. As his anger faded, pain mangled his features.

It was not the first time she had seen that look, but never before had it been so naked or so intense. Always he had come to her afterward. But it had been four years this time. He had not shared her bed since that night at Inveraray. The night before Muriella's wedding.

Elizabeth tensed, thinking she heard his footsteps in the hall, but whoever it was passed her door without stopping. She sipped her wine again, remembering that night. He had stumbled into her room at midnight, drunk. After crawling into her bed, he had lain his head in her lap and blurted out the story of how he and Andrew Calder had tried to kill Muriella.

"But do ye know," he had said, gripping her hand, "I was glad when I saw her come back unharmed. I didn't want to hurt the lass, not really. Do ye believe me?" He had peered at her through the darkness, waiting anxiously for her response.

She remembered the feel of his curls beneath her fingers as she answered, "Aye, I believe ye."

"Are ye certain?" He had pulled himself up beside her so he could look into her eyes. "'Tis all right, then?"

Cupping his face in her hands, she had whispered, "'Tis all right."

He had come to her like a child asking forgiveness. Most of the time he ignored her, or hated her, but she did not think of leaving him, even when her father had begged her to. Because sometimes Maclean would place himself in her hands, as he had done that night, and with his head in her lap he would pour out his guilt. She knew she would never turn him away; she would comfort him, always, because he needed her.

"Elizabeth," he had told her that night, "I'll never hurt ye. No' the way I hurt Anne."

"Hush," she had reassured him. "'Twas no' your fault. And I know ye won't hurt me. Hush." She had run her fingers through his hair, wrapping her other arm about his shoulders, and he was silent. As always, he believed her. He had fallen asleep with his head on her breast.

"Elizabeth?"

She was surprised after all when her husband entered the room. She had not heard the latch move. Peering toward the open door, she realized that the light from the single candle on the bedside table didn't reach the shadows where he stood.

"Elizabeth, I—shall I go away?"

She found him at last through the gloom and smiled, shaking her head. She knew he would leave her if she asked him. When he came to her like this, he seemed to lose his own authority, even his ability to decide. "Come," she murmured. "Will ye have some wine?"

His sigh of relief was almost palpable. He moved toward the bed very slowly, more slowly than usual, she thought. But of course, he had never been so badly beaten before. Watching her as if she might change her mind at any minute, he turned back the covers and slid into bed.

"Ye must hate me," he said, sitting on the far side of the mattress.

"Ye know I don't," Elizabeth asserted.

He could not meet her eyes. "Evan does. Evan thinks me a fool."

Reaching out, she covered his hand with hers. His fingers were cold. "Then *Evan* is a fool," she said. "I love ye. Ye know that."

He turned until she saw that his eyes were burning, wild. He crouched before her as if she might strike him. "No," he declared. "Ye must not love me!"

"Isn't that why you're here, Lachlan? Because ye know exactly how I care for ye?"

"Aye," he choked just above a whisper. Once again he seemed reluctant to meet her eyes, but finally he moved closer, sliding his arms around her waist. "Elizabeth!" he cried, "ye'll hate me in the end. Even ye!"

"No," she repeated. "Never." Drawing the covers over him, she cradled him in her arms. He was shaking.

"I killed her, ye ken. I killed my Anne."

Elizabeth flinched. So it was Anne already. Usually it was early morning before the memories of his dead betrothed began to eat away at him. "'Twas my father's men who killed her, not ye. Ye were only trying to protect her." How many times had she said those same words? How many more would she have to do so before he believed her?

"No, 'twas me. I told her to go. Dear God in heaven, I let her go!"

He moaned and she could feel his hot breath through her thin nightrail. For a long moment he said nothing. Then, "Elizabeth," he murmured as he moved his hand over her thigh, "do ye want me tonight?"

"Aye."

He looked up as he slid his fingers beneath her gown, trailing them over the bare skin of her stomach and higher, to the curve of her breast. "Are ye certain?"

She nodded, fumbling with the strings of her nightrail while his lips met hers. Her head went back and she shivered with pleasure when his moist tongue slipped between her lips. The soft, insistent pressure of his mouth, the movement of his hands upon her body, created a melting warmth inside her that spread through her limbs like the last traces of wine. Deliberately, her husband drew the gown from her shoulders, exposing her breasts, tantalizing her with the languid tracings of his fingers along her naked shoulders.

"Lachlan," she whispered huskily, "please."

He cupped her breasts in his warm palms, ran his tongue along her nipple, making tiny circles on the soft pink flesh. Sucking in her breath, Elizabeth slid down until she lay flat on the bed with her husband stretched out above her. He hovered there for a moment, not daring to breathe, then lowered his body onto hers. She closed her eyes.

All at once, his hands trembled violently, so violently that the tremors seemed to spread through the rest of his body. He dug his fingers into her back, unaware of her shudder of pain as his nails pierced her skin.

"Lachlan!" she cried. "What is it?" Elizabeth tried to push her husband away, but he was too strong and she found she could not stop him.

Maclean entered her roughly, pressing her head into the pillows, covering her mouth with his until she thought she would suffocate. For several moments he twisted above her, heaving. Then he collapsed, rolling halfway off her.

His head lay on her breast and she felt clammy where his skin touched hers. His face was wet; she realized with dismay that he was weeping.

"Elizabeth!" he shuddered. "Forgive me! I shouldn't have let ye go. She's dead, ye know. Anne's dead." He was clinging to her, his fingers bruising her flesh.

"Please," he gasped, "I beg ye, forgive me. I could do nothing else. Do ye believe me?" He looked up, tears streaming down his reddened cheeks. "Please."

She hesitated, too bewildered by his behavior to find her voice. Then she realized that he needed her now more than ever and she could not fail him merely because she did not understand. Closing her arms around him, she drew her husband near. His head fell against her shoulder while the tears ran down her neck and across her chest. She reached out to touch his hair with her fingertips. "Hush," she whispered. "I love ye, Lachlan. I forgive ye."

"But Anne," he mumbled into her hair, "and ye. I betrayed ye—both of ye."

"No, ye betrayed no one. Sleep," she soothed. "Go to sleep."

# 29

The wan morning sun filtered through the windows of the solar but did not quite reach Muriella where she sat at the loom, her fingers flying. The second panel of her Loch Awe tapestry was nearly complete, and as she worked, she tried to lose herself in the wonder of the pattern she was weaving with the soft wool thread. In the center of the panel, the blond woman knelt beside the raging stream, her mouth open in a silent cry of terror, the flowers askew on her head, her hair trailing over the water. Behind her, the valley had begun to disappear beneath the rising river; within the blue and white flow of the water, the chimerical figures of the Kelpies laughed in triumph.

But today the tightly woven fabric held no magic for Muriella. As she gazed at the loom, brow furrowed, a shadow seemed to fall across the image. Something was wrong—something that had nothing to do with John or his anger or her own growing dread. The water seemed to move, to swell beneath her hands. Gasping, she snatched her fingers away. She did not want to know. At last the fabric grew still and the pounding of her heart ceased.

She could not so easily escape her own thoughts. She had dreamt of Hugh again last night, had teased him, run from him, and finally, fallen laughing into his arms. But when she awoke to the watery dawn, the laughter had died in her. Now her own words sounded in her head again and again. *Look at me while ye fall—ye and your women and all your men with ye!*

Muriella closed her eyes to shut out the memory, but it would not go. She should not have said it, she knew, but she had been powerless in that moment. She had wanted to hurt John as much as he had hurt her. She rested her fingers on the lacery of colored threads. Surely it was fear and anger that had made her speak, not the dull ache of betrayal. And yet—

"Megan?" she said.

The servant raised her head from the gown she was hemming. "Aye?" Her gaze was full of compassion and concern.

"I must go to him."

Megan blinked at Muriella in astonishment. She had seen the thunderous expression on Sir John's face this morning, heard the vehemence with which he cursed at any small annoyance, and the servant knew without a doubt that his wife was the cause. As the evening had passed, while Megan cooled the fierce redness of Muriella's cheek with a wet cloth, her mistress had told her of the confrontation in the hall. The servant shivered even now, with the warmth of the fire at her back, when she remembered the words Muriella had spoken. "I don't think 'twould be wise just now. He isn't in a pleasant frame o' mind."

"No," Muriella agreed, "nor is he likely to be. But he's my husband and I can't avoid him forever."

Megan could not argue with that, but still she was uneasy. "What will ye say?"

Focusing once again on the colors of the tapestry, Muriella considered her answer. The humiliation she had felt when John struck her before the men had been deep, but sometime during the night it had slipped away. She had realized eventually that she had left her husband with no other choice. "I don't know," she told Megan. "I only know I have to go."

"Well then, go ye must." But as her mistress rose, smoothed out her pale green gown, and started for the door, Megan closed her eyes and crossed herself in a silent prayer.

* * *

In the music room, John slouched down, one leg slung over the arm of a bowed chair. His casual posture belied the turbulence inside him. He strummed a clareschaw sporadically, but the notes were harsh and discordant to his sensitive ears. He stared into the cold, gray ashes of the lifeless fire which bore no resemblance to the blaze in the Great Hall the day before. That fire had burned too bright and hot, illuminating Muriella with brilliance, searing her shouted curse into the ancient stone.

John gripped the harp too tightly, nearly snapping a fragile string. He had had to strike her. She had left him no choice. Had she shrieked such things at him in private, he might have let them pass, but not in the Great Hall with everyone watching.

"Ye did the right thing," Duncan had admitted reluctantly later, when John sat morose and silent in his chamber. The right thing. Yes.

Why then could he still feel the sting in his hand, sharp as an accusation?

He shifted uncomfortably, remembering the awful silence filled with the sound of Muriella's ringing curse. He remembered too her flushed face and glittering eyes, the long wet hair he had wrapped around his palm. The night before, such thoughts had made his anger flare hotly, dangerously. But now he had had time to think, and what should have been rage had turned to confusion.

Muriella had behaved like a madwoman, but since the rain had gone, and with it the darkness, John had begun to wonder why. He could hear clearly the rasp of her ragged breath, see the unnatural color in her cheeks. She had been deeply overwrought before she entered the keep. What could have happened to make her so distraught, to force her into betraying her pain by shouting foolish threats and demands?

The questions had been haunting him the night through; his righteous anger had been no defense against them. Like it or not, he was troubled by her distress. He raked his fingers across the strings of the clareschaw, making a cacophony of strident notes that did not cover the rustle of skirts.

John turned to stare in astonishment at his wife, who hovered just inside the door. He had not expected to see her today, was shocked to realize from her white braided fingers and wary expression that she had sought him out. She was pale this morning; the flush of yesterday's fire had left her cheeks. In spite of himself, John wanted to speak softly, to ask her what was wrong. But there were things he must make clear.

"So," he said with difficulty, "you've come after all."

Muriella swallowed dryly. Now that she was here, now that John's stark blue eyes were fixed upon her, she could not find her voice. "Aye," she croaked.

Frowning, her husband looked away to regard the cold ashes in the fireplace. He was touched by her uncertainty and could not let her see it. With an effort of will, he turned with a face of stone. "Ye won't speak to me that way before the men. Not ever again, do ye understand?" He said what he must say, not what he wished to say. He could not allow her to challenge him, defy him, even curse him. The men would lose their respect for him as quickly as he lost his own. Nor could he let her frighten them with her predictions of disaster. They were too willing to believe.

Muriella did not answer, but the little color that remained had fled her cheeks, leaving them sallow. Against all reason, John wanted to drop the clareschaw—and his stern demeanor—and hold her. He wanted to take the darkness from her eyes, to *understand.* He rose stiffly, eyes on her pallid face.

When he spoke again, his voice was gruff, but he could not bring the coldness back. "Listen to me. You're my wife and must do as I say."

Muriella knew he was right, but that did not stop the rush of helpless anger. John leaned closer, put his hands on her shoulders. Though she could feel his cool breath on her cheek, she did not lower her eyes or back away. She had come to make things right, but she did not know how, and John's searching gaze did not make it any easier.

"Do ye hear me?"

"I hear." She licked dry lips. "I didn't mean—what I said. 'Twill not happen again." They were the hardest words she had ever spoken.

John released her abruptly. He had expected her to scream at him, to fight, to deny what he knew to be true. Her acquiescence unnerved him, made him regret yet again that he could not simply take her in his arms and comfort her. Even if she had not intended to curse him, she had done so. Not for a moment, since she'd left him the day before, had he escaped the image of her arresting face. She had hovered in the light of the torches, in the shadows, in the deepest part of night, taunting him, always just beyond his reach. "Why did ye do it?" he asked softly. "Whatever were ye thinking of?"

Then, as now, she had been thinking of how her husband looked in the shadows with the light playing over his body. She had been thinking of Mary, with her long black hair, who had lain moaning at his feet. Muriella bit her lip until she thought the blood would come. She turned away so John would not see her face.

"Are ye ashamed to look at me?" he asked.

She whirled. "No! I've already seen enough," she cried. "I saw ye!"

Her husband stared at her in astonishment. "Ye saw what? I don't understand."

She closed her mouth, determined not to say any more, but it didn't matter. John had remembered something. Mary thought she had heard someone in the hall yesterday. He had taken her to the deserted tunnels because it added spice to their lovemaking and because he did not believe, like Colin, in flaunting his women before all who cared to watch. He had laughed at her nervous assertion that someone was nearby. No one went into those passageways anymore, he had told her. No one but his wife, it appeared.

"'Tis unfortunate," he said. "I took her there so ye wouldn't see."

Now he pitied her; she could hear it in his voice. She wanted to move away, but he had taken her hand. Was he waiting for her forgiveness? No. He was sorry she had seen it, not sorry it had happened.

"Let me go!" she demanded.

John's eyes widened. He had hurt her; he could see that. But how? Surely she didn't care that he had other women. She had made it clear enough that *she* did not want him. But that had been a long time ago. He met her gaze and held it, leaning forward until he could feel the warmth of her body beneath his hands. She was driving him mad; she would give him no peace. Overcome by a need so fierce that it burned away the memory of the terror he had once seen in her eyes, he slipped his arms around his wife to draw her close. Before she could turn her head away, he kissed her.

For a moment she stood still, shocked by the heat of his lips on hers, by the pressure of his arms around her waist. She tried to cry out, but he slipped his tongue between her lips, circling the moist inside of her mouth until he forced the breath from her body. She was too surprised to be afraid, and when she put her hands on his chest to push him away, her fingers curved inward, seeking instinctively the dark hair beneath his saffron shirt. Her heart was beating quickly and more quickly; she could feel his hands on her back, drawing her closer while his lips demanded a response.

When she did not pull away, John felt a rush of triumph and began to caress her more boldly. He would learn to know her with his fingertips, make her safe and familiar. Then he could banish her haunting image from his dreams. It was what he had wanted to do since he saw her standing before the fire, damp and lovely, bringing with her the refreshing fragrance of the rain. Carried away by the scent of her hair and the feel of her soft body, he caught his fingers in her curls and pulled her head back with sudden impatience.

When he felt a tremor shake her as he ran his thumb over her breast, he forgot his anger. Nothing seemed to matter but the way she trembled in his arms, the way her mouth opened to his, the longing that he sensed somewhere deep within her. It was the first time she had yielded to his touch, the first time she had answered him with warmth instead of coldness. Dear God, she was a witch indeed to make him forget what had gone before. He wanted her, he realized, with an intensity that frightened him.

Fired by his own rising hunger, John slid his hand over the front of Muriella's gown. He brushed the skin at the low-cut neckline with his fingertips, then reached down to cup her breast in his open palm. Muriella felt her knees grow weak as a strange warmth grew inside her, spreading through her limbs until no part of her remained untouched. The sudden, devastating need that shook her set her head spinning, and she realized she was falling, falling down into the darkness. The water swirled at her ankles, her waist, her shoulders, cold and forbidding. She fought the rushing foam, choking and gasping in an attempt to find some air. Then her body slipped away and it was someone else who fought the sea for one last breath.

"No!" she cried, forcing the image back into the darkness. But the cold terror would not go.

Muriella began to struggle furiously against the arms that held her, while the sweat broke out on her body and the room spun madly. "Dear God, no!"

The cry was wrenched from her with a force that chilled John. Not again, he cursed under his breath. Not now. Then he looked into his wife's pallid face, saw the frenzied expression in her eyes, and realized it was not he she was fighting against. "Tell me what you're so afraid of," he demanded, above the sound of his own ragged breathing. "Ye can't keep running forever."

Muriella's feet were made of lead. She could not escape the confusion of emotions that swirled around her, caught up in the menacing rise and fall of the water. "No!" she repeated, as if that single word could keep the Sight at bay. "I don't want to know."

John took her shoulders in his hands and forced her to look up at him. "Know what?" he demanded. "What's happening to ye?"

He found himself looking into the blank, staring eyes he remembered so well. "You've seen something. Tell me what it is."

She was cold, so still and cold and distant that he thought

she might never come back to him. Then the trembling began. He gripped her more tightly. "Tell me," he repeated.

Muriella was lost in an angry sea, but this time it was not she who was being sucked down into the cold black depths. The pressure of John's hands on her shoulders called to her, forcing her upward, away from the vision of the figure struggling frantically through the storm-ravaged ocean. She gazed at her husband with her dark hollow eyes, her lips moved once or twice, then she reached up, pressing her palms to his chest in a wordless plea. "Elizabeth is in danger," she gasped. "The water will rise. Ye must find her!"

Richard and Andrew Campbell smiled with contentment at the pile of fish lying in the bottom of their boat. The catch had been good today and they were pleased with themselves. They had planned to stay out all afternoon, but the sky was lowering overhead. They decided it would be prudent to return to shore.

As they rowed, Richard sang gustily, his deep voice rolling out over the choppy water.

> I've heard them liltin' at the ewe's milkin',
> For the Flowers o' the Forrest are a'wede awa'.

The wind was creeping inside his damp cloak, so he rowed harder as the drops began to fall from overhead.

"We'd best get back to the keep before gloamin'," Andrew remarked. "Besides, the water looks none too friendly to our little boat."

Richard nodded, continuing his song with even more enthusiasm.

> I ride single in my saddle,
> For the Flowers o' the Forrest are a'wede awa'.

"Ye'd be likely to have your own saddle to ride in, ye fool," Andrew chuckled, dropping one oar for a moment while he drew his hand across his brow. "But we do have the goat Sir John gave ye. Mayhap ye could saddle her and ride her to town." The image of his brother on the decrepit animal's back amused him. "Aye," he chortled, "the goat."

Richard tried to frown but failed miserably. "For shame, Andrew. Yonder is a sad song, ye ken. About the men killed at Flodden. You're to grieve when I sing it, not laugh. For shame."

"And do ye say so?" Andrew replied, shaking the raindrops out of his unruly crop of red hair. As he spoke the sun disappeared behind the clouds and the rain began to fall in earnest. "The Kelpies'll be out tonight, ye can bet," he observed in a whisper. Pulling a blanket from under the seat, he draped it over his already soaking hair.

"Now, laddie." Richard let the oars lie idle while he squinted through the downpour. "Yon bunch of boulders is lookin' mighty odd. 'Tis like there's somethin' that doesn't belong there."

Andrew shook his head. "'Tis the water crept into your noggin, man. Likely the Kelpies mean to lure us there and eat us for supper."

Richard chuckled uneasily. "I don't like it," he insisted. "Look for yourself."

Swiveling on his seat, Andrew cupped his hand over his eyes. "I believe you're right for once," he agreed. "'Tis mighty odd. Looks like a person, ye ken?"

"Aye, just as I thought. And we'd best go see what he's doin' out there with the water risin' all around."

"Now, Richard, my boy, 'tis no' our concern. Ye know Jennie'll be waitin' our supper."

"Andrew Campbell, 'tis no' natural, I tell ye. Somethin's amiss and if we leave it, 'twill gnaw at me the night through." As he spoke, he turned the boat toward the huge rock that rose from the sea between the island of Mull and the shore. The tide was rising of its own and the storm had churned the water about so the rock formation was nearly buried. The closer the boat came, the more uneasy Richard felt.

Andrew rowed in silence, his face creased in a frown of discontent.

"By God!" Richard half rose from his seat. "'Tis a woman!"

Andrew followed his brother's gaze. As the boat drew near the dark outcropping, the brothers turned to gape at each other in disbelief. "She's chained!" Andrew blurted, his voice disappearing into the roar of the angry sea. "Chained to a rock in the middle of the channel. Holy Mother of God!"

For a moment, neither moved; then Richard began to feel under his bench until his hand closed on a heavy piece of iron. "We'll have to get her down, ye ken. We can't leave her like that."

Andrew nodded in reluctant agreement.

"If ye can hold the boat steady, I'll swing up and break the chains. Throw the rope on yonder boulder. That'll keep her still enough."

While Andrew fumbled with the rope, Richard slipped into the icy water.

"Likely we'll all three die of the ague," Andrew muttered.

His brother swam to the edge of the rocks, dragging himself the last few feet. As he stopped to catch his breath, he could feel the rusted chain beneath his hand. "'Tis old," he mumbled, "but still, it won't be easy to break." Hoisting himself out of the water, he climbed up beside the woman, who looked beyond him, her expression blank. Her hair straggled across her face and down her back. The water slid from it in sheets. Richard tried to smile reassuringly, but was too horrified to do more than grimace.

He saw that the chains circled her waist several times, then trailed down the rock. Meticulously, he followed the uneven pattern of the chain across the stone until he found the far end wrapped around a jutting piece of boulder near the waterline. It did not occur to him to speak to her; he only knew he had work to do. Without a word, he began to strike a heavily rusted link with his iron tool.

Andrew's grumbling voice came to him from the water, "Can't ye hurry, man? Would ye have us all drown while ye tinker up there?"

Richard grunted in reply. He could feel the link beginning

to give way and struck harder. Finally he grinned in triumph. "'Tis done," he called down to his brother.

The woman did not move while he unwound the chain from her waist. When he pulled her free, she collapsed against him, as if the rusted links had been her only support.

"There," he muttered in embarrassment. "There now. Ye'll be safe enough with us, ye will."

The woman did not respond. She followed his directions numbly, crawling down the side of the jutting boulders and dropping into the water alongside the boat. Richard slid down beside her, guiding her to a firm handhold on the rocking boat. "Ye'll have to help me, Andrew. We'd no' want the whole thing to tip, and she doesn't seem able to balance herself. Feverish, I think, and no wonder." He glanced back at the rock and shuddered. "What kind of person would do such to another?"

"Save it, Brother. We've business to attend to."

"Aye, just as ye say."

Andrew pulled from above while his brother pushed from below until the woman lay safely beside the fish in the bottom of the boat. Richard followed her quickly, glad to be out of the icy sea.

"Shall I give her the blanket?" Andrew asked as his brother took up the oars once again. "'Twill no' do her much good; the rain's soaked it through already." Nevertheless, he draped the heavy wool over her huddled form. She did not seem aware that he had done so. He would have thought she was dead if he had not seen the occasional rise and fall of her breathing. "By all the saints!" he exclaimed. "Do ye know who this be?" He shook his head distractedly. "We've gotten ourselves into a bundle of trouble this time."

Richard pulled on the oars, waiting for Andrew to calm down enough to impart his news. "Well," he said at last, "who?"

The younger man leaned forward, lowering his voice as if someone might hear. "Elizabeth Campbell Maclean, that's who."

Richard's mouth dropped open. The woman was so bedraggled that he had not recognized her. Or perhaps he had not wanted to. "Holy Mother of God!" He crossed himself, risking the loss of an oar in the turbulent water. Glancing back toward Mull, then toward the shore they were approaching, he said, "We'd best take her to Inveraray. Looks like Maclean has gone gey daft this time. I don't even like to guess what the Campbells will do now."

"Ye don't have to guess," Andrew informed him gloomily. "I'm thinkin' 'tis a lot of sorrow will come of this day's work, and no mistake."

# 30

As the door to the Great Hall swung open, everyone turned to stare expectantly at the man who stood on the threshold. "There be a storm brewin' and it looks to be a mighty one." Adam Campbell paused when he became aware of the number of people watching him. Seeking out John where he sat near the hearth, the man added, "I thought ye should know, m'lord. 'Tis only the storm I came to warn ye about."

John ran his fingers over the strings of his harp. "Thank ye," he said. Though his tone was impassive, the lines at the corners of his eyes and mouth betrayed his unease.

Adam half bowed, then left the hall, swinging the door closed behind him. The men scattered through the drafty room turned away in disappointment. Their dinner had long been cleared away, but they showed no signs of leaving their seats. Now and again, one or the other glanced at Muriella, who sat with her back to the stone fireplace, then, afraid to meet her gaze, quickly looked away. They were waiting, as was John, for news of Elizabeth.

Three hours before, they had been laughing and recounting their successes against the defeated rebels, when John had come down the stairs with his wife, shouting that the men were to form groups to go in search of Elizabeth.

"Sim," he had cried, "take ten men and cross to Duart. David, ye—"

Muriella had taken his arm and he had fallen silent. "They won't find her at Duart," she murmured. "They must look in the water."

John heard the men gasp, but it had sounded far away. He considered his wife's face for a long time before asking, "Are ye certain?"

"Aye," she said.

Sim and the others had not gone to Duart. Those who stayed behind were very conscious of Muriella's presence. They had guessed that the sudden search for Elizabeth had come about because of one of the mistress' visions, but that was something they did not wish to think about.

John and Duncan had played their harps off and on while the hours crawled by. More than once, John found himself wondering why he had chosen to stay at the keep instead of joining the men for the search. The inaction, the minutes that seemed to stretch into hours, were wearing his nerves away. But still he had not gone after the others; he did not want to leave Muriella.

To keep himself occupied, he had taken up his harp and begun to play along with his squire. At first the two had attempted cheerful songs, but soon their music began to reflect the lowering sky beyond the windows.

Muriella sat across the hearth, watching her husband as he strummed the mournful notes. When he and Duncan began to sing together, her thoughts turned back to where they had hovered for the past three hours—in the sea.

Round the old crags of Arthur's Hill,
The tearful mists are slowly creeping
As dawns the morn, so sadly still,
Dunedin's, Scotland's day of weeping.

Her mind painted pictures of Elizabeth being tossed about in the waves, her hair streaming over the gray green water, her body wrapped in chains. Once John had held Muriella by the shoulders, asking, "Will she die?" His wife had answered, "I don't know."

Far murmurs from the city rise,
Of wild distraction, mingled cries
Of wailing and of fear.

Outside the storm was rising; she could hear the rain falling in the courtyard, pounding on the cobblestones. The wind raced above the castle, screaming across to the sea.

Frequent and fast the war-bell tolls,
And up the misty mountain rolls
Its burthen on the ear,
O'er ferny hollow, loch and lea
Replying to the moaning sea.

The water was roiling, crashing against the cliff at the foot of the keep where the seabirds cried their warning. From the heart of Duart, Muriella sensed a bewildered grief that betrayed itself through strangled moans, but that was not Elizabeth. The song ended and Muriella forced her thoughts back to the reality of cold stone all around. She leaned forward to find John watching her. As they stared at each other, afraid to speak, they heard noises in the courtyard.

Dropping his harp, John leapt from his place to move toward the entryway. Muriella was not far behind. As the door opened for the second time, Richard and Andrew came into the hall with a long, gray burden in their arms. Both were sodden to the skin. When Richard saw John, he said, "We heard you're lookin' for your sister, m'lord. Andrew and me, we found her."

John and Muriella stared at the bundle the men carried. Elizabeth was wrapped in a blanket so that only her hair was visible; it fell, dripping, from one end. John focused on Richard's sallow face, framed by dark red hair. "Is she dead?" he asked in a strangled voice.

"Och no!" His hair clinging like seaweed to his freckled face, Andrew answered before his brother could speak. "At least, no' yet. But she's gey ill, or so Richard tells me."

His older brother nodded. "'Twas a terrible thing the two of us saw. Thought we were daft or bewitched. But no, there she was for all the world to see, chained to a rock in the channel."

"What!" The single word seemed to fill the hall before John clenched his jaw shut.

When she saw how her husband's cheeks flushed red, how dangerously his eyes glittered, Muriella forced herself into action. She moved forward, turning back the blanket so she could see Elizabeth's face. Pressing her cheek against her sister-in-law's forehead, she drew a deep breath of concern. She turned to call for servants and found Megan and Mary at her elbow. Glancing at John, she told him, "She's feverish. We'd best put her to bed."

"Aye," her husband agreed. "Take her!"

Megan and Mary lifted Elizabeth's unconscious form from the two men. With Muriella following, the three women began to move across the hall to the stairs.

As they went, Richard declared behind them, "The water was risin', ye ken. If we'd been a bit later—"

For the next several hours, Muriella was busy sponging the salt and seaweed from Elizabeth's body, placing cool cloths on her forehead, and attempting to pour warm wine down her throat. She had long ago despaired of getting rid of the smell of fish that clung to Elizabeth's hair. Muriella had dismissed Mary as soon as her sister-in-law lay shivering on the bed. Now Megan worked beside her, alternately building up the fire and bending over the table to mix herbs together and stir them into the wine. Despite all their efforts, Elizabeth remained unconscious and unmoving.

"She's very ill, m'lady," Megan whispered, as if already in the presence of the dead.

Muriella nodded absently. "Aye, help me with the poultice, can ye?"

Megan lifted the reeking cloth from the bowl while Muriella opened Elizabeth's nightrail and held it aside. When the poultice was in place, she stood staring at her sister-in-law's face. A moment ago it had been deep red and the sweat had stood along her forehead, dripping down into her hair, but now the skin was chalk white and clammy cool.

"M'lady, ye'd best sit down for a bit. There's nothing more ye can do just now."

Her mistress pulled a chair near the bed and sank into it, but did not remove her gaze from Elizabeth's face. The woman's mouth was open; Muriella could hear the breath as it struggled up from her throat and over her parched lips. Sometimes Elizabeth would gasp and choke, but then her breathing would settle again. Muriella was painfully aware of the increasing sound of congestion in her sister-in-law's chest. As she listened in dread, the smell of Megan's herbs began to make her head ache. When the servant placed a glass of wine in her hand, Muriella drank it wordlessly.

Just as she finished the warm drink, Elizabeth moved for the first time. She twisted on the bed, dislodging the poultice and flinging aside the cloth from her forehead.

Muriella sprang to her feet. Taking Elizabeth's hand in hers, she leaned forward, listening. Her sister-in-law moaned, running her other hand over her body at the waist. Muriella caught Megan's eye and winced. Both women had seen the bruises and abrasions made by the chains. The servant grasped Elizabeth's hand and held it tightly.

For a long time, she rolled about, attempting to free her hands and moaning, but did not open her eyes. Then she sat up, crying, "Lachlan!"

Muriella and Megan pushed her gently back until she lay among the pillows. This time they did not look at each other. Both knew it must have been her husband who had chained Elizabeth to the rock, yet she was calling for him.

"Shall I bring Sir John?" Megan asked.

"No!" Muriella said. Then, "Aye, bring him."

When Megan had gone, Muriella poured some of the medicated wine into a goblet and held it out to Elizabeth, who lay staring up at the canopy overhead. "Elizabeth, ye must drink this."

"Lachlan," Elizabeth moaned. "Where's Lachlan? I want him." She began to claw at the bruises through her nightrail, twisting herself in the linen sheets.

Catching Elizabeth's shoulders, Muriella held her until she was still again. Then she reached for the wine, holding the goblet close to her sister-in-law's lips. Elizabeth gaped at her blankly and Muriella realized that in her delirium, the woman did not know her. "Drink," she urged.

Mechanically, Elizabeth raised her head to swallow some of the wine. Then she knocked the goblet from Muriella's hand. The liquid spread over the sheets, staining them red. Elizabeth began to cough and sob simultaneously while the breath rasped in her throat and sobs wracked her body, causing her to double up. And all the time she wailed her husband's name.

Muriella did not hear John come up behind her, but all at once he reached out, clasping Elizabeth's legs. While Muriella held his sister's shoulders, John straightened her legs, then pulled the heavy furs back over her. Megan brought more wine, and although Elizabeth turned her head away again and again, the servant finally managed to get her to drink.

When the wine was gone, John nodded once to Megan and she slipped away. Elizabeth was coughing again, gasping incoherent phrases. But at last the coughing fit passed and she fell silent.

When John looked down at his sister, he felt a tightening in his chest. Her hair was matted; it straggled across the pillow in disorder, except where a strand or two clung to her cheek. Her eyes were yellow, then gray, then the color seemed to fade altogether. The skin was stretched over her bones so that it appeared transparent but for the furious red that came and went in her cheeks. Her breathing was slow and labored and the color had been bleached from her lips. She's dying, he thought. When he looked up, Muriella was watching him, her own eyes gray in the firelight. "Has she told ye aught?" he asked.

His wife shook her head.

"We have to know. I'll have to ask her."

Muriella nodded reluctantly, placing her hand on Elizabeth's forehead in a protective gesture.

Taking both his sister's hands, John murmured, "Elizabeth, ye must tell me who did this to ye."

Elizabeth turned her head from side to side. John was not

certain she had understood him. "Elizabeth," he repeated slowly, "who?"

"He didn't know. He couldn't have known!" his sister cried. "No, 'twas the other two."

"What two?"

"Strangers!" Elizabeth gasped. "Never knew them. Never!"

"No? Are ye certain of that? Ye'd never seen them at Duart?" John persisted.

"At Duart," Elizabeth said as if the idea were new to her. "Aye, at Duart, every day."

John leaned down until he could feel his sister's breath on his face. "Then they were your husband's servants, weren't they?"

Elizabeth looked away. "Aye, they were, but Lachlan didn't know their plans. I swear it."

John shook his head. "Do ye think," he said, "do ye really believe two servants would do such a thing without their master's consent?"

Elizabeth was weeping. "I love him," she cried. "He wouldn't—I love him!" Her voice faded as she began to writhe again.

John stared, too appalled to speak, afraid he might choke on the revulsion that had lodged itself in his throat. His hands opened and closed convulsively about Elizabeth's neck. For an instant, he wanted to crush her voice with the weight of his fists so he need never again hear her anguished cry—*I love him!*

Muriella saw John clench and unclench his hands, saw the anger that darkened his eyes to slate gray. Too frightened to think clearly, she leapt in front of him so her body shielded Elizabeth from his gaze. *"No!"* she cried, pounding her fists against his chest. "Leave her be!"

Gradually, John became aware of the pain in his chest, of the weight of his wife's body pressed against his. As Muriella's face came into focus, the blood ceased its fierce pounding in his head and the tension began to drain out of him. He could not look at Elizabeth's face, gray and bloodless on the pale linen sheets; he could not bear to.

Grasping Muriella's flailing fists in his hands, he tried to move her aside, but she would not go.

"I told ye to leave her be!"

"Listen to me," John said. "I won't hurt her. My sister is safe now," he added, "from all of us." Then, releasing his wife, he turned to leave the room.

All at once, Muriella was too weak to stand. She sighed raggedly as she sank onto the mattress next to her sister-in-law. Reaching out to touch the other woman's cheek, she saw how her fingers shook and drew them back within the folds of her gown. Elizabeth's eyes were once again dark with fever. Perhaps, in her delirium, she had not seen the way her brother's hands hovered threateningly above her. Perhaps she had not seen the violence in his eyes. Muriella could only pray that it was so.

When her body stopped shaking at last, she rose, found the cloth Elizabeth had tossed aside, and dipped it in a basin of cool water. Gently, she pressed the cloth to her sister-in-law's forehead, then her flushed cheeks and throat. Muriella knew Elizabeth was not aware of her ministrations, but she had to do something. She had to try to keep her sister-in-law alive, though she feared it was already too late.

She forgot about the passage of time or the chill of the room or the aches in her own limbs as she sponged Elizabeth's body again and again. Muriella moved from the basin to the bed and back again, stopping only to replace the poultice, straighten the crumpled sheets, or give Elizabeth a sip of wine. She heard someone enter the room behind her, but assumed it was Megan and did not look up from her self-imposed task.

"Muriella."

The sound of John's voice made her stiffen warily, but she did not turn to face him.

"Ye look too weary to stand anymore. Ye'd best sit down for a bit."

"Not 'til the fever breaks," she told him, glancing over her shoulder at her husband where he leaned against the wall. He looked weary too, as if he needed the support of the stone to hold him upright, but she could not think about that now. She had just rinsed the cloth in her hand, but already it had grown warm from the heat that raged through Elizabeth's body. With a sigh, she dipped it in the water and began her task all over again.

John watched his wife work tirelessly until exhaustion drained the color from her face. He wanted to help but sensed she would not let him near. He wondered, as he watched her push the damp hair back from Elizabeth's eyes, if she was not wise. Yet something held him there—watching, waiting, helpless in the face of his sister's pain.

He contemplated his wife's competent, gentle hands as she pressed cool cloths to Elizabeth's forehead. She worked intently, giving her kindness and the last of her own dwindling strength.

Muriella moved more and more slowly, dragging her feet through the scattered rushes. Her breathing became labored and she began to think that to lift her arms once more would be an agony too great to bear. When she stumbled, John was beside her in an instant, supporting her sagging shoulders with the strength of his arm. "Ye must stop. There are servants to do this. Besides, she doesn't even know you're here."

With an effort, his wife straightened, wishing herself free of John's confining arm, yet knowing that without it she would fall. "She knows," Muriella told him softly, "but even if she didn't, I'd stay. If I can't save her, then I can't, but I don't mean to let her die, even if 'tis what ye wish."

Appalled, John turned her to face him. "Ye can't believe that."

"Are ye forgetting so soon? I saw how ye looked at her. I know—"

"'Twas only a momentary madness," he said grimly. "She's a Campbell, and my sister; I don't wish her ill."

Muriella heard the pain in his voice and knew he spoke the truth, but even the sight of his drawn face could not replace the memory of the look she had seen, for an instant, in his eyes. "Please," she said wearily, "I must see to her." When she tried to move away, her knees buckled and she started to fall.

John caught her in his arms and carried her to the low chest against the wall. Seating himself with his back to the cold stone, he settled his wife in his lap. "When you've rested," he said. "'Twill no' help Elizabeth if ye make yourself ill too."

"Ye don't understand," she whispered. "'Tis all my fault."

John stared at her, bewildered. "How—" Then he remembered. *Look at me while ye fall—ye and your women and all your men with ye!* With his hand under her chin he forced her to meet his eyes. "No, Muriella. Even ye don't have that kind of power." But he wondered as he said it if it was true.

How could he be so certain, Muriella thought, when he had never felt the force of the Sight that destroyed in an instant her strength and her will? Yet she wanted to believe him, wanted to abandon her fears, her remorse, and lose herself in the slow, rhythmic beating of his heart. When she rubbed her arms to start the blood flowing through her limbs again, John drew her closer, running his hands over her body, hoping his warmth would chase away the chill from her skin. For a long time he was silent while she sat tensely, staring into the fire across the room.

The smell of herbs and wine hung heavy in the air. Muriella breathed the fumes and felt them running through her blood. She could not seem to move; the rise and fall of her husband's breath was so soothing. At last she succumbed to her exhaustion and rested her head on John's shoulder. His circling touch warmed her, frightened her, disturbed her, but she was tired. Too tired to break away from him.

Drawn by a need she could not explain, she looked up at John's face; its harsh lines had been softened by his own weariness and the firelight that dimmed the bright blue of his eyes. She reached up to touch the springy, dark curls of his beard, and he smiled. Muriella trailed her fingers down his throat to his shoulder, rested her palm above the hypnotic pulse of his heart. Could this man with the comforting hands be the same one who had stood above his sister with murder in his eyes? Before she had a chance to grasp the thought, it swirled away, absorbed by the mist that clouded her thoughts. Closing her eyes, she let the mist enfold her until she drifted into sleep.

Lachlan Maclean spread the parchment on the table, pressing out the creases with careful fingers. Pulling the lamp closer, he stared at the letters until they ceased roving across the page and fell into words and sentences. "January 31, 1514," he read aloud for the third time. With a great deal of resolution, he forced himself to read further.

Lachlan Maclean
Laird of the Clan Maclean

My lord,

Your wife Elizabeth died yesterday, early in the morning. She was delirious with fever for three days before her passing. Her body lies in state at Inveraray, where she will be buried in one week's time.

Sir John Campbell of Lorne,
Thane of Cawdor

Maclean closed his eyes. "Elizabeth died yesterday," he repeated as if he could not understand the meaning of the words. Then, as awareness came to him at last, he began to laugh. So his men had done their work well. She was finally gone and he was free. The debt he owed his old enemy Argyll had been paid in full. Maclean laughed until the tears ran down his face; then his head fell forward onto the table and he wept.

# 31

Twelve Campbell men awaited Maclean at the top of Glen Ara, among them, Richard and Andrew. None of the twelve were armed. It was late afternoon and the sun struck through the leaves, glistening where it met the rain-soaked grass. The trees circled the low, flat area where the Campbells stood; the leaves were so thick they formed a solid ceiling overhead. Some of the men had thrown themselves on the ground. They sprawled in the shade, chewing on blades of grass.

Andrew nudged his brother. "Are ye *certain* Maclean wanted to claim the body? Seems daft to me. He's walkin' right into our arms. But then, he won't come anyway."

Andrew had been saying the same thing for three days now. Ignoring him, Richard shifted the blue and green plaid beneath him. Despite its protection, he could feel the dampness seeping through from the ground. "He'll come," he told his younger brother. "Mayhap because he can't help himself."

"What do ye mean?"

"Mayhap if the curse is still upon him . . ." Richard let his voice trail off suggestively.

This time, Andrew did not laugh at his brother's superstition. He too had heard Sir John's wife curse the Campbells; less than a day later, he and his brother had found Elizabeth chained to the rock. He could not deny what he'd seen with his own eyes. Andrew shivered uncontrollably, though the day was mild and warm.

Just then, Adam Campbell stepped out of the trees. "Maclean!" he exclaimed.

The men looked up in astonishment. Pulling his brother to his feet, Richard nodded grimly. "Ye see."

The Campbells formed two rows of six and stood silent, waiting. When Maclean came from among the trees, they saw immediately that his sword hung at his side and his dagger at his belt. A long look passed among them. He had come armed to the funeral supper. All was not as it should be.

As Maclean walked down the center of the aisle they had formed, the Campbells began to move behind him. The Laird of the Clan Maclean pulled nervously at his red-and-green plaid, draping it farther over his shoulder. They were unarmed, he thought. It was not like the Campbells. Most likely they had their daggers hidden in the tops of their boots. It wouldn't surprise him if he discovered a knife in his back. The Campbells had always been cowards.

As they crossed the last hill and the castle came into sight, Maclean wondered once more what insanity had driven him to come here today. For certainly it was insane. He was armed, it was true, but he was one man—one man among a hundred Campbells, and every one of them his enemy. The group paused while the huge iron gate creaked upward. Maclean took a deep breath. He was doing it for Elizabeth, he told himself. He would take her back to Duart and bury her next to Anne.

As he passed through the courtyard, he noticed there was no one about. The place was silent. Too silent. He stopped when he came to the doors that opened onto the Great Hall. Behind him, he could hear the gate closing, dropping with a final thud against the stones.

One of the men moved forward to push open the massive oak doors. The hinges made no sound. Maclean blinked as he stepped inside. For a moment he was blinded by the change from bright sunlight to cool shadow, then his vision began to clear and he saw that the Campbells stood all around him, watching his passage in grim silence. He noted that none of them wore swords. Nevertheless, their hatred of him was palpable. It followed him as he climbed the stairs, turning to the right then the left as the man before him instructed.

"In here, m'lord," Richard said, indicating a door at the end of a hallway. Then he stepped back into the shadows.

Maclean placed his hand on the latch. As his fingers closed around it, he believed his heart was beating so loudly that those inside could surely hear it. Except for Elizabeth. She would hear nothing but silence. Blessed silence. He pressed the latch until the door swung open.

The hallway had been dark compared to the room he now entered. Torches burned along the walls and there were candles placed at intervals down the long table that dominated the room. Maclean did not wish to look directly at the bier. Instead, he glanced down the walls on either side of the table. They were lined with Campbell portraits. Beneath each portrait flickered a small candle. Beneath each candle stood a live Campbell in full-dress uniform. Maclean noted the regular gleam of metal at each man's waist. Each had a sword, each a dagger. Each stared before him, looking neither to right nor left, and each had his hand poised above the hilt of his sword.

Maclean swallowed noisily, looking at last down the center of the table. To the left stood Muriella, frozen in time, her face a gray mask. To the right stood John with a dangerous brilliance in his eyes. And at the head of the table sat Elizabeth, staring at her husband unblinking across the hundred candles that separated them.

# 32

Maclean drew in his breath with infinite care. So, he thought, the Campbells were not so foolish after all. He could hear the whisper of metal on metal as the men unsheathed their swords.

"Welcome, my lord." John's mocking voice echoed off the walls, covering the sound of the rising blades on both sides of the table. He removed his hand from his sister's shoulder and started the long walk to the other end of the room where Maclean stood waiting. By the time John reached his brother-in-law, he and all the other Campbells held their swords in their hands. "Welcome," John repeated, "and farewell."

Maclean did not move; there was nowhere he could go. When John raised his sword, the blade flashed in the splintered candlelight.

"No!" Elizabeth screamed.

John paused with his weapon above Maclean's shoulder, glancing back at his sister, who stood leaning heavily on the edge of the table.

"Please!"

Muriella turned to her sister-in-law, but Elizabeth avoided her, dodging past the corner of the table. When she came up beside John, she grasped his arm, digging her nails into his skin. "Johnnie, I beg ye, if you've ever loved me, let him go!"

"Ye aren't going to tell me again that 'twas no' his fault,

are ye?" John spoke quietly, fiercely. "Do ye realize what he's done to ye?"

"Aye," she answered with difficulty. "I know." She did not turn to her husband.

"And still ye would have me set him free?" John's face darkened with fury as a new thought struck him. "Ye won't go back to him, Elizabeth, do ye hear?"

"I know," she whispered. "I know. But I would have ye let him live."

God in heaven, how could she ask this of him? The men would be appalled by such an act of weakness; they would snicker behind his back that Maclean had won after all. But as John looked down into his sister's eyes, he found that he could not deny her. Before he could stop to think, he tossed his sword onto the table and commanded, "Let him go!"

The men did not move at once and John eyed them with impatience. "Put your weapons away. I said Maclean will go free."

As they sheathed their swords, the men stared at Maclean, who had not moved since Elizabeth first spoke. His hand still clutched the dagger at his waist; he had reached for it instinctively when John drew his weapon. Now Maclean stood frozen, considering his wife's face as if it belonged to a stranger. When she did not meet his gaze, he took a step toward her.

"Go!" John shouted. "Get out before I change my mind and spit ye like a squealing sow!"

Maclean fumbled with the latch on the door, then hurried from the room.

When he had gone, Elizabeth looked up at her brother, still clinging tightly to his arm. "Thank ye, Johnnie," she said.

John found he could not speak. He shook her hands away and strode out the door.

When Maclean came to the head of the stairs, he paused. Below him, the Campbells stood gaping as if he were an apparition. He knew they had expected a bloody corpse; their anger at finding him alive was evident on their faces. He noticed that some of them had drawn their daggers from within their draped plaids. Perhaps he would not make it out of Inveraray Castle after all.

There was a gasp as all the men released their breaths at once. Maclean looked over his shoulder to find John standing behind him.

"Put the daggers away," John called, his order carrying clearly through the hall. "Maclean goes free." He was not surprised at the expressions of disgust on the faces below him. He himself felt the same. Every muscle and nerve in his body was poised, ready to strike this man dead at his feet. But Elizabeth had chosen otherwise and he had given his word. He wondered if she would ever know how much that decision had cost him. Schooling his features into a mask of indifference, he preceded Maclean down the staircase.

Elizabeth stayed where John had left her, staring at the place where her husband had been a moment before. As the others filed from the room, she did not look at their faces. She knew what she would find there—shock, repulsion and pity. She had seen those things in John's eyes, too. The thought brought the pain up from her stomach and into her throat. Fleetingly, she wondered why she had agreed to the ruse at all.

When, against all expectation, she had recovered from her illness, she had been aghast at the magnitude of her husband's betrayal. At first she had been silent, caught up in her own private cycle of horror, recounting to herself over and over the list of Lachlan's transgressions. Then she had begun to laugh, too loudly, remembering the night when he had come to her and wept. She had forgiven him his sin beforehand, she thought. Forgiven him without knowing. In the end, she had screamed at the walls, pacing the floor like a caged animal. But she had not wept.

Then John had come to read her Colin's letter in which the Earl had planned for Maclean's ignominious death. Elizabeth had chosen to cooperate; after all, her husband had long ago forsaken his right to her loyalty. She had really believed she could make it through to the end when he lay dead at her feet. She believed it until the moment she saw him standing at the foot of the table, facing the Campbells alone. Then it had been too much for her and she had broken her resolve, destroyed John's faith in her, and insured her own inevitable misery. All so that Lachlan Maclean could go free.

From far away she heard the wail of the gate as it wrenched upward. Suddenly, she began to run. Unaware of her surroundings, she fled through the halls toward the door of the eastern tower. The latch was stiff, and she hit it with her knuckles again and again until her hand was covered with blood. When at last the rusted latch came loose, she pulled the door open and started up the stairs. She was heading for the window near the top of the tower. Once there, she paused, her heart throbbing painfully in her chest.

As she tried to catch her breath, she examined the sweep of ground below the castle. It was empty. She was afraid he was already gone. Then he came into view; even from where she stood, she could see that his head was not bowed. No one would ever guess that he was fleeing for his life. She leaned down, gripping the windowsill, knowing she would not see him again. The last of the sunlight struck his red hair, setting it ablaze. As her husband moved into the shadows at the edge of the forest, Elizabeth knelt in the darkness with her head pressed against the unfriendly stone.

Muriella found her sister-in-law standing at the highest window in the eastern tower, staring in silence. The young woman approached quietly, placing her hand on Elizabeth's arm. "Elizabeth."

"Leave me be."

Muriella was shocked by the chill on her sister-in-law's skin. "Ye must come away. Ye'll be ill again if ye don't get warm."

"No." Elizabeth continued to stare out the window. "I won't come away, for I mislike the stairs. Mayhap I'll find another way down."

"Elizabeth—" Muriella could not think clearly. She had spent the last hour sitting in her room, struggling against the compassion and dread, pity and repulsion that warred within her. Even Megan had been shocked into silence. Yet whatever her feelings, Muriella had known she must find Elizabeth; she was certain her sister-in-law was in need of company. But she had not expected this wooden expression, this pair of gray and lifeless eyes.

Under her breath, she cursed John for listening to Colin. She had known how hard it would be for Elizabeth to sit and watch her husband die, had told John that the Earl's plan was cruel beyond words. But he had not listened; his hatred for his enemy had been stronger than his compassion for his sister, at least until the end.

Muriella shivered at the thought. She had wanted to stay away from that candlelit room today, but had guessed that Elizabeth would need her. For her sister-in-law's sake, she had waited with the others for Maclean to arrive. Muriella tried to remember what Elizabeth had said a moment ago. Finding another way down—that was it. She grasped the ledge with cold fingers, turning to look at the ground far beneath her. "Don't talk that way!" she protested.

Elizabeth smiled. "I meant it, little one." Leaning down, she whispered, "There are worse things than death, ye ken. Much worse."

Muriella went rigid. "Don't," she repeated in a strangled voice. "Please come away."

"No, not this time. Ye should have let me die, ye know. 'Twould have been best."

"Surely ye don't believe we would want ye to do this?" Muriella gasped.

"Wouldn't ye? Then tell me, can ye comfort me?"

The younger woman was silent.

"Can ye tell me ye don't pity me? That John and Duncan and the others won't turn away when I see them?"

"Elizabeth—"

"Tell me if ye can!"

Muriella wanted desperately to look away from Elizabeth's steady gaze. Drawing her breath in slowly, she said, "I can't."

With a sigh, Elizabeth turned back to the window. "I thought ye would lie to me. Thank ye for telling the truth."

"Ye don't understand," Muriella continued. "No matter what we feel, it doesn't mean we don't love ye. It doesn't mean—"

"It does. It means everything. I would rather ye hate me. Ye came here to console me for my loss, didn't ye? Do ye really believe ye can save me with your pity? 'Come away, Elizabeth, and I'll weep for ye. And when you're gone, I'll shake my head and wonder how ye could have been so weak and foolish.'"

"Didn't ye pity Maclean because he was one man against many? Isn't that why ye pleaded for him? Do ye think he cares why? 'Tis done; that's what matters."

Elizabeth did not answer for a long time. When she spoke at last, some of the ice had melted from her voice. "You're right," she said. "I pitied him. I thought I wouldn't ever pity a man again, least of all my husband. But you're wrong if ye think he doesn't care. I believe he would've wanted me to let him die. 'Tis what he's wanted from the first day I met him, but I didn't know it. Not until today. When I saw him standing there with the swords drawn all around him, I knew as if he had screamed it to me that he was grateful because I was going to end his guilt. I decided then and there that he would live. I know he'll remember, and his memories will gnaw at his insides until he goes mad. He never loved me, ye see, but he hurt me, and he won't be able to bear that."

Muriella frowned. "If 'twas for that reason—"

"'Twasn't." Elizabeth sighed. "Ye know that as well as I do." Her hands closed on the windowsill until the stone dug into her palms. "I did it because he trusts me, because he's the only person who ever needed me. My father—" She broke off abruptly as she took in the shadowed landscape below. She thought she could feel Muriella shivering.

"It frightens ye, doesn't it? My feelings for Lachlan make ye ill with fear. I'm wondering if you're afraid for me or for yourself?"

"Elizabeth, please."

"Tell me, is it John?"

Muriella did not answer.

"Tell me!" Elizabeth began to laugh in the darkness. "Tell me and mayhap I can pity *ye!*"

Her laughter echoed in the tiny room until it seemed that the stones would crumble.

"Tell m—"

Muriella looked up to see John cross the chamber in two long strides. Without a word, he took Elizabeth in his arms, cradling her head on his shoulder, muffling her laughter in his plaid. The laughter dissolved at last into silence, then to tortured weeping. Elizabeth flung her arms about her brother's neck and sobbed without restraint.

# 33

John rested his head in his hands. Through his fingers he could see the patterns the torchlight cast among the fresh rushes. He watched them in fascination, willing his troubled thoughts into silence.

"Ye needn't stay with me, Johnnie."

He looked up, startled, at the sound of Elizabeth's voice. She had not spoken since he'd brought her to her chamber and settled her on the bed. He had been relieved. He did not want to hear again the unearthly sound of her laughter. "I don't think ye should be alone," he said.

Elizabeth smiled grimly. "'Tis over now, and I've been alone before, ye ken."

John shook his head. "I'll stay."

His sister shrugged in indifference. "As ye wish." After a moment, she propped herself up on her elbow, regarding him through narrowed eyes. "Tell me why ye let him go," she said.

John blinked at her in astonishment. "Because ye asked me to."

"I don't think so. Ye didn't really care what I wanted. Ye sought to make my husband pay for his mistakes and ye used me to do it." Her brother started to protest, but she stopped him with a wave of her hand. "'Tis cruel, aye, but true. Ye needn't bother to deny it."

John shifted on his stool, remembering that Muriella had said the same when she read Colin's letter outlining the

Earl's plans for Maclean. "How can ye even consider such a thing?" his wife had demanded. "How can ye treat your sister so cruelly when she has no strength to fight ye?" She had paused, her eyes bright with anger. "Or mayhap 'tis what you're counting on. Mayhap ye *wish* to punish her for her weakness. If so, ye couldn't have chosen a better way to do it."

"Be silent!" John had told her, furious that she should challenge his decision. It was not until he stood with his sword above Maclean's head that he realized Muriella was right. He *was* punishing Elizabeth by forcing her to be part of this. Punishing her for loving a man she should have hated above all others.

"Mayhap we should have found another way," he told his sister now.

"It doesn't matter," Elizabeth said. She leaned toward him, smiling strangely. "But 'tis odd, don't ye think, that now we're both left with nothing? I don't have my husband or my pride, and ye don't have your revenge. 'Tis a fitting trade, don't ye think, for the life of a man like Lachlan Maclean?"

Chilled by the careless tone of her voice, John rose, kicking his stool away. "Ye don't know what you're saying."

"I do," Elizabeth said. "But since ye don't wish to believe it, why don't ye just go? Ye can't keep your nightly vigil here."

John stared at her. How could she know that he had slept little the past three nights while he waited for Maclean to come? Had she guessed about the thoughts of Muriella that would not let him rest? Elizabeth's expression told him nothing. She closed her eyes in weariness and sank back among the furs with a sigh.

"Please, Johnnie, go. I don't want to fight with ye. I only want a little peace. Please."

"Shall I send Muriella to ye?" He should have thought of it before; he had watched the two women grow closer with each day that passed. Muriella's kindness had never faltered; not once had she been too busy to answer when Elizabeth called.

"No, she's weary. Let her rest." For the first time, Elizabeth smiled warmly, with affection.

John shook his head. Somehow, in the past weeks, Elizabeth had become more like Muriella's sister than his own. His wife was much more than companion and friend; she and Elizabeth shared a kinship, a fragile and invisible bond.

"She'll come if ye want her." It was true, John realized. The Muriella he knew as unapproachable, volatile, moody and changeable, had revealed—for Elizabeth—a well of infinite patience and unfailing tenderness. She gave her sister-in-law a dedication John could not, because, always, his anger and disgust held him apart.

"I know," Elizabeth murmured. "'Tis why I don't need her now—I know how quickly she would come if I called."

John did not answer. There was nothing he could say, though he ached at the sound of his sister's pain, which he could neither soothe nor forgive. Silently, he left Elizabeth to the warm, if lifeless, company of the firelight.

John stood in the library with his hands pressed against the stone. *The Buik of Alexander the Grate* lay open on a brocaded chair, but he had read no more than two sentences before giving it up. Tonight the firelight called him as it had so often of late, conjuring images of Muriella, her face pale and drawn with weariness, her back to him as she spoke to Megan or Mary or Jenny, yet never once let her attention stray from Elizabeth. When, he wondered, had his wife ceased to be a stranger in this keep? When had she made it her home, and the Campbells her family? And why had he never noticed before?

He paced restlessly before the hearth, his boots making no sound on the soft Persian rug. Muriella's face was always before him—her eyes dark with dread, luminous with pleasure, bright with fierce determination. He was bewildered by her complexity, weakened by her pain, impressed by her courage and stunned by his own wildly changing reactions.

His stomach rumbled but the kitchen was too far away,

the hallways too cold. He glanced again at the open book, but it was no use. He could not ignore the unfamiliar tenderness he felt for Muriella, the desire to cup her cheek in his open palm. It made him uneasy. This was not a straightforward battle where he could see the enemy and face him squarely. Perhaps it was not a battle at all, and there was no enemy except his own blindness.

He pounded his fist on the mantel in frustration. He could feel his wife's presence, even half a castle away. He could feel her warmth, hear the tiny, insistent voice that called him, drew him toward her while it warned him away.

In the far shadows of the room, Elizabeth's voice echoed coldly: *Ye can't keep your vigil here.*

Without a backward glance, he abandoned the fire, stepping into the dark hallway. He found his way easily enough, although there were no torches to light the path. For the third night in succession, he passed the door to his chamber and many others after it until he came to Muriella's. For the third time, he put his hand on the latch, then paused, undecided. Above all he wanted to look at her, to see her sleeping with her hair spread on the pillow. But for the third time, he left the door unopened and leaned instead against the wall, waiting for something he could not even begin to understand.

Megan stood beside the shuttered window, looking over her shoulder now and then to see if Muriella still slept peacefully. In the firelight her mistress's face seemed calm enough, but it would not last. Megan was sure of that. The dreams had come every night since Elizabeth had been brought to Inveraray. Every night Muriella woke up shrieking Maclean's name in terror.

Megan pulled her robe closer about her shoulders but did not move nearer the fire. Just now she preferred the chilly air by the window to the heat of the flames. She tried to concentrate on pleasant images that might lull her to sleep, but saw only phantoms that hovered just beyond her reach. She frowned. It was not like her to be disturbed by indefinable fears. But, she admitted to herself, there was something besides her mistress' nightmares that was making her uneasy.

A movement from the bed shattered her reverie.

Muriella was dreaming of a valley, its hills scattered with wild roses and morning glories. She ran across a wide meadow, seeking the burn that rippled by somewhere out of sight. She could hear the pounding footsteps in the distance and knew that Hugh was coming, that soon he would catch her, laughing, tangling his hands in her long auburn hair. When she found the burn, it was already swelling into a river. She paused on the bank, wondering if she dared try to cross by the boulders that protruded from the water, making a bridge to the other side. While she stood, undecided, a hand touched her shoulder.

"Do ye need me to help ye cross?" It was not Hugh's voice, but John's.

To her surprise, she turned to smile at him. His smile answered hers and she was only vaguely aware that the river was rising higher, so that both stood ankle deep in water.

"Come." He took her hand, leading her out to the stones.

The boulders were shiny green with moss and she was afraid of falling, but John coaxed her forward. She took a step, then another, holding his hand tightly all the while. As she picked her way across the stones, the water rose to her knees and the boulders disappeared in the whirlpools the torrent created. When the water reached her shoulders, she turned to look at John for reassurance, but as she did so, she lost her balance and fell headlong into the rising river.

She was revolving in ever-tinier circles. Her hair was swept around her body, her arms and legs tangled in the strands. She could not move. The circling motion coiled her hair around her hips, her waist, her chest. She gasped, choking, spinning toward the boulders on every side. Then, abruptly, she was lifted from the water. Her hair, which a moment before had coiled like a snake around her shoulders, fell back, dripping and limp behind her. Closing her eyes, she breathed dry air and lay still, blessing the arms that held her high above the river.

Someone laughed. She opened her eyes to smile into John's face but he wasn't there. "Maclean!" she screamed. He was laughing at her and his arms fell away and she was falling back toward the black heart of the whirlpool.

Megan had taken a few steps toward her mistress when the door swung open. John did not pause to look at the servant, but went instead to where his wife sat huddled on the bed, her hair falling like a curtain over her face. Taking her in his arms, he held her for a long time in silence.

Megan stood frozen where she was. He must have heard Muriella call out. But how was that possible? His chamber was not nearby. Then he must have been outside, she thought. But why?

She remembered her anxiety during the past few nights, how restless Sir John had seemed, how his gaze followed his wife wherever she went of late. Had he been waiting outside the door? Or had he meant to come in all along? Megan shivered. It was too soon. Muriella's fears, once pushed back into darkness, had rushed into the light once more. If John chose to lie with her now, Megan knew it might destroy her mistress.

The servant stiffened her spine. She would stop him if that were what he intended. Glowering, she moved closer to the bed. John was holding his wife so Megan could not see her mistress's face. He was massaging Muriella's shoulders rhythmically.

"Muriella," he said, "tell me what ye were dreaming of."

His wife opened her eyes, compelled by the sound of his voice, but the webs of sleep still clung, woven into the lingering traces of fear. "The water," she gasped. "The rising water." She choked on the words.

John frowned as his hands moved over her back. Was she thinking of Elizabeth and how she had nearly drowned? Or was there something more? He cupped Muriella's face in his open palms. "'Tis over now," he told her. "Elizabeth is safe."

Slowly, one word at a time, his meaning penetrated Muriella's fogged mind. She was grateful that he could not see inside her nightmare to the real source of her terror. Elizabeth might be safe, but Muriella was not. "I tried to stop it," she cried, "but I couldn't do it."

"Ye had nothing to do with what happened to my sister. I've told ye before, 'tis a blessing that she's free of that man at last."

Muriella shook her head. "'Tis not a blessing, but a curse." She did not give him the chance to contradict her. "Don't ye understand? I *did* curse her, not by causing Maclean to put her on the rock, but by keeping her alive—to mourn, to weep, to remember."

John had no answer for that. He remembered too clearly the chilling indifference in Elizabeth's eyes. "She'll learn to forget. She'll be herself again in time," he said.

"Mayhap," his wife agreed, but she did not believe it. Gradually, her heart had ceased its frantic beating and her skin had grown warm under John's touch. She looked into his eyes, clouded with his own troubled thoughts. "I wanted to thank ye for what ye did today. I know 'twas not easy to let Maclean go. But for Elizabeth's sake, 'twas kinder."

"Was it?" John murmured. "I wonder." He saw that Muriella was calmer, that the effects of the dream had faded away. "Do ye think ye can sleep now?" he asked.

"Aye." The concern in his tone made Muriella want to weep. She could rail against his anger and his betrayal and his lust for blood, but his kindness she could not bear. He brushed his fingertips over her cheek and the simple gesture brought a rush of warmth that frightened her with its power. She made herself breathe slowly, evenly, but could not stop her hand from reaching out to cover his.

"I'll leave ye then," John said. "Ye need to rest." His fingers tightened around hers for an instant; then he rose to draw the furs up to her neck. When Muriella closed her eyes reluctantly, he stepped back and, motioning for Megan to follow, turned to leave the room.

The servant stood for a moment longer, her heartbeat echoing in her ears. What could he want from her? With a single glance at her mistress, she shook her head and slipped from the chamber.

John was waiting in the passage; she could just discern his figure in the dark hallway. She moved forward with care, wishing she had brought a torch.

"Come!" he spoke impatiently from out of the gloom. Then he was beside her, his hand on her shoulder, guiding her through the corridor. When he touched her, she thought that perhaps he intended to take her instead of Muriella. She had seen the hunger in his eyes when he looked at his wife; mayhap this time Mary was not nearby to assuage it. Megan gave no sign of her apprehension. If that was what he desired, what would she do? She had no answer.

After what seemed like hours of darkness, John kicked open a door, leading the servant into the library. At least there was a fire, she thought inanely. At least it was warm. As she moved toward the light of the flames, she heard him stop near the desk. She stared into the fire, braiding her fingers in agitation.

"Megan."

She jumped despite her resolution to remain calm.

"Look at me."

She turned to face him. He was perched on the edge of the desk, his brows drawn together, his hands clenched. "Tonight is the third time," he began, "that I've heard my wife cry out in terror at her dreams."

Megan swallowed with difficulty. So he had been outside the door for three nights.

"I want ye to tell me, if ye can, why she's so troubled in her sleep and why she calls Maclean's name."

It seemed he had not believed Muriella when she said she was dreaming of Elizabeth. Megan opened her mouth, but the words stuck in her throat. "M'lord—"

"The nightmares began when my sister came, didn't they?" John persisted.

"Aye."

"Do ye know what the dreams are?"

"No," the servant said. "She won't tell me, though I have asked her often enough."

"And ye can't guess?"

"No, m'lord."

"What of Maclean?" John persisted. "Why should she see him in her nightmares?"

The servant stared at her hands. By the look in Sir John's eyes, she guessed that his need for his wife had become an obsession. If she wanted to keep him from returning to Muriella tonight, there was only one thing to do.

"Megan?"

She looked up. "Aye?"

"What of Maclean?" he repeated with ill-concealed impatience.

She had sworn, she remembered, but she could not think of that now. "She often has nightmares about him."

John ran his hand over his forehead, leaving a puzzled frown behind. "Does she have reason to fear him?"

"She—I don't—"

Suddenly his control shattered. He leapt up to grasp Megan by the shoulders. "Tell me!"

"Aye," she muttered. "She has reason enough."

John released her, stepping back. "What is it?"

Megan swallowed once more. "Ye remember just before the weddin' when she fell and bruised her face?"

"Aye." The cold fury was already gathering in his face. "Go on."

"She didn't fall."

"Maclean." His voice was without inflection, but Megan recognized the threat beneath the single word. "There were scratches on his neck that night. I remember he tried to hide them."

"I didn't think ye noticed."

He nodded, took a deep breath, and forced himself to ask, "Did he rape her?"

Megan hesitated for an instant. "She said he didn't."

Closing his eyes, John fought to retain control. "But ye don't believe her?"

"I don't know what to believe." The servant moved away from him. She was not certain what he might do next. When he opened his eyes, they glittered cold and silver in the firelight.

"Why didn't she tell me?" he asked at last. For a moment,

he absorbed Megan's startled expression, then looked away. "No," he said, "ye needn't answer." Moving past her, he lowered himself into a chair and leaned forward, resting his elbows on his knees and his face in his hands.

When he spoke, his voice was so low that Megan had to step forward to hear him. "Ye can go back to her now. And thank ye."

He did not look up to see her leave the room. His thoughts were circling around a distant memory. He was staring at the bruises that discolored Muriella's face. Taking her chin in his hand, he had said, *So, little one, ye'll be damaged for our wedding. Are ye sure ye haven't done it on purpose?* Then, on their wedding night—he did not like to remember how cruelly he had taken his wife that first time. No wonder she shrank away from his touch.

He looked up, his jaw muscles tightening convulsively. The image of Muriella's face dissolved and in its place he saw Maclean laughing as the gate opened before him. John sat up, staring unseeing at the fire. "I let him go," he hissed. "I set the bastard free!"

In one swift movement, he reached the door. He wrenched it open and hurried down the corridor to his chamber.

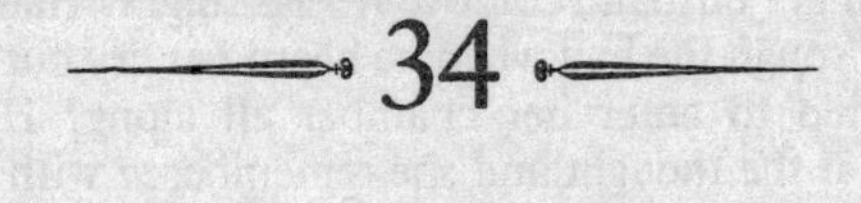

# 34

Muriella paused at the top of the stairs, looking out over the crowded trestle tables strung across the Great Hall. The noise this morning was unusually subdued. Men and servants sat staring before them with no laughter and very little chatter. Muriella was surprised to see Duncan and Elizabeth already seated at the high table; her sister-in-law had not joined them for a meal since her arrival. John, she noticed, had not yet come down. She felt a flash of disappointment that made her hand tremble on the balustrade. She tightened her hold on the worn, smooth wood until the feeling passed. With a steadying breath, she went to join the others.

She sat next to Elizabeth, who smiled wanly. Muriella felt a flicker of hope at the gesture. Touching her sister-in-law's hand, she murmured, "'Tis good to see ye here."

"I couldn't stare at the four walls of that chamber any longer," Elizabeth explained. "'Twas too much like a prison there, ye ken?"

"Aye," Muriella agreed. "I knew ye'd have to come seeking the light soon. 'Tis fortunate that the sun has burned the mist away this morning."

Her sister-in-law looked up at the high slitted windows where the light spilled into the room, softening the mottled gray stone walls. "'Tis late," she observed, brow furrowed. "Why hasn't Johnnie come down yet?"

"I didn't wish to disturb him," Duncan told her. "He

hasn't slept well the past few nights. I'm beginning to wonder what ails him."

Muriella concentrated on the platter of cold meat Jenny handed her, grateful for the excuse to hide her thoughts. She too had begun to wonder. Why, she asked herself again and again, had her husband come to her last night? Had he been passing through the hall when he heard her cry out? Or had he intended to enter her chamber all along? Her pulse pounded at the thought and she remembered with mingled pleasure and unease the warmth his touch had brought her.

Just then, Andrew Campbell came to the head of the table. "I went to wake Sir John, as ye bid me," Andrew explained to Duncan, "but I found him gone."

"Gone? Gone where? Do ye mean he went hunting?"

"Aye, so I thought at first. But I asked the men and it seems no one saw him go and he took no one with him. Then I asked Sim. He was watchin' the gate, ye ken." Andrew leaned forward, full of the importance of his news. "Sim said he opened the gate for Sir John when 'twas still dark night. He was alone and"—he paused in order to hold his audience in suspense a moment longer—"he wore full armor and carried his father's sword. What do ye think of that?"

Duncan blinked at the man, perplexed. "Are ye certain?"

"Aye, so Sim says."

"But where would he be going in full armor in the middle of the night?"

"I'll tell ye, Duncan Campbell. I'll tell ye where he's gone." Elizabeth half rose from her chair, her eyes darting from face to face. "He's gone after my husband. I know it. 'Tis just what he's done."

Taking her hand, Duncan tried to calm her. "Why would he do that? He gave ye his word, didn't he? Ye must be mistaken."

Elizabeth shook her head, sinking back onto the bench when her legs would no longer support her. "Ye won't be convincing me of that."

Muriella closed her eyes and tried to remember what John

had said last night when she told him it had been kinder to let Maclean go. *Was it?* he'd murmured. *I wonder.* She stared at the pitted tabletop, her mouth dry with apprehension. She wanted to tell Elizabeth she was wrong, but could not bring herself to put the lie into words.

John sat in a plush velvet chair, staring at the huge door which led to the living quarters at Edinburgh Castle. He was waiting for his brother. Wearily, he adjusted his doublet. He was not looking forward to this interview with Colin. No doubt the Earl would be livid when he learned that Maclean had left Inveraray Castle alive. But John needed his help. He would just have to keep his own temper under control.

He knew his face had begun to show signs of the strain he had been under recently. His skin was burnt from exposure to the sun and there were dark circles under his eyes. It had taken him two weeks to trace Maclean to Edinburgh—two weeks of riding unescorted to the gates of his enemies' castles and inquiring after the Laird's whereabouts. He had been surprised time and again that not a single man raised a single sword against him. Of course, officially the Campbells and Macleans were at peace, but surely his brother-in-law's relatives knew what their laird had done to Elizabeth, and why John Campbell sought him now. They must have realized that the Campbells would soon regret their impulse to set the man free.

He had asked a multitude of questions at every keep, and each time, although he discovered nothing, he'd had the feeling they would have told him if they'd known. It made him uneasy. When he finally came upon Evan Maclean on the Isle of Tiree, John had been unable to disguise his impatience any longer. "'Tis only your laird we seek now," he'd told the young man, "but if ye shelter him, our vengeance will extend to the whole Clan Maclean."

Evan regarded his adversary with piercing eyes. "Ye want Lachlan Maclean's life, then."

When John nodded, the other man leaned forward, fists clenched. "Well, my friend, take it, and welcome."

John gaped at him. "Ye can't mean that."

Evan's eyes smoldered as he replied, "I do mean it. The man is a fool. He's done nothing but harm to the Macleans for a long time now. The rebellion was his idea, ye ken. We knew it was lost before we began, but no' our laird. He must needs know better than us. And now—" He paused, steadying his voice. "Now that we're finally at peace, he does something that will insure the Campbells are always our enemies." He put his hand on John's arm. "I believe he's mad, and if he lives, he'll eventually destroy us. He thought ye might change your mind, so he's run to Edinburgh to hide. Kill him this time. He's my enemy as much as he is yours."

John shook his head, remembering the vehemence of Evan's declaration. He still could not believe the Macleans had abandoned their laird so completely. He wondered, sometimes, what the Campbells would do if Colin—

"What in God's name are ye doing in Edinburgh?" the third Earl of Argyll roared from across the room. "They told me ye were waiting, but I wouldn't believe them. 'Tis insane to leave Inveraray unprotected with the Macleans ready to slit our throats."

John eyed his brother through half-closed lids. Colin was dressed magnificently in velvet doublet and satin trews. Jewels glittered on his fingers, and the Campbell brooch fastened his cloak to his shoulder. His face, John noted, was purple with fury. Swallowing the bitter response that rose to his lips, John said, "Inveraray is safe enough. I brought no men with me and Duncan and Richard are there if trouble comes. As for the Macleans, from what I've seen, they won't be attacking us at all."

The Earl snorted. "Aye, Johnnie, ye were always so wise. Tell me then, how do ye know they won't attack? And why have ye come?"

"I came to find Maclean, and they won't strike because they want him dead."

"What!" Colin demanded. "To find Maclean? They want him dead? He *is* dead, isn't he? My orders were clear enough." He loomed threateningly over his brother. "What've ye done this time, Johnnie?"

"I let him go," John replied with forced calm. He watched as the lump begin to pulse between his brother's brows.

"Say that again," Colin hissed. "I wouldn't want to kill ye because I didn't hear aright. Say it again."

"I let him go free." With difficulty, John fought the impulse to push his brother away from him.

"Why, in the name of all that's holy, did ye do such a thing?"

Because ye had a cruel and unworthy idea, he wanted to shout. Because Maclean is the deceiver, not the Campbells. But he did not say those things. "I did it for Elizabeth."

"For Elizabeth!" Colin spluttered. "For Eliz— Are ye daft? Ye let an enemy go for the sake of a woman?"

"Elizabeth begged me."

"I don't give a bloody damn what she said or what she felt. 'Twas business, ye imbecile. Business! 'Tis time ye learned there are a great many things more important than your sister's feelings."

Rising precipitously, John moved out of his brother's way. He could see it was time to remind Colin of his purpose here before they came to blows. "I came to Edinburgh to kill the man. I need your help to find him."

"Help ye! I should kill ye where ye stand. Do ye know how many plans you've ruined? I've already negotiated with Campbell of Auchinbreck for Elizabeth's hand. We need that alliance."

John whirled to stare at his brother. "You've what? Her husband isn't even dead yet!"

"'Tis no fault of mine, little brother. That was your responsibility. And the marriage is necessary. Now listen to me, and this time ye'd best do as I say. My men will search Edinburgh for Maclean. When he's found, kill him at once. Then, when you're certain he's dead, go back to Inveraray with this letter in your pocket." Drawing some parchment from his doublet, he handed it to his brother, who stood speechless at last. "Elizabeth must sign the marriage agreement within these two weeks. See that she does. And see that she makes no trouble over this. If ye fail in any particular, if ye so much as breathe without my consent, ye'll be mighty sorry, I guarantee that."

John stared at the letter in his hand. Colin had not even waited until he knew Elizabeth was a widow before selling her to another man. For a moment he was tempted to leave Edinburgh without finding Maclean. He wanted no part of his brother's ambitions. Let Maclean live, John thought, and see how Colin's plans worked then. But Muriella—his stomach clenched with sick rage. No, regardless of Colin's greed, his brother-in-law must die. Crumpling the parchment in his fist, John turned to leave the room. He could not stand to look at his brother's gloating face a moment longer.

The following day, John mounted the rickety stairs at the back of a tavern while the landlord watched him anxiously. The innkeeper did not care for the expression on the stranger's face. "Who do ye seek?" the man asked with as much courage as he could summon.

"No one," John snapped. "I've found him." As he climbed the stairs, he tried to concentrate on his object so he would not notice the rank smell that arose from behind the stairway or the shabby condition of the halls. Maclean had chosen a hell of a place in which to die. But of course, he did not know he was to die.

John stopped with his hand on a rusty latch. Drawing a deep breath, he pushed the door open.

Maclean sat on the bed with a tankard of ale beside him. The sheets tangled about his waist were stained and torn; they had probably not been washed for some time. Besides the bed, there was a lone table with a candle burning on its uneven surface. The air reeked of sweat and ale and the rotten remains of numerous meals. A mass of picked bones was piled haphazardly on the floor at the bedside. With his fingers clenched on the handle of his sword, John looked for the first time directly at Maclean's face.

The man was staring at him, stupefied, his irises lost in the whiteness of his eyes. His Adam's apple moved rapidly up and down the line of his throat.

"How in Christ's name—," Maclean began. Then he stopped. The color returned to his cheeks and he smiled. "Evan told ye, didn't he?"

John clutched his sword more tightly. He had come full of hatred and fury, but just now pity and disgust were even greater. "No. I found ye on my own."

Maclean laughed without mirth. "Are ye afraid of hurting my feelings? I know Evan despises me, as do they all. It makes no matter. So you've changed your mind, have ye? I'm not surprised."

"Quiet!" John cried. His own repulsion threatened to overwhelm him. "Get up!" he ordered. "Get your sword."

"No." Maclean settled himself against the pillows. "No," he repeated, "ye'll have to kill me in my bed. Did ye really think I'd make this easy for ye?"

"Surely ye don't wish to die that way?" John said. "They'll laugh at ye."

"Aye, but what will they say about ye, boy? Don't ye think they'll call ye a coward for killing a man when he had no defense against ye?"

As John moved forward menacingly, a rat skittered across the floor. The candlelight was weak; it did no more than deepen the furrows on Maclean's cheeks. "Ye don't deserve to die like a gentleman. They'll know that."

"Will they?" His brother-in-law laughed again, more loudly. He watched as John advanced toward him, drawing his sword from its sheath. When the blade hung a few feet away, pointing at his heart, he muttered, "I want to die, did ye know that? No," he added when John retreated a step. "I thought ye didn't." He paused, giving his brother-in-law a grim little smile. "Elizabeth knew. Ye take her for a fool, but she's a great deal wiser than ye."

"Be quiet!" All at once the dead Earl's voice echoed inside John's head. *Think before ye act, Johnnie! Think!* But for once he *had* thought. For two long weeks he had thought of the tarnished pride of the Campbells; of Elizabeth, grieving alone while her husband lived free; and of Muriella, retreating inside the darkness of her nightmare. Straightening his shoulders, he took a step forward. This time he had no choice. He met his brother-in-law's gaze for a moment; as he buried the blade in Maclean's chest, he whispered, "For Muriella."

Maclean's eyes widened with brief surprise before the blood gushed over the sword, dulling its silver gleam. He ceased moving and his eyes glazed over until he stared unseeing before him.

John wrenched his father's sword from Maclean's limp body, sickened by the sight of the dead man slumped among the sheets, tipping the ale so it spilled onto the covers and blended with the spreading puddle of blood. Blood and ale dripped over the edge of the bed, falling onto the discarded bones.

Without looking back, John staggered into the hallway. It was done. Maclean was dead and his sister free. And perhaps, just perhaps, Muriella's nightmares were over. The thought of his wife made the mist retreat somewhat, but the horror would not go. Blood and ale, his mind repeated with monotonous regularity. Blood and ale. Blood and ale.

Leaning on his sword, he tried to concentrate on Muriella. Unexpectedly, the mist disappeared. He could go home to her now. His heart, which he believed had ceased to beat, took up its rhythm once again. He would see her. The thought brought with it a sudden clarity, a vibrant memory of how her body had felt in his arms. He remembered the way she had looked at him, her eyes clouded with weariness, and run her fingers from his beard to his shoulder to his slow, beating heart.

John's smile turned to a grimace. Maclean was dead, but Muriella would not thank him for that. She cared too much for Elizabeth. He could envision his wife's face, pale with shock and anger, her green eyes wide with accusation.

She would not welcome him back, could not forget the past so easily. That much he knew. But maybe he could make her forget in time. He would speak to her, care for her, teach her to know him as he learned to know her. And he would not touch her until, when he held her close, her eyes met his and she saw *him*—only him, and not the specter her fear had created.

With an awkward motion, he wiped the blood from his father's sword and turned his back forever on Lachlan Maclean.

So, at least, he chose to believe.

This was in spring, when winter-tide
With his blast hideous to abide,
Was over-driven and birdis small
As throstle and the nihtegale
Began right merrily to sing.

Duncan's voice rose above the clack of the loom, mingling with the rhythm of Muriella's flying fingers. She smiled, grateful for the squire's song, which distracted her from her own thoughts. He had sensed her restlessness since John went away; often in the waning of the slow, endless days, he came to sing and play his harp, hoping it would cheer her.

And for to make in their singing,
Sundry notes and sound-es sere,
And melodies pleasant for to hear.

Muriella bent closer to the forming tapestry, running her palm over the finely woven threads as the notes of Duncan's clareschaw began to soothe her. She did not thank him, for he seemed to understand her gratitude intuitively; sometimes he came and went without either of them speaking a word. He had become a friend who shared with her the silence as well as the songs.

The colors of the third and final panel of the Loch Awe hanging glimmered under Muriella's hands as the fabric shifted in a draft of cold air. Lovingly, she traced the glow of silver moonlight that turned to gold when it reached the water of the loch. She liked this section of the tapestry—woven with the thread the Earl had brought just before his death—best of all; it showed the shimmering expanse of Loch Awe with its wooded islands and tree-scattered shore. In the center of the interlaced blues and greens, the moon made its radiant path of light. In the far corner, a woman with long auburn hair knelt on the bank, looking at a reflection in the water—the face of the woman of the loch who had so often called to Muriella in her high, haunting voice.

> And the trees began to make
> Buds and brightest blooms also,
> To weave the covering of their head
> That wicked winter had them reft.

Muriella almost lost herself in the lacework of colored threads, in the sound of Duncan's voice, in the lilting song of the Highland harp. Almost, she escaped the loneliness that had grown deeper as the days passed. Her friends were with her—Megan, Duncan and Elizabeth—filling the hours with chatter and work and companionship. But it was not enough. The ache inside reminded her always that John was away. The keep seemed strangely empty without the sound of his rage, his laughter, his ceaseless energy. She missed him, Muriella admitted in dismay.

John's face rose before her, blocking the vivid pattern of the cloth, reminding her of the day when he had kissed her in the music room. Her skin tingled at the remembered touch of his hands, and the low, vibrant humming began in her head. Rising abruptly, she dropped the shuttle and watched it swing forward and back across the colored fabric. She stared, mesmerized by the languid movement, by the flickering images in her mind that seemed to take on the color and shape of the tapestry before her. Breathing deeply, she forced herself to look away.

Muriella shivered at a gust of chilly air and moved toward the welcome warmth of the fire. Duncan had finished his song. He turned as she passed so the heat could reach his face. Rubbing his hands together, he leaned closer to the flames.

As Muriella knelt before the deep stone fireplace, an unnerving stillness settled around her, holding her away from the heat of the fire. She was so cold, all at once, so empty. The flames curled around one another, melding, then separating. She peered more closely into the fire. She thought there was something there. Something—her hand shook, her pulse quickened, and the flames leapt unnaturally. Then she saw John, standing in the darkness with a sword in his hand. A candle flickered, revealing Maclean's tangled red curls. The sword moved through the shadows and as the blade plunged into Maclean's chest, John cried, "For Muriella!" The blood gushed out, mixing with a wash of golden ale and dripping over the edge of the bed.

"Dear God!" Muriella cried, while John's voice rang in her ears. As the room spun out of control, she gasped for air, reaching blindly with her sweat-bathed palms for the support of the unyielding stone.

For a moment, Duncan was frozen with fear at the sight of her dark, empty eyes, but he saw that she was falling and knew he had to catch her. With his hands on her shoulders, he pulled her close, running his fingers over her back in slow circles, repeating her name again and again. He did not know what else to do; he was helpless in the face of her disturbing power.

When Muriella shuddered and buried her head in his plaid, he closed his arms around her. He sensed that she did not know he was near, but this time he would not leave her alone with her terror as he had long ago when she first came to Inveraray—the day of the battle with Andrew Calder, when she'd foreseen the deaths of so many men. He fought back his own apprehension, holding her until the shaking eased. Gently, the squire tilted her head back and saw that she was weeping.

Muriella clung to him wordlessly. Maclean was dead. John had killed him, and he had done it, not for Elizabeth, but for his wife. Why? She did not know who held her now, drawing her back to the reality of the airy chamber. She only knew she wanted to forget, to escape the lingering chill of the vision that would not leave her. Muriella leaned closer, seeking the comforting warmth of Duncan's body. His fingers brushed away her memories.

Four days later, Muriella and Elizabeth sat together in the solar. As always, Muriella was bent over the tapestry, which was now nearly complete. She had only to finish the far bank of the loch, the red-haired woman kneeling on the shore, and the indistinct image of the face in the water.

Elizabeth had been working on a bit of embroidery for most of the morning, but now she sat with her hands in her lap. She gazed out the window, her thoughts far away.

Muriella watched her Elizabeth with concern. She had not mentioned the vision of Maclean's death or her own dismay over what John had done. The time was not yet right to tell Elizabeth she had become a widow. Daily, she prayed that John would return and explain his actions, but for now, she could only watch helplessly while her sister-in-law slipped further and further inside herself. Elizabeth had changed a great deal in the past few weeks; her hair hung lank and colorless down her back, her skin was nearly transparent, and her eyes were either wintry bleak or empty of expression.

"What are ye thinking?" Muriella asked.

Elizabeth started as if awakened from a deep sleep. "About my father," she said before she could stop to think. She looked down at her embroidery to avoid meeting Muriella's gaze. With sudden fervor, she began to weave her needle through the fabric.

"Do ye miss him?"

"Miss him!" Elizabeth laughed harshly. "Why should I,

when he abandoned me without a thought? 'Tis hard to care about someone who values power and wealth more than his own kin."

Muriella could not deny it. Though four years had passed since the night when, in desperation, she had faced the Earl across the library, she remembered far too clearly the cold determination in his voice. *Your feelings don't matter. The good of the clan comes first. All the weeping in the world will not change a fact so fundamental.*

Elizabeth looked up, her face strained and pale, but for the first time in weeks, her indifference had slipped away. "I was his favorite, did ye know that? As a child I used to read to him, to sit with him before the fire while he taught me Latin and the Gaelic. In those days I thought he had the most beautiful voice I'd ever heard."

Head bent over the loom, Muriella concentrated on the colored threads to hide her dismay. It hurt her to think the Earl had shared those things with someone else before her. "What happened to change things?" she asked when she could speak again.

"'Tis simple enough," Elizabeth said. "There was a rebellion, and afterward my father gave me to an enemy in order to seal the bargain. He told me he couldn't displease the King, though I begged him to reconsider. Then, after 'twas done, he wanted me to forgive him." She twisted her fingers in the fabric on her lap. "I couldn't do it. He'd hurt me too deeply. Even as a girl, I knew what kind of man he was, but I loved him so much, I never thought he'd betray me that way." She broke off, choking on the words that seemed to stick in her throat. "But ye should know about that," she added finally. "He did it to ye as well."

Muriella's hands trembled and she found she could not answer. "I thought ye loved your husband," she ventured at last.

Elizabeth met her sister-in-law's gaze with an unwavering stare. "Not from the beginning. At first, all I felt was that my father didn't need me anymore, so he'd cast me away like a favorite bauble he'd grown tired of."

"But—" Muriella began, then stopped herself.

"Ye were going to say that Maclean did the same thing, weren't ye?"

Shaking her head, Muriella started to speak, but Elizabeth interrupted her. "You're right, I know." She bit her lip and tears came to her eyes.

Muriella reached for Elizabeth's hand. The older woman clung desperately. After several moments she found her voice again. "But ye see, no matter what happened in the end, Lachlan always needed me. He was so different from my father, who never wanted to let his weakness show. The Earl would never have asked for help. He was too damned strong for that." She gazed out the window, as if she could see the past painted across the billowing waves. "That's why I swore to myself that I'd give my husband the loyalty I'd always given my father. The Earl didn't deserve it anymore."

"And once ye'd decided, ye never turned back," Muriella said. How could she ever have thought Elizabeth weak?

"No," Elizabeth sighed. "Though my family hated me for that choice. Yet not one of them tried to stop the marriage, not even Johnnie. And once it came to me that I loved my husband, I knew I couldn't abandon him, no matter how hard he tried to make me hate him. 'Twas *my* feelings that mattered, not his." She smiled the grim little smile that Muriella had come to dread. "At least Lachlan realized he had wronged me. He begged my forgiveness for his betrayal before he had even committed it." She frowned, her eyes damp with tears. "My father didn't ever understand how much he'd hurt me. He didn't know his sin was greater than my husband's, because the Earl claimed to love me." She smiled with infinite sadness. "I suppose ye think me foolish."

"No," Muriella said, realizing that she spoke the truth. "'Twas no fool who had the courage to stand up to John and ask for your husband's life. 'Twould have been easier to let him die, I think, after all he'd done to ye. But ye never would have forgiven yourself if ye'd done that. I envy ye, Elizabeth. I haven't the courage to love anyone that much."

Elizabeth took her Muriella's hands in a tight grip.

"Och, but ye do. Ye just don't realize it. But I thank ye all the same. You're the only one who really tries to understand and doesn't blame me for failing the Campbells. I love ye for that, Muriella—for everything. For caring enough to save my life, though I can't think 'twas wise."

Muriella opened her mouth to object, but before she could do so, Elizabeth interjected, "And because I care for ye, I'll tell ye this. As a woman, the only thing ye can depend on in this life is that men will try to break ye in any way they can. Before you've recovered from their first blow, they'll strike ye again. 'Tis not really that they're cruel; they just don't know any other way. But remember too, they can only hurt ye if ye give them the power to do so." Elizabeth raised her head and whispered, more to herself than to Muriella, "I don't intend to give anyone that power again."

Before Muriella could respond, before she could remove her hands from Elizabeth's cold grasp, the door swung open and both women turned. They stared, frozen with shock, as John came into the room.

When Elizabeth's hands fell away, Muriella leaned forward, gripping the wooden sides of the loom for support. She was stunned by the rush of joy that flared within her at the unexpected sight of her husband. Then she remembered what he had done. Turning toward her sister-in-law, she saw the mask of indifference settle over Elizabeth's waxen features. Muriella found that her voice had left her. She could only gaze mutely from sister to brother and back again.

Just when she thought the silence would stretch between them until it shattered, Elizabeth spoke. "Where have ye been? To find my husband?"

John frowned. "Elizabeth—," he began.

"Ye needn't try to soothe me when ye don't even know if I'm hurt, Johnnie. Just tell me, is he dead?"

"Aye," he said softly.

"Where?"

"In Edinburgh."

"Do ye think the Macleans will bury him?"

Approaching with caution, John took his sister's hand.

"Ye needn't concern yourself with that. 'Tis over," he told her.

Elizabeth ignored him. "No, of course they won't. They told ye where to find him, didn't they?"

He wanted to deny it, but could not bring himself to lie. "Elizabeth, let me—"

"And did ye talk to Colin?" she pressed.

Taken aback by the question, he regarded her warily. "Aye."

"What did he say?"

John tried to look beyond his sister's cool exterior to the pain he guessed must lie beneath, but even her eyes told him nothing. "He was angry," he said, choosing his words with care.

"But what of me? I'll wager he has another wedding planned, doesn't he? Our Colin isn't one to miss a chance for a new alliance."

"Elizabeth, I know you're upset, but—"

"I'm no' upset. Can't ye see how steady I am? Now tell me."

"Well, Colin said he thought—"

"Is there a letter?" she interrupted.

John gaped at her. Had his sister inherited Muriella's Sight? And why was she so stiff and cold when she should be weeping at the news of her husband's death?

"Give it to me," Elizabeth demanded.

For a moment, John hesitated. "Ye needn't look at it now. 'Tis too soon."

Elizabeth smiled at him pityingly. "Don't assuage your own guilt by keeping me in suspense. I want to know now who Colin has chosen for me. Someone rich, I'll wager, with enough men to give the Campbells a little more power." She turned to Muriella. "As if they don't have enough of that already."

John did not know what to say. She made it sound so calculating, so inhuman. He wanted to put the blame on Colin, but then he caught Muriella's gaze. Hadn't his own wife been sold to the Campbells in the same way—for a little power and a great deal of money?

"I want to see it now," Elizabeth repeated succinctly, as if speaking to a slow-witted child. "Don't play games with me, Johnnie."

John attempted to quell his sudden anger as he pulled the crumpled parchment from his doublet and placed it in his sister's open palm. This was not how he had planned this meeting on the long ride back from Edinburgh.

He watched as Elizabeth read Colin's letter quickly. Then she started to laugh. It was the one reaction he had not expected, and the sound chilled him, despite the warmth of the tiny room. He could not forget that he had heard the same unearthly laughter in the tower that day. "Please," he said, reaching for her hand. "Elizabeth."

"Don't ye find it amusing?" she asked, gasping as she rocked forward and backward. "I'm to marry Archibald Campbell of Auchinbreck." When she saw that her brother and Muriella stared at her blankly, Elizabeth drew a deep breath and explained, "Archibald Campbell—my father's name." She laughed and choked until her face was scarlet and her knuckles on the embroidery frame were white. She laughed until the letter fell from her fingers to the floor, where it came to rest at John's feet.

Muriella sat by the fire in the library with a book of verses open on her lap. Though she tried to concentrate, her attention wandered and instead she found herself staring into the flames, watching the changing patterns of light.

All at once, she raised her head, every nerve in her body tingling with awareness. She knew John had entered the room, though he had not made a sound; she could feel his presence as surely as if his hand were resting on her shoulder.

"Muriella."

As she looked up at him—at his face, burnished bronze from long hours in the sun, and his eyes, touched with gold from the glow of the firelight—she felt the same rush of joy that had come to her when she first saw him that afternoon. She had seen him only briefly since, but she had felt his presence during every endless hour in the day. She smiled at him as he crossed the room to seat himself in the Earl's carved oak chair.

"I wanted to talk to ye," he said, "about Maclean."

She nodded, not trusting herself to speak.

"I want ye to know that I didn't really have a choice. I had to kill him—for the pride of the Campbells and, though ye may not believe it, for Elizabeth. She wasn't truly free until her husband was dead. Ye can understand that, can't ye?"

In the back of her mind she heard again the two words, *For Muriella!*, and knew he was not telling the whole truth; she sensed that he never would. She knew too that she should have been angry that he had broken his word to his sister, but all she could feel was relief. As he had said, Elizabeth was finally free of the chains that had bound her to Lachlan Maclean. Muriella looked into the dancing flames and murmured, "I understand."

"Do ye truly?" John leaned closer, considering her sculptured profile—the curve of her mouth, the gleam in her eyes, the stillness that characterized her features. All at once he wanted desperately to hold her. But he had made himself a promise he did not intend to break. For a long moment, he struggled with the urge to pull her into his arms. He was winning the battle against his own desire when she turned to look at him.

"Aye, I think I do," Muriella whispered, lips slightly parted, brows drawn together. Without thinking, she put her hand on his knee.

John's carefully constructed walls crumbled at his feet. In a single movement, he stood and drew her up against him. Her eyes were luminous, mesmerizing, but this time he felt no desire to escape their power. "Muriella," he murmured.

As she looked up, he kissed her. His lips moved gently against hers and she felt a response stirring deep within her. He drew her closer while his hands moved slowly over her back. Wherever his fingers touched, her skin began to tingle, as though the fabric of her gown were no barrier at all. When he traced the outline of her mouth with the moist tip of his tongue, she shivered, first with heat then with cold.

Muriella felt the longing curl through her body at John's

touch. She trembled when he slid his hand down to her breast and cupped it, stroking the nipple through the cool satin. She moaned and closed her eyes, leaning into the strength of his hand against her back. Hungry, all at once, to feel his skin with her open palm, she pushed aside his saffron shirt to find the dark, curling hair it concealed. Slowly, tenderly, she brushed her hand across his chest, seeking to know with her fingertips the taste and texture of his skin.

He held her closer and her nerves seemed to scream beneath his fingers and his mouth. John kissed the hollow of her throat, trailing his tongue over the pulse that fluttered wildly under his lips. Finally, he tugged at the strings of her gown, loosening them so he could slip his hand inside the satin to touch her bare white skin.

Colors whirled within her, hot and fevered, bright and blinding, setting her heart pounding and her head spinning. She could not control her body; she was certain that the force of her passion would tear her apart. Then the vision of the deadly rising water filled her head and she knew she would never catch her breath again. Stop! she wanted to cry. Stop! She shuddered, unable to bear the torment any longer.

John felt her shiver, and the movement broke at last through the haze of his desire. Pulling away, he saw her staring with her blind, dark eyes and knew that the specter was with them again. He closed his eyes, fighting the impulse that urged him to ignore her fear, to force her to forget the past and remember only the feel of his hands on her skin. But she was quivering, her skin so cold that the chill moved from her body to his. John released her, his breathing harsh and uneven.

Muriella swayed, lost in the rushing, swirling water, and fought her way to the surface where the promise of daylight beckoned. For a long moment, she stood trembling, not daring to open her eyes.

"What in God's name are ye so afraid of?" John demanded.

She heard the sound of his ragged voice, but the words

were far away. Further than she could reach. She opened her eyes to see him standing, fists clenched at his sides in an effort to force his hunger into pain.

Muriella tried to concentrate, to stop her shaking and turn her thoughts away from the memory of the white-foamed water, but it would not leave her.

With a muffled curse, her husband grasped her shoulders, forcing her to meet his gaze. "Every time I touch ye, ye retreat to a place where I can't reach ye, as if the devil himself were holding ye in his arms."

The dead Earl's voice echoed deep in her memory: *Ye hold yourself apart from him as if ye were made of ice and stone instead of flesh and blood.*

"Why?" John demanded. "What are ye afraid of?"

His eyes, like iced fire, burned away the mist that shrouded her thoughts. She swallowed once, then whispered, "Sometimes I see things."

"What things?" When she remained silent, he shook her until her head snapped back. "Answer me, damn ye!"

"I can't."

John's fingers dug painfully into her skin. "Ye mean ye won't."

Muriella looked up at him, and the terror moved within her, too deep, too frightening to express. "No," she said. "I can't."

Her husband turned away, running his hand through his hair again and again. "But the vision is of me," he said to the gray stone wall. When, once again, she did not answer, he whirled to face her. "'Tis me ye fear, isn't it?"

Muriella opened her mouth to tell him it was so, but the words would not come. Never had she seen his face in her vision, yet always it was he—the touch of his hands, his fury, his tenderness—that made the water rise. She saw that he was waiting for her answer, breathing harshly, his face dark with the simmering rage that held him in its grip. That, she thought, was what she feared. Or was it?

"Tell me," he insisted. "Tell me the truth."

"I don't know," his wife said. "I'm not sure."

John advanced on her, eyes blazing. "Then ye'd best think about it, hadn't ye? Ye'd best *be* sure before ye drive us both to madness."

"Aye," she murmured, "before 'tis too late."

Much later, Muriella pushed open her chamber door, entering the light-filled room that seemed to promise peace. Then she saw Megan standing near the bed, smiling in delight. "M'lady!" the servant gasped when she saw her mistress, "just look!"

Muriella moved toward the bed with her heart thumping against her ribs. When she stopped, her vision seemed to come and go with the pulsing of her blood. The furs were hidden under all manner of exquisite fabrics. There were gold brocades, creamy satins, violet silks and fine linens. In the center, atop all the others, was a bolt of deep blue velvet, beside it a paler blue satin. Muriella reached out to run her fingers over the velvet. It was incredibly soft, and blue—not icy, like the sea, but warm. The satin was the exact color of John's eyes.

"Where have they come from?" she asked when she found enough breath to speak.

Megan smiled. "Sir John brought them for ye from Edinburgh. All for ye."

"Tell me," she whispered, "are there any reds among them?"

"Why no, I don't think so. 'Tis strange, isn't it, since red's so popular with the ladies. Why do ye ask?"

"Because," Muriella murmured, half to herself. "Just because." Her fingers closed over the blue velvet; she brushed it over her cheek like a fleeting caress against her cool skin.

# 36

Look, I've nearly done!" Megan cried as she held up the chemise she was making for Elizabeth to wear on her wedding day.

Glancing up from her own needlework on the lilac satin gown, Muriella admired the skill with which the servant had attached the spidery French lace. " 'Tis lovely, Megan. Ye can't even see the stitches, they're so tiny."

Megan's pleased smile turned to a frown as she eyed Elizabeth's slender figure. "I only hope 'twill fit ye, m'lady."

Elizabeth, who had refused to try on the fragile garment, shook her head. "It doesn't matter. 'Tis all just a game anyway." She sighed wearily. "Though I'm grateful for something to keep my hands busy." She indicated the violet silk kirtle she was making to wear beneath her wedding gown. It needed only the hem to be finished.

" 'Tis more than that," Muriella said. "They might have taken away your choice, but they can't take away your pride." Because she believed that, she had chosen two of the finest pieces of cloth John had brought her from Edinburgh and given them to her sister-in-law as a gift. She knew the soft colors would complement Elizabeth's pale hair and gray eyes, and she was determined that the other woman look her best; it would help to hide the torment she was feeling inside. Muriella bent her head, concentrating on the intricate silver leaf design she was embroidering around the square neckline of the gown.

Elizabeth gave her a little half smile. "Ye must think me ungrateful after all you've done."

"No," Muriella said, and meant it. "I understand." Perhaps better than any other, she added silently.

Elizabeth looked away, afraid that the compassion in Muriella's eyes might break the fragile barrier that held back a torrent of unshed tears.

For a moment, a hush fell over the three women. Then the door burst open.

"As ye can see," Colin announced, "I've come for the wedding!"

While Muriella plied her needle with unnecessary force, Elizabeth regarded her brother coldly. He was smiling, his face flushed from the ride from Edinburgh and his own high good humor. He approached his sister, blue eyes sparkling. "Elizabeth, I've brought your groom. He awaits ye in the library."

Elizabeth rose but did not move toward the door.

"Have ye nothing to say, girl? Can't ye greet your brother properly?"

Her expression wooden, Elizabeth came forward, brushing her cool lips over the Earl's cheek. "Welcome back," she added as an afterthought.

Colin grasped her by the shoulders. "Ye won't make trouble for me over this marriage, ye understand?"

"I don't waste my time fighting battles I've already lost," his sister assured him icily.

The Earl's nostrils flared as the lump began to rise between his brows. " 'Tis a splendid match I've arranged for ye with a wealthy and respected man. 'Tis miracle enough that any man should want ye after what happened before. Ye didn't even give Maclean children, and a barren woman isn't much in demand. If ye had a grain of sense in your head, ye wouldn't *want* to fight it."

Elizabeth merely stared at him in silence until he shifted uneasily under her regard. The black look in her eyes disturbed him. She might as well have been looking at an empty wall.

"Well, then," Argyll grunted at last, "if ye won't talk to me, go see to your groom. He's waiting."

"As ye wish," she replied, sweeping him a deep curtsy.

While her head was lowered and he could not see her eyes, the Earl addressed her again. "Are ye really no' grateful, Elizabeth? Won't ye thank me?"

She rose, smiling stiffly, and moved away. As she pulled the door open, she turned back to face Colin once more. "May ye rot in hell," she said softly, her smile fixed and unwavoring. Then she was gone.

"We won't ever be ready in time," Megan groaned, glancing in dismay at Elizabeth, who wore only a robe and was seated on a stool with her hands lying motionless in her lap. The servant turned to Muriella. "She's to be married within the hour and we haven't even begun her hair. Mary said she'd be here early to help. Where *is* she?"

"Here, m'lady," Mary panted as she pushed the heavy oak door closed behind her. "I'm very sorry to be so long, but Jenny didn't wake me this mornin'." With an apologetic look at Muriella, she leaned against the door to catch her breath. "I didn't even have time to bind my hair."

Muriella considered Mary's flushed cheeks, glowing eyes, and the disheveled black hair that fell, unbound, below her waist. A painfully vivid memory stirred—of a tiny chamber full of dappled sunlight across two bodies. She felt the color rising in her cheeks.

"I'm truly sorry," Mary repeated, uneasy at Muriella's continued silence. "Can ye forgive me, m'lady?"

"Aye," Muriella said at last. "It couldn't be helped. But we'd best get started now, and quickly."

"As ye say." Mary breathed a sigh of relief, bent her knees briefly, and moved toward the bed where Elizabeth's wedding clothes lay.

The bride, who had not murmured a word since she'd come to Muriella's chamber that morning, rose from her stool as Megan held out the fine linen chemise. Slipping the robe from her shoulders, Elizabeth put on the delicate garment, which whispered over her naked shoulders and fell to her hips. She bent her head to tie the ribbons, but Muriella took them from her cold fingers.

"Let me do the laces for ye. They're difficult to thread when ye can't see them properly." Deftly, she began to weave the narrow ribbons through the tiny slits in the linen.

Elizabeth did not reply, but let her hands fall to her sides without a word. She remained silent as Megan slipped the high-necked kirtle over her head. The long, tight sleeves clung to her wrists and the skirt fell in soft violet folds to the floor, but Elizabeth seemed unaware of the feel of the silk against her skin.

"Och, m'lady, the gown is so lovely," Mary said, lifting the lilac satin reverently from among the furs on the bed. She ran her fingers over the design of silver leaves Muriella had embroidered around the square neck with such care. "I haven't ever seen anythin' like it." Eyes shining with admiration, she loosened the laces and lifted the gown over Elizabeth's head.

"The color is perfect," Megan declared. She folded back the wide sleeves that fell to a point at Elizabeth's knees. "We'd best begin on her hair," the servant murmured at the bride's continued silence. "I need ye to help with the braids, Mary. I haven't enough hands of my own."

When Elizabeth was seated, the two girls hovered over her, dividing her hair into sections, weaving the sections together. They giggled as they tangled strand after strand and laughed in triumph when each difficult braid was done. Muriella watched, the blood pounding dully in her ears. Then Mary knelt beside Elizabeth, her hair falling over her shoulders and curling among the rushes at her feet.

Muriella took a deep breath. It had happened before—the chatter, the laughter, the flutter of excited movement that could not touch the shell of the woman in its midst. Behind it all was the memory of her own voice saying, *So, it's finally come. There's nothing I can do.* Nothing. Then as now, the walls had closed around her, pushing her down into the darkness.

"Elizabeth!" she cried, drawing the woman up from her seat. "Ye must stand by the window where the sunlight can reach ye." At the startled looks from Megan and Mary, she added, "How can ye see if everything is right with the shadows clinging all around?" Turning her back on their astonishment, she noticed that a rush had been caught in the hem of the satin gown. Kneeling, she worked the fabric free. Despite her determination to hide her feelings, her hand trembled a little.

Muriella felt the brush of Elizabeth's fingers on her bent head and looked up in surprise.

"Don't grieve for me," Elizabeth said softly. "It doesn't last forever, ye ken. The months pass, the hurt eases, and then, one day, ye begin to accept what ye can't change."

"But until then?"

Elizabeth smiled sadly. "Until then, if you're lucky, ye learn to hide your pain so they don't ever guess how deep it goes."

" 'Tis time," Megan murmured, approaching hesitantly. "We must go before they send someone to look for us."

Muriella nodded. Those words too she had heard before. She rose, shaking out her gold velvet gown, and put her hand on Elizabeth's arm.

The other woman shook her head. As the servants left the room, she whispered, "I wouldn't have ye by me today."

Muriella regarded her in bewilderment. "But why?"

Frowning, Elizabeth touched her cheek, then looked away. "Because, my friend, ye know too much, and I don't want to see me in your eyes."

Once again the huge oak doors of the chapel had been thrown wide to admit the guests in their wedding finery. Muriella stood in the courtyard while the women and men brushed past her, disappearing into the musty gloom. The groom, Archibald Campbell, stood talking to Colin in the doorway. Muriella had seen little of him since his arrival; he'd spent most of the time behind closed doors with Colin. Even when he joined the others for meals, he kept to himself. He seemed pleasant enough, even ordinary. There was nothing in his straight brown hair, heavy beard, and hazel eyes to distinguish him from a hundred other men.

Muriella wondered again what had made him choose Elizabeth. No doubt it was the alliance with the powerful Campbells that had tempted him. She looked away. Elizabeth deserved so much more.

She turned her attention to the pipers, who played somewhere out of sight, blowing their keening song into the misted April air. Muriella listened, eyes closed, drawing from the music the courage to move forward.

She felt a hand at the small of her back and turned to find her husband beside her. It was the first time he had touched her since that day in the library. He had been unfailingly kind, had spoken with her by the hour, read with her from John Barbour and Robert Henryson, but he had not taken her hand or kissed her cheek—not even once.

"Well," John said, so low that only she could hear him, "have ye been thinking?"

She had begun to believe he had forgotten her promise. "I've tried," she murmured. " 'Tis all I can do."

John shook his head. " 'Tis no' enough, lass. It's been too long."

It was true; she knew it because a growing sense of urgency within would not let her rest. Always, her husband's face was before her, even in her dreams, and always, in his eyes, was the question she could not answer. "Aye," she said when he drew her to him so the warmth of his breath touched her cheek. "I know." She wanted to cup his face in her palms, to feel the stirring of pleasure his kiss had brought her before the fear had washed it away. When she looked into John's eyes, she felt a tightening in her throat and her hands reached out of their own accord to draw him closer. Just then, the pleasure of standing near him was so great that it was almost pain.

"I want ye," he said, his lips hovering above hers. "Ye know that. But I won't see ye turn away from me again. When ye hear my voice instead of your demons', then I'll come to ye, and not before. 'Tis a promise, lass, to both of us."

The wail of the bagpipes faded as the harps took up their song, but still Muriella stood with her hands on her husband's shoulders. "Come," he said. "'Tis time for the ceremony."

John took her arm to guide her inside and she shivered, chilled by the loss of his warmth. They had barely seated themselves on the front bench when Muriella glanced back to see that Elizabeth was coming.

The song of the harps grew hushed as John's sister started down the aisle toward the altar of silver on carved wood. She held her head high, her skirts flowing behind her over the well-worn stone, the sleeves of her gown swaying with the motion of her body. When she reached the place where Archibald Campbell waited, Elizabeth turned to her groom with no trace of bitterness in the face she raised to his, but Muriella wondered if she saw Maclean's image there.

John grasped his wife's hand tightly as the harps fell silent and the priest began the endless ritual of the marriage ceremony. The three voices filled the tiny chapel, chanting, pausing, repeating the Latin phrases until they rang from the gray stone walls. Then, as Elizabeth and her new husband turned away from the altar, the voices fell silent at last. The bride and groom stood for a moment with the light of a hundred candles on their faces, flickering over the hollows and planes, filling their eyes with moving light. Elizabeth stared before her, seeing nothing, while the couple stepped out of the reach of the dancing flames and started back down the aisle.

They had not moved more than a few steps when the chapel doors burst open. "M'lords, there's a great band of armed men nearin' the keep!" Richard Campbell announced breathlessly. "They look as if they mean to take it!"

"Who are they?" Colin's harsh question reverberated in the tiny, crowded room.

"Macleans, m'lord."

"God in heaven but those bastards choose their times well! I suppose their pride wouldn't let them forget their laird's death after all." He glared at Richard as if the man might contradict him. "Somebody get the women inside," the Earl continued. "Johnnie, ye gather the men. Do ye think we have enough within the castle walls?"

" 'Twill have to be enough," John replied, "but we'll need to hurry if we want to break them before they lay siege."

In a very few minutes, the men had hurried into the courtyard while the women followed. Muriella went to Elizabeth, who stood alone in the center of the narrow stone aisle, and took her arm. "Come inside," the younger woman murmured, "where 'tis safe." Oddly enough, she was not eager to be closed inside the castle walls. Safe the keep might be, but it was also dark and cold and eerily silent.

The doors had barely closed behind the cluster of women when the sound of the battle began. Suppressing her own agitation, Muriella drew Elizabeth out of the crowd and toward the stairway. "Let's wait in the solar," she suggested. "Where 'tis quiet."

Elizabeth had not said a word since the vows she had spoken in the chapel. Now she only nodded, her face as unyielding as white marble.

When the battle had been raging for several hours and neither side appeared to be weakening, John and Colin crouched behind the battlements to discuss the Campbell options.

"They could sit there for weeks, ye ken, until they starve us out. They can't get in, 'tis true, but neither can we get out." Colin sat on his heels, regarding his brother in indecision.

"No," John agreed, "but it seems to me if we could attack from behind, we could scatter them."

"And how do ye suppose we're to get by them without their knowing? Don't be a fool, Johnnie."

Colin's tone rankled; with an effort of will, John kept his fists at his sides. "It makes no difference whether or not they know. Once we're out, they haven't enough men to hold us off."

"Aye, but how do we get out, little brother? They're watching the gate."

"That's just the thing, don't ye see? Most of their men are gathered near the front gate. They expect us to try to attack from there. They wouldn't even be knowing about the little side gate."

The Earl's eyes lit up. "By God, Johnnie, for once you've had a sensible thought. But who will lead the men that way? It'll take mighty careful going if we don't want to alert the Macleans too soon."

"I'll go." John's blood was beginning to speed through his veins as it always did at the thought of battle. "We can lead the horses through the tunnel easily enough without a light. They won't be expecting us at all."

"Aye, well . . ." Colin rocked on his heels, considering whether or not his brother could handle the task.

John leaned forward. "If we wait 'til dark, they won't be able to see us coming. 'Tis two hours away. What do ye think?"

Colin nodded thoughtfully. " 'Tis a good enough plan," he said at last, "so long as ye don't lose your head as ye tend to do. Mayhap I should find some other man to lead."

John laughed. The thought of the pending contest had ruined his brother's ability to wound him. Besides, he knew as well as Colin that the first few men out the gate would be vulnerable in the extreme. Smiling, he leapt down from the stone ledge. "Let me know when ye find one willing," he shouted.

The Earl frowned after his brother's retreating back. Johnnie was right; there was no other.

Head bent over the clacking loom, Muriella concentrated on sliding the shuttle between the taut warp threads. She heard Megan enter the room but did not look up from her task.

"I talked to Duncan," the servant announced. "He says

the men are plannin' to creep out from the hidden gate at dusk to surprise the Macleans." Approaching her mistress, she added, "He says Sir John will lead them."

Muriella bent forward, gasping. She had known John was out there, facing the Macleans' assault, but until now he had had the high castle walls to hide behind. Once he left the keep, there would be no ancient stone battlements to protect him. He would be alone with his sword and his brother's men. Fear rose in her throat, cold and leaden, and her hands grew clammy with sweat.

Elizabeth saw Muriella turn pale, grasping her stomach as if in pain. For an instant, Elizabeth's features lost their waxen appearance. "Megan," she said sharply, speaking for the first time in many hours, "your mistress isn't well. Bring her some wine."

"Aye, m'lady." Shocked by Muriella's pallor, the servant hurried from the room to do as she'd been bid.

When Elizabeth slid onto the bench behind the loom, Muriella whispered, "Do ye think—I mean—'tis very dangerous, isn't it?"

" 'Tis always dangerous in battle," Elizabeth answered carefully, "but John's a good warrior. He won't give the Macleans the victory if he can help it."

"But what if this time he can't help it? What if their anger makes them stronger?" The words were hoarse and indistinct, and she had to struggle to speak them at all.

Elizabeth took Muriella's hand. "If 'tis so, then so 'twill be. Ye can't change that. Ye can only pray that he'll come back unharmed."

Muriella shook her head. "I don't think I remember how."

" 'Twill come to ye," Elizabeth said softly. "I've told ye before, it doesn't last forever. Even the fear goes, in time." Frowning, she contemplated Muriella's averted face. Until now, Elizabeth had believed her sister-in-law to be indifferent to John, if not entirely hostile. She had even felt vague stirrings of pity when she saw how her brother's gaze followed his wife whenever she was near. Yet here

Muriella sat, her eyes shadowed, her skin sickly pale, asking about her husband's danger. Could Elizabeth have been mistaken?

When Megan returned with the wine, her mistress drank it slowly, willing its warmth into her chilled veins, but it could not touch the cold fear around her heart. She peered at the weave of the nearly completed Loch Awe tapestry, hoping to lose herself in the color and patterns she had created. She plied the shuttle to and fro, to and fro, lacing the strands together, building a meshwork of vivid blue and pale peach, but this time the colors changing beneath her skilled hands were not enough to make her forget. The hours stretched out, hushed and endless, with only the rhythmic sound of the loom to break the uneasy silence.

Then, as darkness settled beyond the windows and the torches flared to life, the sound of cheering rose from the courtyard.

Muriella's hands ceased their movement. She met Elizabeth's gaze in apprehension. No doubt the Campbells had won their battle at last. But at what cost? Now, when she needed it most, when she craved the knowledge the Sight could give her, the power had left her.

For the second time, Megan flung the door open and came into the room, her face flushed with pleasure. "The Macleans have fled!" she cried. "The men from the battlements have started comin' in, but Duncan says 'twill be a while before the ones from outside the walls make their way back."

Muriella forced herself to ask calmly, "Ye have no word of Sir John?"

"No, m'lady," Megan told her with regret. "But Duncan says he's better with a sword than any man. No doubt he's safe enough."

"No doubt," her mistress repeated, but she did not believe it. She stared at her nearly finished tapestry; as it undulated in the yellow glare of the torches, she leaned forward, holding her breath. The red-haired woman knelt on the shore, gazing into the water, but the face below her was not pale and lovely, with the blond, flowing hair of the woman of the loch. The face reflected in the gently shifting water was darkly handsome, bearded and sunbrowned, with eyes as blue as the winter sky. Muriella cried out once, then buried her face in the bright, colored fabric.

When the men began to return to the hall, Elizabeth stood waiting to greet them one by one. She had explained to her new husband that she must help with the wounded and he had agreed. "Go," Archibald Campbell had told his wife gently. "Mayhap we can begin again tomorrow."

Now, with Duncan beside her, Elizabeth tended those she could help, doled out food to those who could eat, and learned the names of those who were dead. No one could tell her about her brother. Apparently most of the men had lost sight of him just after the Macleans scattered and fled.

The men had been arriving for nearly an hour when David Campbell staggered into the hall, clutching his shoulder where an arrow had pierced it. While Elizabeth tore his shirt away and bathed the wound, he told her what he could.

"After they ran, Sir John thought we'd best follow for a way to see that they really meant to return to Mull. He was afraid they'd circle back and surprise the keep. We hadn't gone far when some of the Macleans took it into their heads to turn and fight. That's when I got my wound." He pointed to his shoulder with pride. " 'Twas a long skirmish. Seemed more kept coming, despite the number we killed outright. By the time the last Maclean had gone or died, not a single one of us still had a horse. I never saw Sir John, though I looked among the closest corpses. Then my wound started in bleeding, and I thought I'd best come back again."

Elizabeth knew that twenty-five men had left Inveraray

Castle with her brother. It was just past midnight, and she had accounted for twenty-two who were either safe within the keep or dead. Half an hour later, she looked up to see John and another man huddled in the doorway, carrying a third between them. In an instant she was beside them, searching their faces anxiously. Somehow, in the last hours of tending to the wounded, the weight of her self-imposed numbness had left her. For the first time in weeks, she knew she was alive, because the fear was with her again.

"Elizabeth," her brother said, "aren't ye in bed? Or has your groom been wounded?"

John was covered with blood, but his sister could not tell if it was his own. She recognized the second man as Richard Campbell. Leaning down, she examined the third, who was badly wounded. As they dragged him into the light, she saw Andrew Campbell's flaming red hair. His freckles stood out darkly against his pale skin.

"Elizabeth, come away," John said as he took her arm. "There are others to care for him."

She allowed her brother to draw her toward the fire. "Are ye hurt?" she asked at last.

"Och, no! Though the Macleans did their best to see that I was. I've been so long because Andrew yonder fell right next to me. Richard and I thought he wouldn't make it back, so we tried to tend to him there as best we could. We stopped the bleeding, at least, and removed the shaft, but I wouldn't care to guess about his chances."

As he spoke, the exhilaration she had noticed when he first came in seemed to drain from his face. She could see by his furrowed brow that he was tired.

John felt her questioning gaze and frowned. "Tell me, what do ye here? Ye should be asleep."

"I was waiting for ye."

He drew back so he could see her face more clearly. She had not sought him out since his return from Edinburgh, and he could not understand what had brought her to him now. "Why?"

She glanced around to make certain no one was near. "Johnnie," she murmured, "how weary are ye?"

"If you're asking could I fall asleep on the floor with the stones for a pillow, aye, I'm that weary."

"I think"—she paused, searching for words—"I think ye should go to your wife."

John eyed his sister warily. "I don't think she would welcome me in this state." He indicated his clothing, which was crusted with blood. "What makes ye think she would want to see me anyway?"

"I was with her all evening. She was worried about ye. I know she won't sleep 'til she's seen ye. Please, just go to her."

There was a strange expression on Elizabeth's face that John did not entirely like, but he could see no harm in stopping to say good night to Muriella. "All right then," he agreed, "if ye say so. After I wash the blood away. Will that satisfy ye?"

Elizabeth nodded. She smiled as he started up the stairs. He would find his wife waiting, and tonight she would welcome him, because her defenses had been half destroyed by fear. By morning her brother would be bound inexorably by his love for Muriella; his sister had seen it in his eyes. Just now that was all that Elizabeth desired.

Muriella sat in her chamber, gazing out the window. She could see nothing beyond the faint glimmer of stars shrouded with gathering clouds, but she did not mind; the night air cooled her burning cheeks and the cry of the rising wind overshadowed the sound of her own ragged breathing.

Megan sat behind her mistress, sewing in the lamplight. She was listening intently and heard the footsteps in the hall long before Muriella did. When her mistress finally looked up, her gaze met Megan's and held it. Perhaps those steps meant news of John.

As the door swung open, Muriella turned, her heart pounding, to find her husband standing on the threshold in a long saffron shirt and trews. His hair clung damply to his head, and his cheeks were pink, as if he had just scrubbed them. She could see some drops of water clinging to his beard; they caught the light, glimmering as he turned his head. Muriella sank back against the stone with a sigh. He was safe.

Megan rose, looking from her mistress to John and back again. Muriella did not move while her husband stood silent in the doorway, watching her. At last he nodded at Megan and she slipped past him, closing the door behind her.

John listened until the servant's footsteps had disappeared. He thought he had forgotten how to breathe. Muriella sat by the window dressed only in a pale gown with a robe draped over her shoulders. In the lamplight, he could see the curve of her breasts against the gossamer-thin fabric. Her hair, usually tightly braided, fell about her shoulders and down to the floor. With difficulty, he focused on her eyes and the dark shadows underneath. Elizabeth had been right after all; Muriella had not yet slept.

He stood unmoving, waiting to see if she would shrink from his gaze, but she did not. Instead, she rose to stand facing him, her nightrail undulating about her body like a wisp of transparent smoke.

"Holy Mother of God," she whispered. "We didn't hear of ye for so long that I thought ye were dead."

"Did ye really mind so much?" he asked.

When she looked for her fear of him, she found it had been washed away in the wake of an even greater fear—that she might have lost him. "Aye," she said simply.

He took a step forward. "Muriella, I made ye a promise—"

Before he could finish, she grasped his hands in hers and kissed them each on the palm.

He felt the heat of her lips all through his body and with a deep breath, drew her into his arms. For a long time he merely held her, kissing the top of her head, stroking her hair with his fingertips.

Muriella was beyond thought or reason. The evidence of her eyes was not enough; she wanted to see with her hands and her lips that the battle had not taken her husband from her after all. Without hesitation, she put her arms around his neck and stood on her toes, raising her lips to his.

John groaned, then pulled her closer, circling the edge of

her mouth with his tongue. The robe slid from her shoulders as he began to caress her back in ever-widening circles, drawing her gown up as he did so. He trembled at the touch of her fingers on his neck, at the way she teased the still-damp strands of his hair, winding her fingers in the dark curls. With one swift gesture, he drew her nightrail over her head and stood gazing at her naked body. He caught his breath in admiration.

Though her face was touched with sun from her rides across the moors, the skin of her body was pure, startling white. She tossed her hair over her shoulders, revealing the soft lines of her breasts and stomach, hips and thighs. His pulse quickened when he saw the little short breaths she took to calm her excited nerves.

He wanted to pull her to him roughly, to satisfy at once the hunger she had fueled in him for so long. But he knew he must wait a little longer, until he could hold her in the safety of the darkness. His heartbeat slow and labored, he lifted his wife in his arms, smiling when she twined her arms around his neck and nestled closer. As he carried her across the room, he buried his face in the hair at her neck and traced the line of her throat with his tongue.

Muriella shivered, amazed that such a little thing could bring her such pleasure. In that moment, she closed her mind to thought and doubt and fear. When John placed her on the bed and tried to pull away, she clung to him, unwilling to lose the heat of his body even for a moment.

"Wait," he murmured.

She released him and he moved to the foot of the bed, putting out the lamp as he passed. When she heard him remove his clothes, she held her breath until she felt his weight on the bed, then rolled to the center to meet him.

John stretched out and held her, not moving, barely breathing, while her racing heartbeat slowed and she became used to the feel of his body on hers. He was heavy and warm and she responded slowly, circling him with her arms, touching his naked skin for the first time of her own free will.

When she turned her head to meet his lips with hers, John

withdrew from her a little. Leisurely, gently, he took her hands to guide them along his shoulders, down over the thick hair on his chest to his hips and beyond. While he kissed her hair and eyes and mouth, he showed her the strength and the softness of his body through her seeking fingertips. Sometimes he shuddered when her hand strayed to a sensitive spot. When her shyness had begun to pass, she sought those places out, delighting in her power to rouse him with a single touch.

Finally he caught her in his arms, and began to know her body as she had known his. He brushed the hair away from her breasts and ran his fingers over the flesh, which he could see in his memory, though the darkness hid it now. Circling, always circling, he moved his hands over her skin, delighting in its supple warmth and the shivers of pleasure that answered his touch.

He drew her close, nibbling her ear, tracing the lobe with his warm tongue. She could feel every part of him against her sensitive skin; when he found her breast with his lips, she ceased breathing for fear he would stop. With hands and lips and tongue, he caressed her until she trembled, wanting something more, though she did not know what.

"Muriella?" John whispered into the throbbing pulse at the hollow of her throat. "Are ye frightened?"

"No," she answered, surprised at the way the single word vibrated through his body. The blood was pulsing madly in her head, her legs, her chest. The weight of his hands on her body was a pleasure so intense that it left her without breath or words. Now that her eyes had become accustomed to the light, she could see the outline of his face, the fall of his hair across his cheek, the glow of his eyes in the darkness. She felt the water hissing around her, swirling at her shoulders, threatening to pull her under, and knew she should turn away before it was too late. Then John touched her hair, her flushed cheek with his fingertips and the choice was taken from her.

"Muriella?"

She reached up to draw him close—so close that she could hear the pounding of his heart.

John heard her answer in the movement of her body. His breath escaped in a rush as slowly, his hands cupping her warm flesh, he entered her. She gasped, digging her fingernails into his shoulders, shuddered at the sudden pain, then clung more tightly as he began to move within her.

Her vision blurred while the colors whirled and clashed and melded in her head. She knew she could not bear it; she could not. In her wonder, she held him closer and closer still, his heart beating into hers, his breath soft against her ear. Then he cried out once. With her lips pressed to his, she swallowed the sound of his passion and answered it with her own. "Johnnie," she breathed.

When at last they lay side by side, John held her while she trembled, trying to breathe in the stillness that had descended upon them, until the colors settled into familiar patterns, then faded in the darkness. She reached for his hand to grasp it tight, welcoming the heat of his fingers as they twined with hers. "Hold me," she whispered. "Don't go."

His arms closed around her, caught up in the long, damp tangles of her hair.

"I won't leave ye," he murmured. She rubbed her cheek across his chest, then rested her head in the hollow of his shoulder. He said no more, because, just then, there was nothing more to say.

# 

When John awoke, gray morning was spilling through the open shutters. Tossing aside the heavy furs, he reached out to draw his wife near. With his arm around her shoulders, he looked into her sleep-misted eyes and saw that she was smiling. There was no shadowy specter to come between them now.

Muriella moved closer as he brushed the hair off her shoulder to caress the bare skin. She considered the curves and hollows of his face, made stronger by the morning light, and tears burned behind her eyes; always before when he came to her bed, he had left her long before the dawn, but this time he had stayed. She trembled at the rush of joy that shook her as their lips met and clung. His kiss was warm, insistent, tender. She closed her eyes when he slipped his tongue into her mouth. In that moment, as her body met his, a quiver of fear flared in the midst of her happiness and she clung to him more fiercely, her need a wild keening cry inside her.

When John drew away, Muriella moved her hands hungrily over his chest, as if to forge with her open palms a bond between them that could not be broken. She had never before seen his body in light untouched by shadows, and she wanted to come to know by sight what she had already learned by touch. Raising herself on one arm, she explored the pattern of dark hair that almost concealed skin toughened by years of sun and battle but still strangely soft beneath her circling fingertips. She traced the jagged line of an old scar, intrigued by the number of these reminders of past violence that she found on his body.

" 'Tis wonderful hands you've got, lassie," John murmured, his arm tightening around her shoulders, "but I'm thinking 'tis time I left ye for a while. There's much to be done after yesterday's battle."

The flame of fear burned brighter. Muriella cupped his face in her hands, tangling her fingers in his beard. I must let him go, she thought, but she whispered, "Stay a little."

There was nothing her husband would have liked more. The movement of her hands across his chest, the featherlight touch of her fingers in his hair were stirring his need to life once more. But from the light pouring through the half-open shutter, he knew they had already slept too long. "Ah, lass, ye tempt me greatly, but 'tis late and there's much to be done. Before the morning's over we have to bury the dead and see to the wounded. But I'll see ye at breakfast, little one."

Before he rose, he took her in his arms to kiss her one last time. Muriella locked her arms around his neck and her mouth opened under his, drawing a groan of frustration from his parted lips. Then he pulled away and swung his legs over the side of the bed. For a moment he was poised there, frozen in time, the muscles along his back taut with his suppressed desire. Finally, he bent down to scoop his clothes from the floor.

Muriella watched, heart pounding, while he threw on his shirt and stepped into his trews. His body was fine and strong and supple and she wanted to feel it beneath her hands, but she knew a single touch would not satisfy the craving within her.

"Good-bye, lass," John called as he reached the door. " 'Til later."

"Aye."

When he was gone, Muriella closed her eyes, praying for the rapid beating of her heart to ease. She slipped from the bed and found her robe, discarded carelessly the night before. Tossing it over her shoulders, she knelt before the window and looked out at the garden below. It was late spring; long ago the wild roses had taken over the tangled bracken and heather that carpeted the ground, but the profusion of bright flowers could not soften the stark and terrible beauty of the scene before her. In the distance the mountains rose, jagged, black and menacing, outlined against the cloud-filled sky by the shimmering silver sunlight. There would be a storm before the day was out; she could smell the threat of violence in the air, hear it in the rising of wind through the brooding pines. Below her, hawthorn and heather and bracken, roses and wild myrtle undulated in the sudden onslaught of cold, wet wind. Only Loch Awe lay still and untouched, an island of peace in the center of the coming storm.

Muriella breathed deeply, overcome by the power of the landscape that echoed the tumult of joy and fear inside her. It was inevitable, she realized, as inevitable as the pleasure she had known in John's arms. And what of the vision of the rushing water? No matter how much she might wish to deny it, that too was inevitable. She could only wait, powerless, as she had always done. But now the waiting would be sweeter by far—sweeter and more frightening, for now she had so very much to lose.

A cold wind circled through the chamber, waking Elizabeth like the touch of icy fingers on her cheek. She stirred, her mind still clouded with sleep, and opened her eyes with reluctance. When she saw the figure beside her, she sat up abruptly, drawing the heavy furs close. She had forgotten about her new husband—had made herself forget. He'd been sound asleep when she finally came up to their chamber the night before, and she'd been grateful.

"Good morning, my wife," Archibald Campbell said.

He was sitting with his back against the headboard, regarding her mildly. She blinked to assure herself he was real and not some unwelcome figment of her imagination.

"Ye must have been up half the night tending to the

wounded," he observed when she did not reply to his greeting. "How many men were lost, do ye think?"

Elizabeth shrugged. "I'm no' certain, but I do know 'twas not nearly as many as the Macleans lost."

Frowning, Archibald reached out to take her hand. Elizabeth wanted to shrink from his touch, but knew she had no right to do so.

"The Macleans were your own clan for so many years," her husband mused. "It can't be easy to find yourself their enemy all at once."

Elizabeth's eyes widened in surprise. "No, 'tis not easy." She gazed at her free hand, pale and somehow vulnerable against the dark fur. "But 'tis no good to lament what can't be helped." She shook her head in resignation. "I'm afraid the Macleans were glad to be rid of me in the end. It seems I brought them nothing but trouble in the past few years."

"And what did they bring ye?" Archibald asked, squeezing her fingers gently. "I'll wager you've suffered more than any one of the Macleans."

Elizabeth stared at the man who was her husband as if she had never seen him before. In the past week, she had become familiar with his straight brown hair and heavy beard, but she had never noticed how the hair fell untidily over his forehead or the way his dark beard softened the weathered lines of his face. She had seen the hazel of his wide-set eyes, but never recognized the compassion there. She found she could not speak; it had been too long since anyone but Muriella had offered her kindness.

Aware of her discomfort, Archibald released her hand. "I don't know about ye," he said, "but I'm hungry enough for twelve men. And I suspect ye had little to eat yesterday in all the excitement. Shall I call a servant to bring some food? That way ye won't have to dress and go down to the Great Hall quite so early."

Too astonished by his thoughtfulness to speak, Elizabeth could only nod. She *was* hungry, she realized, and that surprised her as well.

"'Tis as good as done," her husband said as he rose and threw on his robe.

When he started to turn away, Elizabeth moved across the mattress, stopping him with a hand on his arm. He turned, one eyebrow raised in question. "Aye?"

She found her voice at last. "I just wanted to—thank ye."

Archibald Campbell smiled and covered her hand with his. "You're welcome, lass," he said.

When Muriella descended to the Great Hall, every bench at every table was occupied. The victory over the Macleans had left the men and wedding guests in a boisterous mood. The shutters had been thrown back and the doors hung open, allowing the sunlight, touched with silver from the threatening storm clouds, to bathe the huge vaulted room. As she moved among the tables, Muriella heard the men recounting with enthusiasm the details of yesterday's battle. They praised John's skill, exaggerated their own, reviled Evan Maclean, jested and shouted with laughter at their own wit. For once, they were not even aware that she passed among them.

She saw that Colin was already seated in the carved oak chair at the head of the high table. His brother sat on his right and Jenny hovered, as always, at the Earl's shoulder. As she stepped up onto the dais, Muriella was met with the sound of Colin's coarse laughter, but she was not really aware of it. Her attention was on her husband. When he looked up and smiled, her heart paused in its usual rhythm. She slipped onto the bench beside him as he motioned for Jenny to fill his wife's platter.

"Here, Johnnie," Colin exclaimed in sudden inspiration, "won't ye kiss your wife good morrow? I'll wager she hasn't seen ye since the battle. Ye should greet her properly."

"Och, but ye haven't been payin' attention, m'lord," Adam Campbell chuckled from the far end of the table. "For unless my eyes deceived me this mornin', she saw a great deal more o' him than she cared to last night."

Heads swiveled toward John and Muriella in avid curiosity, and though she turned pale, she did not allow her smile to waver. She would not give Colin that pleasure.

The Earl eyed his brother with new interest. "Do ye say so?" His gaze flicked from John to Muriella, where it lingered. "Damn me!" he cried. "Then 'tis more of a celebration than we bargained for." Grinning, a malicious glint in his eye, he called to the men below, "What do ye say we have a fête in one week's time? A grand event to commemorate the defeat of the Macleans and anything else worth getting drunk over?"

A cheer greeted his suggestion from the ranks of men who filled the hall. Some waved their chunks of bread in the air to show their approbation. The Earl nudged John with his elbow. "What do ye say, Johnnie, m'lad?"

With an effort, John choked back his anger before he replied, "I say ye should have your celebration, but ye'd best remember that when they're drunk, men sometimes lose all fear and sanity. Likely to do anything, they are." He met his brother's gaze and noticed the lump was in danger of appearing between his sandy eyebrows.

"Are ye threatening me, little brother?" the Earl asked, no longer smiling.

"No' at all. I just thought ye should remember." The gleam in John's eyes belied his words.

Colin was suddenly aware that everyone was watching him with great interest. "We'll discuss this foolishness later," he hissed under his breath.

"Aye," John said, "no doubt. And ye'll see that I have as much to say as ye do."

"M'lord?" Jenny stepped between John and Colin with her back to the younger brother. "Will ye have some sweetbread?" She held the platter out, swaying provocatively in an effort to distract the Earl.

His eyes narrowed while he considered shoving her out of the way, but he decided that John was best left alone right now. He replaced his scowl with a forced smile and took some of the bread.

Muriella released her breath in relief; she had feared that the brothers would come to blows, and that would only have made things worse. She watched her husband struggling to overcome his anger, glaring at his half-empty platter, his hands clenched on the pitted tabletop. When he became aware of her gaze, he turned. "Ye'll have to forgive my brother," he whispered. "I'm afraid my father didn't teach him manners."

"It doesn't matter," Muriella whispered back.

"It does." John turned his attention back to his breakfast; he did not trust himself to discuss Colin's behavior further.

Muriella began to eat the cold beef and sweetbread Jenny had served her, but when she heard a murmur of curiosity rippling through the men, she looked up. A disheveled stranger stood in the doorway, looking about him. He had obviously been riding hard; his hair was windblown, his body covered with a fine layer of dust, his face strained with exhaustion. He held a leather packet under his arm.

John looked up and saw the man in the same instant that his wife did. He knew the messenger at once. Glancing at Muriella in apprehension, he cursed the man's poor timing.

As the stranger started toward the high table, John rose, intending to stop him before he'd crossed the hall, but he had barely swung his leg over the bench when Colin called, "Where have ye come from, man? Do ye bring me letters?"

"I come from Cawdor, m'lord, and my letters are for Sir John."

Annoyed, the Earl stood, ignoring his brother's angry exclamation. "Not again!" Colin snapped. "Don't tell me there's *more* trouble brewing in that little keep in the north."

"Aye, m'lord," the stranger said. "There's trouble enough."

Out of the corner of his eye, the Earl saw Muriella lean forward, suddenly intent. He smiled to himself. "What is it now?" he demanded. "Another murder or another scandal?"

"Whatever it is," John hissed in fury, " 'tis my business, not yours." He saw what his brother was trying to do, but John did not intend to let this touch Muriella. "Come," he said to the messenger, who had paused at the foot of the platform. "We'll discuss your news in the library." With a sidelong look at the Earl, he added, "Where 'tis quiet and a man can think." Before he left the table, he tried to smile reassuringly at his wife but knew he was unsuccessful. As he joined the stranger and started to wind his way through the rows of trestle tables, he could feel Muriella's bewildered gaze burning like a brand into his back.

# 39

The dream began as it always did. Muriella was a child again, happy and without fear, running with the wind in her hair on the hills near Kilravok. Laughing into the cool morning breeze, she lost herself among the rustling shadows of the leaves in the forest. She had to hide before her cousin found her and won the game.

"Muriella!" Hugh called softly, as he ducked beneath the low branches of an oak. "I'll find ye in the end," he whispered, his voice warm with teasing.

She moved deeper into the woods, where she could watch him yet not be seen. Holding her breath, she smiled when he paused to listen, the speckled sunlight dancing over his bright red hair. Then she blinked and he vanished, his raw leather boots making no sound on the soft earth of the forest.

Muriella crept from behind the oak that had concealed her and stood peering among the hawthorns, pines and oaks. She tried to catch a glimpse of Hugh's red hair, but saw only the green of the leaves and the gray of the shifting darkness. Then she heard a shout of glee and her cousin was behind her, winding his hands in her long auburn braids. "Ye see," he said, "I told ye I'd find ye!" He tugged on her hair, swinging her around. She went gladly, laughing as she turned to meet his triumphant gaze. But when she saw his face, the laughter died in her throat.

This was not her beloved Hugh, but the grotesque mask of

a stranger. The eyes were sunken, hollow, the skin black and scarred. The mouth was twisted into a leering smile of contempt.

Muriella awoke, gasping, but even when she opened her eyes, the image of the ghastly face would not leave her. Always before, the dream had left her with a feeling of peace, but this time the contentment had turned to a deep foreboding that lingered and grew in the enveloping darkness.

Instinctively, she turned, reaching for the reassuring warmth of her husband's arms, but he was not there. With a rush of despair, she remembered; it had been a week since he'd held her after the battle, but he had not come to her again. Almost from the moment the messenger arrived from Cawdor, John had been away. He left before dawn each morning and returned long after the keep had fallen silent for the night. Muriella was sure his absence had to do with the trouble at Cawdor. Hour after hour, Colin's words rang in her head: *What is it this time? Another murder or another scandal?* She would have given much to know the answer. But more than that, she thought, hands clenched against the inevitable pain, she would have given much to know why John had not held her again, kissed her, made her forget her fear in the rush of her newborn joy.

Unable to sleep, she knelt at the window, throwing open the shutters in an effort to get some relief. Even in the darkness, she knew a deluge was coming; she could feel the seething moisture in the air. The storm she had expected had not yet broken, but every day the mountains grew bleaker, the clouds darker and more threatening. And every day the emptiness inside grew until it consumed her from within and there was nothing else.

On the floor by the open window, Muriella waited for the dawn, then rose, put on her mauve silk gown and kirtle, and made her way downstairs. She had not thought anyone else would be about, but when she reached the Great Hall, she saw that several men were coming and going from the room on the far side where the weapons were kept. Though their voices were raised in excitement, Muriella could not make out the words; without conscious thought, she turned in that direction. Long before she'd reached the place where the men were gathered, she heard John's voice above the others. "Are ye sure this time?"

Muriella paused. It seemed like an eternity since she had heard that voice. Its power mesmerized her for an instant.

Then Richard answered, breaking the spell. "Aye. I told ye, I took care to make certain."

"Then we'd best be on our way as soon as possible. Are the horses saddled?"

"Aye, m'lord."

Moving forward soundlessly, Muriella stopped on the threshold. She had never felt comfortable in this chamber, whose walls were lined with broadswords and daggers, claymores and spears. She felt uneasy among the implements of war, but she saw at once that John was at home here. He stood in the center of the bare stone floor, arms akimbo, waiting with impatience while Duncan adjusted the wide, strong leather of his master's sword belt.

Her husband, like the others in the room, was armed for battle in his long saffron shirt, leather doublet, and thick wool trews. His father's sword hung at his side and two large daggers had been thrust into his belt. Muriella felt a strange constriction in her chest. Somehow in the past week, she'd forgotten how broad John's shoulders were, how dark and wild his hair—forgotten, too, how harsh and unyielding his face became when he was angry. That he was angry now she had no doubt; she could see it in every rigid line of his body, in the energy that seemed to radiate from him in waves until it touched every other man in the room. The sense of foreboding grew more insistent and she had to force herself to breathe evenly.

At last, one of the men noticed Muriella hovering in the doorway. He froze with his sword in midair. Slowly, one by one, the men sensed his discomfort and a hush fell over the room.

John looked up. "What the devil—" He broke off abruptly when he saw his wife.

"I'd like to speak to ye," she said.

His eyes gleamed with an emotion she could not understand and the lines of his face hardened. For a moment, she thought he would refuse her outright. Then, with a curious twist of his lips, he nodded at the men. No one said a word as they took their weapons and left the room. Duncan was the last to go.

"I can't linger," John said, before the door had closed at the squire's back. "What is it?"

He struggled to speak calmly, but could not disguise the tension in his body or the shadows under his eyes. He had not been sleeping any better than she, Muriella realized. "Where are ye going?" she asked.

Her husband looked away, running his hand through his hair in agitation. "There's something I have to do. Something that can't wait any longer."

"But why do ye need your sword and shield and leather doublet?"

His answering smile was grim. "'Tis wise to have them when ye go to surprise an enemy before he surprises ye."

"What enemy?" his wife asked in desperation. "Why must ye speak only in riddles?"

John saw the dread in Muriella's eyes and hesitated. There were things he must tell her that had nothing to do with his sword and his shield, things that must be said with gentleness and care. Just now he found it impossible to summon such feelings. He had to be away, before it was too late.

She was waiting expectantly, nervously. Even through the slow-simmering rage in his blood, he ached for her and wanted to take the confusion from her eyes. But the memory of her tortured voice came to him like a warning: *The horror is here, inside my own head. I can't close my eyes and make it go away—the images only become clearer. I can't run because they follow. And I can't bear it anymore. I can't!*

She had known enough fear; he would not add to that lingering horror. He had made a silent vow to her, and he would honor it now. "Muriella," he said, keeping his voice steady with an effort, "when a man is too blind to see that he's gone too far, 'tis time to show him the error of his ways. And I intend to do just that before the day has grown much older."

He closed one hand tightly around the hilt of his sword and with the other, stroked his dagger in a fierce caress.

The feeling of foreboding was now so great that Muriella thought it would choke her. She lunged forward, grasping John's doublet in her hands. "Please don't go!" she cried. "There's danger waiting for ye; I know it. Please!"

John stiffened, stepping backward until her hands fell away. "Don't ask that of me," he said harshly. "Not ever. Danger or no danger, live or die, one thing I won't ever do, even for ye, is give up my honor."

*I wouldn't ever stain the name of Campbell by hiding like a coward in my keep. What I do, I do because I must—for honor.* How often, Muriella wondered, would John echo his father's words? But as she met her husband's implacable gaze, she knew that, no matter what he said, it was not concern for his honor that drove him now. The look that glittered in his eyes was rage—pure and bright and coldly menacing.

"I've come to say farewell."

At the sound of Elizabeth's voice, Muriella looked up from the tapestry laid out on the floor of the solar. For the past few hours she had been kneeling on the cold stone, stitching together the slits between the different colors on the back side of the finished hanging. "The trunks are ready?" she asked her sister-in-law.

Elizabeth closed the door behind her. "Aye, at last. Once Megan took over, things went much more smoothly. Thank ye for giving her up for a morning."

"I would have come myself—" Muriella began.

Elizabeth shook her head. "I told ye, I couldn't have borne that. I didn't want ye there, reminding me—" She broke off and busied herself brushing the rushes aside then seating herself on the floor.

"I wouldn't have spoken a word if ye didn't want me to," Muriella told her.

Smiling gently, Elizabeth said, "Ye needn't say a word to make me remember. I told ye before, 'tis in your eyes." She glanced away. "'Tis difficult enough to start for Auchinbreck so soon, but my husband says his men are restless and he doesn't wish to leave them for so long. 'Tis odd," she mused, looking around the small stone chamber pensively, "when I first realized they'd brought me to Inveraray, I wanted to be anywhere but here, yet now I don't want to go."

"Mayhap ye'll find ye like it at Auchinbreck, once you've made it your home."

"Mayhap," Elizabeth murmured. "But that doesn't make it any easier to leave ye. 'Twas ye, after all, who kept me alive when I would have given up."

Brow furrowed, Muriella regarded her sister-in-law in concern. "Ye said once that I should have let ye die."

Elizabeth shivered at the memory. "I was mad with grief then. Things are different now."

Muriella could see that it was true. Elizabeth had clearly been sleeping better; the shadows under her eyes were fading and the color had begun to creep back into her cheeks. "You're looking well," the younger woman said. "Mayhap your marriage suits ye better than ye expected. I've been watching ye over the past few days, and it seems as though 'twill no' be so hard after all to accept what ye can't change."

Elizabeth frowned at the thought of her own words. Had it only been a week ago that she had stood in Muriella's chamber and felt the world dissolving into darkness at her feet? It seemed a lifetime had passed since that cold, gray morning. "Sometimes Archibald frightens me," she admitted in a whisper. "Not because he mistreats me, but because he doesn't. I don't know how to fight his kindness."

Muriella stared at the needle threaded with blue wool in her hand. "Mayhap," she said at last, "ye don't need to fight anymore."

With a sigh, Elizabeth settled herself more comfortably on the floor. "I try to tell myself I must. I warn myself to think, to remember how much they've all hurt me before. But sometimes I forget, just the same. This morning I did." Her eyes misted over, and she struggled to find her voice.

"Archibald came to me and told me he'd had my things sent from Duart to Auchinbreck. I'm sure the Macleans weren't happy to give them up—my father had given me some wonderful jewels before I left Inveraray, and many of the gowns were worth a great deal."

She paused to look up at Muriella. "Archibald says they gave him no trouble, but I'm certain 'tis not the truth. He only said it because he didn't want to distress me. I know he had to threaten them somehow."

"So the trunks will be waiting for ye when ye reach Auchinbreck?"

"Aye." Elizabeth took a deep breath. "I'm not certain I have the strength to look inside them. Before I could tell him so, my husband said that if I never want to open them, I needn't do so. But if I find, in time, that the past is easier to bear, then my things will be there—waiting." She gazed at her hands, clasped tightly in her lap. "When he told me that, I wanted to weep."

Even now her eyes filled with tears, yet she smiled. And for the first time there was no sadness in her smile, no bitter realization, no regret. Muriella, moved by her own aching memory of a chamber emptied of scarlet and filled instead with green and gold and brown, put her arm across the other woman's shoulders. "I'm glad for ye," she said. "Mayhap Archibald Campbell is exactly what ye needed to make ye forget."

Elizabeth nodded. "Ye know, at first I thought 'twas cruel beyond words that my husband shared my father's name. But now I sometimes wonder if the second Archibald Campbell isn't meant somehow to make up for all the pain the first caused me."

"I hope 'tis so," Muriella whispered.

"Aye." Once again the two women glanced away from one another. Seeking a distraction, Elizabeth turned her attention to the tapestry spread across the width of the chamber. "I've watched ye work on this so often since I came to Inveraray that I can't believe 'tis finished at last. May I see it before I go?"

Muriella rose, hands trembling as she lifted the huge

tapestry, then drew one end up and across the other so that, when she reached the far side of the chamber, the front of the hanging was visible. No one but she and Megan had seen the completed design, and she awaited Elizabeth's response with eagerness and apprehension.

Eyes wide with admiration at the vivid colors, Elizabeth knelt beside the first panel, in which the bubbling burn flowed by while the Kelpies watched from the protection of their leaf-shrouded bower. In the distance, the golden-haired woman led her friends as they rode to the hunt, laughing, their plaids caught up in the wind behind them. "'Tis lovely," Elizabeth murmured. "Ye can almost hear their laughter."

She moved to the second panel, where the water swirled around the woman's waist as the burn swelled into a deadly torrent. Her mouth was open in terror, the wreath of flowers askew on her long, flowing hair. Within the rushing water, among the leaves and in the darkness beyond, the Kelpies laughed and danced, celebrating their victory over the lady who had ruled their valley for too long. Elizabeth shivered at the gleaming triumph in their eyes.

Finally, she came to the last panel. She leaned forward to look more closely at the sweeping grandeur of Loch Awe. The islands of birch and larch were lovely in every detail of earth and bark and shadowy leaves; the water rippled gently, the moon shone down in silver radiance, and the path of golden light touched the water with ethereal brilliance. Elizabeth held her breath, running her fingers over the fabric, marveling at its fine weave and subtle shading of color. Then she noticed for the first time the red-haired woman kneeling on the near bank, staring at her reflection in the water. But it was not her reflection. It was— Elizabeth's hand grew still above the image of her brother's blurred but vibrant face. She looked up to find Muriella watching her, eyes dark with grief. Neither spoke for a long moment.

Muriella looked away, breaking the stillness at last. "Do ye know where he's gone?" she asked.

Bewildered by the desperation in her sister-in-law's voice,

Elizabeth shook her head. "Even when we were close, my brother didn't tell me his plans." At Muriella's look of disappointment, she rubbed her chin and tried to think. "But I heard Archibald say something—I believe Johnnie's gone after a man who has been giving him trouble for a long time. I'm afraid 'tis all I know."

"Aye," Muriella said, "John told me he was going to meet an enemy. But he wouldn't say who."

"Ye saw him today?" Elizabeth asked in surprise.

"Just before dawn. I found him in the chamber where the weapons are kept. He was armed, the men were armed, but he wouldn't tell me why."

Elizabeth frowned. "Why should that frighten ye? 'Tis no' unusual for men to keep their battles and their grudges to themselves. They don't think we care or understand about such things."

"It frightens me because I saw the look on his face. 'Twas the look of a stranger, and his eyes—they were blind, as if I weren't there, as if there were nothing in the world but his own rage." Muriella shuddered at the memory of those cold, implacable eyes.

Spreading her hands helplessly, Elizabeth said, "'Tis the way things are with Johnnie. 'Tis no' in his nature to feel anything halfway." She paused, choosing her words with care. "Mayhap he didn't tell ye more because he didn't want to upset ye."

"Doesn't he realize that the waiting, the uncertainty are the worst? Doesn't he see how hard it is to be left behind?"

"Ye know he doesn't," Elizabeth murmured. "He's a man. How can he understand that the walls of the keep ring with silence when the men are gone? How can he when he's never heard the chilling stillness for himself? How can he understand the boredom of inaction when his life is all motion and danger and excitement?" Sighing in compassion, she said, "Ye mustn't ask the impossible of a man like Johnnie. He can't know what ye feel any more than ye can know what he feels. He won't change, my friend, and neither will ye. Ye'll be happier by far when ye come to accept that."

Muriella could not argue with what she knew to be true,

but that did not ease the dread that lay like a fist of lead in her chest. A hush fell and the two women stared at the dust motes dancing in streams of sunlight that fell through the wide solar windows. Finally, Elizabeth rose. "I must go now. My husband will be waiting."

"Aye," Muriella breathed. Not until that moment did she realize how much she would miss the companionship she had shared with Elizabeth over the past few months.

Elizabeth and Muriella faced each other, suddenly at a loss for words. Then Elizabeth whispered, "Ye'll come to visit me at Auchinbreck, won't ye? Soon?"

"I'll come," Muriella told her. "And mayhap now ye won't be afraid to return to Inveraray."

"No," Elizabeth agreed. Her gray eyes steady, she met Muriella's gaze. "I think that soon I'll find I'm not afraid of anything anymore."

Her sister-in-law nodded mutely.

Eyes damp with tears, Elizabeth and Muriella embraced one last time, while at their feet, the afternoon sun shone on the softly undulating waters of Loch Awe, frozen forever in a pattern of glowing silk and colored wool.

# 40

The Great Hall was ablaze that night with a thousand candles. Most of the tables had been removed and the rushes dragged into the courtyard so the floor would be free for dancing. Muriella stood at the foot of the stairs, surveying the crowds of jeweled men and women who rotated before her. Until tonight, she had not believed there were that many jewels in all Scotland. She touched the pendant at her own throat. For the first time since the wedding over four years ago, she was wearing the golden flame that had been her gift from John.

She had no trouble picking out Colin where he stood across the room. His doublet was of deep wine satin, his shirt was ivory, and he wore a jeweled belt at his waist. When he gestured, his hands were collections of colored flame in the candlelight. He had discarded his plaid for the evening and wore instead a burgundy velvet cloak. He was by far the most magnificent among the men, but Muriella was not impressed. She wanted to laugh at him. He was playing king and those who danced before him were his subjects.

"So here ye are, my wife."

Muriella started at the sound of John's voice. She had not known he had returned to the keep. Anxiously, she turned to find that the furious stranger had gone; her husband's eyes were clear, untarnished blue, the rigid lines of his face had softened, and his lips were curved in a pleased smile. He was dressed for the fête in a black doublet and trews, his plaid wrapped gracefully around his shoulders. The clothes were simple, but his dark looks were far more memorable than Colin's blond splendor. Muriella's heart began to beat unsteadily.

"As ye can see, ye had nothing to fear," he said as he took her arm in a warm grasp.

"Ye haven't been wounded?" his wife asked, examining his shirt and trews for the telltale bulk of a woven bandage.

John's smile broadened and he drew her toward him with both hands cupped under her elbows. "Not even a scratch." Eyes sparkling, he brushed her cheek with the tips of his fingers. "I've missed ye," he said huskily, as if a week of frustration and loneliness had never come between them. "Will ye forgive me for my neglect?"

Muriella trembled with pleasure and dread as her husband slid his arms around her back. She had missed him too—more than she'd realized. More, perhaps, than she could bear. John's hands were circling slowly over her back, bringing her skin to tingling life, and she made herself speak again before her courage burned away beneath his magic touch. "What happened today to change ye so much? This morning—"

"This morning things were different," he interrupted. "Ye were right to think that there was danger, but ye needn't concern yourself anymore." His voice was little more than a whisper a breath away from her parted lips. "The danger has passed."

Just for an instant, when his mouth met hers, he made her believe it. Muriella swayed toward him, sliding her hands up to his shoulders. She could feel the texture of his satin shirt, strangely cool beneath her heated palms. Her breasts brushed his chest, and even through the fabric of her gown, they ached for his touch. His lips caressed hers, gently at first, then more and more fiercely until Muriella's doubts were consumed by the stirring movement of his hands across her back. As he drew her closer, the wild yearning rose within her, warm and blinding and fearfully bright.

"We'd best leave off, my little one, or I'm sorely afraid

we'll disgrace ourselves before the guests." As he pulled away from her, she saw that his cheeks were flushed and the finger he ran along her cheek quivered just a little. "If we leave now, Colin won't ever cease his taunting, so we'll stay. But I'll come to ye later."

"Aye," she said. There was no other answer she could give.

"Since we must be here, we might as well enjoy the evening," John murmured. "Shall we have a dance or two?" When she nodded, he led her out onto the crowded floor.

She was hardly aware of the laughing tilt and sway of the dancers around her, or of the magnificence of the many lights that had at last destroyed the chill in the cavelike hall. The warmth of John's fingers on her skin made her giddy. As she whirled in his arms, the candles and the flaming jewels seemed to merge into one gleaming, flickering mass of color. Her body rose and fell with the music; the lights danced magically before her eyes. Each time the intricate steps brought John near, she smiled, and each time his grip on her grew tighter. The song of the clareschaws was running through her blood; John's breath was brushing across her cheeks. She rotated rhythmically in the candlelight, her skirts swirling about her legs.

When the harps fell silent, Muriella leaned against her husband while she steadied her breathing and her pulse began to slacken. After a moment, he looked down at her, smiling, and said softly, "I've been thinking that now 'tis safe again, 'tis time to go back to Cawdor."

She blinked as if she had not heard him properly. "Ye don't mean—" Stopping in confusion, she tried to find the words to express her distress. "But 'tis barren there, and long abandoned. There're neither hangings on the walls nor rugs on the floors."

John shook his head. "I've taken care of that. Ye'll find things have changed a great deal since your last visit."

Looking away, she murmured under her breath, "They couldn't have changed enough."

"Muriella?" her husband asked. "What troubles ye?"

She drew away from the shelter of his arm to meet his

questioning gaze. "I don't think I can face Cawdor again. The memories are too strong."

"Even now?" he whispered.

She nodded. "Even now."

Before he could respond, Colin appeared from among the weaving dancers, calling, "Johnnie, where've ye been hiding?" When John did not answer, the Earl reached out to grasp Muriella's free hand. "Ye wouldn't deny me a dance with your wife, would ye? I've been waiting all evening." He did not stop to hear his brother's response but pulled her toward an opening in the press of moving bodies.

For a moment, John kept his hand on Muriella's, as if he would not let her go, but when he realized some of the guests were watching, he released her. Bowing with elaborate courtesy, he said, "As ye wish, Brother. But take care of her."

Colin smiled as he faced his new partner. He had not missed the underlying threat in John's voice. However, his brother did not intend to pay John any mind. The Earl had found, at last, that he was bored with Jenny, and his eyes had begun to wander. He had not failed to notice that Muriella was magnificent tonight. She wore a deep blue velvet gown with satin ribbons, and as she rotated in the dance, the skirt parted in front, revealing her sky blue kirtle. Her auburn braids were wound around her head, with pale blue ribbons twined among them. At her throat the ruby glowed in its gold setting. Colin squeezed her fingers, and when she came near to circle with him, he moved his hand above her waist. "I was hoping Johnnie wouldn't return before dawn," he said. "Then I could've had ye all to myself."

Muriella whirled away as the dance demanded, but when she faced him again, she said, "He wouldn't like to hear ye talk that way."

"Do ye think I care what Johnnie likes? Ye forget that *I'm* the Earl. My brother is nothing."

Muriella stiffened and took a step back. "Nothing," she said, "except my husband."

Forcing himself to smile, Colin closed the space between them. "'Tis no' wise to scorn me, ye know. If I want ye, I shall have ye."

"Ye sicken me," she said.

"Do I?" His voice was cool but she felt the rage underneath. "I suppose ye prefer my little brother."

She faced him squarely. "Aye."

"Then you're a fool," he hissed. "He's more interested in hunting down his enemies and making them cry for mercy than in visiting your chamber. He knows, no doubt, what he'll find in your bed, but out there, with a sword in his hand, my brother plays a game he thinks he can't lose. Or hadn't ye noticed his gloating smile tonight?"

Muriella withdrew her hands from Colin's grasp. "What do ye mean?"

"Didn't he tell ye? I'd have thought he'd be bragging about his triumph to anyone who'd listen. Ye see," he said in an exaggerated whisper, "The Devil Afire will burn no more."

Muriella regarded the Earl curiously. She had heard the name before but could not remember where.

Colin saw her confusion and leaned forward until she could not escape the cold gleam of his eyes. "Surely ye know of the one they call The Devil Afire? 'Tis the outlaw, Hugh Rose. Or at least, 'twas 'til today, when Johnnie killed him."

The foreboding was with Muriella again, so all-enveloping that it took her breath away. "You're lying," she choked.

"No, my blind little fool, 'tis the truth. Haven't ye realized yet that Johnnie's determined to make certain there's no one left to challenge his right to Cawdor?" The Earl smiled when he saw the color fade from Muriella's cheeks. "Hugh Rose was in his way—and now he's dead."

The room began to spin as Colin drew her back into the dance. When she bent her head, the sound of John's voice came to her like a grim, distant warning. *There's something I have to do. Something that can't wait any longer.* She circled and bowed, skipped and turned, but all the while her husband's furious image was before her. Why had he never answered her questions?

With a start, Muriella realized that Colin was leading her off the floor toward the place where John waited. For a moment she thought she could not face him, then a rush of bright anger restored her courage.

"Muriella?" her husband asked, disturbed by the strange flush of color on her cheeks.

"I would speak to ye privately," she said.

Eyes narrowed, he regarded her in silence for a moment before taking her arm. "As ye wish."

Together they climbed the stairs without a word. When they reached the top, John drew Muriella into a hollowed niche in the thick stone wall. "Well?"

The curve of the passageway blocked the torchlight; Muriella looked up at her husband, noting the way the shadows clung about him, darkening his face and disguising the expression in his eyes. "Where were ye going when I found ye this morning?" she demanded.

John stiffened, his fingers closing more tightly around her arm. "Have a care for the way ye ask your questions," he warned. "Mayhap the answers won't please ye." When she continued to stare at him, unblinking, he frowned. "As I told ye then, I was on my way to meet an enemy."

With an effort, Muriella kept her voice steady. "'Twas my cousin Hugh, wasn't it?"

For a moment, her husband was shocked out of his anger. "How did ye know?" Then he remembered the smug grin with which Colin had relinquished Muriella. John clenched his free hand into a fist that made his arm ache to the shoulder. "Aye," he said.

Muriella could not breathe, but fought to make herself go on. "Ye killed him, didn't ye?"

Cursing his brother under his breath, John put his hands on his wife's shoulders. He had not meant for her to find out this way, had never meant for her to know what Hugh Rose had become. "Listen to me—," he began.

"Is it true?" she cried. "Just tell me if 'tis true."

"Aye," he said in resignation. "I killed him."

"Why?" she asked. Seeking support for the weakness in her knees, she pressed one hand against the stône.

"Because," John told her softly, "he was an evil man."

"No!" She looked away and covered her ears with her hands. "I won't listen."

Forcing her hands away from her head, her husband said, "Ye asked for the truth and now ye'll hear it. Hugh Rose was a thief and a murderer who didn't deserve to live anymore. I only destroyed him before he could destroy me."

Muriella closed her eyes. It seemed that killing Hugh was not enough for John; he wanted to kill her memories too. It was then that she saw again the blackened face that had haunted her dream. She had thought it was the image of some ghastly stranger, but now she understood; the leering mockery of a face had been her cousin's death mask. Suppressing a single, anguished cry, she turned away from her husband.

"Where are ye going?" he demanded.

"To my chamber. I've lost a childhood friend tonight. Mayhap ye'll allow me a moment to grieve alone." Sensing that he would not try to stop her, she slipped past him to disappear down the narrow, twisting passageway.

She did not see Duncan stop as she passed and turn to stare after her in dismay. He cried out once, "M'lady!" but she did not even hear him.

"Well, what's so important that it couldn't wait 'til morning?" Colin asked in impatience as he faced his brother across the crowded library. "My guests are waiting, ye ken."

John sat on the edge of the desk, clutching the wood with unnecessary force. "You've been meddling in my business again."

The Earl noted with misgiving the gleam in his brother's eye. Maybe he had gone too far this time. "What business? Make yourself clear, man."

"I'm talking of Muriella, as ye damned well know! What did ye say to her?"

Colin's smile was mocking. "I merely mentioned that she was looking particularly lovely tonight. I'm afraid she doesn't take compliments well."

"So ye were angry when she didn't fall for your charm and ye decided to get back at her, is that it?"

The Earl laughed uneasily. "I don't know what ye mean."

Releasing the desk and flexing his hands to stop the tingling in his fingers, John took a step toward his brother. "I think ye do. Now tell me, damn ye, what did ye say to her?"

Colin tried to think of the wisest answer, then with a shrug, decided to tell the truth. "I told Muriella ye'd gotten what ye wanted from her and left her for the pleasure of the hunt, with Hugh Rose as the prey."

John gasped in disbelief. When he caught his breath again, he had to fight to control the rage that left him shaking. "I knew ye were low, but—"

Smiling crookedly, Colin regarded his brother in unconcern. "Don't try to abuse me just because ye aren't man enough to keep her happy, Johnnie. 'Tis no' my fault."

In an instant, John closed the space between them, grasping his brother's doublet in his hands. The fury boiled in him, clamoring to be released. "I warned ye before to leave her alone, ye bastard."

"'Tis no' me who's the bastard, and well ye know it. I've heard they don't have real feelings like other people. I just thought I'd see for myself."

At Colin's bland smile, John's control finally snapped. He released his brother and, with all his strength, slammed his fist into his brother's jaw. Colin, third Earl of Argyll, staggered briefly, then slumped to the floor, unconscious.

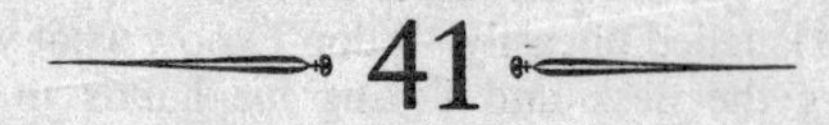

# 41

Once she had left her husband behind, Muriella ran without stopping until her chamber door was closed and the bolt slid into place. The fire had died down, so the chamber was cold, but she did not revive the flames. Collecting several candles from around the room, she lit each from the torch and set them in a circle she had cleared on the floor. Numb with shock, she sank to the stone with the candles as a wall of fluttering light around her. They seemed to isolate her from the people and music and laughter that swept through the keep beyond her door. Feebly, the flames attempted to push back the gloom to the corners of the room.

Closing her eyes, she felt the glow of the candlelight against her lids as she tried to bring the image of Hugh's face into her mind. But all she could see was the blackened shell of his death mask. Soon, even that faded as John's face rose to cover it. Her heart slowed and she tried to free herself of the image, but it would not go.

It would be with her always—in her dreams and her nightmares, in the sunlight and the darkness, even in the Loch Awe tapestry, where she had woven her husband's face without knowing. Why could she not escape it? The answer came to her in the flutter of the candlelight through the shadows—because she loved him.

Muriella gasped, pressing her hands against the floor as if to keep herself from falling. She had been blind; she should have known it long ago, but she had shut her eyes to the truth. She had not wanted to face the turmoil of her feelings for John: the frantic beating of her heart, the ache that never ceased to come at the sight of his face. The hopeless, joyful, cruel, intoxicating force of her love, and at the center of all those things—the fear that would never leave her.

The solid stone room began to sway, tilting wildly from side to side as her heartbeat grew labored. Slowly, inevitably, the coldness settled in her bones. She was struggling with the darkness that closed around her until it became the water, rushing, white and chilling, about her body. It would sweep her away; she had no strength left to fight it anymore. She clawed her way upward, choking and gasping, but the water pulled her down and down and down, sucking the last of the breath from her body.

She shuddered, arms wrapped tightly across her chest. It was a long moment before she realized that the water had retreated and she was sprawled on the floor in her chamber within the ring of candle flames. The sweat rolled down her face into her hair as she rubbed her arms in a futile attempt to chase away the chill. She thought her heart had ceased to beat, that it might never again take up its rhythm, but then she felt the painful thumping in her chest and knew that she had survived the vision once again.

Long after the chill had left her and the trembling had stopped, the image of the rushing water lingered—cold and bright and menacing, like the rage that glimmered in John's eyes.

She had first seen it on the afternoon when the Campbells arrived at Cawdor and he'd come crashing toward her through the river. She saw it always in his love for the chase, the hunt, the inevitable kill. The fury that drove him to hunt down his enemies until every last one of them was dead—Andrew Calder, Lachlan Maclean, Hugh Rose, and countless others whose names she did not know. *'Tis no' really that they're cruel,* Elizabeth had murmured. *'Tis just that they don't know any other way.* Yet it was that very intensity of feeling that had tempted John, for a moment, to silence his own sister because he could not bear her weakness. The rage that was his God ruled him, obsessed him, changed him—the rage that might one day be turned against Muriella herself.

There was another John, a tiny voice whispered from out of the gloom. A man who saw her needs and cared for her and tried to understand. But that John frightened her even more, because, when he came to her and held her, he could make her forget. *Sometimes Archibald frightens me. Not because he mistreats me, but because he doesn't. I don't know how to fight his kindness.*

Muriella buried her face in her hands. When John had made love to her, when he'd held her and taught her to know his body, the joy had rushed through her in waves, overwhelming her wisdom. As he caressed her skin with his gentle hands, she'd forgotten, for an instant, that those hands were covered with blood—and always would be. *Ye can't ask the impossible of a man like Johnnie. He won't change, my friend, and neither will ye.*

Muriella was choking on the smell of must in the tiny, airless chamber. She had to get away from here—from the maudlin shadows the candles painted across the walls. Away from the voices screaming inside her head like disembodied spirits singing a frighteningly beautiful song.

She had to leave it behind before it consumed her. She would go to the loch, because there she would find peace. Moving awkwardly, as if her limbs were not her own, she rose, went to the door, and slid the bolt open. Turning toward the darkened end of the corridor, she groped through the shadows for the door through which Megan had taken her on her first morning at Inveraray. When she found it, she dragged it open, hoping to lose herself in the dank, curving passage beyond. She did not look to see if she was followed.

Muriella ran incautiously, brushing against the moist walls, stumbling on the steep downward path, but she did not slow her pace. She dared not take the chance of pausing, or the weeping voices might overcome her. At last she came to the final door. She slid the bolt back with both hands, unaware that it stained her fingers with streaks of rust.

When she emerged into the lower garden, the cold wind rushed at her, nearly forcing her to her knees. She embraced the chill because it dulled her senses, dimming the clamor of voices to a dull, persistent murmur.

She had meant to follow the battlemented walls of the keep and find her way through the darkness to the loch, but when she heard the sound of the river, she paused. Its voice was loud enough to sweep away the other troubling noises. Muriella turned toward the deafening roar. As she approached, she saw that the river lashed within its banks, discontent and deadly with the swollen bravery the melting snows had given it. She stood on the bank, feeling the spray that drenched her face, her hair, her deep blue gown. As the water cooled the heat in her cheeks, the river seemed to call to her.

She swayed forward, fascinated by the rush and thunder of the water swirling over the tumbled rocks. She could feel it closing around her shoulders, drawing her under. The terror welled within her, stopping her breath, but still the water called, echoing with its hypnotic voice her own long-ago words to Megan. *'Tis the waiting that's the worst,* it roared. *The waiting. . . .* The slow, wearing agony of not knowing when or where or why. . . . The river laughed and groaned, throwing the words in her face time and again, until she moved closer, mesmerized by the swift-flowing image of her fear. *'Tis the waiting, the waiting, the waiting that's the worst.* The water wooed her, lured her, called for her to come . . . *come know the chill, swirling heart of your terror so it need not haunt you anymore. Come. . . .*

If she answered, if she let the water take her, then the waiting would be over and she would be at peace.

Drawn by the call of a nightmare too powerful to resist, she plunged, unthinking, into the river. Then the icy water closed around her and the shock of the bitter cold woke her from her trance. As her legs were swept from beneath her, she cried out, realizing in horror what she had done, but her voice was drowned by the force of the rushing river. The water dragged her, struggling, in its path. Though she flung her arms out, reaching for the shore, she could not free herself from the furious torrent that had her in its grip at last.

Then a sharp sound broke through her terror. She looked up to see Duncan stretched above the river on a heavy branch. In the clear, cascading moonlight, she saw that he was weeping, and the thought of his tears was more painful than the rocks and bushes that tore at her. Choking on the water that filled her eyes and throat, Muriella reached for his hand as the current swept her beneath him.

He closed his other hand around her wrists and they swayed there, balanced precariously, while the branch shifted under their weight. Duncan lay still, holding her as best he could, while he waited for the movement to subside. The river was only inches away, tumbling beneath them with a fury that made him shiver. Afraid as he had never been before, Duncan found a strength he had not known he possessed. While Muriella dug her fingers frantically into his shoulders, he slid his arms around her waist and drew her up beside him. They clung to the heavy branch of the oak, trying to catch their breath, then, slowly, an inch at a time, began to crawl backward away from the water.

When he reached the trunk, Duncan dropped to the ground and stood waiting to help Muriella as she made her way down in her drenched skirts. Leaning awkwardly against the rough bark, he pulled her dripping body close to his own. He rested his head on her hair, then did not attempt to move again.

Muriella clung to him, wet and bruised, blood running down her forehead. She did not think, and although she was chilled, she did not shiver. With her head on Duncan's heaving chest, she gave herself up to the memory of his tears. She did not notice that the blood ran more and more freely over her face, and she slipped into unconsciousness without ever having looked into his eyes.

Duncan felt her slump against him. When he tilted her face up, he saw where a rock had cut her forehead at the temple. Pushing her gently away, he tore a long strip from his shirt to wind around her head, hoping it would slow the bleeding. When he began to breathe normally again, he lifted her in his arms and started toward the castle.

She was heavier than he had thought and the path to the keep was long and steep. He struggled with his burden, stopping to rest now and then against a nearby tree. Gradually, as he left the river behind, the fear began to slip away and his mind to work once more. Thank God she was safe, he thought. Thank God he had had the presence of mind to recognize her distress when he saw her running from the fête. He'd waited outside her door, then followed her with increasing dread when she left her room to disappear into the passageway. He remembered with a chill the horror he had felt when she'd thrown herself in the water.

It took the squire a long time to find his way through the gloomy passage. When he finally pushed open the inner door, he paused, relaxing for a moment against the stone wall. Then he continued down the hall, noticing with relief that the door to Muriella's room was ajar. With his foot, he kicked it open.

Megan stood in the center of the room, a ring of burned-out candles at her feet. Beside her stood John, his face drawn and gray. At the sight of his cousin, Duncan stopped on the threshold, aware, for the first time, of what he must now face. He wanted to turn and run, but his burden was too heavy and it was already too late.

John raised his head, blinked, and froze where he stood. "What in God's name," he roared, "have ye done with my wife?"

Duncan trembled, intensely aware of the weight of Muriella's head against his shoulder. He thought he would not be able to answer, but then his voice returned. "I—didn't do it," he stuttered. "I—only—found her." Furious at his own weakness, he swallowed once and spoke more calmly. "Before I explain, I think she needs care. Her head—"

With an effort, John got his anger under control. He could see from the blood seeping through Duncan's makeshift bandage that his wife did indeed need care. He crossed the floor in two long strides, lifted Muriella from the squire's arms, and carried her to the bed, where he laid her among the heavy furs.

"We'd best get her wet gown off before she falls ill," Megan whispered behind him.

"Aye," he said, unable to pull himself away from the image of his wife's ashen face. She lay with her skirts twisted about her, dripping over the mattress and down the side of the bed. She was breathing unevenly, her lips slightly parted. Her skin was translucent—pale ivory in some places, gray in others. The blood trickled over her forehead and into her wet hair.

"M'lord," Megan said.

John turned away abruptly. "I'll get Mary to help ye see to her." Brushing past the squire, he stepped into the corridor and shouted, "Mary! Where the devil are ye when I need ye, girl? Mary!"

When the servant finally appeared, John ushered her into Muriella's chamber; then, motioning for Duncan to follow him into the passageway, he closed the door with a bang. "Now," he said sharply, "tell me."

Duncan shifted from one foot to the other, staring down at his damp, mud-stained trews. How could he describe what had happened when he was not even certain himself? He frowned, searching for words, though he knew that there were none. "Your wife's been in the river, m'lord. I think she hit her head on a rock and that's why—"

"How did she get there," John interrupted, "and how is it ye were there to find her?"

He spoke without inflection, but Duncan recognized the threat beneath the softly spoken words. "I saw her run from her chamber earlier. She—" He paused, running his tongue over his dry lips. "She seemed distraught. I saw her go to the door, the one that leads to the tunnels below, and I followed."

"Why?" John waited rigidly for his cousin's reply.

"I don't know. I thought she might come to some harm.

'Twas late and I couldn't understand why she should be going outside."

"How did she come to fall in the river?"

This was the question Duncan had feared. He considered lying, but was not certain what Muriella would tell her husband when she awakened. If she had been serious in her attempt, then John should know the truth. "She didn't fall."

Mechanically, John moved toward his cousin, his sword swinging against his leg. "What are ye saying?"

"She jumped. I believe she intended—"

"No! Ye must be wrong." John's hands were shaking as he took Duncan roughly by the shoulders. "Tell me," he demanded, "are ye certain of this?"

"Aye, m'lord."

For an instant, John thought if he strangled his cousin, cut off the source of the news he had just received, then it would no longer be true. His wife had fallen, he told himself. Just that. Fallen into the river at midnight, four hundred yards from the keep? No, Duncan must be right, damn him! His fingers closed bruisingly on the squire's shoulders.

Duncan gasped at the look in his cousin's eyes and felt his palms grow damp with sweat. "M'lord!" he cried in desperation, "I've only told ye the truth!"

John winced and released the squire at once. *'Twas only a momentary madness,* he had told Muriella once. But a moment, he realized, was long enough. "Forgive me," he said. "'Tis not your fault, I know." He turned away in an effort to steady his breathing.

Sensing that the danger had passed, Duncan sighed in relief, then touched his cousin's arm. "There's something more ye should know," he said softly. "Your wife must have changed her mind when the water closed around her, because when she saw me, she reached out to take my hand. I don't know why she threw herself in, but I do know she wanted me to save her. 'Tis no' much," he said when he saw the look on John's face, "but 'tis something."

John raised both fists to his forehead and closed his eyes against the dawning realization that his wife had tried to take her own life. Somehow, his mind refused to accept it. He shook his head again and again in denial. "Thank ye for all you've done," he said. His face clouded over as he added, "Don't tell the others what's happened."

"No, of course not."

Looking at Duncan's lanky body, covered with mud and leaves and a trail of blood that began at his shoulder, then disappeared into the saffron folds of his long shirt, John told him, "Ye'd best get out of those clothes. And have Jenny draw ye a bath."

"Are ye sure ye wouldn't have me stay?"

Wearily, John shook his head. "Just now I would be alone. I have to think what to do." As he turned to stare at the heavy oak door that shut him away from his wife, he realized that he could not think. His mind was blank from shock and pain and a despair so deep that he dared not recognize it.

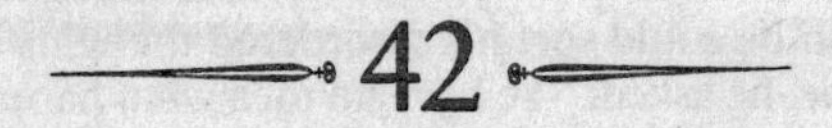

# 42

Muriella moaned. As her dreams retreated, she tried to think where she was, but her mind was operating from the center of a dense fog; around her everything was dark. She sensed movement nearby but did not know what it meant. Slowly, with a great deal of difficulty, she opened her eyes. Her vision was cloudy; she could discern only shadows and vague shapes that had no meaning. But she felt a presence just above her. As her vision began to clear, a face appeared, scowling, troubled. She blinked several times before the face came into focus; then she drew a name up from her memory. John. She felt a rush of joyous relief at the sight of his familiar face. He was safe. Or was it she who had been in danger?

Her head began to ache at the thought. She noticed that though her husband's hand was resting on the bed next to her shoulder, he was not looking at her. In the same moment, it came to her that the long-awaited storm had broken at last; she could hear the wind moaning as rain slashed furiously against the walls of the keep. No wonder the light was so strange and silver tinted. No wonder John's face looked so gray and haggard. But perhaps that was not it at all. Perhaps something was very wrong. "Johnnie?" she murmured.

His head snapped up. For a long moment, he simply stared at her. "Why did ye do it?" he asked at last.

She did not understand. "Do . . . what?"

Drawing a deep breath, John leaned closer. He could see the confusion in her eyes and knew that it was real. "Ye don't remember, do ye?"

"Remember?" Muriella's heart began to beat unsteadily.

John ran his hand through his hair, smoothing the untidy strands as if he could sort his disordered thoughts as easily. After a time, he asked, "Ye have no idea what happened last night?"

His wife frowned, trying to think. She remembered the room full of swirling dancers, the way John had held her in the fragmented light, and the stirring warmth of his lips on hers, but then—nothing. "I don't think—," she began, but a distant, troubling memory made her stop. It hovered before her, just out of reach. Perplexed, she drew her brows together and felt a strange discomfort across her forehead. Muriella reached up to touch the thick linen bandage, wincing at the pressure of her fingers on the wound beneath. As the pain sliced through her head, it all came back to her—John's face, the candlelight, the darkness, and, finally, the river. "Dear God!" she cried, turning away.

"Muriella."

The sound of his voice brought the flaring pain up through her limbs. She was shaking and could not stop. She felt him touch her shoulder, curse under his breath. Then he was gone and the coldness was with her again. "Johnnie," she called, "don't leave me!"

She did not know if he had heard her. She closed her eyes, pressing her hands into the warm mattress, hoping to still the trembling. Just when she thought it might never end, John reached from out of the unnatural stillness beyond the bed to offer her a goblet of wine. "Drink."

She took the cold pewter in her hands, raised her head, and drank. As the soothing warmth began to move through her veins, the shaking eased until, at last, it stopped altogether. Only then did she find the courage to look up at him.

"Now," her husband said, setting the goblet aside, "tell me."

She could feel his breath on her cheek and it made her

want to weep. "I didn't really wish to die," she told him, knowing it was not enough, that nothing she could say would ever be enough.

"Then why, in God's name, did ye do it?"

"'Twas—" She tried to think, but the throbbing in her head defeated her. Then, in the midst of the numbing pain, came the memory of something he had told her once. Grasping a wolf pelt in her cold fingers, she said, "'Twas only a momentary madness. The river hypnotized me and I didn't have the strength to resist."

It was not what he wanted to hear; she knew by the way he retreated, his expression hidden by half-closed lids. All at once, she wanted to draw him close, to smooth the pain from his face with the touch of her hands. "I swear to ye, I didn't mean to do it."

He stared at the rushes at his feet until the power of her gaze was too great to ignore any longer. "If 'tis so, then tell me why ye left the keep in the middle of the night. Why were ye even near the river?"

"I had to get away," she replied without thinking.

John winced as if she had struck him. "From me?"

"No!" she cried. "But mayhap—" Her eyes clouded with confusion. "I don't know."

Massaging his forehead as if it pained him, her husband sank deeper into a chair beside the bed. Muriella wanted to take the hand that rested on his knee, but she sensed that he would not welcome her touch. The constriction in her throat nearly choked her and tears burned behind her lids.

John ran his hands over the soft wool of his trews as he tried to find an explanation for his wife's behavior that he could understand. He knew she had wanted him when he held her at the foot of the stairs; he had felt her response when his lips met hers. As they danced, she had been happy; he remembered clearly the radiance in her eyes each time she looked at him. But afterward, something had gone wrong. He looked up to find Muriella watching him in tense silence; only the thunder of the rising storm outside disturbed the stillness. "Was it because of Cawdor that ye ran away?" John asked. "Or was it Hugh Rose?"

Muriella blinked at him in astonishment. She had forgotten Hugh completely. "No," she told him. "'Twas neither of those things."

"Then why?" John reached out to take her hand. "In God's name, tell me the truth!"

His wife felt his desperation, and though she formed the words of a soothing lie, her lips would not utter it. "I don't think ye really want to hear the truth."

He looked up then, his face drawn and pale. "I can't stand the waiting any longer. Tell me."

Muriella stared at his strong, sunbrowned hand for a long time before her fingers closed around it in a plea for understanding that she knew he could not give. "I did it because of ye," she said. "Because ye will destroy me."

The pain that rose within him was so great he had to look away. She had admitted at last what he had always suspected. He realized, as he released his wife's hand, that she was right; he did not want to know. "So," he said in a tone so still it frightened her, "*'tis* me ye see in the vision that comes whenever I touch ye."

Muriella bit her lip. The time had come when she could no longer avoid answering his questions. Her mouth was dry and her empty hands trembled as she whispered, "The vision is of my own death."

"Your death?" he repeated blankly. Then he realized what she was saying. John rose from the chair and kicked it away. "But that can't be," he said, knowing he was fighting a battle he had lost long ago. "I love ye too much."

Muriella gave a strangled moan and turned her head away, but not before he saw the bitter realization on her face.

"Were ye such a fool that ye didn't know that?"

"Aye," she muttered. "Just such a fool."

John began to pace in agitation. He had to think, but his thoughts were clouded by hopelessness and, beneath that, a violent denial. The Sight had never been wrong before, but— He turned in sudden determination. "'Tis not true," he declared. "I wouldn't ever want to hurt ye."

She wanted to believe him, but the sinking in her stomach

told her she dared not. "Just as ye never wanted to hurt Elizabeth?"

John stopped still, thumbs hooked in the wide leather of his sword belt. He could not deny it; he remembered the overwhelming rage he had felt as his sister lay ill, calling Maclean's name. And Muriella did not even know how near he'd come to hurting Duncan the night before.

Muriella waited for him to speak, to tell her she was wrong, to repeat his assurance that he would never hurt her, but John simply stood there, staring before him, appalled. His wife quailed.

John saw her shiver and he looked away. "I assume," he said carefully, in a voice without inflection, "that ye want me to go away so ye'll be safe."

Terror of a new kind shook her then. "No! I don't want to be safe."

Finally, inevitably, his control snapped. He leaned down, pressing his hands into the mattress, trapping her head between his two arms. "Then what, in the name of all that's holy, *do* ye want?"

It was there in his eyes again—the rage that made him into a stranger. She wanted to push him away, to free herself from that glittering stare. And yet—Elizabeth's warning pounded in her ears: *Remember, they can only hurt ye if ye give them the power to do so.* "I don't know," Muriella said.

John's shoulders sagged in defeat. He straightened slowly, releasing her from the prison of his hands. She sensed he was going to leave her and knew she had to stop him. Muriella reached up to grasp her husband's hand before he could slip away. "Please!" she cried.

She had made that plea before, but now, as then, he did not understand what she was asking for. Her fingers were warm and beguiling on his; against his will, he met her gaze. She held him immobile with her eyes; he could not look away. It had always been so. She tortured him, tempted him, enchanted and denied him. Her eyes were wild and green and fathomless and he knew, in that instant, that he had to break free—before she dragged him into the sea of her terror and they both drowned in the waves. "I've done what

I can," he said, withdrawing his hand from her grasp. "I don't know what else to do." He turned away.

"Johnnie!" Muriella cried, but he did not pause. He crossed the chamber in three long strides and the sound of the door slamming behind him echoed from the damp gray walls. Muriella closed her eyes. She should feel relief, she told herself. He was gone and she was safe. But she knew as she lay there struggling with the darkness that she could not bear his absence.

Colin awoke with a painful grunt. Gingerly, he touched his swollen jaw, wincing when he opened his mouth. He moved his lower teeth back and forth, hoping the motion would loosen his sore muscles and relieve the pain somewhat. John had done a thorough job, he thought, glowering. Now that it was too late, he remembered the warning his brother had given a week ago: *Ye'd best remember that when they're drunk, men sometimes lose all fear and sanity. Likely to do anything, they are.*

But John had not been drunk. The thought disturbed Colin. If necessary, he could deal with an intoxicated fool, but he did not know how to deal with a man who had been neither wild with drink nor weak with fear. Fear was the only thing the Earl really understood, the only method he knew to control the men under his command. But he had lost that control over his brother; John did not fear him anymore. And Argyll did not like it.

"M'lord? Are ye awake?" Sim poked his head inside the door warily.

Colin leaned back behind the bed curtains so the servant would not see his bruised face. "Aye!" he snapped. "What is it?"

"I wouldn't disturb ye, but a man came with a message from court. He said you're to see it right away."

"Well, don't stand there dithering in the corner. Bring it here, man!"

Reluctantly, the servant came forward, keeping his eyes lowered.

"Can't ye move any faster?" Argyll snarled. "Would ye have me wait all day?"

"Forgive me, m'lord," Sim muttered as he handed over the sealed parchment with shaking fingers. "I didn't mean to keep ye waitin'."

Colin noted with satisfaction that Sim did not look up. Now here was a man who knew how to approach the Earl of Argyll—a man who could not even meet his master's gaze out of fear of what he would find there. Grasping the note, fixed with the royal seal, Colin cuffed the servant on the ear for good measure. "Be gone!" he said.

Certain he would be obeyed, the Earl opened the parchment to find a request from the Queen Mother that he return to Edinburgh at once. There was trouble at court. He frowned. As if he did not already have trouble enough. On the other hand, he would not really mind leaving the damp halls of this keep for the luxuries at court. Only when he heard Sim shuffling from one foot to the other did he realize the servant still stood at the bedside. Brows drawn together in anger, he said, "I told ye to go."

"I heard ye, m'lord. But there's somethin' else I think ye should know."

"Out with it!" the Earl demanded.

The servant swallowed nervously. "I thought ye should know that Sir John left Inveraray an hour since."

"Left? To go where?"

"No one knows. When Duncan asked where he was goin' and when he would return, Sir John said 'twas no' anyone's business but his own."

"Did he now?" The Earl rose at last, throwing a robe over his shoulders as he moved toward the fire. "He was angry then?"

"No' exactly. He was—" The servant fumbled for words. "Still, ye ken, and silent, with cold, cold eyes. But he frightened me more this mornin' than he does when he's in one of his rages, I can tell ye that."

With his back to Sim, Colin touched his battered chin as

he gazed thoughtfully into the flames. "Do ye have any idea what happened to make him that way?"

Sim coughed, hoping the Earl had not seen him staring at the dark, ugly bruise on the side of his face. "I did hear 'em sayin' in the kitchen that Sir John's wife threw herself in the river last night."

"She did what?" Colin turned so he could see the servant's face.

"Jenny says she heard Duncan tell Sir John that his wife threw herself in the river."

"She isn't dead, is she? Someone would've informed me, surely."

"Och, no! She hurt her head, I'm told, but 'twas only after she awoke and Sir John spoke with her that he went away."

Colin's eyes narrowed. "So," he murmured. "Where is she now?"

"In her chamber. Jenny said she isn't likely to leave her bed today."

Running his fingers over his jaw, the Earl murmured, "Leave me now."

"As ye say, m'lord."

When the servant had gone, Colin stood pressing his hands against the stone above the fireplace. He had meant to punish John for his behavior last night, but his brother had already slipped out of his grasp. And Argyll did not have time to track him down just now. The Earl smiled crookedly when he thought of Muriella trying to take her life. He did not wonder why; he had given up long ago trying to understand her motives. Besides, this time she had made her husband miserable enough without Colin's intervention, it seemed. Perhaps it was better, for the moment, that *she* make John pay for his error in judgment.

His brother had said they'd be leaving for Cawdor soon. By the time the Earl returned, they would be gone; he would see to it. Then there would be peace again at Inveraray.

But with Muriella at Cawdor, there would be no mistress here. Colin frowned, rubbing the good side of his chin with two fingers. Perhaps on his way home, he would collect Janet and the children and bring them to the castle. His wife had asked to come often enough. The voices of his children might even make the keep seem a little less empty.

Argyll clenched his hands into helpless fists. What foolishness. Inveraray was full of Campbells, all of whom looked up to him with respect—and dread. Except for mad Johnnie and his fey wife. Glowering into the fire, Colin thought he would be happy to see the last of those two.

Megan drew away from the window as a flash of lightning blazed across the sky, illuminating the distant peaks with a brilliance that made her shiver. Quickly, she closed the shutters against the storm. "I don't like to think of Sir John out there in the rain," she said.

In spite of the storm, Muriella's husband had left Inveraray; she would have known it even if Megan had not come to tell her an hour since. Already the bleak gray walls had begun to ring with the sound of his absence. "He knows his way over these hills, even in this weather. He'll take care," she said, praying it was true. But she knew in her heart that John was in a dangerous frame of mind and not at all likely to take care. She feared the storm inside him was greater than the one without.

Turning away from the window, the servant returned to Muriella's side. For a long moment, she stared down at her hands before asking hesitantly, "Why did he go, m'lady?"

Muriella could not meet Megan's troubled brown eyes. "Because I didn't give him any choice."

"But Sir John isn't the kind of man to let his wife make choices for him."

"No," Muriella murmured, "but even *he* isn't strong enough to fight the power of the Sight and win."

Megan retreated a step. She did not want to think about that. "Do ye think—" She looked down at her hands again. "Do ye think he'll come back?"

"I don't know." Muriella found it difficult to speak around the lump that had formed in her throat. All at once, she knew she must be moving. Throwing the furs aside, she slipped from the bed.

"M'lady, please. Ye aren't strong enough to be up yet."

Muriella shook her head. "I can't stay still." At Megan's frown, she added, "But thank ye for caring, my friend."

"Am I your friend, truly?"

Stopping to meet the servant's searching gaze, her mistress smiled sadly. "Aye, from the first day they brought me here, I think. I'm grateful for that, Megan. For everything." Before Megan could respond, Muriella turned and started slowly over the rushes, shivering when the cold from the stone beneath penetrated through to her bare feet. While the servant hovered anxiously nearby, she slipped into a gray kirtle and gown—to match her mood, she thought. As she dressed, she bit her lip to keep her teeth from chattering. She had not yet shaken the chill that had settled in her blood from the icy water the night before.

"What are ye goin' to do?" Megan asked.

"Go to the library, I suppose. I only know I can't stay here." Where the sound of his voice still lingers, she added silently. Where the memory of his face hovers always before me. *Don't grieve for me,* Elizabeth had said. *It doesn't last forever, ye ken. The months pass, the hurt eases, and then, one day, ye begin to accept what ye can't change.* Muriella could not make herself believe it, not while the vision of the endless, empty days stretched out before her, making a lie of every word of comfort she had ever heard.

"Come," she said abruptly. "Let's be gone."

With Megan behind her, she stepped into the passageway. To her surprise, she found the hush there even harder to bear. She realized too late that the icy water had taken more from her than she'd supposed. For a long moment, she stood with her arms wrapped around her body, unable to make herself move forward, shivering uncontrollably. Then, when she tried to take a step, she lost her balance and started to fall.

A callused hand reached out to steady her. "M'lady? Are ye ill?"

She looked up into Richard Campbell's troubled face and noticed that, where it touched her arm, his hand trembled. He was afraid of her. "No," she said, "but I thank ye for being here to catch me. I don't seem to have any strength today."

Richard frowned. "Ye look mighty pale. And your head must pain ye. Don't ye think—" He stopped, realizing he had no right to question her.

Muriella shook her head. Though he could not disguise his unease in her presence, he also would not shirk his duty. And that duty was to protect her, no matter what his feelings were. "I can't stay still," she told him.

When she started to move again, her knees wobbled. Once again Richard took her arm. "Will ye at least let me help ye then?"

"The only way ye could help would be to bring my husband back." The moment the words were out of her mouth, she regretted them. Her problems with John were no concern of Richard's.

Richard blinked at her in surprise. "If ye didn't want him to go, why didn't ye cast a spell to keep him here?"

She sighed wearily. "Because I don't have that kind of power."

Something about the raw pain in her voice made him believe her. He looked at her more closely, noticing how her hands trembled, how pale her cheeks were and how deep the shadows under her eyes. Just now, it seemed she was no longer a woman to be feared, but rather a girl to be pitied.

After a moment's hesitation, he whispered hoarsely, "M'lady, I'm sorry."

She stared at him in astonishment. "I don't understand."

He shifted from one foot to the other, his face flushed with embarrassment. "I have had unkind thoughts of ye," he explained haltingly. "But mayhap I was wrong."

"I told ye so time and again," Megan interjected, "but ye wouldn't listen to me."

"Mayhap some things a man has to see for himself." He turned back to Muriella. "Do ye think ye can forgive me?"

The lump was forming in her throat again. "Ye had reason enough to believe what ye did, and I didn't try to tell ye different. But now ye see"—Muriella spread her hands to indicate her own slender body—"I have no power beyond the power of the Two Sights, and that I would forsake today if 'twere my choice." She saw that Richard was listening, brow furrowed. "I want ye to know that no matter what I said, I never meant the men any harm. Can ye believe that?"

"I can try." Then, before she could stop him, he leaned down to kiss her hand. It was the first time in over four years that one of the men had touched her of his own free will. The simple gesture made the tears ache in her throat. "Thank ye," she murmured.

Richard raised his head. "I must needs see to my brother's wound before the mornin's out. Can I go, m'lady?"

It was the first time, too, that one of John's men had asked her permission even for a thing so small. "Aye," she said in a strangled voice.

He bowed and, with a tentative smile, left them.

John would be pleased, Muriella thought. But John was not here, she reminded herself; he might never be again. As Richard disappeared down the passageway, she found that she could hold back her tears no longer.

# 44

Later, after her tears had dried and Megan had insisted she sit by the fire and eat some broth, Muriella ventured again into the hall. The chill in her blood had finally begun to dissipate and this time her legs were strong enough to support her. The two women found their way to the library in silence.

While Megan sewed by the light from the single window, Muriella settled herself in the Earl's carved chair and tried to read. She found, to her dismay, that the carefully transcribed parchment pages might as well have been written in a language she could not understand. The only words that had meaning for her were the ones John had spoken that morning while the world outside her window went mad with the fury of the storm. *What, in God's name,* DO *ye want?* If only she'd had an answer to give him.

The rain had raged at last into silence and the clouds had parted to reveal the pale blue sky, but the freshness that rose in the wake of the storm only made Muriella's loneliness deeper. She opened the worn manuscript of John Barbour's *The Bruce,* tracing the familiar words with her fingertips, as if to recapture the warmth she had once shared with the Earl while they recited it together. But he was dead. Today even his memory could not reach her. She had just rested her forehead on the desktop in despair when she heard the door open.

Muriella looked up to see Duncan seat himself on a stool nearby, his Highland harp in his hands. Before she could speak, he began to play, and though she leaned closer, he shook his head. "I've only come to see that you're safe."

As he spoke, he ran his hands over the strings of the harp in a soothing rhythm. He sat on the stool in his long saffron shirt, his fair head bent forward so his hair fell into his eyes, but he did not push it away. In the sunlight, the pale strands glimmered, but she saw from Duncan's pallid skin that he had had a restless night. Because of her. She started to speak again, but again he shook his head.

"Some things are too difficult to say and even more difficult to hear," he told her softly.

"But I must tell ye—"

Without raising his head, he stopped her with a wave of his hand. "'Tis enough to say that last night I did what I thought was right. 'Twas my duty to ye and to my cousin." He looked up then, his brown eyes steady. "I'm grateful to see ye here, but please don't talk, because I don't think I wish to know if ye feel differently."

The tears threatened to betray her again. Muriella blinked them back. "Did ye think I would blame ye for saving my life?"

The squire shrugged. "I didn't know. How could I? But it doesn't matter now, so long as ye're safe."

"It matters," Muriella said, but he only smiled and bent to concentrate on his music once more.

The notes rose clear, sweet and pure, weaving wordless stories in the sunlight. In spite of herself, Muriella fell under the spell of the music. As the song washed over her, she became aware of the magic Duncan's fingers created—a filmy tissue of interwoven notes that hung suspended in the air, softening reality like an undulating gauze curtain. Muriella smiled her gratitude, and when the squire looked up to meet her eyes, he seemed to understand.

A loud knock on the door shattered the moment, and the fine, clinging notes of the song faded, so that everything came once more into sharp focus.

"Aye?" Muriella called.

Mary opened the door and stood with her hand on the latch. "M'lady, there's someone to see ye."

"Who?"

"I wouldn't be knowin'. He wouldn't say. But he swore he must see ye."

With a curious glance at Megan, who shook her head, Muriella said, "Bring him, then."

"Aye, m'lady." Mary curtsied before leaving the room. She had not been gone long when the door opened again and Alex the Gypsy stepped over the threshold.

"M'lady," he said, bowing.

Muriella gaped at him. She tried to speak, but found that she could not.

Alex glanced quickly around the room. "Could I speak to ye alone for a time?" he asked.

Megan rose, a half-finished shirt in her hand. "Ye don't think—," she began.

The Gypsy interrupted her. "Ye want to help her, don't ye?"

"Aye, but—"

"Well, I can do it. Ye can't. But ye must leave us alone."

At last, Muriella recovered her voice. "Please, do as he says."

Megan wanted to protest, but the sight of Muriella's face stopped the words in her throat. There was a new light burning in her mistress's eyes, and she could see that this man's arrival had distracted Muriella from her depression for the time being. "If 'tis what ye wish." But she was clearly reluctant to go.

Alex put his hand on Megan's shoulder. "Your mistress will be safe with me."

Suddenly she remembered where she had heard that melodic voice before. She looked into Alex's eyes for the first time in four years and, instinctively, she trusted him. It was strange that it should be so, she thought, but she did not stop to wonder why as she left the room.

When, at Muriella's nod, the squire rose to follow, she said softly, "Thank ye, Duncan, for everything."

With an uneasy smile, he nodded and stepped into the hall, closing the door behind him.

While she tried to collect her wits, Muriella considered the Gypsy in silence. Alex had not changed much in the past four years. His weathered face was the same, aged beyond his years by day after day of sun and toil and the weight of his special knowledge. His clareschaw was slung over his shoulder as always. Just as she remembered, his silver hair and beard curled over the shoulders of his green-and-gold Gypsy shirt.

"You've been gone a long time," she said at last.

"Too long, it seems."

She grasped the carved arms of her chair. "I don't understand."

"I think ye do," Alex said quietly.

She had forgotten the power of his eyes that changed from green to gray and back again in the path of the shifting sunlight. She wanted to look away but could not do it. "Why have ye come back?" Muriella asked.

Alex seated himself unhurriedly on the stool Duncan had abandoned. "Because ye need me," he said, brushing a strand of hair back from his seamed face.

She did not bother to tell him it was not so; she knew he would see the truth in her eyes. "How did ye know?"

He smiled. "Ye asked me that once before, I think. My answer is the same now—I dreamed of ye last night."

"But—"

"Our camp isn't far from here," he interrupted. "As I also told ye, people talk to the Gypsies. I know that your husband has left Inveraray. I know too that ye tried to take your life. So, I came."

Muriella took a deep breath but it did not still the sudden trembling in her hands. "Why should ye care about that? I'm not your concern."

"Somehow you've become my concern, though why that should be so I can't say. Mayhap 'tis because of the burden we share." He leaned closer, reaching out to brush her furrowed brow with his fingertips. "Because of this"—his fingers traced the hollows of her cheeks—"and this"—the rigid line of her mouth—"and this"—and came to rest on her eyelids as they had done four long years ago.

Muriella sat for a moment, eyes closed, aware of the featherlight touch of the Gypsy's fingertips on her lids. She remembered so clearly that distant afternoon when she had known for the first time that another understood her pain, because Alex had felt it too. Then he drew away. She opened her eyes to find him regarding her intently.

"'Tis because of that," he said, "that ye'll tell me what happened yesterday to make ye seek the comfort of the river."

His searching gaze held her immobile, though she fought to free herself from its power. Against her will, she murmured, "It started, I think, when my husband received a packet of letters from Cawdor. I knew something was amiss, but he didn't tell me what it was. He didn't come to me at all." That was not what she had wanted to say, but the words seemed to spill out, welling up from a secret place within her that the Gypsy had uncovered with a single, telling glance. She laced her fingers together in her lap. "But the real beginning was the dream."

"Aye," Alex mused. "So I should have guessed." His hands resting on his knees, he leaned forward—waiting.

"I'd had it before, but 'twas no' the same. My cousin Hugh and I were young again at Kilravok, and happy, before I'd ever heard the name of Campbell. Always in the end, we fell together, laughing, but this time when I turned to Hugh, I saw only his blackened death mask. 'Twas a warning, ye see." She swallowed, wishing the Gypsy would look away for even an instant, but his steady gaze did not waver. "My husband killed Hugh yesterday."

Considering her in silence, Alex finally shook his head. "'Twas only for that? Ye hadn't even seen the man since ye left Cawdor."

"No, but I'd lost something precious just the same. In

all the years since I've come to Inveraray, 'twas my only dream untouched by fear. And now that dream too has become a nightmare. I couldn't bear to lose Hugh that way."

The Gypsy moved closer as, unblinking, he said softly, "The Hugh in your dream was a child. People change."

"I can't believe he could change so much. I don't want to believe it."

Thoughtfully, Alex ran his fingers through his heavy beard, catching them in the tangled strands. "Is that why ye tried to end your life—because Sir John had taken your childhood friend from ye?"

"No," she whispered.

"Then why?"

"Hugh's death—somehow it made me realize—" She stopped, but his gaze burned into her, exacting the truth regardless of her will. "I realized how much I—care for my husband."

Alex leaned back, sighing deeply, and his eyes lost some of their luminous intensity. "I see."

Released from his spell at last, Muriella looked away. "This time I don't think ye do."

The Gypsy frowned. "Do ye know *why* Sir John killed Hugh?" His hair had fallen into his face again and he pushed it back impatiently.

She shook her head. "It doesn't matter now."

"But it does. Mayhap the reason ye fear your husband is because ye don't understand him well enough."

Muriella stiffened. "I didn't say I fear him."

"Didn't ye?" Alex murmured. "I thought ye did." The Gypsy reached out to raise her chin with one callused finger. "My child, ye can't understand your husband 'til ye know the truth—unclouded by doubt or fear or the memory of a once-pleasant dream. Ye said there were some letters from Cawdor. Mayhap if ye read them 'twould help ye see things more clearly."

"Mayhap," Muriella replied warily. "But I don't know where they are. And I don't think—"

"Aye?" the Gypsy murmured. "What don't ye think?"

Once again she tried desperately to look away, but the light in his eyes had captured her and would not set her free. "I don't think I want to know."

Smiling grimly, Alex drew away from her. "And that, above all, is why ye *must* know."

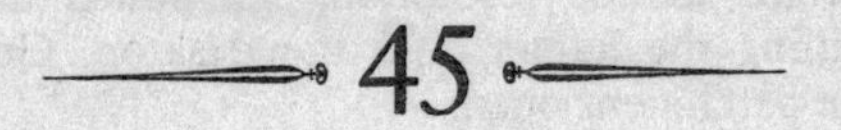

# 45

A short time later, the Gypsy entered the library again. "Here they be."

Muriella surveyed the packet he had thrown onto the desk, but did not reach out to take it. "How did ye get them?"

"Duncan helped me find 'em among Sir John's papers."

"Why would he do such a thing?" she asked, half to herself. "Surely he knows John would be angry."

Alex shrugged. "He didn't like it, but I told him how important 'twas for ye to see 'em."

"Do ye think he understood?"

The Gypsy shook his head. "No, but he tried. You're lucky to have such a friend."

Muriella thought of all the gifts of song the squire had given her—and one gift more. "I know."

"Would ye have me stay while ye read?"

She noticed that the strained energy which had characterized Alex earlier had gone. Now he did not seem at all intimidating, only very, very tired. "No," she said. "'Tis best if I'm alone, I think."

"As ye wish. But I'll be nearby."

"Thank ye."

"Ye may no' wish to thank me when ye've seen 'em." Before she could respond, he slipped out, closing the door without a sound.

For several minutes, Muriella sat staring at the square of

faded yellow against the dark leather cover of a manuscript. She waved her hand over the folded parchment as if to make it disappear into the shimmering sunlight. *What, in God's name, are ye so afraid of?* John had asked her once. What indeed? With sudden resolution, she pulled the ribbon loose, spilling the letters onto the desktop. Gently, she spread the parchment open.

"John Campbell, Lord of Lorne, Thane of Cawdor," it read.

My lord,

Your enquiries surprised me, for I thought that matter had been settled in your father's time. 'Tis true enough that Hugh Rose has been spreading the rumors far and wide, and mayhap the people fear him enough to believe him. Or mayhap when he stands above them with his sword poised and ready to strike, they tell him only what he wants to hear. But even that won't give him the power to bring the case to light again. There can be no question of illegal proceedings, for all concerned signed fully attested legal documents. Ye need not bother further with Rose's slanders against your wife's name, for your right to Cawdor is unquestioned.

But I warn ye, when The Devil Afire sees that his rumors aren't succeeding, he'll resort to the sword soon enough. Still, if as ye say, ye intend to come here soon, I believe your presence will do a great deal toward keeping the outlaw in line.

Your obedient servant,
Robert, Precentor of Ross

Muriella's vision blurred, though whether with tears or confusion, she was not certain. Laying the letter aside, she chose another.

My lord,

There's been much unrest between the Calders and Roses of late. The old feud is stronger now than it has been in many years; the young Hugh Rose has seen to that. He's been heard to say more than once that ye cheated him out of his rightful fortune by stealing his bride. I won't repeat the foul things he's been saying about your wife (though there are others less delicate than I). But I'll tell ye this: I don't think she will be safe at Cawdor so long as Hugh Rose lives. Nor will ye.

The outlaw will never forget the humiliation ye gave him last October. By showing him mercy, ye only fed his rage. His right arm is useless since the blow from your blade, but he makes no secret of the fact that he's been working with his left. From what I hear, his hatred of ye gives him more strength than a normal man. He is feared as much now as he was before. He says when he's ready, he'll come for ye and your wife. I warn ye, he isn't to be trifled with. 'Tis a dangerous situation here 'til he's been dealt with. If you're coming indeed, I pray 'twill be soon, for I mislike the smell in the air.

Ever your servant,
Archie Campbell
Cawdor Castle

Muriella gripped the parchment in cold fingers. She could no longer deny how much the Hugh she had known had changed. It seemed that this time John's rage had been justified, and it had been as much for her sake as for his—perhaps even more. *Have a little faith,* Alex had told her once. She should have listened. Dropping the crumpled page, she reached for the last letter.

Dear Cousin,

I've spoken to a great many people in the past few weeks, just as ye bid me. It's taken time, for, as ye instructed, I've taken care that no one will repeat my questions after ye and your wife arrive at Cawdor. I believe that, other than the threat from Hugh Rose, 'tis safe to bring her. The servants at the castle don't appear to listen to Rose's rumors. The few who wonder if the rumors are true tell me they don't care, for they hate the Calders with a passion and the Roses as much. The two families have caused a lot of bloodshed with their constant feuding, and those who are neither Calder nor Rose wish your wife the victory.

As for the other matter, I had to ask a great many more questions with a great deal more care, for I knew the Roses held the secret if any did. I'm afraid ye'll be disappointed at my news, for there is nothing definite, as Isabel Calder has been dead this past month. I believe she was the only one who knew for certain. But one of her sisters, Glenna, seemed particularly troubled by my interest, so I pressed her. After many hours, she finally told me she was aware, all those years ago, that her sister loved a man besides her husband. She did *not* know whether Isabel had "known" the man, nor did she know his identity. Apparently, Isabel Calder was very discreet. But Glenna did say that, on her deathbed, her sister said something which made her believe the man must have been a Gypsy. As the Gypsies come and go so irregularly, I don't believe 'twould be possible to trace one nameless man. I advise ye to let it rest. For even if, after years of searching, we were to find him, 'twould not answer the one question that Isabel alone could have answered.

Your loyal cousin,
David Campbell

The air in the library was warm, but Muriella's hands were icy cold. How could it be that no one had told her about Isabel's death? She conjured up the image of her mother bent over the loom, fingers flying, singing the songs she created as she worked. Muriella remembered how Isabel had so often kept boredom at bay with her talk of magic and the Kelpies and the wonder to be found in the patterns of colored thread. But now her mother was gone and Muriella had never really had a chance to know her. She closed her eyes against the grief and regret that welled within her.

But there was something more. ". . . the man must have been a Gypsy." Dear God! *People in trouble sometimes seek out the Gypsies, so your mother came to me.* Dear God in heaven. *Somehow you've become my concern. Mayhap 'tis because of the burden we share.* Her fingers curled inward until the nails dug into the skin of her palms. *Ye see, lass,* he had whispered once in his melodic voice, *that ye aren't alone.*

As the sound of that voice faded into silence, Muriella found she could not move. Outside the door, Alex was waiting.

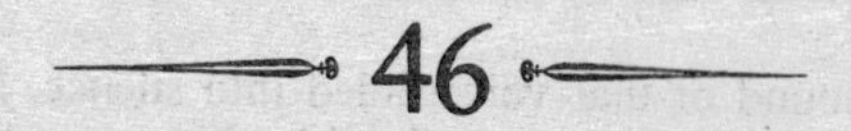

# 46

Elizabeth sat with her new husband in the library at Auchinbreck. She was reading a book of poems by Robert Henryson while Archibald looked at a treatise on strategy. The silence they shared was a comfortable one; now and then Elizabeth looked up to smile at the man beside her. Somehow she was always surprised by the sight of her husband's face—so pleasant, so ordinary, so warmly familiar.

Archibald felt her gaze and glanced up, answering her smile. When a servant appeared in the doorway, he turned sharply; he had left orders that they were not to be disturbed. "What is it?"

"Sir John Campbell's come from Inveraray to see ye, m'lady."

Closing the book in her lap, Elizabeth glanced at her husband before asking, "Is aught amiss?"

"I don't know. But from the look on his face, I'll wager the whole Clan Campbell is on the brink of ruin."

Elizabeth tensed, and when her husband took her hand, she gripped it tightly. "Bring him here," she said.

The servant hurried away as Elizabeth turned to Archibald. Before she could speak, he said, "I'll leave ye to talk to him alone. If there's any danger, I'll learn of it soon enough."

She smiled in gratitude. "Ye don't mind?"

Brushing a light kiss over her cheek, he rose. "No' at all. I'll be waiting in the hall if ye should need me."

She smiled as he left her, but when her brother entered the room, the smile disappeared.

John stood on the threshold with his hair in wild disarray. Although his cheeks were flushed—from heavy riding, she guessed—beneath the color he was ghostly pale. For the first time in all the years she had known him, she noticed that there were lines etched in his skin from his nose to his mouth, and deep furrows across his forehead. His eyes were a turbulent blue gray.

"Johnnie," she said, "tell me!"

When he did not respond, she left her chair to move forward. Taking his arm, she drew him to her husband's chair. Then, while he sat staring at his hands, she poured him a goblet of wine. He drank it down without pause, clearly unaware that he had done so. Elizabeth turned her chair to face his and waited, her fingers laced together in her lap.

"Muriella—," he began, then stopped. He seemed unable to form the thought.

His sister felt a chill of foreboding run down her spine. "What is it?" When he still did not answer, her heart began to beat erratically. "Tell me what's happened, Johnnie, please!"

"Muriella tried—to take her life."

Elizabeth gaped at him in disbelief, but her brother would not meet her eyes. Finally she whispered, "Is she all right?"

John gazed down at his hands helplessly. "She still lives, if that's what ye mean."

"But she's been hurt?"

Her brother ran his hand through his hair in agitation. "I begin to think the inner wounds are greater than the outer."

Elizabeth felt a sinking in her stomach. "Don't speak in riddles, Johnnie, not about this. Is your wife hurt?"

"She has a cut on the forehead, mayhap a chill, but no more."

"Thank God." Weak with relief, his sister sank back into

her chair. She watched in concern as John rose and began to pace up and down the room, glaring at the rushes beneath his feet as if they were enemies to be conquered. For a long time she did not have the courage to break the silence, but then, at last, she murmured, "How?"

John stopped with his back to her. "She threw herself in the river."

"No!" The color drained from Elizabeth's face. She had thought the horror was behind her, but John's toneless statement had brought it rushing back. Struggling for breath, she fought the memory of those crawling, endless hours chained to the rock while the water rose in fury all around her. "Muriella couldn't have done such a thing!" she gasped.

"So I thought too. But it seems we didn't know her as well as we thought."

Elizabeth clutched the arms of her chair until her hands ached. She was afraid if she let go, she would fall. She saw John move toward the wide embrasure. Placing one booted foot on a low chest, he gazed blindly out at the courtyard below. She realized he was not aware of her distress.

Unable to find her voice, she rose and went to the shelf where Archibald had left a flagon of wine. Holding a pewter goblet in her shaking hand, she filled it with the dark liquid and drank it down. As the wine began to affect her, the mists of memory receded and the shock dimmed a little. Her heartbeat slowed to normal while the silence stretched between brother and sister—thin as a single thread, and as fragile. Elizabeth closed her eyes, wondering why John had come to her at all. When at last she turned toward him, her face was still and expressionless.

"So," she said calmly, "what have ye done with her?"

John turned in surprise, as if he'd forgotten his sister was in the room. "Done with her? I left her at Inveraray."

"Just that? Nothing more?"

Her brother gazed at her, perplexed. "What would ye have me do?"

"'Tis a terrible sin to try to take your life," she said, moving toward him, her gown rustling about her ankles.

"The Church will surely excommunicate her if they hear of this. Will ye tell them?"

"No!"

Elizabeth was unmoved by the single explosive word. "But after what she's done, no one would blame ye."

"I wouldn't be caring if they did. I won't do it, that's all."

"Why?"

Eyes narrowed, John regarded his sister intently. "Elizabeth—"

"Then will ye lock her in a tower?"

"No, by God!" He moved toward her menacingly, but she did not retreat.

Raising her chin, she said coolly, "Our father would have done so, after he beat her bloody, no doubt."

John clenched his fists and fought the urge to strike her. "Damn our father! She's *my* wife!"

"But surely ye'll punish her."

"Elizabeth, I warn ye—"

He was so close that she could reach out to touch his face, a face distorted by anger, but still she did not quaver. "Ye don't seem to realize, 'tis a *sin,* Johnnie!"

"I don't care."

"But—"

"She's my wife, damn ye, and I love her!"

Brows drawn together, Elizabeth repeated stubbornly, "But if she tried to take her life—"

She broke off abruptly when John grasped her by the shoulders. "Stop this madness, Elizabeth, before ye push me too far. I love Muriella, do ye hear? Whatever she's done!"

His sister's eyes glittered, but she spoke without inflection. "I see."

He noticed then the odd expression on her face. She was smiling knowingly and seemed to be waiting. But for what? Then, all at once, he heard a distant echo—the sound of his sister's voice weeping, *I love him! He wouldn't—I love him!*

He released her and his hands fell to his sides. "Dear God," he murmured. "Elizabeth, forgive me. I thought—"

"Ye thought I was a fool and weak besides. But now ye see, don't ye? I was just as ye are."

Running his hand across his forehead, he sank back into the chair. "Aye, just as I am," he muttered in despair.

His sister smiled a little. "'Tis a curse on our family, don't ye think? This compulsion to love someone to the point of madness? Muriella once said she admired that in me, but I didn't believe her."

"Muriella," John repeated. The sound of the name brought his anguish rushing back. He stared at the floor in silence.

Elizabeth watched her brother slump forward, defeat in every line of his body. She was surprised to find that she pitied him. Never had she seen her brother so helpless before. Kneeling beside him with her hand on his arm, she said, "I think this has affected ye more deeply than ye realize. Mayhap ye don't want to admit it, but you're horrified by what she's done."

"Doesn't she even fear the wrath of God?" John demanded.

Unable to bear the sight of his confusion, Elizabeth looked away. "How can she, when she's already lived in hell?"

John closed his eyes but could not disguise the pain that transformed his face. "Hasn't she ever been happy, even for a moment?"

Elizabeth gripped his arm. "I didn't mean that, Johnnie. Of course she's been happy."

He met her compassionate gaze fiercely. "When?" he demanded. "Name me one day when she wasn't haunted by her demons."

"There were many, as ye'd know if ye asked her. But I don't think I've ever seen her as happy as she was the morning after my wedding and the battle that followed. She was so full of joy that day that her face shone with it and her body could barely contain it all."

"Oh, God!"

Elizabeth drew away. "I'm sorry. That only makes it more difficult for ye, doesn't it?"

He could not answer. His despair was choking him.

Elizabeth rose to pace before the empty fireplace, conjuring Muriella's face before her, trying to understand the hopeless tangle of her friend's feelings. "Did she tell ye why she did it?"

It was a long time before John answered. "She said she'd had a vision, that she was afraid I would—" He could not bring himself to say the words. "That I would harm her someday."

Elizabeth paused as a strange stillness descended upon her. "Can ye really blame her for thinking that?"

John looked up sharply at the bitterness in his sister's voice. She was staring at him, her gray eyes wide with unsettling memories. Those eyes carried him back to that moment when the madness had overtaken him as he stood above Elizabeth while she lay ill, calling for her husband. "Ye knew," he whispered hoarsely.

"Ye thought I was delirious, but I knew."

Her steady, unblinking gaze was more than he could stand. Rising abruptly, he moved toward the window. "I don't know what to say to ye. I don't know how to explain—"

"No, Johnnie," his sister interrupted. "Ye don't need to explain. 'Tis past now."

John shook his head. "I don't think 'twill ever be past."

Elizabeth crossed the room until she faced her brother. "I've tried to leave those days behind—I had to. Mayhap ye should do it too. 'Tis Muriella who matters now. What are ye going to do about her?"

Her brother looked away, rubbing his fingers over his brow as if to ease the pain within. "I don't know."

Elizabeth's heart contracted in compassion. "Do ye think ye can live without her?" she asked softly.

John turned, his face haggard with care in the soft evening light. "'Tis hard to know."

"I'll tell ye something that ye may not believe, but 'tis true just the same. I doubt that Muriella can live without ye."

John's eyes widened. How *could* he believe it? "Ye don't seem to understand. She fears me too much. She thinks I'll hurt her."

"Then go back to Inveraray and show her she's wrong."

John gaped at his sister in astonishment.

With a sigh, Elizabeth put her hands on his shoulders. "Listen to me, Johnnie. I know you've killed many men in battle, mayhap more than I can count. 'Tis the way ye survive. But murder—I don't think you're capable of that."

John struggled to find his voice. "*Ye* can say that?"

Her gaze did not waver. "Aye."

"But ye saw me—"

"I saw what ye *wanted* to do. 'Tis no' the same as what ye would have done. Stubborn ye may be, passionate in your rages and desires, mayhap even cruel sometimes, but ye simply aren't the kind of man to hurt someone ye love."

"Ye really believe that?"

"I do."

John felt a constriction in his throat. For the first time in his life, he wanted to weep. "Why? After all I've done?"

"Because on the day when Lachlan Maclean last came to Inveraray, ye let him live." Her brother started to interrupt, but she stopped him with a wave of her hand. "Ye had far more reason to want *his* life than ye did mine. He'd long been an enemy to me, to ye, to our father and the clan and the King. All he'd ever given the Campbells was years of trouble and betrayal. Yet when I asked ye to, ye set him free."

"But I killed him in the end."

When he would have turned away, Elizabeth held him with the touch of her hands on his shoulders. "I spoke to Megan the day after ye left Inveraray. I know why ye did it. I know too that Lachlan had to die. He'd pushed us all too far too often. I knew that even in the beginning. 'Twas just that I couldn't bear to watch it happen."

John stared at his sister as if he had never seen her before. *Ye take her for a fool,* Maclean had said, *but she's a great deal wiser than ye.* Strange that, in the end, the husband who had mistreated and despised her should have known Elizabeth so well. And yet, John himself must have trusted his sister more than he realized or he would not have come to her now. "You're Muriella's friend; ye understand her best. Do ye really think I should go back to her?"

"'Twill break her heart if ye don't." Elizabeth gazed thoughtfully into her brother's eyes. "But I wonder. . . . 'Twill no' be easy to win your wife if ye can't forgive her for all the pain she's caused ye."

"That doesn't matter now."

"Doesn't it?" Elizabeth asked softly. "Are ye certain of that?"

When John moved away from her, she did not follow. He turned once more to stare out the window at the languid movements of the men in the courtyard below. Though he tried to close his mind against it, the memory of Duncan's words rang in his head: *I don't know why she threw herself in, but I do know that she let me save her.* It was that knowledge which had gnawed at John's insides since the moment he left Inveraray. He knew with a certainty that appalled him that if it had been he waiting on the riverbank to pull Muriella from the water, she would have drowned rather than reach for his hand. She had made a choice, in that moment, to give Duncan something she could never give her husband—her trust. And for that John could *not* forgive her.

# 47

Muriella leaned on the library windowsill, staring out at the sea below. The clouds had crept around the sun again, and the light had the strange silver cast that always came before a storm. She did not turn when she heard the door open; she knew without looking that Alex had come into the room.

"I'd begun to worry," the Gypsy said. "Ye didn't make a sound for so long."

"I was thinking." She concentrated more intently on the forming patterns of rain clouds in the graying sky.

"Did ye learn what ye needed to know?"

He was coming closer—she could hear his soft footsteps on the thick rug—but still she did not leave the window. "Aye. I learned much more than that," she murmured.

The Gypsy paused a few feet away from her. "Why won't ye look at me, lass?"

Releasing her painful grip on the stone, she turned to find him watching. His weathered face was lined and careworn, his gray green eyes full of concern. Those eyes. With an effort of will, she met his gaze.

"What is it?" Alex asked. "What's troublin' ye?"

His gaze was not holding her now; she could have looked away if she wanted to, but she did not do it. She wondered if she could draw the truth from him as he had drawn it from her a few minutes before.

When she did not speak, he took another step forward. "Tell me."

*My child,* he had once called her. Her heart was beating too slowly; the blood was hardly moving through her veins. His eyes, she thought. His strange, compelling eyes. "Are ye my father?" she said at last.

Alex gasped as if she had struck him in the chest. The color drained from his face and faded from his eyes, leaving them pale and lifeless. For a long time she thought he would not answer.

Finally, he said stiffly, "No. I met your mother when she'd just begun to carry ye." He forced himself to meet her doubtful gaze. "Ye must try to understand what was between us and no' think badly of her. Isabel needed a friend, and I was there for her. What we shared was rare in this cold, heartless world."

Muriella was surprised to realize she was not disappointed in her mother. Perhaps it was because she had never known Isabel's husband, had never seen John Calder's face, except once in a painting. Her father had given her Cawdor, but that had never been cause for gratitude. But Alex had shared so much with her. He had given her understanding, compassion, consolation. He was the only one who had told her truths she did not wish to hear. And he had given her music. She understood too well what his friendship must have meant to the lonely Isabel, because Muriella herself had so often felt alone and bereft since her arrival at Inveraray. "Please tell me about it," she asked softly as she drew him toward the chairs in front of the empty fireplace.

The Gypsy sat down and spread his hands before him, examining the palms in the shifting gray light. "I don't remember the day or even the year we met," he said wistfully. "To me 'twas as if I'd always known Isabel Calder. Ye could say 'twas she who brought me the Sight when I was a boy."

Muriella frowned, seeking a distant memory. *I was standin' above a river,* Alex had told her the first time they met, *starin' into a pool of clear water, and I saw the face of a woman I didn't know. When I leaned down to fetch her out, 'twas no one there.* "Hers was the face in the water, then?"

Alex nodded. "She followed me in dreams, ye see, even before I met her in the flesh. And then—" He hesitated. "I couldn't have changed what happened between us, even had I wanted to. She was an extraordinary woman, your mother." He gazed beyond Muriella to the bright, remembered image of the woman he had lost. "Every year when the Gypsies moved south, I had to leave her behind," he continued, unable now to stop the flow of painful memories. "And every time the partin' was more difficult to bear. But I couldn't stay away. I didn't have that kind of strength."

"Is that why ye came to me? Because of what ye felt for her?"

"No' entirely," the Gypsy replied. "Ye see, we were much together in those days while ye rested in her womb. We used to talk like ye *were* my bairn. 'Twas her wish that 'twas so, and mine as well. With your father dead and unable to defend ye, I swore to Isabel that I'd protect ye as if ye were my own. 'Tis what I have tried to do."

Muriella nodded and touched his hand in answer to the question he had not asked. "Did ye see her again after my wedding?"

Pushing the hair back from his face, Alex gathered his thoughts carefully. "Aye. I was with her soon before she died. We'd been travelin' far from home, south through England. By the time we came north again, she was very ill." He did not try to hide the grief that ravaged his face. "I was a fool, ye ken. I waited too long. I thought since ye were finally married and grown up safe among the Campbells, that she might have come away with me then."

"Had ye asked her before?"

"Och, no! 'Twould have been cruel to offer her a choice she couldn't make no matter how much she might want to."

Leaning forward, Muriella murmured, "Because of me?"

Even through the weight of his sorrow, Alex smiled. "Aye. Ye were the one true joy in her life. She was determined that nothin' should ever hurt ye, so long as she had the power to stop it."

"But she never sent a single letter—" Muriella stopped before more words escaped, betraying the depth of her bewildered pain.

But Alex did not need to hear the words. "We talked long and often before she drifted at last into the mist. She told me a great many things. She said she'd never told ye the truth about your father or your guardian because, for a long time, she thought ye were too young to understand. Then one day she saw that ye were all grown up, and 'twas too late. She didn't want to lose your trust when she knew that someday soon she'd lose ye altogether.

"She knew when her father said ye were to marry Hugh that she should have sent word to Argyll sooner. She felt the danger always around ye, though she tried to hide it so ye would not feel her fear. No' for a moment were ye really safe with the Roses, but the Earl had left ye with her, and she couldn't bear to give up the gift he'd given her."

"But surely after my marriage she could have sent word."

Alex winced at the raw longing in Muriella's voice. "I think her guilt kept her silent more than anything else. She told me she had been selfish and careless for so long, that when at last she let ye go, she had to let ye go completely, though it broke her heart. She wanted ye to have no ties to the Campbells' enemies, no ties to a past that was gone forever. She made the hardest choice in her life that day—to set ye free, absolutely and forever. But ye must no' think that for a single moment she forgot ye."

Muriella struggled to understand. "But I wrote to her. I sent letters—" She broke off, feeling foolish in the face of her mother's sacrifice.

"She never saw them," Alex asserted. "She told me she'd always hoped ye'd forgive her and send word. But when ye were silent, she accepted that too."

"I don't understand."

"Perhaps her father, Hugh Rose, made certain she never got your letters. 'Twas the kind of petty cruelty that would have given him pleasure."

Muriella looked away as an ache of sadness filled her chest. Why had she never known how much her mother cared for her? It had always been Lorna who laughed with Muriella, taught her, listened to her troubles. She closed her eyes at the hot pain that still flared at the thought of her childhood companion. Was that why Isabel had never been more than a figure weaving shadows in the background? Muriella had memories—few and precious and strangely vivid—of the hours spent in the solar learning the magic of the loom, but suddenly that was not enough. Not when Isabel had given up so much to insure the happiness of her troubled daughter. Not when she had given up Alex.

The Gypsy rose, massaging his eyelids with his fingertips. "Forgive me, lass, but I can't talk more of her now. Even to say her name—" He broke off, turning so she could no longer see his face.

"You've already given me more of her than I had before," she told him. "I thank ye for that."

When Alex turned back to her, his face showed no sign of his inner turmoil, but his eyes were shadowed with grief. Those gray green eyes met and held hers for a long moment and she drew her breath in sharply. It was as if she were looking into a mirror at the luminous reflection of her own suffering. For the third time in a single day, tears burned behind her lids.

"I lost your mother," the Gypsy said, "but it doesn't have to happen that way for ye." He motioned toward the letters still scattered over the desktop. "Can ye understand now why Sir John did what he did?"

Muriella nodded, abandoning with reluctance the subject of her mother. "Ye were right," she admitted. "Hugh had changed. He was evil, just as my husband claimed."

Brow furrowed, Alex paced across the blue Persian rug. "Then mayhap," he said, speaking slowly, to be certain she understood each word, "the face in the dream wasn't your cousin's death mask at all. Mayhap 'twas your first true glimpse of the kind of man he had become."

Muriella bit her lip. Could that grotesque face have been the image of Hugh's blackened soul? Then she realized it must have been. Death masks were cold and still as stone, but in her dream, Hugh had been horribly alive. She shivered when she remembered his chilling, triumphant laughter.

Too restless to stay still, Muriella rose and returned to the window to stare out at the wind-whipped ocean far below her.

Perplexed by her reticence, Alex regarded her more closely. "None of that matters to ye, does it?"

Muriella shook her head. "Understanding what happened in the past can't change what's to come."

The Gypsy noticed the rigid line of her back, the way her hands gripped the stone sill until her fingers grew pale from the strain. All at once, he thought he understood. "You've 'seen' something, haven't ye?"

"Aye." The word fell hollowly from her lips toward the raging sea beneath her. "Over and over again. Even in my dreams I can't get free."

The Gypsy sank back into his chair, his hands locked together. "I should have guessed it." For a long time there was silence while he stared at the floor, gathering his thoughts. "Ye'd best tell me."

"I don't think I can."

"I know how hard 'tis to put your fear into words," Alex told her. "But 'tis a risk ye'll have to take if ye want me to help ye."

She knew it was true, but that did not make it any easier. Closing her eyes against the image of the silver-streaked sea, she curled her fingers inward, seeking a depth of courage she did not think to find. She could hear the thunderous crashing of the waves on the rugged cliff, smell the clinging scent of salt in the air, feel the moisture rising to meet her. Her heartbeat seemed to echo the churning fury of the distant water. Muriella fought to steady her breathing. When she turned to Alex, her face was unnaturally calm. She moved to take the chair across from his, then leaned forward, pale and rigid. "In the vision," she began hesitantly, "I'm surrounded by water."

"Go on."

"I'm drowning in the waves that are rising all around me—" She broke off, closed her eyes to renew her strength, then continued more slowly. "The water is dragging me farther and farther under until I can't breathe. I try to stay afloat, but 'tis stronger than me and I can't win. I know—" She shuddered, choking on her own voice. "I know that someday 'twill take me down so far I won't ever rise again."

Fingers caught in the strands of his beard, Alex asked, "When does it come to ye?"

Muriella concentrated on the interwoven pattern of her fingers against the dove gray skirt of her gown. "When my husband touches me . . . or . . ." She bit her lip and tried to remember exactly. "Or when he moves me somehow." She looked up, her face ashen. "I feel myself drowning and it terrifies me."

"So."

When the Gypsy said no more, Muriella whispered, "Ye must think me mad for throwing myself in the river."

"No, lass. I think 'twas the only way ye could find to put an end to the waitin'."

She froze, her fingers locked in a painful grip. He had always known so much about her. Perhaps too much. Muriella rose and began to pace the floor in agitation. Suddenly she whirled, hands extended toward the Gypsy in a silent plea. "Can't ye change a vision once you've seen it?" she demanded in desperation. "There must be a way!"

"I don't know for sure," the Gypsy murmured, his voice hoarse with compassion. "But I do know this. If there *is* a way, 'tis to meet it head-on."

"I don't understand."

Choosing his words with care, he said, "Ye follow the vision through to its natural end."

"No!"

"Listen to me!" In one swift movement he had left his chair and grasped her shoulders in his hands. Only when her eyes had locked with his did he continue. "Ye won't ever change the future by fightin' it this way. To conquer your fear ye must face it once and for all."

From somewhere out of the stillness that fell between them came the echo of her own troubled voice. *I don't think I can face Cawdor again. The memories are too strong.*

"Ye never went back to Cawdor, did ye?" Alex said.

Muriella's eyes widened at the ease with which he had read her thoughts. She suppressed the urge to shiver and back away. "No," she said shakily.

"Mayhap ye need to do just that."

"I don't think—," Muriella began.

Alex increased his grip on her shoulders until she winced. "'Tis long past time ye *did* think. And not just about Cawdor. Before Sir John comes back—"

"He may not return at all."

"He will," the Gypsy assured her. "He can't help himself. But before he does, ye should consider something with a great deal of care. Remember that your visions aren't always what they seem. The dream of Hugh wasn't; mayhap 'tis true of this one as well." With one gnarled finger he raised her chin, capturing her once more in his compelling gaze. "Think of this, Muriella. Think long and hard. Mayhap 'tis no' your husband ye fear at all. Mayhap 'tis yourself."

# 48

John stayed at Auchinbreck for one week. On the seventh day he sought out Elizabeth to bid her good-bye.

"Do ye know what ye'll do now?" she asked him.

Her brother shook his head. "I can't say for certain."

"You've missed her, Johnnie. I've seen it on your face."

He looked away. "Aye, that I have. Sometimes I think just to see her again would be enough for me. But then I begin to wonder—"

"Don't think so much," Elizabeth warned him. "You've always been guided by your feelings before. Ye should know by now that they won't lead ye astray." She tucked a strand of pale hair behind her ear and smiled up at him. "Just remember Muriella needs ye even more than ye need her. Give her a chance to tell ye so."

"She may not want to see me at all."

"Ah, Johnnie," Elizabeth murmured, brushing his cheek with her fingertips, "ye haven't heard a word I said."

John took her hand and smiled down at her. "I heard ye, and I thank ye—for everything." He tilted his head, contemplating his sister's face in a new light, coming to know it all over again. "We've been strangers for far too long," he said at last. "But things will be different now."

Elizabeth nodded. "I don't think I realized until ye arrived a week ago how much I've missed ye since I first went to Duart. I don't think I wanted to admit, even to myself, how lonely I was there."

"But now that Duart's behind ye, are ye any happier?"

"Happy?" his sister repeated thoughtfully. "My life is comfortable now, even pleasant. But happy? I don't think I know what that is. And yet—" She smiled at the memory of the spring roses she had found strewn across her bed that morning. "Mayhap I'm learning about it after all."

"'Tis time ye did," John said fervently.

"'Tis time we all did."

Drawn by the smile in her eyes, John took his sister in his arms. It had been so long since he'd seen her smile.

For a moment she was too surprised to respond, then she returned his embrace, resting her head, for a moment, on his shoulder. "Take care," Elizabeth whispered. "And Johnnie," she added as he turned away, "God go with ye."

"Andrew, ye shouldn't be out of bed!" Muriella cried when she saw him leaning weakly on the balustrade at the foot of the stairs in the Great Hall. The heavy bandage beneath his loose saffron shirt was unstained with red, but that did not mean it would remain so. "If ye don't have a care, your wound will re-open and then where would ye be?" In the two weeks since the battle with the Macleans, the gaping wound in Andrew's shoulder had begun gradually to heal, but she could see from his sallow face, covered with pale freckles, that he was still too weak to be about.

"So long as I'm no' locked away in that tiny room, I don't care," he told her. "Ye can't think how quickly a man can go daft with only his brother to keep him company." He paused to catch his breath; it was the longest speech he had made in many days. Then he smiled crookedly. "I wanted to see if there was still life in the rest of the keep. And I thought it couldn't hurt to come down for supper this once."

When his hand slipped on the balustrade and he began to sway, Muriella hurried to his side. "You're daft indeed to take the risk," she said, "but if ye must, at least let me help ye so ye don't fall into the rushes."

"Ye needn't bother about me," Andrew whispered, smiling weakly. "No Maclean is going to get the best of me! And where," he added as his knees threatened to buckle, "is my brother when ye need him?"

"Here, ye fool," Richard said, bracing Andrew against his strong shoulder. "I'll see to him, m'lady, or I'm sore afraid ye'd end up draggin' him across the room to lay him on a table, dead to the world."

"Much ye know about it," his brother snorted. "'Tis good for a man to move about when he begins to mend."

Muriella stepped out of the way, turning to the men at the nearest trestle table. "Ye'd best clear him a place here. I don't think he'll make it much farther."

Sim and Adam moved aside as Richard settled Andrew gingerly on the bench.

"Ye'll find the seat a little hard, no doubt, after your soft pallet," Sim called. With a smile, he pushed a half-full tankard of ale over the marred tabletop.

Andrew leaned forward to catch the tankard, grimacing at a twinge in his shoulder. "To tell ye the truth, since the Earl's gone back to Edinburgh, Richard's had nothin' to do but sit by my bed and play with the straws from the mattress. I told him to have mercy, but he *would* keep chewin' them one at a time 'til I was through to the floor." Looking around, he whispered behind his hand, "The bench is much more comfortable than the cold stone, I can tell ye that."

While the men laughed, Muriella motioned for Mary to bring more food. Grinning in spite of his pain, Andrew said, "Thank ye, m'lady, for rescuin' me from Richard's cruel hands. He pretends to help, but he only does it to torture me, ye ken."

She smiled, noticing that Richard too was grinning.

When Sim shifted on the bench, Adam wagged a finger at him warningly. "Don't be shovin' that way, man. Ye'll start Andrew's wound to bleedin' again, and *I* won't be the one to carry him upstairs."

In the midst of the general laughter that followed, Richard reached over to touch Muriella's arm gently.

"M'lady," he whispered, nodding toward the huge double doors to the Great Hall.

Muriella looked up and caught her breath.

John stood in the doorway watching in astonishment. He had never before seen the men laugh with his wife, never seen her move among them, apparently at ease. Thumbs hooked in his belt, he saw how she bent to assure Andrew's comfort, how quickly she ordered his food to be brought. He saw too that several strands of hair had fallen free from her braid to curl over her cheeks, which were flushed from the heat of the fire. Her gown had a smudge on one sleeve that told its own story. To him she had never been more beautiful.

But he had not yet come to a decision. The hours of hard riding through the mist, over rushing streams that flowed beside magnificent, rugged hills, had done nothing to clear his thoughts. Then his wife looked up.

With a cry of surprise she broke into a wide smile. Color darkened her cheeks, touching them with a warmth he could feel even from across the room. Her eyes sparkled, green and clear with welcome, relief, and something more. All at once, there was no longer a choice to be made.

John crossed the hall slowly, making his way with difficulty between the uneven rows of tables. He had been too long without his wife; now the few moments before he reached her side seemed endless. Yet not once did her smile waver; it seemed to reach out to him, drawing him inexorably forward toward the remembered warmth of her slender body. He could not have turned away from her in that moment even if he wanted to.

As he approached, he realized that the men had fallen silent, watching with curiosity his passage across the room. He had left without explanation, he remembered. No doubt they would wonder why. He would deal with that later.

When he reached the table where Richard and Andrew sat, before he could speak to Muriella, Duncan came to greet him. "'Tis glad to see ye I am, m'lord," the squire told him. "Since your brother left the men have been running wild."

"Don't tell me," Andrew groaned. "I missed all the fun!"

Though John wanted only to take his Muriella's hand, he turned to Andrew. "How are ye healing?"

Glancing from right to left as if someone might overhear him, Andrew said in a whisper loud enough to reach the vaulted ceiling, "Richard would have killed me by now if 'twere no' for your lady wife. She has magic hands with a wound, that lass."

John looked up at her in pleased surprise. Clearly she had spent the time while he was away mending her relationship with the men as well as mending Andrew's shoulder.

"Besides," Andrew continued, "'twas so still in that chamber I thought nightly that the Kelpies would come and take me away."

John did not hear him. He was looking at Muriella; she had taken a step toward him and her eyes never left his face. Her gaze devoured every familiar curve and plane.

"I've told ye more than once," Richard hissed to Andrew, "that ye don't know when to close your mouth. 'Tis time ye learned that lesson."

Disgruntled, Andrew looked up to see John close the distance between himself and his wife, then take her hand. The man's eyes widened in sudden comprehension. "As ye say," he murmured.

"M'lord, you're just in time for supper!" Mary cried, arriving just then with Andrew's bread and stew. "We didn't know ye were comin', but there's plenty of venison, and stew besides."

John nodded absently. All he could hear was the sound of Muriella's breathing; all he could see was her radiant face. "Shall we go up?" he murmured, taking her arm.

"Aye." They turned to start toward the dais but Muriella paused, frowning. "But Johnnie—"

"Later, my wife, there will be much to say. For now just let me have your company to enjoy." When he slipped his arm around her shoulders, Muriella leaned closer. He could feel the rhythm of her heart beating against his, and an ache of longing rose within him.

"I missed ye," she said so low that only he could hear.

"And I ye, lass. And I ye."

Only Duncan, Muriella, and her husband sat at the high table that night. While he ate, John touched his wife's arm often, to reassure himself that she was really beside him. Though she smiled whenever his eyes met hers, though the air between them crackled with the knowledge of their need, they did not speak of these things. Instead, John discussed with his squire what had happened at Inveraray since he had been away.

They had finished eating and were sitting with their goblets of wine in hand when Alex and two other Gypsies took their instruments and moved toward the fire. Every night since Alex's return, he and his friends had entertained the men after supper.

"Ye didn't say the Gypsies had come back," John said, turning to his wife in surprise. "'Tis glad to see them I am. No others understand music as they do." Smiling down at Muriella, he asked, "Will they be staying long?"

His wife shook her head in regret. "I don't think so." Just that morning, she remembered, as she knelt in the solar finishing the binding on the tapestry of the loch, she had felt Alex's gaze upon her and turned to see the sadness in his eyes. "Ye won't be here much longer, will ye?" she'd asked quietly.

Alex had shaken his head. "No. Soon enough we'll be on our way."

With an effort, Muriella kept her voice steady as she murmured, "When?"

"I can't say for certain," he told her, "but I promise ye this. Ye'll know when the time comes."

She stared down at her hands. "Once ye go, will I see ye again?"

The Gypsy smiled. "I don't think ye can help but do so."

Muriella reached out to touch his arm. "Alex—"

He stopped her with a single glance. "'Tis the way with us, isn't it, to hear things that haven't been said?"

Muriella looked into his eyes and saw there all that she wanted to say and all that she wanted to hear. "Aye."

"So be it. We've said enough." She'd thought there was a quaver in his voice but she could not be certain.

Now she watched him settle himself by the fire, strumming his harp softly. When John recognized the notes of a familiar song, he rose. At the question in his wife's eyes, he explained, "I miss the magic of the clareschaw and would find it again tonight."

His voice was low and husky with promise. Muriella smiled as he brushed his lips over her cheek. "Soon," he told her. Then he was gone.

As John made his way toward the fire, Muriella felt Alex's gaze upon her and looked up. There was a message in his gray green eyes, but she could not guess what it meant.

When a servant had brought John his harp, he sat by the fire with the hollowed gray stone at his back. He listened for a moment, then began to move his fingers over the strings. Eyes closed in concentration, he played the notes as if they were a part of his blood and bone. Muriella locked her hands together on the tabletop and leaned forward, listening. Then, softly at first, her husband began to sing.

> An thou were my own thing,
> I would love thee, I would love thee.
> An thou were my own thing,
> How dearly would I love thee.

Muriella bit her lip. She had heard the song before; she could not remember when. Resting her head on her braided fingers, she let the sound of John's voice enwrap her.

> To merit I no claim can make,
> But that I love; and for your sake,
> What man can, more I'll undertake,
> So dearly do I love thee.

John looked up until his eyes met hers across the crowded room. Then all noise ceased—the chatter of the men, the scratching of the dogs beneath the tables, and the clatter of pewter on wood as the servants removed the last of the meal. The clinging notes of the clareschaw were all that was real. In that moment, John's clear blue gaze drew her back in time to a distant memory: the dark passageway, the flickering candles, Alex at the harpsichord, and her husband singing in a voice that had made her shiver with its beauty. She realized then that the Gypsy had chosen this song in order to make her remember.

An thou were my own thing,
I would love thee, I would love thee.
An thou were my own thing,
How dearly would I love thee.

John's eyes never left his wife's face. With his song and his voice and the sensual movement of his fingers on the strings, he seemed to echo her thoughts and her need. Muriella rose at last to make her way toward him.

While love does at his altar stand,
Have thee my heart, give me thy hand,
And with this smile thou shalt command
The will of him who loves thee.

Her heart beat in time with the slow, enticing cadence of the song as she moved between the tables without knowing she did so. She knew only that her husband's voice was calling her, mesmerizing her as it had done once before. Without so much as a touch of his hand, he was drawing her toward him, weaving an invisible web of notes with which to bind her.

How dearly would I love thee.

She reached the place where John sat and knelt at his feet, one hand on his bent knee.

My passion, constant as the sun,
Flames stronger still, will ne'er have done,
'Til Fate my threads of life have spun,
Which breathing out, I'll love thee.

Slowly, slowly, his music dispelled her fears, scattered them like dry forgotten leaves in the October wind. John's fingers lay still on the strings, yet the notes seemed to linger in the air for a long moment. Muriella leaned closer, her fingers warm against his knee, her thick braid falling over her shoulder.

"I think—" he began.

"Aye," she murmured.

Without another word, he set his harp aside. They rose together, joining hands. Muriella felt an ache in her throat when she looked up at her husband's dark, bearded face, touched now with shadows, now with light as he guided her out of the reach of the fire. At the foot of the stairs, Muriella stopped and turned to Alex with a smile of gratitude.

But the Gypsy was gone. She did not look at the wide oak doors that opened into the starless night, for she knew he would not be there. *Ye'll know when the time comes.* Too soon, it had come. She felt his loss in the painful dragging of her heartbeat and the tears that burned behind her eyes. Yet, as John slid his arm around her waist to draw her close, she smiled, if a little sadly. For days, Alex had been beside her, trying to ease her sorrow and make her understand her fears, but now, she realized, he'd done all that he could; in the end, inevitably, he'd turned away, delivering the choice back into her hands.

John and Muriella did not speak, not even when her chamber door was closed behind them and they stood alone. For a long moment, palms cupped around her flushed cheeks, John simply looked at his wife—at the luminous green of her eyes, the soft curve of her parted lips, the graceful line of her neck. He caught his breath in admiration and wondered how he could have believed, even for an instant, that he could live without her.

The stillness whispering around him like a wordless invitation, he reached for the leather thong that bound Muriella's hair. She stood, eyes closed, face tilted toward the light as he worked the thong free, then slowly, one long, gleaming strand at a time, began to unbind her heavy braid. When her hair hung rippling down to her knees, he ran his fingers through it again and again, kissing the curling tendrils as they fell across his callused palms.

Then, with his hands still caught in her hair, he moved so near that she could hear his shallow breathing in her ear. Muriella opened her eyes and took his face in her hands, burying her fingers in his heavy beard. Without a sound, she drew him closer until their mouths met and clung together, warm and moist and fierce with need. The tangle of his beard brushed her sensitive cheeks and she sighed with pleasure as he slipped his tongue between her parted teeth. Unexpectedly, John drew away, smiling a promise that needed no words. As slowly as he had unbound her hair, he now untied the laces of her gown.

Muriella could feel the movement of his fingers, kept from her skin by the soft barrier of fabric. She shivered at the need that rose within her, a blinding white heat that stopped her voice in her throat. She had never wanted John so much before, never known how bright an agony her yearning could be. She dug her fingers into his shoulders in a silent plea, but he would not hurry.

When the laces came free in his hands, he lifted the gown over her head, then drew the kirtle up an inch at a time. The cool satin clung to her, caressing her hips and thighs like the mist that curled softly through the night beyond her window. She groaned and reached for him, but he only smiled as he bent to open her chemise. At last he pulled the filmy garment free of her body, then knelt and began to brush aside the strands of her hair with the movement of his lips over her naked skin.

The spinning began deep within her—the hot whirl of colors that stole her breath away—while John kissed her thigh tenderly, then trailed his tongue upward to her hip, the curve of her waist, her stomach and, finally, her small white breasts. He was torturing her with an agony too sweet to bear. When his warm, circling mouth reached the hollow of her throat, she cried out, pulling him to his feet. He caught her in his arms and held her, but she was not satisfied. With her hands curled against his shoulders, she guided him back toward the curtained bed. Somehow he lifted her onto the furs and, pausing only long enough to discard his own clothes, moved up beside her.

Skin to skin, he kissed her recklessly, his lips as searing and demanding now as they had been gentle before. With a gasp of pleasure, he slid his hands over her back, seeking the quivering of her body that told him her need was as great as his. With her tongue, she followed the line of his neck to his ear, then touched her lips to his again.

She was shaking from the white darkness that whirled within her, from the paths of liquid heat John's hands traced over her bare skin, from the wild, tender pressure of his mouth. With willing hands, she traced the curling hairs on his chest. Drawing her close, John twined his legs with hers and rolled with her across the mattress, while her hair wound itself around their bodies, binding them together in a fine, soft web. Sinking her fingers into his flesh, Muriella cried out, knowing her desire was too great, that the spinning would grow so bright and hot within her that, eventually, her heart would burst. But she did not care.

With a groan, John entered her at last. He began to move against her, rocking, rocking, tangling himself in her rippling hair. He was with her everywhere; no part of her remained untouched. As she gasped and closed her eyes in wonder, the bright darkness shattered and fell in glimmering fragments, filling the aching emptiness inside her.

Muriella sighed as John shuddered once more, then drew her into the curve of his arm while his rasping breath caressed her damp forehead. When he closed his arms protectively around her, her eyes filled with tears.

Her husband felt her tremble and looked up to see the

shimmer of moisture in her eyes. Leaning down to trace the path of a single teardrop with his tongue, he whispered, "Why?"

"Because I'm so happy to have ye back."

He felt a constriction in his throat that would not let him speak. Almost, it was enough to make him forget.

# 49

They awakened to a morning that, for once, was free of storm clouds. Muriella lay in her husband's arms while they talked of Andrew and Inveraray and Colin's return to Edinburgh. They talked of Elizabeth and her husband and the changes in her since the wedding. By unspoken consent, they did not mention Muriella's fear or what it would mean when they left the warm safety of her chamber for the cool misted brilliance of the world beyond.

When at last they fell silent, John drew away from his wife so he could see her face. "I've been thinking a great deal about Cawdor," he said.

"And so have I."

He brushed a strand of hair off her cheek. "We don't really have a choice," he said. "We have to go back. We've lived on my brother's sufferance for too long, and Cawdor is where we belong. Besides, the keep has been too many years without a master."

"I know," his wife agreed. "'Tis not only Cawdor that's suffered from our neglect. I *need* to go back, though 'tis not a pleasing thought. But mayhap there . . ."

"Mayhap what?"

Muriella contemplated John's face, cloaked with morning shadows. "Mayhap there I can begin to understand."

John nodded but did not trust himself to answer. He was thinking how lovely she was in the gray morning light. Her hair was a splendid, glittering web across the pillow—a woven net that enwrapped him and would not set him free. She was not human, he thought. She was of some other world—a Kelpie, a witch who bound him with the magic that glowed in her hypnotic eyes.

Muriella's gaze met his—dark with secrets, bright with desire—and in that instant, he felt that they were frozen in time. They could not go back, because they knew too much. Yet they could not move forward until she was ready to do so. In a way he was glad; the waiting would give him time. Time to prove to her what he now knew with certainty: whatever his wife had seen, whatever she feared, whatever she believed, he could not hurt her—ever.

Three weeks later, John stood in the center of the crowded courtyard amidst a melee of stamping horses and excited men. The servants came and went with bundles and baskets, hanging them from the backs of the animals and trying to avoid the hooves of the restless horses. The morning mist had not yet burned away; it clung in the corners and draped itself over the rough cobblestones, making the servants, still half asleep, stumble about, laughing and shouting when they blundered into one another. The cool, damp air rang with curses barely muffled and the panting of horses long past ready to be moving.

John surveyed the scene with a shake of his head. It was a good thing he had sent the bulk of their possessions to Cawdor beforehand or the confusion would have been worse now. He glanced up when he heard Richard's familiar voice.

"Out of my way, ye fool, before your horse tramples me underfoot. Your bags are secure. Ye should be waitin' outside the gate where ye aren't in danger of takin' several lives at any moment."

"Besides," Adam called down from the back of his restive animal, "I prefer the dangers of overcrowdin' to the sound of yer naggin' voice."

Richard snorted and turned away to bully a servant who had dropped a basket at his feet.

John smiled to himself. He had been touched when Richard and Adam and several others had asked if they could accompany him to Cawdor. Even Andrew had insisted he would not be left behind. The men could have stayed at Inveraray where they were comfortable and secure, but they had chosen instead to go to a place where the people would not welcome the Campbells, where their lives would be a struggle for more than a little time to come.

"Ye could have ordered us to go, but ye didn't do it," Richard had explained with a shrug. "Besides, we can't leave ye alone at the mercy of the Calders and Roses. Then again," he had added, grinning, "there hasn't been a battle here for weeks on end and the men are cravin' some excitement. We thought we just might find it at Cawdor."

John had grasped the man's hand firmly. "Thank ye," was all he'd said, but it had been enough. Now he looked up sharply when he saw Duncan leading his cousin's saddled horse.

"He's more than eager for a long ride, m'lord. I can't keep him still any longer."

"I'll take him now. Ye should see to your own animal. We'll be leaving soon."

"Not soon enough for me," Duncan called over his shoulder as he headed back toward the stables.

John smiled after him. Apparently his cousin was also hoping for some excitement. "Have ye seen my wife?" he called to Megan when she drew her animal up beside his.

"She said she was goin' to bid farewell to the loch."

Nodding, he told her, "All is nearly ready. Richard will tell ye when 'tis done and then ye and the others can follow. I'll go find Muriella now."

"Aye, m'lord. We'll be along soon," Megan called after him.

Muriella sat on the ridge overlooking the wide expanse of Loch Awe, where swirling mist hovered above the water, wrapping the wooded islands in drifts of cool white magic. In that moment, the woods, the water full of shifting secrets, the silver-touched leaves of the trees all around made her shiver with their mysterious beauty. Beyond the trees she could see the jagged mountains, their sides streaked with streams of silver white that shattered the brooding blackness. Frightened and enthralled by their magnificence, she turned to see the hills reflected in the shimmering surface of the loch.

She tilted her head, listening, and peered at the softly undulating water, but today there was no lovely face captured in the waves. Today there was no high, lamenting voice, too beautiful and piercing to be real. Today, in the stillness of early morning, there was only a whisper of memory to tell her that the face had ever been there.

"Muriella!"

The sound of her husband's voice broke the spell that held her in its grasp. With the ache of parting strong within her, she pulled the reins, guiding her horse down the ridge the way it had come an hour since. Moving slowly but without hesitation, she turned her back on the woman of the loch and started back in time toward the nightmare that was Cawdor.

Muriella had lost count of the hours. As they rode through the woods for mile after wandering mile, she'd grown more and more withdrawn. She'd been grateful for Megan's lively chatter, which had kept her mind off the stillness within her.

"Look at the hills, m'lady," the servant exclaimed. "They're so gentle and low that they don't frighten me like the mountains near Inveraray."

Muriella nodded but did not speak. It was all so painfully familiar—the hills, the green moors, the groves of oak and hawthorn and pine. Strange that she should remember so well what had passed in a flurry of terror that afternoon four years ago.

"Och, 'tis so lovely and peaceful here," Megan continued, undeterred by Muriella's reticence. "Why didn't ye tell me there was such a world outside of Inveraray?"

Her mistress smiled at Megan's obvious delight. The servant's enjoyment helped ease Muriella's mood a little.

Long before the horses came upon the river, she sensed that they were nearing Cawdor. Her heartbeat quickened then slackened, and her hands grew clammy. She would see it again—the wall, the tower, the river. She could see them now inside her head in every vivid detail. It was as if the violence of her emotions that day had burned these landmarks forever into her memory.

The riders followed the river as it wound through the rolling hills and disappeared beneath the thick canopy of trees. When they came at last within sight of the castle, Muriella slowed her horse so the animal fell behind the others. Oddly, she felt nothing; her feelings were cloaked in a protective veil that left her numb. Then John was beside her, leading her wordlessly under the gate toward the huge, square tower that was Cawdor Castle.

As she entered the courtyard, Muriella paused at the sight of the movement and color of men and women scurrying about their tasks. It had not been this way the last time she was here. Then it had been quiet and eerily still, as if the keep itself were waiting, as were they all, for the tragedy that could not be avoided. When they had dismounted, John stood beside her for a moment, his arm about her shoulders, while she fought to catch her breath.

"I must see to the men and horses," he said at last. "Will ye be all right on your own?"

With a thin smile, she looked up at him. "Aye, I think 'twill be best that way."

John nodded, motioned to Megan, then left the two women to make their way through the throng of people into the wide-open doors of the Great Hall. This too had changed, Muriella realized with a shock. The bare stone walls had been covered with tapestries and the floors with fresh rushes. The hall, which had once been cold and echoing and empty, was crowded now with trestle tables, beneath which the dogs had already settled themselves and begun to scratch. The servant girls hurried to and fro with cushions and platters and bundles of fresh vegetables. Their chatter rose toward the high, curved ceiling, filling the room with motion and warmth.

Muriella stared, unable to take it in. Why had she thought this keep must always be as bleak and abandoned as the last time she had stood here? Then Megan touched her arm and she looked up at the high table. It was strong, heavy oak, with two ornately carved chairs at either end. But that was not what made Muriella catch her breath in surprise. Behind the raised platform hung the Loch Awe tapestry.

"Sir John said 'twas so lovely that he couldn't bear to leave it at Inveraray," Megan told her. "He ordered it hung where all could see it."

Muriella bit her lip. So John had understood how much the hanging meant to her. Only gradually did she become aware that the servants had fallen silent and stood staring at her.

"Is't her?" she heard one woman whisper.

"I don't know," another answered. "But we'll soon see."

The women fell silent and, one by one, the other voices stilled as the servants turned to regard Muriella in frank curiosity. There was a flutter of movement at the far end of the hall. An expectant hush fell over the room as a woman descended the curving stairs and stood at the bottom, her hand on the iron balustrade. When the servants turned to her, Muriella followed their glance, narrowing her eyes as she caught sight of the woman who paused, silent and still, waiting.

Then Muriella met the woman's gaze, and a jolt of painful memory went through her body. She knew well that broad, gentle mouth and those soft brown eyes. She remembered every detail of that tightly coiled brown hair. Only once, perhaps, it had not been streaked with gray and the lines on her face had been less harshly defined. Lorna.

As Lorna began to move toward her, the servants seemed to draw in their collective breath. Muriella stood frozen, unable to force her limbs into motion, her throat strangely raw.

Lorna stopped, glancing briefly at the tense and watching faces of the people all around her. Then, with a silent prayer, she reached for Muriella's left hand.

Muriella drew back to avoid her touch. Then she heard the servants' indrawn breath of surprise and knew that, much as she might wish to, she could not avoid this moment. Biting her lip to still her trembling, she offered her hand to the woman who had once been her friend.

Lorna breathed a sigh of relief, then slowly examined the younger woman's hand. She stared at the scarred, rigid finger, then touched it gently, regretfully. Releasing Muriella, she dropped to her knees, murmuring, "Welcome home, m'lady."

The servants expelled their breath in a rush; then a cheer rose from those nearest the door. The others caught it up, one after another, until the hall rang with the sound and it spilled into the courtyard. Men bowed, women curtsied, and each spoke their own message to the lady of Cawdor Castle. "Welcome indeed." "M'lady, 'tis glad to see ye here at last, we are." "May ye bring peace with ye to Cawdor."

Muriella hardly heard them. She was transfixed by the expression on Lorna's face as she stared at the bent finger. "I would have known ye anywhere," the older woman whispered in anguish. "How could I not with those eyes of yours?" There were tears in her eyes as she added, "Can ye ever forgive me?"

Above the uncertain sound of her voice, Muriella heard a faint echo from long ago. *Think how much she must have loved ye to do such a thing.* She found she could not speak through the tightness in her throat. Tears burned behind her own eyes, but they would not fall.

Lorna bowed her head in acceptance of Muriella's unspoken condemnation, then rose from her knees. Silence had fallen once more, and she rushed to fill the awkward stillness. "We've been ready for ye for so long, ever since your husband sent word ye were coming. I waited and hoped every day 'til long past dusk. I watched from the window in the tower. I know 'twas silly, but 'twas how I remembered ye, sitting on the ledge looking down at the river. That's why, when ye finally came, I missed ye altogether. 'Twas no' 'til I heard the horses in the courtyard that I knew." She faltered. "I never really thought to see ye again."

Muriella felt the first rent in her protective veil as the numbness began to slip away. This was no stranger who had abandoned her in a distant past. This was the woman who had once been everything to her—mother, friend and confidante. The woman who had recognized Muriella's danger and cared enough to let her go. This was Lorna, who loved her. Muriella felt a moment of wrenching sorrow, then a surge of joy that Lorna had not forgotten after all. Her tears spilled over at last.

Lorna started away. "I'll leave ye to your rest."

"Don't go." Muriella's voice was little more than a whisper, but it stopped the other woman still.

Lorna looked back just as Muriella reached toward her. Then they were in each other's arms, clinging together, weeping so that their tears met and mingled.

Muriella shivered at the tumult that erupted within her as she felt her friend tremble with relief and sadness together. Suddenly, her head was full of voices, warnings, memories that she could neither bear nor stop. She drew back, crying, "I must go."

Lorna regarded her intently through her tears. "To the river?"

"Aye."

"Do ye think 'tis wise?"

"I don't know if 'tis wise or no'. I only know I have to do it," Muriella replied.

Lorna nodded in understanding. She understood so much. "Go then, but don't linger. The past can hurt as well as heal, ye ken."

Without another word, Muriella left behind the curious glances of the servants, the bittersweet smile of her friend, the warmth and life that filled the hall. The echoing voices in her head guided her back in time, across the remembered dust-strewn rooms to the heavy oak door that led to the river. Working the stiff latch free, she pulled the door open and stepped out into the blaze of the afternoon sun. Her heart thudded in her chest as the image of a long-ago day came back to her, carried in the murmur of the rushing river. Here she had stumbled toward freedom, laughing as the shadow of the keep fell away behind her. Here she had run with the flowers brushing her legs, and found the peace she sought in the murmur of the water. Retracing the steps she remembered so well, she turned first toward the tiny clearing where the trees closed whispering around her.

The copse was as cool and dark as she remembered and the ground as soft. The ferns grew wild beneath her feet, carpeting the clearing with damp, green tendrils. She stood at the foot of the tree where she had lain beside Lorna and listened to the story of the building of Cawdor Castle. *He had a troubled life, your father, and ye have inherited so much that was his.* Muriella had not understood then, but now it was all very clear. This place had been the source of all her trials. Because of Cawdor she had lost everything she once held dear. Because of Cawdor she had become a prisoner. Could she ever be happy here now? *Ye won't ever change the future by fightin' it this way. To conquer your fear ye must face it once and for all.* But what if, in the end, it broke her?

She stared at the dancing leaves overhead, mesmerized by the moving light and shadow on her face, by the memories she could no longer escape, and by the muted rumble of the river just beyond the trees. The water called her as it had once before, enticing her with the rhythm of its unchanging song. Now, as then, she could not resist the summons.

With measured steps, she moved from the safety of the copse toward the riverbank. Here she had knelt, listening to the water, and heard the horses coming toward her. She knelt again, trailing her fingers through the water, feeling the chill as it moved up her arm. Shuddering, she made herself remember the moment when Lorna had cut her finger so brutally. Then there was nothing but the searing pain and the fury of John's voice as he came splashing toward her, cursing. She closed her eyes, but the horror would not go; in her mind her blood spread over the surface of the water like a dark, rippled stain.

Muriella raised her hands to her cheeks and found that she was weeping. Now that her protective veil lay in shreds at her feet, the fear and pain and loss came welling up inside her, choking her as she rocked, her arms clasped tight across her chest.

Then she realized she was not alone. Her head came up and she spun to find John approaching, cloaked by the shadows of shifting leaves. She stood, gasping for breath, tears streaming down her face unabated. "Johnnie!" she cried.

This time she did not put the plea into words, and yet this time, he understood. In a moment, John covered the ground between them and took her in his arms.

"Thank God you're here!" When she felt his arms close around her, the relief was so great that for an instant her heartbeat seemed to cease. With her head on his shoulder, she leaned close, pressing the weight of her memories against his strong body. He was there for her, she realized, and always had been. Just as Lorna always had.

"I don't care about the future," she whispered, "or the fear of what might be. I only know I don't want to lose ye."

"Ye won't lose me," he told her fiercely.

She raised her head, seeking the warmth and comfort of his lips on hers. He kissed her, swallowing the salt taste of her tears.

Muriella moaned and wrapped her arms around her husband's neck as the memories retreated. At the heated pressure of his lips, the whirling began in her head—the magic, the wonder, the fear that raged together inside her, spinning, always spinning, until she thought she could stand no more. *Mayhap 'tis no' your husband ye fear. Mayhap 'tis yourself.* John's hands drew their stirring patterns over her back while Alex's words spun within her until they echoed the rhythmic pulse of the water at her side. *Ye'll always create your own nightmares. Ye and no one else are at the heart of all your terror.* Mayhap, the river whispered, 'tis yourself, yourself, yourself. . . .

Then John touched her lips with the tip of his tongue, and a keening cry of need whirled within her. *Ye follow the vision through to its natural end.* She wanted to shout a denial, but John's lips and his circling hands would not let her. Her hunger screamed through her and she held him tighter, tighter, while the words rang warningly in her head. Mayhap 'tis yourself, the river whispered. Ye follow the vision through. Face it, her heart throbbed as she began to fall. Face it once and for all.

Then the words were drowned by the roar of the rising water. It was up to her shoulders, her neck; it was choking her. She fought, gasping for breath, against the swirling foam, but it drew her downward to the dark, raging center of the water. When a single breath sent a sliver of fierce, bright pain through her head, she cried out and gave up the struggle. She no longer had the strength to fight, so she let the water take her down, down, down into the murky depths. For a moment more, it roiled and spat, then the spinning stopped, the roaring ceased, and the waves grew still around her. In the sudden cessation of fury, in the clear blue calm that was left behind, Muriella began to float upward toward the distant brightness she had thought never to reach. As she moved, the darkness dissolved and the light burned over her face.

"Muriella!"

Slowly, very slowly, she opened her eyes to the image of John's face. In that moment, in the still crystal heartbeat when sound and motion ceased, the joy swept through her in a torrent. "Johnnie!" she cried breathlessly. "I'm free!" Then she spun away, kicking up the pine-scented earth as she went. All at once she was weightless, exultant, so full of jubilation that she could not stay still. Her shoulders, curved for so long under the burden of her fear, were unbowed at last.

John watched, astonished, unable to comprehend her erratic behavior. Then she turned, her face glowing with joy, her eyes so clear and green that they seemed lit by an inner light. Tripping over the uneven ground, she came back to him and threw her arms about his neck.

"My lord," she said, "I love ye so much."

Only then, as the ache of tears rose in his throat, did he realize he had thought never to hear those words. "And ye aren't afraid, are ye?"

Muriella threw her head back, smiling and weeping both together. "Never again," she said. She felt dizzy with a happiness that left her trembling, a joy so intense that she thought her legs might collapse beneath her. "I realize now that 'twas no' my death I saw. And 'twas no' ye I feared," she added when she could speak through her tears. "'Twas no' ever ye, but only my feelings for ye."

Her husband shook his head, uncomprehending.

"They're too strong, ye see. I thought I couldn't bear them. I thought if I let them take me, they would destroy me in the end. But I was wrong."

John took her chin between his thumb and forefinger, forcing her to meet his eyes. "Are ye telling me ye nearly drove us both to madness because ye were afraid—"

"That I loved ye too much."

He stared at her in disbelief. Could they have suffered so much for so little?

"But today," Muriella whispered before he could find his voice, "the demons are gone. Now there is only ye and me."

She was smiling and he found he could not escape the glow of her elation. It was as powerful as her fear had once been, and as irresistible. Her body quivered, her lips parted, and without a word she drew him with her toward the river—toward the bright, jubilant cascade of glimmering liquid light.

"Johnnie? Do ye think ye can ever forgive me?"

When he did not answer at once, she moved closer, reaching out to touch his cheek. "I love ye so much that I ache with it," she said. "But 'tis a sweet pain, and one I don't wish to live without."

He drew her hand away from his face, holding it in his open palm. Her eyes were deep green, like the sea in the heart of a storm, and there were fresh tears on her cheeks. Like the sea, her eyes swept over him, catching him up in the storm of her own creation. He raised her hand to his lips and kissed her scarred and crippled little finger.

Muriella leaned toward him and his arms closed around her. In that moment, as their bodies came together, his breathing matched the murmur of her pulse, and of the wind that dipped, sighing, through the woods and across the rippling water.

# *Afterword*

Although *Child of Awe* is a work of fiction, it is based in historical fact. John and Muriella were the founders of the Clan Campbell of Cawdor and their names are carved into the stone mantel at Cawdor Castle. I have seen and examined that mantel. I have stood in the tower, looking through the high embrasure at the canopy of trees which hide the rushing water. I have walked the sloping path from the base of the tower to the river. But even before my trip to the Scottish Highlands, this book had become more than simply a story I wanted to tell; it had become an obsession.

My fascination with *Child of Awe* began in 1976 when, from dozens of books on Scottish castles, I jotted down three separate stories that interested me as the possible basis for my first novel. Only when I began serious research did I discover that the stories—an account of Muriella's abduction, an account of Elizabeth's brutalization, and the legend of the making of Loch Awe—were intricately intertwined, the three strong threads which became the fabric of *Child of Awe*.

I have taken certain liberties with the dates and ages, and the events did not always occur in the order presented here. The scarcity of historical records from this period makes it difficult to describe specific events for which there is often conflicting evidence. For example, the story of the kidnapping has several versions in Scottish tradition. Some claim it was Muriella's grandmother who "marked" her by branding her on the hip with a red-hot key. There are also many popular traditional accounts of Maclean's ill-treatment of Elizabeth; there is a rock in the channel between the Isle of Mull and the shore that is called, to this day, The Lady's Rock. There is even a song about the manner in which John killed Lachlan Maclean, entitled "Take Up Maclean and Prick Him in a Blanket."

The story of John and Muriella is only one segment in the dramatic and often bloody history of Cawdor Castle and the two families—Calder and Campbell—who have held it since its construction in the fourteenth century. According to *The Book of the Thanes of Cawdor,* Muriella and John lived the rest of their lives at Cawdor, where they had many children and a happy marriage.

From the beginning, the writing of *Child of Awe* has not been easy—just as Muriella's life itself was never easy. In many ways, it has seemed like the long and painful birth of a child, lasting for nearly fourteen years. I have rewritten the novel again and again, reshaped it repeatedly with loving care, "finished" it more times than I can count. Most recently, after several years of working on other projects, I returned again to *Child of Awe.* Encouraged by the enthusiasm and faith of my publisher, I looked at the novel with new and more mature eyes. I saw things which have always been there, but which had eluded me until now, and which have transformed the book of my heart once more. I will not say, this time, that it is finished. *Child of Awe* will never be finished. It will haunt me always.